Shadows of the Anunnaki:
Time Rewound

KUDOS FOR SHADOWS OF THE ANUNNAKI: TIME REWOUND

Time Rewound is a well written, satisfying conclusion to the "Shadows of the Anunnaki" trilogy by Janice Dietert. Each book is a wonderful reading experience in its own right and *Time Rewound* is no exception. Time travel, space travel, romance, political intrigue, the microbiome and multiple dimensions, this book has it all. In this conclusion to an intellectually stimulating trilogy, Janice Dietert explores current science speculation and theory while delighting the reader with interesting characters that develop and grow throughout the book as well as the trilogy. Highly recommended.

- K. Hauger

WOW! Another fantastic read for this series! For me, I found this book extremely fascinating and even plausible! In some ways, this information can open doors in your own mid that can blow your current concept of life to smithereens!

There are many things going on in our universe we, as the general public, know nothing about. Our very "adept and honest" leaders are embroiled in the lust for greed and power. I find it encouraging to imagine a world where we have more connection to the universe and understand we are ALL ONE within it. It takes love, understanding, respect for others and cooperation to really change things that benefit everyone!

Even though Ginny is the human who notices things are not quite right, it appears the hybrids are the real heroes. Even though they were created for a specific purpose, the creators of the hybrids FORGOT that these hybrids had feelings, dreams, talents and a multitude of other things which made them unique and vital to the solutions needed to move forward. By combining their unique talents in the spirit of cooperation, the hybrids come up with ideas to change their future history.

At any rate, I thoroughly enjoyed this book.

- J. Shaw

Also by Janice Dietert

Way Shower: Light and Shadow
Way Shower: Redemption
Way Shower
Shadows of the Anunnaki: Earthbound
Shadows of the Anunnaki: Origins on Nibiru
Between Two Worlds
Son of the Star

Coauthored with Rodney R Dietert, PhD

Science Sifting
Strategies for Protecting Your Child's Immune System
The Edinburgh Goldsmiths I: Training, Marks, Output, and Demographics II
Compendium of Scottish Silver II
Scotland's Families and the Edinburgh Goldsmiths

Cover Art by: Kip Ayers
       www.kipayersillustration.com

Shadows of the Anunnaki: Time Rewound/

ISBN 978-0-578-16359-8

Dietert Publications
Lansing, NY

ACKNOWLEDGEMENTS

I want to thank Gaye King. She started all this fun with the Anunnaki and Guardians and Masters. If not for her, there would be no trilogy, no reason to write.

A big thanks to my hubby, Rod Dietert. He knows what "writing mode" means and what to do when I've been too immersed to have a "plan for dinner." He's also read every-single-word of every-single-story I've written. Bless his heart. He even likes most of them.

Reviewers

To my faithful reviewers, Kat and Jean, not only do you read the books and apparently like the books, you're so helpful with your comments and I'm so grateful for the kudos you let me put in the books.

Mentors

Some of you may not realize how influential you've been to my thinking.

Colleen Kiley - you taught me there's more than one way to vision, and more than one way to obtain answers. Do you see any of those ways in this book?

Dr. Richard Bartlett and Melissa Joy Jonsson, the two of you taught me to notice the novel that most people miss, to look for alternative realities to show up and that the past can be changed to influence the present. You also taught me to stop being so serious, to play and have fun!

Raymon Grace, you taught me more uses for dowsing than I knew were possible, and that there's more than one way to change the past and make it stick.

And to my wonderful, intuitive, talented artist, Kip Ayers - I'd never have an attractive book if it weren't for your powerful, amazing cover art. Thank you so much for all the times you've fit my projects in between your own work.

Shadows of the Anunnaki: Time Rewound

TABLE OF CONTENTS

PROLOGUE   1
CHAPTER 1   LOOMING DISASTER   6
CHAPTER 2   JOURNEY TO THE PAST   11
CHAPTER 3   UNLIKELY ROMANCE   22
CHAPTER 4   THE UNVEILING   31
CHAPTER 5   CHOICES MADE   41
CHAPTER 6   PAIRINGS INTERRUPTED   50
CHAPTER 7   ERRORS OVER TIME   56
CHAPTER 8   CORRECTIONS TO MAKE   61
CHAPTER 9   NASDATAL'S STORY   66
CHAPTER 10   GATHERING ALLIES   80
CHAPTER 11   RESCUING NASDATAL   87
CHAPTER 12   WHAT HAPPENS NOW?   97
CHAPTER 13   NEW TRAJECTORY   103
CHAPTER 14   PUSHING GROWTH   114
CHAPTER 15   CHANGES AND CHOICES   122
CHAPTER 16   EMERGING PROJECTS   131
CHAPTER 17   FIRST PAIR   138
CHAPTER 18   DEMONSTRATIONS OF POWER   145
CHAPTER 19   PROJECTS ON DISPLAY   154
CHAPTER 20   NEW WORLD OF EDUCATION   164
CHAPTER 21   UPSCALED EXPERIMENTS   172
CHAPTER 22   WILD ADVENTURE   179
CHAPTER 23   OF NYMPHS AND LOVE   186
CHAPTER 24   EFFECTS OF THE POWER UP   193
CHAPTER 25   THE ONES WHO JUDGE   200
CHAPTER 26   MASTERS OF THE UNIVERSE   206
CHAPTER 27   STATE VISIT   215
CHAPTER 28   ENHANCED AWARENESS   223
CHAPTER 29   ROYAL MACHINATIONS   230
CHAPTER 30   ESCAPE   241
CHAPTER 31   WELCOME HOME   249
CHAPTER 32   LAST PIECE OF THE PUZZLE   257
CHAPTER 33   MANY PATHS TO CHOOSE   264
CHAPTER 34   EVICTED   276
CHAPTER 35   THE HIGH LIFE   283
CHAPTER 36   PROMISES FULFILLED   292
CHAPTER 37   OUT MANEUVERED   300
CHAPTER 38   HOME OF THEIR OWN   310
CHAPTER 39   FINDING BALANCE   318

CHAPTER 40 WAY FORWARD   329
CHAPTER 41 PREPARING THE WAY   338
CHAPTER 42 LIVING PACT   348
CHAPTER 43 OFF WORLD   361
CHAPTER 44 NEW LAND   371
CHAPTER 45 EMBRACING CHANGE   379
CHAPTER 46 BUILDING ANEW   386
APPENDIX NOTES   396
APPENDIX A   397

PROLOG

Hundreds of thousands of years ago, a planet in our solar system with a 3,600 year elliptical orbit around our sun supported a race of people whose existence was in danger. When it approached the sun at its closest, the planet grew quite hot, while a dark winter fell when it reached its furthest distance from the sun. In order to sustain life, vast volcanoes had belched massive amounts of ash into the sky creating a thick, protective atmosphere around the planet.

Over time, the volcanoes grew dormant and the thick atmosphere was not replenished with ash. Gradually, a hole developed in the atmosphere, its size growing larger with every pass near the sun. On this planet, known as Nibiru, weather patterns became extreme, crops withered in the fields and the women became barren.

Out in the vastness of space, a group of five Multi-Dimensional travelers had been watching this planet and its inhabitants' struggles. Having barely survived the destruction of their own world eons ago, they knew the people of Nibiru would die within their lifetime without aid. Cloaked in planes of invisibility, they observed the rulers of Nibiru. When a royal prince possessing integrity took the throne of the combined kingdoms, the Multi-Dims, as they termed themselves, sent one of their own, Emissary, to offer their aid.

These desperate days of Nibiru and their search for a solution on our Earth were recorded by Sumerian scribes and kings claiming to have

1

been taught the first language. They knew the inhabitants from Nibiru as lords and gods with the Supreme god being Anu. This same Anu was the king of the combined kingdoms of Nibiru.

The scientists of Nibiru determined that large quantities of gold, which Earth had in abundance but of which Nibiru had scant quantities, could heal the hole in the atmosphere if processed correctly. This would, however, take a lot of time, which they didn't have. And there was no guarantee the results would be permanent. So, the Multi-Dims offered to create a race of hybrid beings capable of using the elements of nature as powers. They could permify the healing of the atmosphere if the hybridization included genetic material of both the Multi-Dim race and that of Nibiru's royal family.

Desperate for a solution, Anu agreed and signed a pact with the five Multi-Dims - Nasdatal, Marne, Giramusen, Zalkur and Emissary. From this science, 501 hybrid beings were born; a prototype, Enmarsikil, and exactly 250 men and 250 women.

The original plan was to raise them to maturity on Nibiru, teach them how to use their formidable elemental powers, heal the hole in the atmosphere and anchor that closure permanently to Nibiru. However, rivalries within the royal house threatened Anu's reign. When his rival, Alalu, found gold on our Earth, the 10th planet of their solar system, the plan was changed.

Suddenly, the hybrids were paired for life using objective tests to measure the compatibility of their powers. Generation-by-generation would be sent to this planet they knew as Ki. Immediately, upon touchdown, catastrophe beset the oldest generation of hybrids. Their own attunements to the elements were frequencies that were dissonant to the elements of Ki. They were so incompatible with the world around them that that they lost the ability to hold their form together. Within hours, they all lost their bodies and became the elements their powers represented.

Though a crushing blow, the Multi-Dims held to their plan to send the rest of the hybrids to Ki. They tested samples of Ki's elements, used neural implants to adjust the hybrids' resonance to Ki's elements and paired the second generation. However, it became obvious that one hybrid, the eldest and prototype, would have no mate unless something were changed. So, Nasdatal gave Enmarsikil the option of choice. If he found one of the hybrids attractive, and she was also attracted to him, she could be freed of her pairing contract once she had completed her service on Ki.

Enmarsikil accepted what little he was offered and discovered that the youngest hybrid, Astara, was not only whom his heart was set on, but that she cared for him in return. They signed their own pact but were forced to wait millennia before she was finally free of her obligations.

Though the goal was for the hybrids, better known as the Guardians and Masters, to work in partnership with Anu's sons, the Anunnaki, in truth they were treated more as servants. For their part, the Anunnaki were at best thoughtless in their treatment and at their worst, ruthless and cruel in their quest for dominant power. No one amongst the Guardians and Masters remained unscathed as the Anunnaki wantonly exploited their abilities often traumatizing the Guardians and Masters in the process.

However, the Anunnaki didn't stop at just exploiting the Guardians and Masters. Because work in the gold mines was so difficult and there were no more men arriving from Nibiru to take the workers' places, Enki, Ninhursag and Ningishzidda partnered together to create another hybrid race. Taking the DNA and genetic material of an Anunnaki man and using a female from an existing Earth hominid, they created a slave race, the first of which was the Adama. These new beings were intelligent enough to communicate with the Anunnaki and strong enough to do the work in the mines as well as be the hunters and home servants the Anunnaki sought to ease their lives on Earth. The two hybrid species came into contact very little at the behest of the Anunnaki.

After tens of thousands of years of servitude, the Guardians and Masters began to fade as their internal power weakened. Nasdatal and Enmarsikil had prepared a secure Facility in a remote location for this very purpose. Those who were fading heard the bell of the locator beacon and, following its signal, were conveyed to the Facility where Enmarsikil tenderly laid each sibling to rest placing them in suspended animation. Some day, when their life force was completely recharged, the Facility was set to awaken them.

But in case something went wrong - from equipment failure to environmental disasters to unforeseen discovery by hostile forces - the Multi-Dims took genetic material from all 501 hybrids and entered it into humans. Thus, the elemental frequencies would be entirely harmonized with those of Ki with no further need for neural implants. The genetically enhanced humans were distributed across the globe with the hopes that, should the Guardians and Masters not awaken in their true forms, they would surface and awaken in future humans.

Several thousand years later, many human holocausts had greatly reduced the genetic pool of humans with the enhanced DNA. Worse, the Guardians and Masters remained in stasis in the Facility. As wars enveloped the world and shockwaves hit human consciousness, Guardians and Masters began to wake only to find themselves in human bodies sharing consciousness with an often resistant human soul. Worse, the amnesia of their long sleep often occluded their identity and purpose. They struggled mightily to rediscover their origins and experiences.

Possibly the most devastating realization upon recognizing themselves was finding their former great powers shackled to human flesh and learning that the traumas of their own past had been repeated in some form during their human counterpart's life. Their human partners all needed serious mental and physical healing before they would be able to take up the charge to aid the world in its hour of need.

Some hybrids had been through brutal horrors. Unscrupulous Anunnaki had abducted them conducting genetic experiments on them to learn the secrets of their powers. One in particular, Marduk, Enki's eldest son, even sought to make his own hybrids but was unable to give them bodies of flesh. He sought other means of embodying them. Once the Guardian and Master DNA was incorporated into the human genome, those humans were now susceptible to being overpowered and invaded by unseen assailants, Marduk's Multi-Dim warriors.

In this time all the hopes and plans of the Multi-Dims were on a fast track to doom and no one seemed aware. Only one hope remained; Enmarsikil's special team whom he had personally trained on Nibiru. He had set alarms for them in the distant past, and they were sounding now. From their beds in the Facility, they would energize the DNA to awaken in resonant humans. If things went well, they'd be drawn to one another in human form. Then the mission could begin.

But it was hit or miss when they found each other. Ki and Astara were the first to gain realization of who they were. Then came Aiya, Ushumgal, Erumgal and Kumzubar But the most satisfying meeting was when Astara recognized Enmarsikil in the man her human embodier planned to marry. Slowly, he was drawn out into the knowledge of who he really was.

Most discouraging was the way the awakening team seemed to collapse in upon itself, and the people moved in and out of each others' lives. Enmarsikil, frustrated that nothing could move forward, considered aborting the mission. Unless something drastic were discovered and action taken, the few who were awake and engaging the mission would be useless against the rising culture of terror and would die purely human

4

deaths.

Astara's human embodiment was Ginny and, together, they may just have stumbled upon an idea so implausible, so impossible, it just might work. Now, could they make the Guardians and Masters around them and even those in the past understand the desperate conditions? And would any who heard and understood them have the courage to undertake implementing the only solution?

The time to find out was now.

CHAPTER 1 - LOOMING DISASTER

A blue-eyed, red head in her late forties sat at her computer in the home office she shared with her husband. Above her on the wall hung the painting of a dragon reading a book that her cousin had created just for her. As she gazed at it, she smiled with fond memories. Behind her, sun shone in the double window, its light dappled as it filtered through the branches of the spreading red maple that shaded that corner of the house. The maple was Ginny's favorite. Every now and then a bird would call, and she would spin around to watch Blue Jays, Cardinals, Goldfinches, Chickadees, Woodpeckers and the occasional Mourning Dove line up on its branches awaiting their turn at the feeder on the deck.

Right now, Ginny was reading a new science article her husband, Ted, had forwarded to her from the university where he worked as a research scientist. The article was an epigenetic study in rats that could point at the origins of irrational phobias people are often born with. For Ginny, who had been Ted's science editor for the last decade, getting the latest scientific news flashes was one of the perks of reading otherwise long, boring manuscripts.

Right now, Ginny wore a frown as she read. A petite, strawberry blond with a gentle bluish aura about her pursed her lips as she peered over Ginny's shoulder and read along with her.

"So, let me see if I get this straight," the blond named Astara said. She straightened up and, as she did, the air around her shimmered. "When the mother rats were young, researchers exposed them to a certain odor at the same time they were having an unpleasant experience."

Ginny spun her chair, glanced up and nodded.

Astara peered past her and read further. "Ok, then the rats were mated, conceived and gave birth to pups," she continued.

"That's right," Ginny affirmed, still periodically amazed she could see and talk to someone most people weren't even aware was there.

"Then the researchers exposed the pups to the same odor only without them having had the experience. But they reacted to the odor the exact same way their mother had after having had the bad experience," Astara concluded.

Ginny nodded. "Without ever having shared their mother's experience and long before she had been mated, they still had the same avoidance reaction to the same odor."

Astara shook her head. "How? How is that possible?"

"The researchers haven't yet discovered the mechanism," Ginny replied. "What they hypothesize is that the mother's experience somehow altered some aspect of its genetics so it passed her odor avoidance behavior to her pups, even though they had no reason to behave like that."

"All genetics," Astara pondered as she followed Ginny to the kitchen while she poured her second cup of coffee. "Now, here's the thing," Astara said slowly. She stared out toward the front yard through the Belgian lace curtains on the kitchen window as she thought. "This was a simple life experience for the rats. What about more intense life experiences? Would they be passed on too?"

"I suspect so," Ginny replied, "especially if they were emotionally intense or traumatic."

Ginny headed back up the hall to the office with Astara following. The air around her shimmered even more than usual.

"Intense?" Astara asked. "Like traumas, abductions, experiments?" she wondered slowly.

Ginny set her coffee cup on her desk and stared at her counterpart. "Wow! That's a thought. All the experiences you Guardians and Masters had eons ago would be prime for rewriting human genetics that would get passed through the human lineage through which it was inherited."

"Then what effect would the tens of thousands of years of Guardian/Master traumas have on the humans our genetic material was implanted in?" Astara pressed.

Idly picking up her coffee cup, Ginny headed down the hall and out onto her back deck. She sat in the sun with her dogs, an older Bichon and a younger poodle mix, at her feet. "That is a very good question," she said at last.

She sipped her coffee while watching a pair of hawks circle the five acre meadow behind her house. Her mind went back to when her friend, Gayle, was told by a psychic that she was very powerful and was part of a lineage known as Guardians and Masters. The psychic suggested Gayle read the works of Zechariah Sitchin, which Ginny had immediately dumped in her lap since she had the whole series of his books. Gayle had been convinced by his research into Sumerian and Assyrian texts. Ginny had been blown over by the tape the psychic had made and Gayle had loaned to her. It had been too shocking when he read Gayle's past life information, and as Ginny had listened chills had skipped down her spine. She could remember having been there, too; could see the scene as if it were only yesterday.

Curious about what happened in the past, Gayle and Ginny meditated and experienced shared visions. Slowly, they pieced together the lives and histories of the Guardians and Masters. That was when they discovered Ki and Astara, Guardians who had leant their genetics to Gayle and Ginny respectively. More interestingly, when Ginny started dating Ted, tall and toned from dancing, over a decade ago, she had recognized the energy and Astara, with whom she was now acquainted, recognized Enmarsikil, her lost love, in Ted.

Ginny, Gayle, her husband Dan, and Ted had all worked to break down the barriers between the Guardian/Master part of themselves, as they called it, and make their counterparts more available, nearer to the surface of their consciousness.

For Ginny, she had developed a cooperative living situation. Though Astara seemed to reside inside her, there were often times when Ginny could bring Astara sufficiently close to the surface that Astara could step outside of Ginny as a phase-shifted element of her.

"Do you think any of this is impacting humans now?" Astara asked breaking Ginny's musings.

"I'm sure it is, only exactly how it's happening is a bit of a mystery," Ginny replied.

"Maybe time will show the how," Astara decided.

"It's a puzzle and we have to wait for all the puzzle pieces to be able to see the whole picture," Ginny concluded.

Several days later, Ginny again stared hard at her monitor as she read a news article about a dangerous criminal who had attacked people in their home while in the midst of a drug-fueled, psychotic break. Astara peered over her shoulder as usual, the frown on her face darkening by the minute.

"That is not normal human behavior," she fumed.

"That's why he was deemed to be psychotic," Ginny replied reaching for the notes she'd taken during a recent dowsing workshop.

As she flipped through her legal pad, Ginny's mind immediately brought up the image of the stalwart mountain man. Plain spoken and to the point, Reg was an articulate speaker without the need for superfluous ums and uhs. What made him fascinating was his view of dowsing and his methods of applying it.

Could he find water? Sure. He could also take a well poisoned by arsenic and clean the water so no traces were left. Furthermore, he realized that ancestral beliefs created patterns passed down through the generations that could still impact individuals now. That had been too close to the olfactory rat study she'd read recently. He had ways of using dowsing to clear those patterns. Ginny had been all ears. This was some of the most practical dowsing she'd ever learned.

Now, she was looking in her notes for information on possession. While a lot of people still didn't believe in demonic possession, she'd read that the Catholic Church was seeing an increase in requests for exorcism. Reg had a technique for that and believed that for the most part possessions were the deceased looking for an opportunity to continue to enjoy something they liked while alive, like alcohol. In order to do that, they needed a willing body to participate. In other instances, though, real evil could take over. Ginny had a hunch one way to open the door was through substance abuse, like cocaine, and that's what created the psychotic break so the evil could act on the world.

Since they in some ways 'shared' a mind, Astara was aware of her thought process.

"They aren't just evil," she pointed out. "It's Marduk's Multi-Dim Warriors. It's the only way they can have any form in this world since he couldn't fully duplicate his father, Enki's, process of creating us."

Ginny nodded. "What gets me is something Reg was saying. Dowsers lately have been finding people who either don't have a soul at the moment or who were born without one. A woman at the workshop wondered how the body was being animated without a soul. Reg admitted that he and the other dowsers didn't know."

"You do, don't you?" Astara asked.

"I suspect."

"Multi-Dim Warriors?" Astara pressed.

Ginny nodded. "Let's face it. Trying to inhabit human bodies only works so long for them because they burn out the body. Now, a soulless body would be nothing more than a meat suit and they the puppeteers. The human would last longer."

"Which do you think that guy was?" she asked pointing to the guy's mugshot on the screen.

"Host," Ginny replied. "Apparently he has a non-violent record stretching back for petty theft. You don't suddenly make a jump from stealing a purse out of an open car window to a brutal attack in the wee hours of the morning unless something else is forcing that issue."

"The problem with a Multi-Dim Warrior animating a soulless human," Astara said pensively, "is that one warrior can control many suits."

"That skews things far in their favor," Ginny agreed. "They don't have to wait for genetics to combine just so."

"There's one other piece to this," Ginny said.

"Hm?"

"There hasn't been a Guardian or Master whom I've met and journeyed into the past with for whom their Guardian/Master experiences hadn't found a way to play out in their present life. They're all traumatized in some way," Ginny explained.

"But some of those experiences, like being abducted by and experimented on by Marduk means in this lifetime they're even more susceptible to influence by Multi-Dim Warriors," Astara concluded.

"How much do you think wars around the world are clearly influenced by the susceptible people overrun by those warriors?" Ginny wondered. "Humans need to be strengthened against this unseen army."

"You do things that take you into the past to change things," Astara pointed out.

Ginny nodded. "There are ways and I've learned some."

Astara stood up fully and crossed her arms.

"How would we know the point at which to make a change?" Ginny asked.

"Use my lifeline. Go back to my birth and follow my line forward. There has to be a point at which interrupting the process will make sense," Astara suggested.

Ginny nodded. "This might just work."

"Next week while Ted lectures in Tennessee?" Astara asked.

"It's a date."

CHAPTER 2 - JOURNEY TO THE PAST

Ginny drove Ted to the local airport, pulled up to the unloading zone, gave him a hug and kiss and wished him a safe trip. She watched his tall, dark-haired figure walk away with his satchel in one hand and rolling luggage at his side in the other hand. A lump rose in her throat. Every time he left to give a lecture or attend a conference, a piece of her worried he might not come back. She was certain she'd inherited that worry from Astara.

She drove back home, packed up the dogs and met her pet sitter at the front door a half hour later. Ginny wanted no distractions while Ted was away this time. She and Astara had serious business to attend to.

Once everyone was out of the house, Ginny did her usual straightening up while she waited for Ted's periodic phone calls from airports along the way. When he finally arrived at his hotel and they had their last chat for the day, Ginny ate a light meal, cleaned up the kitchen and prepped coffee for the next morning.

"Ready?" Astara asked from the downstairs as Ginny headed toward her.

"Ready as I'll ever be," Ginny replied.

They crawled into the king bed and got comfortable, Ginny put in her ear buds and turned on her double drumming recording on her iPod then adjusted her eye mask.

"Ok. We're going to my healing circle," Ginny announced.

Astara grabbed her hand and they were whisked down a long tunnel. They were unceremoniously dumped onto a plateau that overlooked a broad Bay. Where they presently stood was in the middle of a flat rock stone circle. On the side away from the Bay stood a stone bed. The rest of the circle appeared empty to the naked eye.

The two women still clasped hands, but Ginny stretched out her right hand and closed her eyes in concentration.

"Past life lines," she called, the wind whipping her hair and carrying her voice.

In moment a doorway appeared in front of her and to the left and an archway beside it on her right. Ginny opened her eyes and looked at them. The door on the left opened giving a glimpse of a suspended walkway that stretched deep inside. Off to either side, movie screens hung suspended in mid-air. Since that led to past life lines in humans, Ginny mentally closed that door.

Now she turned to the archway. Fine silver filigree work ran up both sides and across the top. The door parted down the middle and slid back revealing another tunnel. This presented like a horizontal tornado that swirled with cream, mint green, and blue streaks in the whitish cloud-like sides.

Ginny looked over at Astara. "You ready to revisit the past?"

Astara studied the archway and gave a slight nod.

The two women stepped into the archway and were sucked into the tunnel. After a while they felt themselves slowing. With a jerk, they suddenly found themselves in a house made entirely of light. In the middle of the entry hall stood a gold pedestal on which a dolphin of shimmering silver remained in perpetual mid-leap. Marne, a tall slender woman with flowing blond hair and a rippling blue dress, faded into view from the doorway to their right.

"I've been following your intent," she told the two women. "If you both enter Astara's time stream, you will automatically change the past from her inception."

"And that isn't what we came to do," Ginny assured her.

"What else can we do?" Astara asked.

Marne motioned for them to follow. Ginny and Astara walked through the room where Marne had stood and passed through another door. Ginny glanced back at the larger, outer room. It was sparsely furnished as if Marne either had few needs here or didn't understand decorating. She ducked into the next room, which was something like a holodeck only with space and stars all around.

12

"If you and I stand on the platform," Marne said pulling Ginny up beside her, "Astara can re-enter her own timeline while we observe. Sections I will narrate but it will be useful at times to take hers or others' perspectives, and you will be able to enter their experience without altering anything."

"Sounds complex," Ginny commented.

"Merely a matter of layering dimensions of reality in a construct within the Web of All."

"I'll take your word for it," Ginny remarked.

Astara stood below on the transparent starry universe-scape.

"Are you ready, Astara?" Marne called.

Astara glanced up and nodded.

In a blink, she was gone and a scene began playing all around them. Enmarsikil as a young boy stood on a portico looking out over a courtyard. Marne picked up the narration.

As the firstborn, Enmarsikil achieved all the firsts. When he was younger and watched his siblings struggle with what he had already accomplished sometimes he felt the superiority of a conqueror, but mostly he felt compassion. He reached out and helped them as much as he could and was often surprised by the tweaks they managed to incorporate. Secretly, he would try out those tweaks and play with the new ideas.

However, as he matured the time came when he no longer felt able to share his growth with the others. Mainly, it was because the changes he felt in his body were new and not entirely in his control. Plus, his powers began surging in unpredictable ways that took Teacher long hours and much patience to help him harness.

The one thing no one could help him manage was an unfamiliar desire that had sprung up. He'd watch the older girls, feel his heart race and longings flush through him. While Teacher explained those changes to him as well in dry technical terms, Enmarsikil was certain there was more to his desires than mechanics, so he broached them with his mother.

I talked to him of love, of the joining of heart and soul and not just body. I talked to him, yes, of powering up. But I also talked to him of a bond no one could break. And in the night when he lay on his bed to contemplate things, his heart yearned for the experience I had described.

Marne paused sighing. The scene shifted away from Enmarsikil and Marne picked up the narration.

Astara, on the other hand, was the baby of them all. Born last, she watched her siblings try out everything first and by the time she was old enough to attempt the same, she had the technicalities all worked out. A little practice and poof! the work was done. This did not necessarily endear her to the older children who had struggled for the achievements she sneezed at. As a result, she sought out time alone where she practiced the things that popped into her head or she sat and day-dreamed.

At first, her dreams were merely of fitting in or of being so marvelous, the others were amazed and looked up to her. When they teased her, instead, she gave up that dream. However, her proclivity for learning things easily, and her frequent disappearances drew the attention of the trainers. Some, like Giramusen, got annoyed when Astara couldn't be found. I, on the other hand, saw the spark of difference and individuality as a trait to be nurtured.

Then word was whispered around that a special team was being auditioned. Enmarsikil, himself, would choose individuals to try out and, if they were good enough, they'd get special training. Astara had always looked up to the eldest brother. When he was demonstrating techniques for others, she watched him closely. A keen empath, she couldn't miss the loneliness in his eyes or the kindness of his actions. Now she wished she dared to dream he would choose her, but she was the youngest, and there were so many others older, more experienced and better than her at everything else that her chances were slim.

As Ginny watched Astara's past, she felt a shift and her perspective now seemed as if she were right there in the Guardian past. She was aware, in particular, of Astara's feelings.

Astara sat in a lecture hall listening to Teacher's voice drone on. She was about to drift into one of her familiar daydreams when she felt a prickle up her neck. Whipping her head around, Astara was surprised to see Enmarsikil standing in the Lecture Hall doorway. The tall, wavy haired young man wore his usual focused expression, though in his few relaxed moments, his full lips were known to curl into a smile, and his crystal blue eyes to sparkle like sapphires. Right now, he looked at Astara intently and suddenly the distance between them shrank.

"Follow me," he whispered, his voice echoing.

With a soft gasp, she snapped back to reality at her chair and shook her head to clear it. Slowly, with her heart pounding, Astara gathered her belongings, slipped out of her row and raced up the stairs. She met him in the corridor outside. As she began walking beside him towards the gymnasium, the walk took on the surreal quality of slow motion. Even the dust motes in the sunbeams seemed to slow almost to a stop in mid-air. The world of her dreams, the ones where she was chosen as an equal, and her real life were colliding. As they stepped inside the wooden-floored gym with its doubly high ceilings, things sped back up to normal.

Older siblings from the other generations were already gathered inside. They glanced their way as Enmarsikil led Astara inside. Whispers seemed to flutter about her like a thousand birds all flapping their wings at once. Immediately self-conscious, Astara shrank back against the far wall to avoid their taunts. But Enmarsikil's eyes and ears were sharp. He tolerated no disrespect on his team. One sharp glance about the room quelled any teasing. The group lined up to begin work, and Astara found a spot with the others. As she followed the others through Enmarsikil's drills, her confidence grew and she came out of her shell.

In that gymnasium, Astara found her true home. Every day she entered, Enmarsikil had a warm smile and an affectionate pat on the head for her. Every achievement she made, he cheered her on. It didn't matter that he praised all of the trainees' efforts; it was the fact that someone finally praised hers. She persisted through all of the trials making all of the cuts. After two shars of training, her proudest moment came the day when Enmarsikil named her to his final team. She beamed when he put the chain and medallion around her neck. She had a home, a place where she belonged and a purpose. No longer just the youngest; she was finally part of a group and accepted.

The eldest generation of children were now teenagers. Already the trainers were beginning to talk of bonding, and pairing and mates. Enmarsikil listened with a frown on his face. During the big lecture gatherings, he carefully counted all of the hybrids. He shook his head and recounted. Something seemed missing because there were 500 of them and one of him, in all an uneven number unless.... He tried to dismiss the thought that he'd been forgotten for this part of the process, but the idea had gained a foothold and would not be ignored.

Then, too, the Multi-Dims determined that unusual measures would have to be taken to ensure that his team awakened from some long sleep they were to take in time to perform their special mission. He was to know; they were not. He was to report on the implants affects on the them to Teacher; but not say a word to Father Ea. A young man of great integrity, the duplicity gnawed at his gut and kept him awake at night.

15

"Enmarsikil shouldered heavy burdens at Teacher's bidding," Marne said as if from a distance.

The focus of the scenes became directed at observing the older teens.

After discussing the implants with the other Multi-Dims, Teacher sought out Enmarsikil. The older man was by far the tallest of the Multi-Dims with flowing black hair to his shoulders that matched his long cape. His chiseled features accentuated the intensity of his gleaming black eyes. At the moment Teacher found Enmarsikil standing on a portico watching the other hybrids socialize by generation and gender. Teacher eagerly explained the next phase of the mission.

"Then what do I tell them about the implants?" Enmarsikil asked, ready to round up his team.

"You don't," Teacher replied.

"What?"

"For their own good, they cannot know any of this. When working with the Anunnaki, they must have nothing to hide," Teacher explained.

"Then what do I tell Father Ea?" Enmarsikil wanted to know.

"Ea and Anu also must not know. There are too many political implications to this project already. Anu has a delicate balance to maintain amongst his people, and Ea is the one force he can use to maintain that stability. They, too, need to be free to do their jobs."

Enmarsikil set his jaw, his eyes dark. "I cannot lie to Father Ea. He always asks me for a report of the hybrids. If something is done to them, I must tell him."

"The chosen ones will be brought to the Healing Wing for a special physical as part of the testing of their enhanced powers," Teacher explained patiently. "That's all Ea needs to know."

Enmarsikil began pacing. "I don't like to lie. My integrity is at stake."

"You will not have to lie, son. You will not tell Ea anything that is not the absolute truth. You just will not tell him everything."

"And when he asks me 'Is that all?' then what do I tell him?" Enmarsikil demanded, his eyes blazing.

"You tell him yes and inwardly think, 'That is all I can tell you for the safety of the others.'"

Enmarsikil clenched and unclenched his fists. "Is that all I am good for? As a go between? The one who takes the chances first, so the
16

others don't have to?" he demanded in a low growl. "Am I just the lab animal? I suppose you'll put an implant in me first to make certain it works before you risk the procedure on the others?"

Teacher blinked and took a step back. The words echoed those Marne had attacked him with when he first altered baby Enmarsikil's growth cycle.

"No, of course not!" Teacher sputtered.

"Really? Then why are there exactly 250 girls and 250 boys?" Enmarsikil challenged. "Why are they being tested, even now, for whom they will be paired with...for their mate? Why have I no mate?" Enmarsikil demanded, his body trembling with fury, "unless I'm expendable, and they are not."

Teacher stood before the distraught young man in shocked silence. "You are not expendable, son," he said huskily. "You are all I've got."

"Then why do you test everything on me first? Why do you teach everything to me first?" Enmarsikil cried, slapping his hands against his chest. "Why do you keep asking me to bear heavier and heavier burdens alone...always alone?"

Teacher backed up and sank onto a stool. Marne's words from cycles ago rang through his ears, and he groaned at the realization of their truth. *"You will sacrifice the one for the benefit of the many."*

"Oh my. What an error I've made," he groaned covering his face with one hand. "Despite my far-sighted vision, I was so focused on the mission we'd undertaken, that I didn't see the need in front of my face." He shook his head.

"That's it? That's all?"

Teacher raised his eyes to meet Enmarsikil. "I am so sorry. I have failed you, my only son."

"You can't do anything?" Enmarsikil pleaded, fear creeping into his heart.

"I will try," Teacher promised. "At this point, I don't know what I can do, but I will try."

With that he rose stiffly from the stool and slowly shuffled inside.

Enmarsikil spent long days in a darkness of spirit. No one could reach or soothe him, not even his mother's hug. Almost, little Astara's smile touched him but it was if even that bright ray of sunshine was no match for the darkness inside. At the same time, Teacher absented himself from everyone and everything. Enmarsikil felt more alone than he had ever felt. He was the solitary odd man out, Teacher had admitted it. All the others would be paired up to act out Teacher's dreams, and he would

17

grow old in the gloom alone.

Several cycles went by. With little enthusiasm, Enmarsikil put his team of hybrids through their paces then spotted Teacher as they filed out. He turned and made his way to a secluded porch where the Multi-Dims frequently met in private. Teacher followed. They stood silently looking out over a garden area, neither willing to be the first to speak. Finally, Teacher cleared his throat.

"I have come to right a great error to the best of my ability," he said quietly.

Enmarsikil merely nodded.

"Everything you charged me with is true. I was so focused on the project, I forgot who you were as an individual. I sacrificed the one for the many, and I am deeply sorry for my error."

Enmarsikil neither moved nor spoke.

"I called you my son but I have never treated you as such. I intend to remedy that," Teacher continued.

Still no response.

"You were right in charging that I ask you to bear great burdens without giving you a mate to ease their weight. Unfortunately, even with our technology, the changes the Anunnaki have made to this project mean that no more hybrids can be created."

Enmarsikil stiffened, his eyes reddening, but he still maintained his silence. Teacher took a step closer.

"It took me long hours of searching, but I saw a future time...a time when it could be possible for one of the girls to become available to be your mate. We can set up the conditions under which this would be possible. I can write it into the final bylaws for the Anunnaki's use of the hybrids on Ki so that all would have to honor the change."

"And how will all this come about?" Enmarsikil asked skeptically.

"As I sifted through the planes, I saw a time when an enemy of the ruling family will arise from within," Teacher said.

"One of the clan will betray their own?" Enmarsikil asked incredulously, turning towards Teacher.

"His lust for power will override blood ties."

Enmarsikil shook his head in disbelief.

"It will be a dark time for the Anunnaki and hybrids alike Their loyalties will be called into question and they will be sorely tried."

Enmarsikil grimaced and looked away.

"However, if one of the females chooses to remain loyal to Anu, his family and her siblings, in spite of the desperateness of her own

18

situation, she can be freed of her contractual partner at her request. Then, if she wished, she could choose another mate or live free."

"And how does that help me?" Enmarsikil wanted to know.

"Study the hybrids now. If there is one woman you feel particularly drawn to, we will arrange for you to get to know her. If she is equally attracted to you, then I would educate that woman as to her potential destiny before she left for her assignment on Ki."

"And what if she rejects me? Or forgets me? What if the test is too much for her?" Enmarsikil asked.

"There is no guarantee that the future I saw will occur, that one of the girls will return your affections, or that she would hold the course. But no future I see in the Visioning Sphere is ever certain, son. All I see are the outcomes with the highest probability of occurring. But it is the best I have to offer you, and I will do all within my power to make it so."

Enmarsikil took a deep breath and sighed. "Thank you...for caring. If I see someone I like and she returns my affections, I will let you know." He turned to leave.

"And Enmarsikil, don't...."

"....tell Ea," he finished. "I understand."

And with that vague promise offered, Enmarsikil went about his daily tasks with little more hope than before. Instead, he threw himself into research and his special team and tried to forget.

Being the first to try everything, being the go between between the trainers and the Anunnaki, being the responsible one were just a few of the things Enmarsikil hated about being the eldest. He particularly hated being told of developments concerning his siblings and not being able to warn them. On this occasion it was a matter of learning that, as once happened to him, their growth and maturation were going to be sped up by 7-10 years. Even as Teacher droned on, he stopped listening to the explanation that the entire mission had changed because of Anunnaki politics. Cold fear for his siblings' well-being gripped his stomach. He couldn't get out of his mind that none of them were seen as individuals but only as disposable tools. Part of him was very angry.

In order to effect the growth changes, the trainers hosted a dance for the hybrids. The easiest way to make the changes was to allow the dance music to act as carrier waves to transmit special frequencies to the hybrids' brains. The Trainers decorated the large ballroom with sparkles and floating, multi-colored lights. Strings of blinking gold lights were wound around the solid support columns throughout the room. At one of end of the festive hall, a table was laden with refreshments. However, the

Trainers made certain to keep Enmarsikil apart from the others and made him wear specially filtered earplugs. As the eldest, his brain and body had already matured; only harm would come to him if he experienced the frequencies.

Enmarsikil stood alone on a railed platform and watched his unsuspecting siblings dance. After a while, he spotted the youngest, the girl from his special team. She stood apart from the others and scanned the crowd. His heart always went out to her when he saw her. She was exquisitely sensitive and highly intelligent and every bit the loner that he was.

Now, she glanced up and headed toward the platform. Still apparently unaware of him, she climbed the steps and tried to peer over the railing. Even though she was now nine, she was petite. Enmarsikil watched her struggle for a moment then walked over and bent near her ear.

"Do you want a boost up?"

Astara glanced up and smiled at him. "Please."

Enmarsikil wrapped his arms around her waist and lifted her high enough so her knees rested on the railing and he merely had to support her. She scanned the crowd intently.

"I must remember them," she murmured.

"You will never forget your brothers and sisters," Enmarsikil assured her.

"Marne said there may come a day when the memory is too faded to recall. I must remember their energy patterns," she explained.

He frowned. "Oh."

Astara continued to gaze at her siblings then let herself down from the railing, her pretty face very serious. "This mission is all too big for us," she told him earnestly. "We're too few."

A chill ran down his spine as she echoed his own concerns. "You'll grow up," he heard himself say as he tried to sound reassuring, "and then you'll be big enough for the task."

Her blue eyes searched his. "I really hope that's true."

Enmarsikil gave her a smile and a pat on the head.

She smiled her thanks and the bright cheerfulness of her smile and sparkling blue eyes flew straight to his heart.

"Too bad she's the youngest," he thought as she turned to descend the platform's stairs.

Just as her foot hit the first step, the music changed, and so did her body. Enmarsikil did a double take because with each step, she seemed to age a year or more. A wave of dizziness passed over him, and he grabbed

20

the rail to steady himself.

When he looked back up, Astara hit the main floor, turned back toward him, smiled and waved. He swallowed hard for she looked now to be 3-4 years older, and her flat chest had definitely been replaced by the curves of impending womanhood. He had expected his siblings to change, but 3-4 years in less than a minute? He left the platform to find Teacher and interrogate him. Part of him was angry at how fast their growth was being pushed; yet, another part of him held a speck of hope.

CHAPTER 3 - UNLIKELY ROMANCE

Several cycles after the growth enhancement treatments, the changes had slowed. For the older hybrids who had already been closer to maturity, the changes had stopped and their powers had stabilized. For Astara's generation, and especially for the youngest hybrid of all, the changes continued. Now closer to a 15 year old, she struggled with the magnitude of changes the growth treatments had brought.

Since the hybrids would be accompanying the Anunnaki to Ki, Teacher had decided they would give a demonstration of their powers. Everything from martial arts to healing, creating realities via harmonics to dance. Astara took part all the way through but was dreading her final dance number with Marki. He wasn't musically or rhythmically inclined, and you need excellent musicality to make the courtship dance sizzle.

To add to her problems, the stress of performing was causing further internal growth. She could feel it all day so it came as no surprise to her when she went to put on her dance costume that it would have to be let out in the bust and the hips again. However, when news came that Marki had been injured in an earlier demonstration and had been taken to the Infirmary, Astara rushed out to find Marne.

She crouched down and crawled to the edge of the viewing stand. Thankfully, Marne was seated close to the edge, and it wasn't hard to get her attention. Astara hastily whispered her dilemma then went back to the dressing room to wait.

22

Enmarsikil hadn't noticed the minor commotion at the side of the viewing platform. He was enjoying the choreographed dance his siblings were performing and the special effects their combined fields produced. Suddenly, he heard Marne's voice inside his head. He turned toward her, and she beckoned him over.

"Astara's dance partner was injured in the sparring and she is supposed to present the finale," she whispered to him.

"What can I do?" he wondered.

"Be her partner."

"What?" he almost squeaked out loud.

"Quickly, go to the dressing rooms and get changed."

Enmarsikil slipped off the stand and headed toward the staging area still somewhat in shock. The girls inside put Marki's suit up against him, and the size discrepancy was readily apparent. Frantically, they searched the wardrobe area for something of a better fit and found a silver, one-piece jumpsuit with red flames streaking up the legs.

Unused to the chaos of open dorm living, Enmarsikil ducked behind a clothes rack, shed his clothes and struggled into the jumpsuit. Moments later, he reappeared feeling highly self-conscious in the body-hugging outfit. The girls appraised him with a critical eye. Aiya, a fiery tempered brunette, grabbed a long red scarf, wrapped it around his waist like a sash, and let the longer end drape down the front. Satisfied, she pushed him out the door toward the edge of the stage where Astara nervously waited.

Enmarsikil took his place beside her, looked down and gulped. In place of her usual leggings and tunic, she was wearing a body-revealing costume. A tight, short-waisted bodice of gold pushed her breasts together and up revealing deep cleavage. He stared for several moments before even noticing anything else. Finally, his eyes traveled down along her exposed midriff to the low slung skirt of filmy, sky blue gauze.

Feeling an uncomfortable tightening in the crotch of his costume, he tore his eyes away and watched the choreographed story-dance that was nearing completion. He leaned sideways trying not to see too much.

"What dance are we doing?" he whispered near her ear.

Astara glanced up, saw who she was now partnered with and smiled broadly. "The courtship," she replied hastily as the dancers in the courtyard took their bows and began to file off.

"What?" Enmarsikil exclaimed. "But...I...."

"Just lead it," Astara said hastily as the last of the previous dancers left the courtyard. "It's up to me to do the rest."

With his heart pounding in his ears, Enmarsikil let her lead him into the center of the large, paved courtyard. He drew her in close with one hand holding hers and the other cupping the bottom of her shoulder blade while she lightly rested her free hand on his shoulder. The music began, and he swayed with her for a couple of measures getting the feel of how she moved her body. The tempo was slower, sensual and syncopated. Alone it was a very sensual piece; as part of a dance, it was designed to complement and augment the passion of the dancers' movements. Feeling woefully underprepared, Enmarsikil took a deep breath and began.

What he had intended to be a simple left side pass to an anchor point behind him, Astara turned into one of the most sensual moves he had ever seen. She swayed her hips seductively as she passed by and rolled her body up from toe-to-head like a sinewy wave when she anchored. On the next pass by him, she hijacked the move when she was directly in front him. She stopped, placed her hands on his upper thighs and rolled her hips in figure eights in front of him while she leaned her upper shoulders and head against his chest.

Fire seemed to shoot through him from his groin spreading outwards. He felt a little dizzy, and it was all he could do to remain standing. He had never experienced the dance like this before. Then again, his mother had always been very modest while teaching it. Now, though, he was experiencing full, unbridled passion in all its throbbing glory. This petite young hybrid was making him feel things he hadn't suspected were possible, and it was all he could do to keep his head straight enough to lead the dance.

On the next pass, he caught her back and whipped them around in a one-arm spin. She locked her gaze with his, and he swallowed hard. Desire blazed in her eyes and seared him through her touch. His mind spun wondering if she could be feeling the passion she was creating on the dance floor with him.

Hope, that dangerous emotion, caught hold of his heart much as the passion of the dance had taken over his libido. Enmarsikil's mind raced. They were pushing her growth. Before long she would be fully mature. They'd always shared a close bond. He'd always thought she was special. He'd never thought about her for a mate because she was the "Little One." However, as she ran her fingers through his hair, over his shoulders, down his chest then shimmied down his legs, Enmarsikil knew there wasn't much little about her anymore.

He needed to catch his breath, gain a moment to straighten his thoughts. He spun her towards himself, caught her, wrapped his arm

24

around her back and slow-danced. In response, Astara gazed lovingly up at him. He fought the urge to kiss her rose-red lips. She leaned her head against his chest and sighed contentedly.

The music shifted, intensified and he pressed her close to his body. His gazed locked with hers as they ground pelvis-against-pelvis in slow hip circles. She caught her lower lip in her upper teeth, her eyelids drooping languidly. He dipped her back, sweeping her long hair against the flagstones. Then he snapped her back up, and she wrapped one leg around his hip, crotch meeting crotch.

The pressure and the heat were exquisite and unlocked desires he'd kept tightly bottled. For a moment, he felt the urge to roll her to the ground and grind himself against her. But the music changed, and he snapped her into an intense pattern of movements across the courtyard during which their eyes rarely left each other's face. Moments later, he dropped down to one knee draping her back over it. The End! The onlookers applauded; they rose and took their bows. The dance was over.

Enmarsikil returned backstage with Astara. He peeled the silver jumpsuit off and slipped back into his own clothes. Astara hadn't had a chance to change yet; the other girls gathered around congratulating her on a sizzling performance. She spotted Enmarsikil, broke away from the others and caught his arm before he could leave. She reached her arms up around his neck, pressed herself against his chest and gave him a lingering kiss on the cheek. If she'd had any idea how little self-control he had left after that dance, she might have been less effusive. He kissed her back then hurriedly left.

Enmarsikil sped away to his research gardens trying to busy himself in the familiar. The gardens encompassed a series of branching, meandering gravel paths. Some led to food crops, others to beds of flowers and trees, and the main path wandered from the back door of the research wing to the large fish ponds way in the back. High brick walls surrounded the gardens helping to maintain an even temperature inside.

At the moment, Enmarsikil tried working in the beds with food crops. But he dropped tools and kept bending down to pick them up with shaking hands. A twig snapped behind him, and he spun around to see Teacher coming toward him down the walk. He straightened fully to greet him.

"You saw?" Enmarsikil asked desperately trying to hide his eagerness.

Teacher nodded.

"What do you think?" he pressed hardly daring to breathe.

25

"By all appearances it would look as if she were interested in you," Teacher conceded laying a hand on the young man's shoulder. "Just remember, she has undergone enormous changes in a very short time. She may have been reacting to them and not to you."

"But the way she looked at me...." Enmarsikil protested.

"Is the way she might look at any man right now given the acceleration of maturational factors," Teacher cautioned.

Enmarsikil's face fell and his shoulders drooped.

"You need more than that dance to go on," Teacher said squeezing the young man's shoulders.

"That's hard to come by when I spend so little time with the others," Enmarsikil mourned.

"We'll find a way," Teacher assured him. "I promised you this opportunity."

Enmarsikil nodded and watched his mentor leave. He set down his tools and made his way to his room. Large and spacious, he had filled it with books, apparatus of varying designs, specimens and seer's tools. However, he had what he called his dreaming corner. Here he would open a plane and transfer a memory he wanted to replay and relive. Then, at any time in the future, he only had to open that plane and step inside, and he could relive it as he wished.

Now, he opened a plane, transferred his memory of the dance and entered into it moving and feeling as he had earlier. He changed just one thing, though. At the point where he brought Astara close, he kissed her. He wasn't sure exactly how a kiss would feel, but he hoped it was something like what he felt in his imagination.

Astara had been giddy when the dance ended. So much went through her head. The dance had been a huge success and everyone was congratulating her. However, it had aroused feelings and sensations in her body that were foreign and unexpected. Then there was the way Enmarsikil had looked at her during the dance. His eyes had suggested that she was the most desirable woman he knew. At one point, she could have sworn he would kiss her.

She closed her eyes at the thought, her breath coming in soft pants. She could feel his hands on her bare skin again, and when they had done the groin-grind something hard had pressed against her igniting this heat inside. She'd gotten hot and moist and longed for...something. When she had whipped her leg around his hip for the crotch press, her supporting knee had nearly given out. Whatever he had, her body craved it. It called

26

to her in a hungry voice, and her own desires screamed yes.

Marki caught her daydreaming about the dance the next day and taunted her. She dashed off crying. *Maybe he's right*, she thought. *I mean, I am the baby. Who am I to hope Enmarsikil would desire me?*

She ran across the field on the mountain side of the compound just beyond the Academy walls. She was following the walls around the research center idly wondering what lay beyond. Suddenly, she spotted an old door partly off its hinges behind an old, gnarled tree. Glancing about, she hurried over, pulled the door back farther and squeezed inside.

She entered a magnificent garden filled with all types of trees, plants and birds. Astara spun about trying to take everything in at once. She caught a flash of iridescent blue in a nearby treetop and took a step backward to get a better view. With the second step back, she stopped cold, or better yet was stopped cold by a warm, upright body.

Stifling a scream, she spun around to face Enmarsikil.

"Oh!" she cried bringing her hand up to her mouth. "I'm so sorry. I shouldn't be here." She backed toward the door in the wall preparing to flee.

"No! No!" Enmarsikil countered quickly reaching out to stay her flight. "It's all right. You can stay. I'd love the company."

Astara stopped and studied him. Her heart skipped a beat when she saw the hopeful, soulful look in his eyes. The heat flushed to her cheeks and reddened her lips when she appraised his taut, chiseled body and full, slightly quivering lips.

Quickly, she inhaled a breath of fragrant air and tried to calm her racing pulse. "What do you do here?" she asked allowing him to slip his arm behind her, guiding her with a hand placed between her shoulder blades

Enmarsikil glanced about the garden wondering in which direction to take her. "I research different types of plants...try to create better strains."

"Why?"

"To make things grow under different conditions...produce better fruit..."

"For the mission?" she asked, blue eyes sparkling.

"I suppose," he replied.

"What are these?" she asked, taking his hand and drawing him over to a nearby bush.

Dazed by her soft touch, he followed temporarily tongue-tied. "Um...that's...a-a new strain of fruit," he finally managed.

"And this?" Astara asked spinning toward a well-pruned tree.

Enmarsikil happily followed her about his garden answering her questions and describing his work. At last, Astara glanced at the garden chronometer.

"I really should go now," she said. "I have instructionals in a little while."

Crestfallen, Enmarsikil refused to relinquish her hand. "Will you come back?" he asked hesitantly.

"If you'll let me."

"You're welcome any time you're free," he replied walking her toward the garden door.

Astara paused gazing wistfully up into his eyes. When he remained stoically beside her, she turned and slipped out the door. He waved as she took off across the field.

Enmarsikil went back to work on his latest flower, one he had been cross-pollinating when she arrived. He worked for a while longer whistling and smiling, a dreamy look in his eyes.

Astara returned to instructionals as dreamy as ever. Since that was nothing new for her, nobody noticed anything unusual. Had they, though, they might have caught the light flush that periodically crept into her cheeks. It was gradually erased by a frown of confusion as instructionals turned toward a discussion of the pairing process.

When the next mid-cycle break came again, Astara headed back to the door in the garden wall. She slipped inside and quietly made her way along the garden paths seeking Enmarsikil. She heard splashing and quickened her steps. Rounding a corner, she spotted him scooping leaves out of a fishpond. When the twig she stepped on snapped loudly, he dropped the skimming net and spun around.

"Sorry," she apologized. "I didn't mean to startle you."

"That's ok," he replied, picking the net back up and dumping out its contents on land. "I'm just glad to see you. I thought maybe you wouldn't come back."

He pretended to check out a fish that surfaced in order to avoid her gaze.

"Oh no. I wasn't staying away on purpose," Astara quickly assured him. "Teacher and Marne were talking about some sort of pairing exercises. It's all very confusing."

A jolt shot down his spine as Enmarsikil realized exactly what exercises they might be. For a moment he squinted his eyes tightly closed

28

and breathed heavily. He considered asking Astara to leave. But he remembered Teacher's promise, glanced up and caught the merry glint in her eyes. He swallowed hard.

"I'm sure it will become clearer over time," he managed.

She laughed lightly and its music lifted his spirits. "That's what the trainers keep saying."

Astara moved closer and peered into the water of the pond. "What's in here?"

Enmarsikil felt her shoulder brush his arm and warmth spread through his chest. "These are some fish I've been breeding. I've separated them into several ponds depending upon gender and age."

"Kind of like a fish version of us hybrids," she remarked off-hand.

He frowned at the analogy; the likeness was too close for comfort. Pushing the idea out of his mind, he led her from pond-to-pond showing her the different fish.

Coming to the pond with his best fish, he pointed out one with especially pretty markings. Astara leaned out over the edge of the bridge on which they stood attempting to get a better glimpse. Suddenly, she wavered and started to fall forward.

In a flash, Enmarsikil reached out, grabbed her around the waist and leaned back with his full weight. She teetered for a moment falling back against him with a soft thud. For a moment, they stood there her back to his front until he carefully turned her around.

His chest rose and fell heavily. "Are you all right?" he asked, his voice husky with concern.

Still shaking from her near fall, Astara nodded breathlessly and gazed into his clear blue eyes. Enmarsikil's strong arms trembled as he held her. In response, she leaned more fully against his muscular chest.

All she could think was that this felt every bit as good as the dance. She had watched the other boys, particularly the older ones who hadn't picked on her much growing up. None of them made her catch her breath, or made her heart sing, or engendered the heat that Enmarsikil did. She bit her lower lip wishing he would kiss her and looked up at him through her long lashes.

He had her in his arms. He trembled with the effort to keep from sweeping her off her feet. He'd dreamed of this moment, wished for it, longed for it. But would she let him? He gazed at her upturned face and her full red lips.

Hesitantly, Enmarsikil bent his head toward hers as time seemed to stand still. At last their lips touched, and he felt like he could hardly breathe. He slipped his hand behind her head prolonging the moment any way he could and loathe to let her go. Finally, with a deep sigh of satisfaction, they pulled apart.

"Mm, that was...special," Astara remarked happily.

"Yes, just like you are," Enmarsikil replied.

"I'm special?" she asked, eyebrows raised in surprise.

He nodded. "You're sweet and kind and inquisitive," he said, inwardly thinking 'and unbelievably sexy.' He smiled. "I appreciate your coming to see me."

"But I love coming to see you," Astara replied enthusiastically. "I love listening to you talk about your work. And I like spending time with you."

Hope took root and sent shoots into his heart. "I'm glad," he said. "I feel the same way about you."

Enmarsikil slipped his arm around her waist and led them over to a tall, spreading tree. They sat on a mossy patch with their backs against its trunk. He took her hand and held it in his, thrilled to know she at least liked him. While they chatted about inconsequential things, he periodically paused to christen her lips with another kiss.

All too soon the garden chronometer showed that it was time for her to return to the Academy. Enmarsikil walked her back to the door in the wall but was loathe to let her go. He pulled her back for one last quick kiss before watching her squeeze outside and race across the field.

Enmarsikil watched her go with mixed feelings. On the one hand, his heart was singing and dancing a giddy jig to know that the attraction between them was mutual. If it led to love, Astara was all he could have hoped for. But the knowledge that she would first have to be paired with another and would have to undergo dangerous tests in order to be with him weighed heavily on his heart.

He tried to forget, to only think about the hopeful possibilities, and buried himself in his work.

CHAPTER 4 - THE UNVEILING

The next series of instructionals were a break out of the pairing process. Astara paid careful attention to what the criteria were for personality harmonization, power synergization, interpersonal physical chemistry, augmented clairvoyance and the like. When she visited Enmarsikil, she intently scrutinized her interactions with him to see how they measured up to the standards talked about in the lectures.

Meanwhile, every visit she made to him, he unveiled more and more aspects of himself. He secretly attended many of the lectures and knew how far into the process they had progressed. Sometime soon, Astara would realize she would be paired against her will, and he would give her the choice option. But, he decided, if he was going to ask so much of any woman, he wanted her to see every aspect of himself. He couldn't afford to be too embarrassed about anything. It would be cruel to hide a "wart" as it were, have her go through the agony of the tests, only to discover she had made a mistake in the end.

When she visited next, he escorted her through the different labs in which he ran experiments. She always showed interest, asked questions and displayed an amazing aptitude for the work. On another visit, he told her about his lonely childhood, about being the first hybrid things were tried on before being used on the others. She frowned while he spoke and at times blanched at the things he related. When she left, he was almost certain it would be her last visit.

The chronometer marched on, yet he heard her cheerful call again, much to his relief. This time he told her his memories of the siblings as they grew up. He was always trained apart from them and brought in to demonstrate and coach. There were many days when he felt far removed from the others even though they all shared DNA.

Now, Astara had come again, and Enmarsikil took her into his most private space, his suite of rooms where he slept and studied. He curiously watched her almost tiptoe into his bedroom and gaze in awe about the room. Here he kept everything from the sublime to the grotesque.

Astara gazed in amazement at the sheer size of the rooms. How marvelous to have so much space all to yourself and not have to share it with siblings. She scanned the bookshelves along the right hand wall to see what tomes Enmarsikil read and referenced. There was one on male-female interactions including sex. That was a topic instructionals would soon cover. Without thinking, she pulled it off the shelf and leafed through it. The page suddenly opened to the reproductive body parts, complete with pictures. She stared at the page wide-eyed then, suddenly aware of his close presence, snapped the book shut. Enmarsikil had turned aside, glad she couldn't see his beet red face.

Recovering herself, Astara gazed at the large crystal orb set into a sunken retainer in the floor between the shelves and the bed. She knelt down to get a closer look, and Enmarsikil knelt beside her explaining how the Visioning Sphere worked.

After a while she moved on running her fingers lightly over a harp in beautiful harmonics. She turned the corner to the right entering a small alcove filled with more shelves and a desk in front of the window. On it was a telescope pointed skywards and she bent down to take a peek. Straightening up, she spun around and gave a sharp gasp because the shelves that lined the back of the alcove were filled with specimen jars of all types. With morbid curiosity, she checked out bugs, small animals, his collection of animal eyeballs (which made her shudder) and a collection of parasitic worms she wished she'd never laid eyes on. Suddenly, she stopped and stared. There in a large jar, an unborn baby bobbed in fluid.

"What is that?" she asked.

"A fetus," Enmarsikil replied. "It's mother couldn't carry it to term, and it was too young to live on its own."

Astara reached toward the tiny fingers and toes. "Were we this small once?" she breathed.

He nodded. "We all come from embryos too tiny to see with the naked eye."

She puzzled over it for a while. "The baby gets inside after a couple join?" she asked.

"Y-yes," he stammered feeling the heat rise to his face.

She stopped and straightened up. "I wonder what it's like to have one inside. Will that happen to us as well when we're paired and we join?"

It was such an innocent question that it took him off guard. Yet, he was certain she wouldn't like the truth.

"We are hybrids, Astara," he began technically.

"Yes." She turned and looked up at him with big, innocent eyes.

"Hybrids are...sterile," he told her.

She knit her eyebrows. "What does that mean?"

Enmarsikil ran his hand through his hair. "Sterile means none of us can procreate."

Her face remained blank, and he was beginning to sweat.

"We cannot make babies," he finally said flat out. "Our bodies aren't able to."

Astara's face fell as she glanced back at the fetus. "Oh. I...I didn't know."

To take her mind off the tiny baby in his collection, he gently guided her to what looked like an empty corner of his room. A round, stepped up platform stood there, and the air above it was strangely viscous.

Astara frowned and stepped around it. "What is this?" she asked, her intense curiosity back in a flash.

"This is my dream corner," Enmarsikil said. "If I have a memory I'm particularly fond of and I want to relive it, I create a plane for it here and store it. Later, I step back into it and re-experience it all over again."

"Really? Show me!" she urged, her eyes sparkling.

Enmarsikil started with a fairly safe memory, the day he caught her on the bridge and they kissed. Her face beamed as she watched. Then he let that one go and opened another. In an instant, the dance began again, and she gave it her undivided attention, until one particular moment occurred.

"Wait!" she cried. "We didn't kiss. I would have remembered if we'd kissed."

Enmarsikil was sweating profusely now and blushing heavily but there was no turning back. "I can alter the memory if I want to."

"You changed it so we kissed?" Astara whispered.

He nodded.

"You wanted to kiss me then?" she asked hesitantly. "You...you liked me even back then?" she probed.

He released that memory and brought up dozens more floating in air like giant bubbles. Astara studied them carefully letting out a soft gasp.

"These all have me in them? Why?" She turned toward him half-hopeful, half-afraid.

Enmarsikil looked down at the floor for a moment struggling with what to say. "Please don't think me foolish," he said at last shyly looking back up at her. "But I always thought you were special. Your smile used to buoy my spirits even when you were little, and I kept a collection of your smiles and laughter."

Astara's eyes flew wide open. She glanced toward the collection shelf in the other room then back at the bubbles of memories.

"When I would get lonely or feel down, I would open a bubble and relive your laughter," he continued. "It always seemed to flood my heart with sunshine."

Astara reached towards the bubbles and heard her own laughter. "I...I hardly know what to say. I only knew you made my heart sing, and you were easy to laugh and smile around. I had no idea I meant anything to you. I'm so used to being the baby nobody wants underfoot."

He took her hands, drew her close and kissed her forehead. "You've never been underfoot to me. You've always been my ray of sunshine."

The next instructional had a different air about it. There was a nervous tension in the room as the first generation filed onto the lecture platform. The Multi-Dims were all in attendance that day, but Marne in particular watched the gallery rows above. She spotted Astara and quickly got Teacher's attention.

Pay close attention to Astara's reaction, Marne told him mentally.

Teacher glanced up and grimaced. *If Enmarsikil is right, today will come as a shock,* he agreed.

But you don't want to overwhelm her, Marne warned him. *If we see her struggling, you need to call for a break...give her a chance to leave.*

Teacher nodded imperceptibly then faced the gallery and opened the session. "Today we are going to have the first pairing tests," he announced. "We will be testing men and women for their ability to augment one another's powers, to balance one another, for their psychological compatibility, sexual compatibility, and overall ability to

34

create synergy between them."

He paused as the fist man and woman stepped up to the first testing station.

"When two are determined to be most compatible through these tests, they will be given a mating contract and will be together for life. While we understand that you don't really know each other well or that you may already know of someone you're attracted to, these pairings have a purpose that is greater than personal interest. Your powers are needed in their maximized form for the job you must perform on Ki. For some of you, the match may lead to love and we hope it does. But it is not something we can guarantee."

The hybrids glanced at one another in dismay, the truth finally sinking in. Astara felt like someone had just hit her chest with a battering ram. Tears welled in her eyes, and the color drained from her face.

Marne prompted Teacher below, who quickly glanced up.

"Ok, one demonstration round, then we break," he said loudly.

A young man and a woman from the first generation volunteered. They stepped up to the platform in the well and began a series of psi-tests. When it was apparent that their energies didn't mesh, the volunteers stopped. The young woman sat down and another went up to take her place. This time the psi-test went well, so the pair were approved to move on to the next station.

In the gallery, Astara fought the urge to scream, *No! I already know who I want.* Now she realized that being with Enmarsikil would never be a reality. She glanced at the exit door dearly wishing she could escape the sudden torture.

Marne gave Teacher a sharp glanced, and he cleared his throat.

"The first generation are required to stay. I strongly urge the second generation to remain as well, but the third and fourth generation are dismissed," he announced.

Astara bolted up from her chair and out the door fleeing as if from a predator. Marne made a clone copy of herself who followed Astara from a distance. The distraught girl was beyond thinking of using a concealment plane to cloak herself, so Marne's copy produced one for her. As expected, Astara headed for the old door in the garden wall, and Marne maintained the cloak until she was safely inside.

Enmarsikil spotted her wandering along a path. He gave her a hug and took her to where he had created a new strain of poultry, chatting on about the cross breeding and difficulty getting it right. But she seemed not to hear him. A couple of times when he glanced up, he thought he saw a tear trickle down her cheek. Finally, he let his words trail off. He pulled her down beside him on a nearby bench and took her hands in his.

"Astara, is something wrong?" he asked tentatively. "Have I said anything that hurt you? You've been so quiet."

She shook her head and stared at her lap, her face drawn and pale. "We watched the older generation start going through the pairing tests. That's when Teacher told us that whomever the tests showed we should be paired with will be our mate for life. Did you know about this process?'

He nodded glumly.

"We can't choose a partner," Astara cried softly, tears rolling down her cheeks. "Birds and animals...even bugs get to chose their own mates," she added as a lacy-winged bug flew by, "but ours are chosen for us. It's not fair!"

"We were created for a purpose to do a specific job," Enmarsikil reasoned. "There are explanations for what they are doing."

"But how we feel about it doesn't matter?" Astara protested.

"I don't think it's part of the formula," he admitted.

"And for life! How long is that?" she asked, turning anguished eyes toward him. "Does anyone even know if we die? Are we like the Anunnaki who sleep in their graves or are we like the Multi-Dims who don't seem to die unless violence assails the universe? How-long-is-our-life?"

Enmarsikil stared at her in shock. No one, not even he, had thought of that question before. A weight pressed down against his chest.

"I'm not sure Teacher and they know how long we will live," he admitted frankly.

"Then how can they mate us for life?"

With his heart pounding against his sternum, Enmarsikil took a deep breath. "What if there were a way to be released from that contract someday and to be able to choose your mate for yourself?"

Astara snapped her head around to look at him, her eyes narrowed skeptically. "What do you mean? How?"

Enmarsikil took another deep breath to quell the nerves in his stomach. He was taking a huge risk, but he had to tell her all. "When they created me, they never even thought of a mate for me. There are 501 hybrids. I'm the one standing alone."

Astara's eyes widened in sympathy. "Oh, Enmarsikil. Here I've been worrying about wanting to choose who I get paired with, and you have no one at all?"

He shook his head and studied the ground for a moment while he

36

gathered his courage. "I asked Teacher, and he found out they can't create someone for me now, either."

"Oh, Enmarsikil. I'm so sorry," she said laying her hand on his arm.

"But he gave me one possibility."

Astara held her breath waiting for him to continue.

"If a woman returns my...affections," he said, his voice cracking and his mouth dry, "there is a way that we could be paired...in the future," he stammered nervously.

Her blue eyes growing intense, Astara studied him intently. "How?"

Enmarsikil licked his dry lips inwardly searching for the right words. "Teacher has seen a future time when rivalries within the House of Anu will create danger. He told me that if the woman I love remains loyal to Anu in spite of her difficulties, there will come a time when she may ask to be released from her contractual mate and can then choose whom she wants to be with."

"In other words, if she passes the test, she gets to claim the prize," Astara said wryly.

He nodded dismally.

Astara sat in silence for a long while thinking about all the things she had learned that day. "You told me this, why?" she asked. "Are you saying you're in love with me?"

Enmarsikil took a sudden gulp of air. "Oh my. Yes...yes I guess I must be."

"The kisses...the memory bubbles...you've loved me for a while," Astara pressed.

He rubbed his sweaty palms on his pants. "I don't think I knew what I was feeling until recently."

She turned toward him and held his gaze. "Are you asking me to be that woman who passes the tests and chooses you?" she pressed.

Enmarsikil rubbed his face and swallowed hard. This was his moment, his one chance at future happiness. But when he studied her earnest face, the knot in his stomach became a rock.

"I've tried to work myself up to this moment," he admitted. "This is my one chance to someday find happiness, but...."

"But what?" Astara asked laying her hand on his shoulder.

"The more I grew to love you, the more I knew I could never ask you to make such a sacrifice for me," he told her glumly. "I just can't do it."

He sighed and his shoulders sagged in defeat.

Astara put her cool hand against his cheek and turned his head till their eyes met. "Do you wish it?" she asked quietly.

His pained eyes said it all.

She kissed his cheek then sat back in contemplative silence. "It would be a sacrifice," she admitted after a while. "But it also feels like a ray of hope."

He studied her more closely.

"I-I've dreamed you were my mate," she confessed blushing, "both when I was asleep and when I was awake. It was all I could do to keep from crying in instructionals when Teacher said they'd pair us for life. I felt like a battering ram had slammed into me, like some horrible curse had been cast upon me, and I couldn't bear its weight."

His bright blue eyes registered his concern.

"But this is a possibility I thought I was being denied...the ability to choose."

He nodded barely daring to breathe.

"It's such a huge decision to make," she whispered.

"Astara," Enmarsikil said clasping her hands. "There is no pressure...understand me? No pressure. I would be thrilled if you chose me, and I would treasure you forever. But, I will not ask you to do this. It's a monumental decision, and only you can know if it's worth the risk."

She nodded smiling gratefully and squeezing his hands in thanks.

"Take your time to think about it," he urged. "You are in the youngest generation, so it will be some time before you go to Ki. Take the time to make sure you know your heart."

"But you do love me?" she asked seeking reassurance.

He brought her fingers to his lips and kissed them. "With all my heart."

"You've never asked if I love you," she pointed out softly.

"Th-that's more than I could a..." he began before she covered his mouth with her lips and kissed him like never before.

When they finally came up for air, his pulse was pounding throughout his body.

Astara put her lips near his ear and whispered, "I love you."

When Astara returned to the Academy, she sought out Marne's quarters to ask her for guidance. The door to her library was ajar. Astara knocked lightly then pushed it open wider. Marne looked up from her solid, carved oak desk, smiled and motioned for her to enter. Astara

38

stepped inside and shut the door behind her.

Nervously wringing her hands, she approached Marne's desk and sat in a chair opposite. She suddenly realized that to ask her question, she had to admit to sneaking out.

"Um...I've kind of broken rules," she said at last.

"Enmarsikil has told me he's had a very sweet visitor for a while," Marne responded calmly.

Astara's jaw dropped. "H-he told you?"

Marne nodded. "I'm easier to talk to than Nasdatal."

"I-I'm not in trouble?" Astara squeaked.

"Not if you're here to ask what I think you'll ask," Marne replied.

"About one girl having the chance to choose to be with him?" Astara asked.

Marne nodded.

"Is it for real...I-I mean the whole thing?" Astara stammered. "Contractual mate...tests...choice...Enmarsikil?" she added breathlessly.

Marne held her gaze. "The option is for real," she said steadily. "Teacher realized too late his oversight in preparing a mate for Enmarsikil. This is the only way he can see clear to make up for his error. Has Enmarsikil offered this to you?"

Astara nodded. "But what do I do?"

Marne studied her. "How do you honestly feel about Enmarsikil?"

Astara took a deep breath, dropped her eyes to her lap for a moment then looked back up. "Ever since I can remember, Enmarsikil was always the older brother. When all of the older kids just teased me or ignored me, he never did. He always listened to me, smiled at me, made me feel valuable. Wherever he was always felt like home to me. The thought of being without him makes me feel homesick. I don't know if that's love, Marne. It's not just a flutter feeling or the passion I felt during the dance. It feels deeper than that...more permanent."

Marne appraised the young woman before her. "For being the youngest, you certainly do come by a lot of wisdom," she remarked.

Astara blushed. "But how do I make this decision? It seems like there's so much to consider."

"There is," Marne agreed. "The pairing process is a life-changing event. But a decision like this would be as well. In one case, the choice would be made for you. In the other, you could make the choice."

"I need some time to think...some quiet...privacy," Astara said thinking of the noisy, crowded dormitory where she and the other girls were housed.

"Then take a few cycles," Marne offered. "You're known for going off on your own during rest periods. Take a few cycles to seek the time alone that you need."

"Thank you," Astara said rising and slipping out the door.

She hurried to the dorm, grabbed items she would need, stuffed them into a satchel, then slipped out the door. She climbed over the low spot in the compound's walls and dashed across the field disappearing in the trees on the slopes of the hill behind the Academy.

Astara wandered along game trails listening to the soothing sounds of nature. She hiked along a ravine that was home to a swiftly flowing river. Soon she came to a roaring set of high falls. Leaping from rock-to-rock above them, she made her way out to the center of the river and stood staring out over the precipice.

The mist billowed up to meet her and dappled her face. She thought of all the injustices she and her siblings faced, most of all having to be separated from Enmarsikil and joined with another. Her tears flowed freely and were wicked away on the wind.

When she could cry no more, she turned and retraced her steps to the shore. There she dried her eyes and left the roar of the river for the muffled peace of the forest. She walked on the padding of needles and fallen leaves following a slow-flowing stream deeper into the woods. As if instinctively seeking solace in her primary element, Astara's gaze rarely left the gurgling brook.

The land began rising and she climbed the rocks beside the stream like a mountain goat. At last she reached an upland pool where the water collected before spilling over the lip of a flat rock. She dropped her satchel onto the bank even as she stepped into the clear, cool liquid. Astara waded in and melted into the water becoming one with her element.

CHAPTER 5 - CHOICES MADE

While Astara melded with her element and let it wash the grief and anger from her heart, Enmarsikil stood on the bridge overlooking his fish ponds. He heard the crunch of gravel and barely turned his head. Marne walked closer and put her hand on his arm.

"Have faith, Enmarsikil," she said quietly.

He swallowed a sob and turned away. "It was so much to ask."

"She wanted you to ask."

"How do you know?" he asked.

"Because you are the only brother who has ever made a difference to her. If you hadn't asked and she had heard of the option later, she would have been very hurt and angry," Marne explained.

"But I've visioned and what she will have to go through...." he protested.

"Is not by our design," a bass voice interjected.

Enmarsikil turned to see Teacher standing beside Marne.

"We would not choose those tests were it up to us," Teacher assured him. "And I cannot explain why the future presents itself thusly."

Enmarsikil took a deep breath and nodded. "It's just...the more Astara came to mean to me...the less I wanted to see her hurt. I would rather suffer the sacrifice than put her through pain."

"And thus you know you selflessly love another," Marne told him with a hug.

"Does love always feel like this?" he asked.

"Only when it's the real thing and not just your head or your libido talking," Teacher told him.

"Oh."

"But think about this, son," Marne added before they turned to leave. "As much as you would spare her pain, she would willingly undergo that for you."

"How do you know?"

"It is written in every fiber of her being," Marne assured him.

She and Teacher turned, started walking down the garden path toward the research wing and disappeared into the mist.

When Astara finally felt cleansed, she pulled herself together in the pool and began moving toward the shore. At first, she appeared as a form oozing up from the water. But her shape took on greater solidity as she approached the shore. Finally, she stepped onto dry land, scooped up her satchel, headed toward a bright glade and lay down.

The ground was warm under her back, and she settled in against its firm support. The sky above was an open expanse with branches waving leaves along its fringes. Birds flitted back and forth overhead, and the languid buzz of insects filled her ears.

Astara closed her eyes and dreamed. She saw battles and struggles, unknown catastrophes and deception. She saw herself fade but also reawaken. For a moment of time, she held a lapis lazuli tablet in her hand feeling its smooth face. She saw Enmarsikil, older and changed, and felt his comforting strength as she leaned against his chest. A soothing warmth filled her, and he felt like home. She breathed in that sense deeply and smiled.

Opening her eyes, she found her heart and mind clear of confusion, her path laid out straight before her. Without hesitation, Astara picked up her satchel, rose from the ground and headed down out of the hills with the firm step of someone who knew her way.

Crossing the field, she stopped and looked from the Academy to the garden wall. Cloaking herself, she hurried over to the door in the wall and slipped inside. After a bit of a search, she spotted Enmarsikil sitting on a tree stump overlooking a fish pond. As she neared, he sensed her presence, stiffened, stood up and turned around.

He barely breathed as he silently observed her. He could not determine what her response might be and steeled himself for the worst. He had played this moment over and over again in his mind. He would

42

see her stand there for ages, then she would drop her head, turn around and walk away for good. And he'd prepared himself not to call out to her, not to call her back to him. But each time he saw that image, his heart shattered irreparably.

Astara gazed at the motionless figure a few yards away. She'd never seen Enmarsikil look so stoic, so pained, so scared. With one final burst of energy, she chose. She dropped her satchel on the ground, took a step toward him breaking into a run. Enmarsikil saw her coming and suddenly inhaled sharply. As she drew closer he stretched out his arms and she leapt into them. He swept her up hugging her to his chest. No words were needed as he gazed into her clear blue eyes. He kissed her losing himself in the joy of the moment.

For many long moments, they stood there wrapped in each other's arms. Finally, Astara swayed and Enmarsikil caught her.

"Are you all right?" he asked, his voice full of concern. "Are you sick? Have you eaten?"

She leaned against him. "Hungry I guess. I didn't want to chance being seen by going to the kitchens for food to pack."

"You haven't eaten?" Enmarsikil asked, alarmed.

"Not for a few days," she admitted.

He scooped her up in his arms and carried her towards the research wing. "We'll remedy that right now," he declared.

Carrying her inside, he took her to a small kitchen in his suite of rooms. He sat her in a chair at the table and quickly rummaged through the cupboards and cooler for breads, fruit and drink. He set a plate of food in front of her and got one for himself. He didn't touch his, though, but watched to make sure she ate and was feeling stronger.

After a few bites, Astara glanced at his worried countenance. "Are you going to eat, too?" she asked. "If your pallor is any indication...you didn't eat much while I was gone either."

Enmarsikil looked down and nodded. "My stomach was in too many knots."

"And now?"

"Flutters and nerves," he admitted.

"Or hunger pangs," she pointed out.

He smiled, looked up and grabbed a piece of fruit taking a bite. "I just want to make sure you're ok," he told her.

"And I don't want to make sure you're ok, too?" she countered.

A startled expression crossed his face. "You're...trying to take care of me?" he asked.

"Every bit as much as you're trying to take care of me," she told him.

Tears welled in his eyes and he fought to hold them back.

Astara reached out and tenderly caressed his cheek. "What's wrong?"

He kissed her hand then shook his head in his struggle against the flood that threatened to burst over the dam. "No one...no one's ever taken care of me," he whispered.

She slipped her arm around his neck and pressed her cheek to his. "But isn't that part of loving another? Wanting to take care of them and seeing that they're happy and healthy?"

He nodded still finding speech difficult. "It's just that...."

"We'll always seek to find ways to take care of each other," she assured him. "Even when we're apart. We'll find ways."

He nodded giving her a tight smile.

Though they finished eating in silence, they entwined their legs and smiled at one another. There was a simplicity and innocence just in being in each others' presence that they absorbed like sponges. Finally satiated, Enmarsikil picked up their plates and took them to a sink.

"We should probably go see Marne," he said.

Astara nodded. "I'll have to get my satchel."

He stayed her with an outstretched hand, turned it palm up and mentally "called" to her satchel. In moments, it navigated itself into the room and Astara plucked it out of thin air.

"I haven't seen that trick before!" she exclaimed impressed.

"It takes the manipulation of several elements. Since I'm attuned to all of them, I have all of them equally at my command," he explained.

"Wow! Cool trick."

With that, he slipped one arm around her waist and with his free hand wrapped a concealment plane about them. He led her through the labs and out into the Academy proper. They made their way to Marne's library, entered and shut the door. Dropping the concealment plane, they saw that Teacher was already there with her.

Marne and Teacher waited silently as the couple entered and gathered their courage.

"We...have something to tell you," Enmarsikil said at last.

"Astara came to me seeking guidance several cycles ago," Marne said. "Were you able to find clarity?"

Astara nodded. "I think I knew my decision before I left," she responded. "I just needed to muster the courage."

44

Marne smiled and nodded.

"And your decision is?" Teacher asked.

Astara turned toward Enmarsikil for support. "When I am with you," she told him softly, "you feel like home to me. When we are apart, I am homesick. My heart belongs to you even though duty will call me elsewhere."

She turned back to Marne and Teacher. "If there's even the slightest chance that Enmarsikil and I can be joined one day, that's a chance I want to take."

"This path will be arduous," Teacher warned her.

Enmarsikil, who stood behind her with his hands on her shoulders, squeezed gently.

"I had dreams of the future when I was gone," Astara replied. "I have seen the struggles. And I am willing to endure them," she said with simple honesty. "If there is a chance I can someday be with Enmarsikil, then I choose that."

She turned and gazed up at him. "You are worth the struggle."

His eyes misted with tears, and he pulled her into a close embrace. "Thank you," he whispered.

After a moment, Astara pulled from his embrace and turned to Teacher and Marne. "What must I do to make my decision formal?"

"Choose a symbol to be your own and affix it to this document," Teacher instructed.

Astara chose an eagle, rolled the cylinder in ink then rolled it onto the bottom of the document. Enmarsikil followed suit choosing a phoenix to be his symbol.

"There is a chance that as time passes and events occur, your memory may dim," Marne cautioned. "We need to devise physical triggers to awaken your memories."

"I have programmed a pendant that, once you receive it, will send you a strong awakening signal. You will know Enmarsikil as your chosen mate when he gives you this emerald," Teacher explained, laying an emerald pendant on a fine gold chain before her. "Enmarsikil is less likely to forget, so I think if he would devise something unique that he could give you, it would be a potent trigger as well."

He glanced up at Enmarsikil, who nodded.

"While we encourage you to continue seeing each other and building your relationship, any consummation of your relationship must wait until that future time," Marne warned.

The couple nodded their understanding and compliance.

"Now, go your separate ways and no word of this to anyone else. It is just between us," Teacher added.

Enmarsikil turned Astara towards him and lightly kissed her. "I will wait for you no matter how long it takes, and you have my prayers to the Creator of All."

"I will be true, Enmarsikil," Astara declared with conviction. "No matter what happens I will be true."

"I know you will," he replied, then kissed her forehead and left the room.

Several days later, Astara entered the garden to find Enmarsikil tending a flower he had planted in a specially designated section of ground. He smiled at her approach.

"This flower is special," he declared cutting off a deep red bloom and presenting it to her.

She took a deep breath of its sweet fragrance feeling the silky softness of its petals on her nose. "How so?"

"I created it to try to capture your beauty and radiance," he replied. "I began shortly after the dance. It has only now reached full maturity."

"Like me," she responded peering up at him over the mass of petals.

He nodded then slipped his arm around her shoulders. They strolled through the garden until they came to a mossy hillock where they sat.

"Things are different now," Astara told him.

"Because of the contract?"

She nodded. "I feel more hopeful, less cursed and doomed."

Enmarsikil smiled and squeezed her shoulders.

"But it will be a long time before we get to live that contract."

He nodded in acknowledgement of the unpleasant reality.

"Sometimes at night," she continued, "I see images of what may come. Our path isn't going to be easy."

"I've had premonitory dreams, too," Enmarsikil admitted. "Dreams of times you are hurt or are in danger, and I can't reach you."

Astara leaned her head against his shoulder. "I've seen that, too."

"Astara, I don't want you to hurt just for me," Enmarsikil said. "At times I feel it has been a very selfish thing I've done."

Astara's head snapped up and her eyes widened. "You don't believe the love we share is worth fighting for?"

Enmarsikil tenderly cupped his hand over her cheek. "I worry that

46

you will be worn out in that fight. I would protect you from all hurt if I could."

She placed her hand over his and leaned into his palm. "I know you would protect me, but you can't. No one can once the mission begins. It may be that our love and the hope of a future together is all that keeps me going when the way gets difficult."

He leaned forward and gently brushed her lips with his.

When it came time for her to leave the garden, she gave the flower back to him.

"But I mean for you to keep it," Enmarsikil protested.

"I can't," she replied shaking her head. "When others asked where I'd found it, what could I say? It grows nowhere else."

With that, she slipped through the door and was gone.

Enmarsikil went back to the hillock, sat down and stared at the flower. He remained in that position losing track of time. He could not even give the woman he loved a simple flower or their love would be betrayed. Tears welled in his eyes, and he squeezed them closed with his thumb and forefinger to prevent a flood.

"Enmarsikil, I missed you in the lab," a deep voice said quietly from close behind him. "Did you forget?"

"I guess I must have," Enmarsikil replied furtively wiping the tears away with his sleeve.

"You have never forgotten lab work before," Teacher said sitting beside him on the hillock. He glanced at the rose in his hand. "She didn't like it?"

Enmarsikil shook his head. "She couldn't take it with her for fear it would betray us," he replied turning to Teacher. "I can't even give the woman I love a simple flower when, were it in my power, I would give her the world. All I can give her are words."

Teacher pondered this in silence for a while. "Sometimes words are the most powerful gift."

"What can words do?" Enmarsikil queried morosely.

"The right words spoken with the right intent can bond two people across time, space and dimensions," Teacher replied.

Enmarsikil lifted his head to study his mentor.

"My people have a powerful ritual that, once performed and the words spoken, exchanges the essence of the couple. From there on out no matter the distance, the time or the dimension, they are forever in contact. If you wish, I will give you these words."

Enmarsikil thought hard. "How might it work between Astara and myself?"

"Were she in trouble, you would sense it. Though you might not be physically present, you could lend her strength when she most needed it. And wherever you went that bond would always draw you to her. No matter how long apart, how far the separation, you would sense her and be drawn to her...."

"And find her," Enmarsikil breathed, hope lighting his eyes.

"It is our most precious gift, and we only give it to our true mate. It binds two people for all eternity. It can never be undone," Teacher explained.

Enmarsikil thought hard. "I would like to offer her that. That feels foundational...more than just words...actions even in absence."

Teacher nodded and taught him the words and the simple ritual that accompanied them.

A few days later, Enmarsikil walked through the garden and spotted Astara bending over the roses he had created in her honor. Though a smile lit her face as she breathed their fragrance deeply, a lone tear trickled down her cheek. She lovingly caressed the petals jumping when he stepped on a twig.

Enmarsikil reached out and wiped the tear away, then engulfed her in his arms and kissed the top of her head. Finally, he drew her to his side and they slowly wandered the garden paths. They began to cross the bridge where they first kissed, but he paused in the middle.

"That was a poor gift I gave you the last time," he confessed.

"Oh no, Enmarsikil. It's beautiful," she hurried to say.

"But not something you can carry with you," he replied.

"No, but that's just how it is," she responded with a little shrug and looked away.

He placed his finger under her chin and turned her face back toward his. "What if I could give you a gift that stayed with you always?"

Curious, she gazed up at his intense blue eyes.

Enmarsikil explained the ritual Teacher had shared with him. "It could never be undone," he warned her, "but it would mean if you were ever hurt or in danger, I would know it and I could lend you my strength."

"And when you were lonely, I'd feel it and could send you some reminder of myself?" Astara asked with growing enthusiasm.

Enmarsikil nodded. "Is this something you would like?"

She nodded fervently.

He placed one hand over her head and his other hand over his heart. "Put your hands over mine," he instructed. "Then repeat after me."

48

"My honor for yours, nothing will be lost.
My soul for yours, never forsaken.
My strength for yours in your hour of weakness.
Though time and distance and dimensions separate, yet ever and
anon *will I hearken to your voice.*
Should fading come, will be my life for yours.
My gift is given."

At the moment they spoke, the fabric of existence seemed to melt. Astara felt her soul leave her body and enter his, while his soul deftly moved into her heart on a breath. She felt his essence mingling with hers then the two souls returned from whence they had come. Only now she felt different. A warmth burned through every fiber of her being; she was no longer alone.

She looked up at him; Enmarsikil's eyes were glowing.

"We can never be parted now, not for all eternity," he said with calm assurance. "Wherever you go, part of me will always be with you."

"And part of me with you," she whispered as he bent to kiss her.

CHAPTER 6 - PAIRINGS INTERRUPTED

As Ginny watched, the scene shifted to an office inside the Academy. A messenger hurried toward Teacher, a tablet in his hand. Teacher stopped, took the tablet and read quickly. He looked up at the messenger.

"Are you certain? Ea's ship is nearly ready to travel to Ki?" he asked.

The messenger nodded.

"Thank you. This news is important," Teacher said.

The messenger clicked his heels, spun around and hurried out the door. As soon as he was gone, Teacher placed an internal call to the rest of the Multi-Dims. In moments, they entered his office.

"I just received a message from Ea," he explained. "His ship is nearing completion for its mission to Ki."

"What should we do?" Giramusen, a tall willowy woman with bird-like features and flaming red hair, asked.

"We should gather the hybrids by generation," Emissary suggested. He was a man of vague description, medium in height and build, silvery hair and cloak, easy to miss in a crowd or the shadows.

"Yes," Teacher agreed. "It is time the eldest were paired and prepared to leave Nibiru."

In one cycle, all four generations filed into the largest lecture hall and took up seats by sections. They awaited their instructors, hushed whispers echoing around the room.

As Ginny watched, her mind raced. If the first generation was paired and went to Ki, her Earth, they would be lost and the cycle of history would begin all over again. She pursed her lips. If there was ever a time to intervene, now was it.

As Teacher had the first generation rise and prepare to come down front for the formal pairing tests, Ginny inched forward on the platform. Without any warning, she suddenly launched herself forward into the hologram. Marne reached for her, her hand missing her by just an inch. Instead, Ginny felt Astara grab her from the other side of the hologram, and they materialized side-by-side at the head of the instruments table, solid and visible to all in the hall. A collective gasp went up from the tiers of stadium seats in the wood paneled auditorium, and the Multi-Dims stared in shock.

"Stop!" Ginny shouted, staring directly at the First Gens. "Stop and step back! If you come forward, take these tests and go to Ki with Ea, you'll be lost. You don't survive!"

Teacher immediately stepped toward her. "Who are you?" he demanded forcefully. "How do you know they perish?"

The other Multi-Dims pressed in behind her and suddenly Ginny felt assailed by unseen forces.

"I'm a human from Ki," she said struggling to get the words out.

Spongy bubbles of energy pressed forward probing into her mind and body unbidden. She shook from the effects and her eyes rolled back in her head.

Without warning, future Astara stepped out in front of her, threw up her hands to ward off the Multi-Dims' probes and put up a solid bubble of energy around herself and Ginny to shield them.

"I'm Astara awakened in her human form," she announced with a nod to Ginny. "You planned for that to happen someday."

The Multi-Dims took a step back and relinquished their energy probes. However, they had maintained them for too long. Ginny's knees buckled and she slumped toward the floor. Marne rushed to catch her just before she hit the floor.

While Teacher dismissed the Guardians and Masters, Marne whisked Ginny from the lecture hall, through the corridors with their vaulted ceilings to a dark wooden door on her left. A slight motion of her hand and it popped open. Marne carried Ginny through her office to a door on the right and into her bedroom. She lay the weakened woman on her bed and immediately began checking her vitals as well as energy levels at the chakras.

Giramusen entered. "Would you like some help?"

Marne nodded while continuing her intense focus. Giramusen started bringing energy into her hands then entering it into the soles of Ginny's feet. Gradually, Ginny's heartbeat strengthened and she took deeper breaths.

A knock at the door sounded before Emissary entered the room. "Nasdatal sent me," he announced quietly. "When she has stabilized, he would like to see all of us in his quarters."

Ginny blinked her eyes open then stared wide-eyed at the beings around her. "You're Marne," she said pointing, "and Giramusen...and Emissary."

"Yes, but how did you know?" Giramusen challenged.

"Astara and I have journeyed back through her life, and I've journeyed with other human/hybrid symbiots. I've retrieved as much of their history as I could. And I've seen you all in those journeys," Ginny explained in a loud whisper. "I just...didn't expect you all to be so real."

Giramusen raised an eyebrow but said nothing more.

Astara came in with a gilt cup of water. Marne helped Ginny sit up, and she drank from the cup as Astara held it.

"That's not normal water!" she exclaimed.

"Nor is that a normal cup," Marne said setting it on a nearby stand. "How do you feel?"

Ginny sat up fully and swung her legs out of bed. She stood slowly and took a couple of hesitant steps.

"Not too bad," she replied.

"Then we shouldn't keep Nasdatal waiting," Emissary insisted.

The others gathered around Ginny and led her out of Marne's suite down the hall to the left and to a door with the pattern showing a universe on it. It opened before they could touch it.

Ginny cautiously stepped inside and gazed about her in awe. Gradually, she became aware of being under intense focus. She swung her head to the left and caught her breath. Enmarsikil as a young man stood staring at her and Astara.

Ginny leaned toward Astara. "Do you remember him like this?" she asked.

Astara's smile was dreamy. "Oh yes," she breathed. "And I remember how much I loved him."

52

They had no further time for musings. Zalkur, a stolid mountain of a man with a bushy beard and cloak of browns and greens, brought a large, wooden, straight back chair with armrests and positioned it in the middle of the room. He motioned to her, and Ginny gratefully accepted the seat. The others took their places in an arc around her, folded their legs and sat on cushions of air.

Teacher studied her for a moment. "Is the future of my children as dire as you predict?"

"We really are living representatives," Astara said.

He sighed heavily. "We must know. We must hear what goes wrong."

"Please, tell us," Marne urged.

All eyes were on Ginny and again she felt the pressure of their will bent towards her. Astara once more put up the shield.

"You must pull yourselves in or you will drain her again," she warned them.

In a moment, Ginny could breathe more freely.

"The best I can do is start with the First Gens and give you a synopsis of the rest."

Teacher nodded slowly and encouraged her to continue.

"You said they were lost," Enmarsikil said in a tight voice. "How?"

Ginny looked over at him. "Your frequencies as elementals are in dissonance with those elements on Ki. Once the First Gens left the ship and started exploring the land, they literally could not retain their form. They became their elements and largely disappeared."

Enmarsikil blanched.

"How did we resolve it?" Nasdatal wanted to know.

"You and Ninmah inserted neural implants into the others while Ea sent back readings of Ki element samples. That way you were able to adjust the other generations' frequencies. They had to permanently reside on Ki after that."

"Never come home?" Enmarsikil breathed in alarm.

Ginny shook her head.

"But there's more, isn't there?" Giramusen charged.

Ginny nodded. "The Second Generation fared well with Ea in his territories until Enlil's forces waged war on him. Some of the Guardians and Masters were used in the defensive lines. The first one to fade did so due to injuries he sustained in those battles."

"They were never intended for battle," Zalkur declared hotly.

"And yet, you have us show off our martial skills to the Anunnaki," Astara pointed out. "Why wouldn't they then think we can be used for battle? I volunteered at one point to stand with Enlil's son, Ninurta, because of a coup from outside the royal house."

The others looked to each other obviously carrying on a mental conversation at the speed of thought.

"Does it get worse than this?" Marne wondered aloud.

Ginny hung her head. "Much worse."

Cries of dismay went up around them. Nasdatal raised his hand to signal for silence.

"What more happens?" he asked.

"Enmarsikil nearly fades too soon because he doesn't have a mate," Ginny said tersely while glaring at Teacher. "All the Guardians and Masters are left to fend for themselves during a planet-wide Deluge. Fighting between the Anunnaki becomes so bad when Ea's son, Marduk, finally lands for good on the planet, that the ancient fire weapons are dug up. Our Ki is tricked into pressing the detonator switch, and Enmarsikil only reaches her side in time to shield her from the radiation. The rest of us hide underground, but whole settlements are wiped out and many of the Masters are injured to the point of fading."

"Ki and I were trapped replacing crystals in a planet stabilization center when Marduk let the roof collapse on us. Marki had just enough energy to lead Kumzubar and Enmarsikil through another set of tunnels to reach us but faded once the rescue was made," Astara told them.

"And don't forget, Marduk found samples and notes that Ea left behind," Ginny reminded her. "He tried to create hybrids of his own but didn't know how to get the transplanted embryos to take in a woman and couldn't embody them."

"So he experimented on us," Astara declared through clenched teeth.

"And that's why we're here," Ginny added. "When the DNA of the hybrids was added to the human lineage it was altered by the Guardians' and Masters' experiences. Those experiences are now being played out in parallel in their human lives making them susceptible to and vulnerable to possession by Marduk's Multi-Dim Warriors."

"If you don't make changes now," Astara said, "the future is bleak."

"Right now, life on Ki is about to implode. You've got to make changes or neither the first or second missions are successful, and Marduk's children will rule the world," Ginny warned them.

54

Now the Multi-Dims and Enmarsikil spoke animatedly between themselves.

"This cannot be!" Enmarsikil declared aloud. "We are not to be exploited and abused like this," he said, his eyes staring defiantly at Nasdatal.

"No, no, I agree," Nasdatal hastily replied. "I somehow missed this in my visioning. Please, tell us what we must do differently. These atrocities must never come to pass."

"I think I've boiled it down to six major areas of change," Ginny replied. "But it starts with not sending the First Gens now!" she stated emphatically.

CHAPTERS 7 - ERRORS OVER TIME

The group encircling Ginny waited patiently as she gathered her thoughts. Astara brought her more of the energized water. Ginny drank thirstily, handed the cup back and took a deep breath.

"I think the one thing I really don't understand," she began, "is how such amazingly powerful beings as yourselves lost control of this project."

Nasdatal's eyebrows raised and the tips of Giramusen's hair flamed like so many lit candles.

"No, seriously," she continued. "You had a goal, a worthy endeavor. But you let yourselves get caught up in Anunnaki politics."

"We cannot force our will upon others," Emissary explained quietly.

"What force would you have needed?" Ginny retorted. "At the point when things became a choice of continued Anunnaki financial support for the hybrids or their intent to search for gold, you could have just let them go find gold while continuing to hold to your original purpose. Are you seriously going to tell me you needed their permission and financial backing?"

The Multi-Dims glanced at one another uncomfortably.

"And when the hybrids were sent to Ki, you would threaten dire consequences if the Pact were broken, but none ever came. Marduk broke it dozens of times. Enmarsikil finally had to step in to enforce it, but the Pact was between you Multi-Dims and the House of Anu," Ginny pointed out. "What's with that? It seems like you were ensnared into Anunnaki politics, hypnotized into their funding scheme and impotent to enforce your own Pact."

"Now see here...." Zalkur rumbled.

"No!" Astara said sharply. "I bear the scars of Marduk's experiments and Ginny has lived them out in her human life. Things went very badly wrong, and we took the brunt of all of it."

Enmarsikil frowned heavily but said nothing.

"What else?" Nasdatal asked evenly.

"You should have held to your purpose," Ginny insisted. "There is no reason that, once gold was shipped from Ki, that the hybrids couldn't have been incorporated as Master Alchemists or whatever term you wanted and refined the gold dust so that more could be done with less and the results permified."

Zalkur rumbled under his breath. "The thought had crossed my mind."

"If you," Ginny said pointing at Nasdatal, "hadn't felt some need to appease Anu, the hybrids would have been safer and far more useful."

"But, if we never went to Ki, you would not be here," Enmarsikil pointed out.

Ginny glanced aside at him. "There's no reason the hybrids couldn't have gone to Ki later, once Ea sent back element samples so you could have tested the effects on them and made adjustments to the hybrids first. And by the time they got there, they wouldn't have needed to be in Anunnaki employ unless they specifically contracted with them. They could have had their own agendas, managed their own projects, missed out on being traumatized and exploited repeatedly."

"You keep saying they were traumatized and exploited," Marne spoke up. "How?"

Astara stepped forward. "I was traumatized by Marki from the moment we were paired. We had to be paired on Ki by Ninmah. Every night was a shouting match or worse for eons. We could rarely achieve power up, our hatred for each other was so great."

Marne was aghast.

"My only refuge was Ninmah's healing facility at Shurrupak. Had I not been assigned there, I'm not sure what would have kept me sane. And I wasn't the only one."

"Our own children mistreated each other?" Marne asked in

shocked amazement.

"Is there more?" Giramusen probed.

"When Enlil came, he wanted us to become invisible to the humans that Enki created," Astara replied, "but how it was done hurt us. Enmarsikil and Teacher had to come fix it. Down in Enki's territories in the Abzu, hybrids were used in battle and the scars they carry into the human lineage means they have a tendency to either battle, be embattled or tune out the world. And then we go back to Marduk's torture. Keep the hybrids working on their own project designs from the start and give them permission to defend themselves," Astara finished.

"Give them permission to be real live people," Ginny insisted. "You have no idea how important this is."

Nasdatal raised an eyebrow. "I think I do."

Ginny narrowed her eyes. "Are you versed in human epigenetics?"

He turned his head to one side, and her mind filled with a myriad of hurried whispers. Finally, he turned back to her.

"For the sake of argument, let's say I'm not," Nasdatal said evenly. "Make your point."

"One of the reasons Astara and I decided to come back in time is based on an epigenetic study we just read," Ginny replied.

Nasdatal nodded for her to continue.

"The study was based on rodents, rats to be exact," Ginny began. "Researchers took young female rats, put them through a traumatic experience while exposing them to a particular odor, mated them and let them give birth. When the pups were weaned, the researchers exposed them to the exact same odor but without the experience. However, the pups reacted to the odor as if they'd lived through the experience themselves."

"They had the same trauma response as their mother had before she'd even conceived them," Astara added.

"But...that would mean," Enmarsikil spoke up, his brain working frantically, "the experience had to have altered the mother's DNA."

"Exactly!" Ginny and Astara chorused.

"You can't be suggesting that what our children experienced has been passed onto the humans," Marne cried in alarm.

"That is precisely what I've found," Ginny replied, "both for myself and for other people whose DNA hold Guardian or Master heritage. And for humans, they don't just have reactions; they attract experiences into their lives that directly mirror the events from their Guardian and Master lives. Those life events often don't stop cycling until someone manages to tap the hybrid line, go back in time and alter the past."

"You've done this?" Giramusen asked.

Ginny nodded. "At first I had to for my sake and my friend's sake. But soon we identified others and it took work, a lot of it dangerous to the practitioner."

"But there's one other issue at stake," Astara inserted. "The hybrids who confronted Marduk's attempts to enter his Multi-Dim Warriors into them had a permanent vulnerability after that."

"The Multi-Dim Warriors have found ways to exploit that vulnerability in humans," Ginny added. "They find openings when humans' souls are shocked out of their bodies during traumas like accidents or surgery."

"Or when they take drugs," Astara said.

"And you know this how?" Nasdatal asked skeptically.

"Ted, Enmarsikil's human counterpart, and I were attacked by one in the night in our own home," Ginny replied quietly. "We almost didn't survive."

"But they've started doing something else since humans burn out too fast with a Multi-Dim Warrior inhabiting them," Astara interjected. "They have found a way to remove the souls of humans and animate several shells simultaneously from the outside."

"It makes this new breed of humans particularly dangerous," Ginny concluded.

"This is all very serious," Zalkur groaned.

"This certainly isn't right," Enmarsikil chimed in.

Giramusen studied Ginny. "There is more on your mind."

Ginny nodded, took a deep breath and squared off with Nasdatal. "I think one of the most short-sighted, hypocritical things you did was to misrepresent the hybrids both to yourself and to the Anunnaki."

"How so?" Nasdatal demanded, his eyes sparking dangerously.

"From the very beginning you created living beings but called them tools. Because you denied them the acknowledgment of being living souls, you misused them as if they were objects," Ginny pointed out, her voice getting tight. "For your information, a tool is an inanimate object built by intelligent beings to be used for a designated purpose. They have no soul, no life, no feelings, no hopes and no dreams."

"But we are living beings," Astara declared hotly. "We have souls, life, hopes, dreams and loves."

"You didn't create tools," Ginny charged holding Nasdatal's gaze.

"You created a race of slaves whom you misused and abused from the very beginning."

The Multi-Dims gasped.

"And all the time we kept telling ourselves that surely you had a reason or you wouldn't ask us to go through these horrors," Astara said hoarsely, tears coursing down her cheeks. "Only you were off elsewhere and rarely knew what we were enduring."

Nasdatal blanched, flinching as if physically slapped.

"But where was I?" Enmarsikil cried, a knot tightening in his stomach. "Did I do nothing?"

Ginny turned and looked at him kindly. "You were there and you did everything within your power to help. At one point you even shortened Marduk's lifespan and literally made him allergic to the hybrids so he could never come near them again."

Enmarsikil heaved a sigh of relief.

"But what if extreme measures like those had never needed to be used?" Ginny pointed out.

Nasdatal seemed to turn inward for a while. Finally, he sighed heavily and hung his head. "If all you have said is true, then I have failed miserably."

Ginny pursed her lips and shook her head. "It always seems like your ideas are sound. It's just their execution that goes off track."

"But why?" Emissary wondered. "He is our Seer. Yet, it would seem that his visioning is diminished."

"The First Generation who were able to retain their consciousness within an elemental form and found us have a theory," Astara announced.

"We all think that Nasdatal is missing his core," Ginny added, "which means his visioning is less clear, his judgment is flawed and his execution falls short."

A shocked silence fell over the room as they all took in this possible reality.

"I never knew," Nasdatal said shaking his head remorsefully. "But now that I place my attention there, I find my children are right. What can possibly be done to correct these errors and prevent such gross injustice from taking place?"

Ginny smiled. "Oh we didn't come empty-handed."

"We came with ideas," Astara confirmed with a firm nod of her head.

CHAPTER 8 - CORRECTIONS TO MAKE

"Tell us your ideas," Giramusen urged. "If we can prevent any of these tragedies from occurring...."

"We must," Marne whispered.

The other Multi-Dims looked quite sober.

Ginny took a deep breath. "Nasdatal, you need to go back in time and hold to your original plan to have the hybrids help heal the atmosphere on Nibiru."

He nodded, stretched his legs rising upwards in the air and became a blur before disappearing from sight. In the multi-dimensions, he found the thread leading back to the Secret Council chamber. He waved his hand and the wall grew transparent before him. Nasdatal watched until the moment was fast approaching his decision to change the hybrids' purpose. For a split second everyone in the room froze, and he took his younger self's place.

Now, Nasdatal sat at the table with Anu, Ea and Ninmah all waiting for his decision. He glanced toward his comrades, sent them a quick mental message, then turned his attention to Anu.

"I understand that your people cannot financially support both operations," Nasdatal said evenly. "However, we don't require your financial support. We choose to hold to our original purpose for the hybrids. Our children are attuned to Nibiru and for now they will stay here."

Anu shook his head. "But the Academy. It's on military ground."

"Bequeath it to us," Nasdatal said. "We can maintain its upkeep ourselves and, when we no longer have need of it, will return it to your care...in better shape, I might add, than what we acquired it in."

Anu considered this.

"But if we acquire gold on Ki," Ea said, "what use will we have of your hybrids?"

"You will have to return the gold to Nibiru," Nasdatal replied. "The hybrids can refine the gold so that it is more stable for its purpose and can permify the results in a way your scientists cannot."

"Then you do believe there is more gold on Ki?" Ea asked breathlessly.

Nasdatal nodded.

"And you would continue in this venture even without our backing?" Anu marveled.

"We did not offer help on the condition we had your support," Marne pointed out.

"We don't need your help," Giramusen sniffed.

Anu narrowed his eyes. "Then why do you help us?"

"Pure altruism," Zalkur replied.

"It is a trait we hope to pass on," Nasdatal added with a hint of a smile.

Satisfied that a new thread had been woven into the fabric of time, Nasdatal released his hold on that moment, transited forward and reappeared amongst the others in his quarters. He resumed his position and nodded to Ginny.

"Continue."

Though a little startled at his sudden disappearance and reappearance, she began again. "The second biggest issue is pairing the hybrids. Those tests are fine as far as objective measures of their powers go and they could help weed out severely mismatched pairs...."

"But we need a say!" Astara piped up.

"It's unconscionable to dictate a partnership for life if that lifetime lasts for hundreds of thousands of years," Ginny added. "Did you choose your partners or were they chosen for you?"

Marne glanced at Nasdatal and cleared her throat. "We chose for ourselves."

Ginny crossed her arms, raised an eyebrow at Nasdatal and tapped her foot. "So, it's ok for you to choose whom to love but beings with a broader emotional range should suffer forever?"

"We were looking for the best augmentation of their powers," Giramusen explained.

"While ignoring any heart bond they may have already established?" Ginny growled. "That's just cruel and irrevocably harmful."

Astara froze knowing Giramusen's flaming temper all too well.

Marne hastily intervened. "What would you suggest their lifelong purpose be?"

Ginny turned her attention away from the red head with steam rising in puffs from her shoulders.

"Even after they help heal the atmosphere on Nibiru, they could be sent to Ki. However, they should determine their own purpose independent of the Anunnaki. And if there are any who are unwilling to leave Nibiru, they should remain here."

"Plus, they should travel and work independently of the Anunnaki," Astara added. "We can create our own space vehicles. We don't need to use theirs."

"If the hybrids do decide to partner with the Anunnaki on a project, there should be firm boundaries set," Ginny continued.

"And if you say breaking a pact means they die...," Astara said, her eyes flashing.

"Then they should die," the women chorused in unison.

"But will we still fade?" Enmarsikil wondered. "What if one of us were on Ki and began to fade? What then?"

"Two Facilities were originally built," Ginny said, "one on each planet. "I'd still do that and I'd still enter hybrid DNA into the human genome. I'm convinced that it's the one thing that could give the humans a fighting chance against the Anunnaki. Just make certain that the hybrids' life experiences are healthy and fulfilling. Doing that would inject a whole different pattern into the human experience."

The Multi-Dims looked at one another then back at Ginny and Astara.

"What you suggest is quite reasonable," Emissary noted.

Nasdatal nodded. "Our children are mostly adults now. Perhaps it is time to include them in the decision-making."

"But for them to make good decisions, they need to know our origins," Marne suggested. "Our beginnings are part of their history. Knowing that will help them better understand their purpose."

"We shall gather them after a period of rest," Nasdatal agreed.

"And then I shall share my story."

With that, the beings uncrossed their legs and once again touched their feet to the ground.

"Do not forget that we still need to retrieve Nasdatal's core," Emissary reminded them as they headed for the door.

"Oh yes," Marne agreed. "But where would it be?"

"I'm sure we'll discover the moment and place," Nasdatal assured her as they watched the others leave his suite.

While the Multi-Dims went their own way, Ginny and Astara followed Enmarsikil back to his labs. The younger Astara waited nervously inside at a large lab desk. The older Astara squeezed Ginny's arm and slowly made her way toward her. Ginny watched the two women begin talking.

She turned and slowly scanned the high tech lab. A man cleared his throat to her left and she spun toward him. Enmarsikil stood studying her obviously bearing a question. Ginny moved closer so they could keep their voices low.

"Wh-what is my human self like?" he asked hesitantly.

Ginny smiled and laid her hand on his arm. "Your future self, Ted, is a gentle-hearted man with impeccable integrity," she told him. "He has a sweetness about him that is innate, but if you harm someone he loves, you will regret it. He's a scientist and well-known in his field. Yet, he is not so rule-bound that he boxes himself in. Instead, he's always stretching his horizons, opening to new possibilities."

Enmarsikil breathed a sigh of relief. "Good. That's really good. Um...is your relationship with him...satisfactory?" he carefully probed.

Ginny laughed lightly and he blushed. "Enmarsikil, when I finally found Ted it was after some pretty horrible experiences. I didn't know they made men like him, but now that I know, I could never be happy with anyone else ever again."

Ginny stood on tip toe and kissed his cheek.

Astara headed toward them while her younger self watched from the lab desk. "We should probably go back."

Ginny nodded.

Astara looked up at Enmarsikil trying hard to keep her composure. "When Teacher calls you to the Lecture Hall to tell his story, will you send me a signal? I think Ginny and I will want to hear this."

He nodded then watched as the women turned, began walking and merged into a single blur that disappeared.

"I think," his Astara said approaching, "that this is all very weird."

64

"I think," Enmarsikil replied slowly, "that we're seeing what we're capable of doing in action. I never considered time travel."

CHAPTER 9 - NASDATAL'S STORY

Ginny and Astara were instantly sucked back through the tunnel the moment they set the intent to leave. They were flung backwards out of the arch and landed in Ginny's healing circle on the hard stone. An instant later, the arch's door snapped shut and instantly disappeared.

"Well," Ginny said getting to her feet and dusting herself off, "that was interesting."

"I hope we chose the right time," Astara said joining her and preparing to return to Ginny's room.

"What other time would have been better?" Ginny asked taking Astara's hand.

"Perhaps," Astara said quietly, "we weren't meant to be born."

Ginny gazed at her counterpart with concern and shook her head. "When you go making changes, you don't want to completely rip a whole segment out of history," she explained. "Any corrections should be the ones weighted as the highest probabilities."

Astara knit her brows. "I do recall Enmarsikil having said something to that effect once," she admitted.

"Even the human teachers who've taught me time travel say that," Ginny replied. "Ready?'

Astara nodded.

"Return," Ginny called.

Almost instantly, the women were whisked away from the plateau and the Bay back through the darker tunnel. Before they knew it, they opened their eyes in Ginny's room on Ginny's bed.

A week went by as they waited for some signal. Ted came home from his lecture trip with a white paper of the proceedings to write a segment for. In between his writing and Ginny's editing, she tried to describe her adventure. He heard her but work emails flew fast and furious so she was really on her own.

Life had mostly returned to normal until one day Ginny heard an odd bell-like sound that wouldn't go away. Thinking it was her blood pressure, she checked it with a monitor but found it was normal. The next tone was like a low bull horn. She shook her head. Astara watched her curiously.

"How do you know that's not Enmarsikil contacting you?" she asked at last.

"Oh!" Ginny exclaimed blushing. "I guess I thought the alarm would be in words."

"We were always tone and harmonic tuned," Astara explained. "But if it's him, that means the generations have been called to the big lecture hall."

"Guess we ought to head there soon."

They went down to Ginny's room and she turned down the covers of her bed. "Perfect timing. I'm ready to sleep and Ted's out of town again."

She set her iPod for White Noise Lite extreme rain, slipped under the covers and let Astara guide them back. Before she knew it, they popped into the Great Hall and took seats in the first row off to one side. Soon the Multi-Dims entered and the low chatter in the room quieted to a hush.

Nasdatal took the center of the main floor. "In an effort to better acquaint yourselves with your origins and purpose, I've been requested to tell my story. With the help of my colleagues, we've created a plane on which the story will unfold holographically. I'll narrate as we go."

The other Multi-Dims positioned themselves at intervals on the main floor, made some movements with their hands, and the room suddenly appeared to be hurtling through space toward a point that was growing bigger as they neared it.

"Our race is a very long-lived one by anyone's standards," Nasdatal began. "When I was a young child, I recall one ancient philosopher who died...a very rare event. Those who knew the antiquarian said he had known that day would be his last. He had stretched out upon his bed, taken a deep breath and expired on the spot. Family members who were on hand said his essence departed as flecks of crystal, and his body shriveled down to the bones. His family gathered his bones for internment in the great necropolis outside the city."

"I remember that day as if it were yesterday," he continued. "It was the day that changed my life forever. All the city's inhabitants gathered on the broad, flagstone courtyard within the U-shaped, terraced necropolis. A platform had been erected in the bow of the 'U', and the governor stood on the platform to hold a Remembrance."

As Nasdatal spoke, the other Multi-Dims brought in the scene in a way that made them all feel like they were in the middle of it.

"Remembrances were usually held once a year in the necropolis as a matter of course," Nasdatal continued. "They helped solidify the images of our deceased ancestors in the collective mind of the populace, enhancing the memory for the elders and building memories of the past for the young. On this day, the Remembrance was designed to do those things as well as add the most recently departed to the collective memory."

"The governor instructed the gathering to begin at their left and focus on blank blocks of white stone. As we did so, the holographic image of the person interred therein formed like a sculpture in place of the block."

As the hybrids watched, white standing stones gradually began taking the shape of this person and that.

"The throng slowly shifted their focus from one white stone to the next with each new image being added to those before it until the necropolis appeared to be populated by gleaming white statues," Nasdatal said.

"Once all the ancestors had been imaged, the philosopher's family came forward, set his bones in the waiting receptacle, and a clean, white stone was slid into place over top. His friends and family took many long moments gathering his image in their minds and projected it onto the stone. As they did this, the stone gradually took on the departed's form. Finally, they backed away from the stone so everyone else could take in the image and commit it to memory."

The hybrids watched as a small group of people with bowed heads lifted them and eased back. When they did, the new stone bore the image of the newly deceased.

"At last the governor instructed us to once again view the ancestors as we had at the beginning. Only, this time, I noticed images and scenes playing out beside the stones; each scene looked like a movie of the person's life. I said nothing while we were at the necropolis. Once the internment was over and my family returned home, I sought out my father and asked him about the scenes I had witnessed," Nasdatal told them.

"At first my father was shocked and dumbfounded. He probed me with questions and more questions. Afraid that something was wrong with me, I said no more about the images I'd seen and things seemed to return to normal at home. Yet, a few weeks later, my father bundled me up and took me to the large University on the far side of the city. There were several universities in the city arranged at spokes' ends from the city center. The seats of learning seemed to circle the city. One probed the depths of science and being. Another studied the intricacies of mind and multi-verses. One championed the arts. Yet another probed the depths of the unseen world. A road like a spoke on a wheel ran from each to the hub in the city center where the government square was housed."

As the hybrids watched, first it seemed they flew overhead viewing the mammoth city from the air and seeing the roads fan out about the city center. Then they swooped down along one road culminating at an imposing gray building.

"My father whisked me along the long corridors with their arched, column-flanked halls and vaulted ceilings that were all part of the University of the Unseen Worlds and Dimensions. We entered the domed, circular room of one of our world's foremost Seers. The elderly gentleman who retained the title of Preeminent Seer sat on a tall chair that appeared to be raised on stilts. From that vantage point, he had a perfect view of a huge purple crystal that hovered just above an opening in the vast, black granite stone floor. I remember staring at the man as he slowly hovered off his chair and came down to the floor to greet us," Nasdatal reminisced.

"After brief introductions, my father commanded me to once again share the story of my experience in the necropolis during the philosopher's internment. Feeling quite afraid, I haltingly told the strange old man what I had seen that day. The Seer watched me carefully, though it seemed he was less viewing me, instead seeing something just to the side and above my head. He showed me different objects and asked me what I saw. I spoke truthfully, though I was frightened. Several times my father frowned and squinted as if trying to see something that was not there.

"In the end, the Seer determined that I was as gifted as he was and that my gift was both rare and highly prized. The gift frequently skipped hundreds of generations before popping up in the least looked for places. Ninety generations ago, the University of Science had discovered a Seer who was now directing and driving theoretical research there. Now, it was the turn of the University of the Unseen to discover a Seer."

Nasdatal paused as if collecting his memories.

"My father 'gave' me to the university on the spot as some sort of living donation. I watched with sad eyes as my father marched away down the long corridor and left me there to stay and train with the ancient master. I would now live out my days in those halls. I only returned home once for a rare festival. But by then, my training had become so advanced that I couldn't interact with my friends or family without instantly observing intimate, hidden details of their lives. It was embarrassing to all and I was shipped back to the University before all the days of the festival had been fulfilled. At that moment, I understood that I no longer had a family or a home."

A somber quiet filled the lecture hall as the hybrids took in this news and a heart-felt vibration pulsed on a low frequency offering comfort to the lone man up front.

Nasdatal picked up the thread. "Though I was lonely, I locked that part of myself away and applied myself to developing my gift. Inwardly, I vowed that one day I would have a son whom I would personally instruct. I vowed never to abandon him to strangers."

He looked straight at Enmarsikil as he said this and a tingle flew down the younger man's spine. All the days his father had kept him at his side observing his siblings. All the times he'd desperately wanted to join them but his father had coached and mentored him in private. He finally understood.

"Early in my training, I had visions that often came in unbidden flashes. However, I couldn't discern where within the time stream they were located," Nasdatal continued. "Even when the Seer taught me to project the images into the crystal sphere, they were more often raw blasts of vision rather than coherent streams of images. As I grew older and more able to handle the power overload, the Seer periodically gave me portions of his own powers to help me learn control and focus. Gradually, like turning a kaleidoscope in my mind, I was able to bring my visions into alignment."

Nasdatal tilted his head upwards and stared off into space. "I remember the first time I produced the time streams myself. The Seer had just given me an extra portion of power. I recalled feeling it surge through my brain leaping from neuron-to-neuron like some maniacal spark. Yet,

70

that did the trick and, suddenly, the images I'd been seeing appeared in the crystal sphere like perfect streamers of light. All the images were lined up neatly in their own story arcs on their own time streams positioned according to the possibility they showed. I was elated, too elated to notice the great weariness that descended upon the Seer. What I did notice was the strong metallic taste that filled my mouth and hung around for days."

The images of scenes illuminated from within the great crystal filled the room with flickering light. Enmarsikil realized that the crystal in his own suite was but a smaller version of this one.

"At different times each month, the students from all the Universities would join together in the city center," Nasdatal recalled. "Traveling with their Masters down the spokes to the hub, they could hear lectures and watch demonstrations from every field that was represented. There I soaked in information on every subject and mingled with others my own age.

"In time I met a group of sisters - nine in all - who were each some elemental fraction of water. Even in silence they were impossible to miss for their long, flowing blond hair in successive shades that always seemed to move as if blown by a breeze or carried on a current. And when they talked or laughed, it seemed as if music filled the air." Nasdatal's face softened at the memory and the corners of his mouth turned upwards. "While it was impossible to miss them in a group, I rarely registered them all. I only had eyes for one, the youngest, Marne." He turned to gaze at his beloved companion. "Her water element seemed to be that of a still, quiet pool, and her mere presence both soothed and excited me."

Marne smiled sweetly at him, the shared memory obviously special to them both.

Nasdatal turned back to the hybrids in their seats. "I also met young men my age from the University of Science - Zalkur, V and X - and another student from the University of Government and Diplomacy. Already a junior Emissary, this young man was adept at melting into a crowd and only being a wisp of a memory upon those he passed. Yet, whatever words he chose to convey carried great weight and depth and remained ringing in his listeners' ears." Nasdatal glanced at Emissary before continuing. "The group of us, men and women, grew closer as we continued our years at our Universities.

"The day finally came when, having passed a grueling round of visionary exams presented by the Seer, I proudly took the title of Teacher. While I could not convey my gift to others, I could teach the younger students how to find, access and eventually manipulate the multiple dimensions in which we lived."

As Enmarsikil watched his father mentoring young people, he realized how well prepared Nasdatal was for the job he'd undertaken with him and his siblings. Nasdatal's voice filtered into his mind.

"I began my new career while continuing ever more arduous visioning studies," Nasdatal related. "And the Seer pushed me hard to learn. One day, I met my friends in the city center. The students from the University of Science were presenting 'doctoral' research projects, and this was a particularly proud day for V. On this day, the Master Science Seer was to formally announce his support of V's project, an ambitious effort to create a universe from scratch and to mold its evolution according to all the tenets of life devised by the best minds of each of the Universities.

"I was truly proud of my friend. We had become as close as brothers in our youth. Now, my chest swelled with pride for him as the Master Science Seer invoked his aura of approval around V."

The hybrids watched as a blue glow with gold sparkles swirled around a tall, lean young man.

"As a hush fell over the gathering, V chose his interdisciplinary team - Zalkur and X from Science, me from the Unseen, Marne and two of her sisters from Arts, Giramusen from Environment and Emissary from Government. Together, we were tasked with creating the foundational guidelines upon which the new universe would be formed.

"Yet, even as I stood on the platform with my friends and heard the roar of the crowd, it all seemed to fade away as a sense of darkness descended about me," Nasdatal confessed. "I shook it off as anomalous but remained uneasy even as the mantle of responsibility was placed about my shoulders."

He sighed heavily. "In the months and years that followed while working on V's project, I discovered that it wasn't my visioning abilities that I was wanted for. I was the top adept in Multi-verse Manipulation. I could pass between multiple dimensions like water slipping between the cracks in stones. I could cloak myself in one dimension only to appear in another. I could use one dimension as a creative lab and bring my vision through to the inhabited dimension in solid form.

"V had studied all of our abilities with care, but he particularly coveted one. I could do something that few preceding adepts could do. I could decide that I needed a multiverse for a particular purpose and create that very one, thus dispensing with the need to seek for and call up one that was already established. It was this ability that V coveted most for his project."

72

Nasdatal shook his shoulders appearing to attempt to rid himself of an uncomfortable mantle.

"When I wasn't in V's lab or teaching my own classes, I spent as much time as I could with my friends. While the water sisters seemed to ebb and flow together, Marne more often separated herself and sat quietly beside me in the gardens around the city." Nasdatal turned and stretched out his hand to her. She eased over and placed her hand in his. "I couldn't help but notice her delicious presence, yet I couldn't bring myself to act." He took both of her hands in his and gazed into her languid blue eyes. "I wouldn't even permit myself to sample any future visions concerning her. I couldn't face the possible disappointment of learning I might not have a place in her future," he confessed.

Marne smiled her encouragement to him. He kissed her fingers, squeezed her hands then let them go.

"As time pressed on, V needed most of us less and less. He had already gleaned the essence of our knowledge and abilities. Now, he kept Zalkur and X close to him as they began to actually build the project. Periodically, he brought in Giramusen or debriefed Emissary so he could keep the government informed of this or that progress. Finally, he unveiled a controlled exhibition of the project. As V operated the controls in the middle of an open-air arena to give the surrounding crowd a demonstration of what the final version would achieve, I stood with the other team members and listened as the Master Science Seer spoke of the work in the most glowing terms. The crowd about us hung on every word, mesmerized by the demonstration and the Seer's glowing words."

Before them, those in the lecture hall watched a model of the universe project come to life and seem to grow before their eyes.

"But something was not right," Nasdatal remarked. "Marne and her sisters looked at one another with pale faces. Clutching each other for support, they hurried off the platform and away from the arena. Meanwhile, the darkness once again descended over me. Suddenly, as if an internal light switch had been thrown, I could see the project for what it was. Overcome by horror, I was assailed by images of people screaming only for the screams to be abruptly cut off by intense, searing heat. An instant later, the flames died as an immense pressure crushed in on every side. I held my head with one hand and reeled to one side only to find the pressure released a second later by a catastrophic explosion that roared in my ears.

"Ignoring my friends and the crowd around me, I staggered off the stage and away from the arena. Stumbling, I nearly sank to my knees, but

Zalkur and X had followed me and caught me on either side. Together, we hurried to a small park where we saw Marne and her sisters. Giramusen soon joined us."

The hybrids watched as the individuals all converged in a secluded nook of the park, lush foliage otherwise concealing them from view.

"We talked amongst ourselves for a while, all of us finally agreeing that something terrible and devastating was in the works and that the City was totally mesmerized by the Master Science Seer's speech. Marne and her sisters related how they had felt like particles of pollution were entering their bodies and sickening them, which was why they had left so hurriedly. Meanwhile, Giramusen wondered at the crowd's rapt attention and whole-hearted agreement of the project. I said nothing of my own experience until Zalkur mentioned the speech had left a metallic taste in his mouth. The others concurred.

"A cold tingle zipped through my brain. I clearly remembered my last experience with that unpleasant, metallic taste. I realized that the Master Science Seer was expanding pure power, his own power, possibly amplified mechanically, to sway and hold his audience. I questioned Zalkur and X about the Master Science Seer's visioning. They admitted that since the project's inception, the Seer had spent his energies promoting his protégé's vision rather than expounding on any of his own.

"Fearing the worst, I took leave of my friends and hurried to find my Master. I hastily shared the news and asked the aging Seer for advice. First, the Seer had me share my visions with him by using the crystal sphere. I asked what he had seen himself, and the Master replied a profound darkness lit only by a flickering flame."

Nasdatal paused, a darker expression crossing his face. Taking a deep breath, he continued, "My Master Seer said that he suspected the Science Seer's visions had faded with age, and that he was hiding the fact by promoting V's ideas. When I asked what we should do, my Master fell silent for a long while. At last he admitted that he had considered laying himself to rest as his own years weighed heavily on his shoulders. However, now it was obvious that I would still need him, for though I'd been promoted to the rank of Teacher, I was still young by our kind's standards. If I tried to present my visions against those of a venerable Master Seer, my voice would never be heard. My Master decided to conserve his personal energy and had me build special contrivances for that purpose. Then he gave me the remainder of his considerable power and called Emissary to him.

"The day after V's demonstration, the Master and I entered

the government complex at the center of the city and stood before the governing body. I shared with its members my alternative visions concerning the project. The Science Seer and V were called in and a heated debate ensued. My Master had been right; had he not accompanied me, the governing body would have dismissed my visions. But, when my Master concurred that he had shared my visions, the statesmen were thrown into disarray and a long debate was enjoined.

"While the government debated, V continued his work. However, my friendship with him was irretrievably broken. We went our separate ways though my heart was heavy and sad. I turned my back on my friend and left with my feet feeling like lead and my head and spirits hung low," Nasdatal confessed.

He looked again to Marne. "But in my time of darkness, I felt a gentle hand on my arm that soothed me, for Marne was by my side."

She slipped her arm around his back as he spoke.

"With a warm, caring gaze she melted the gloom from my heart and brightened my vision. Suddenly, I felt an urgent need to check the probabilities for her life, and I came up in a preponderance of those time lines. Feeling hopeful, I asked her to join with me as my mate. In a simple ceremony attended only by our closest friends and her sisters, we were partnered."

Ginny leaned toward Astara and whispered. "Now, why doesn't he teach you guys to check the timelines or check the timelines for couples seeking to be partnered? Wouldn't that make a lot more sense than all this mumbo-jumbo about pairing exercises? Seriously, I hope he's paying attention to his own life story...and when did he forget it?"

Suddenly, Ginny felt the world get sucked away from her and all she saw was Nasdatal.

"Yes, remembering makes me ashamed of the path I've chosen to date," his voice echoed in her mind. "You are right. There are other ways of pairing that are not mechanical."

The world around her finally returned and she shook her head to alleviate the uncomfortable sensation the experience had given her.

"From then on," Nasdatal said, "we worked together with our friends on a plan of our own to diminish the damage we saw would come."

The scene changed to a view of the Combined University at the city's center. A large darkened area that seemed like a sea of black punctuated by a platform on which a small, spotlighted figure came into view.

"V's project began to take shape," Nasdatal said. "The people could walk by the Combined University and watch the work or view an interactive demonstration as it replayed like clockwork. Zalkur and X provided more details to us as we watched the various steps play through."

Zalkur stepped closer to Nasdatal. "V's idea was to open two black holes; one in the University Center and one in the midst of a dark matter 'pool.' He would link them via a wormhole stabilized within a containment field. He had a number of multiverse adepts that would work in shifts around the clock maintaining the entrapment field."

"Yes, and the fact that I would not be among them was V's main sore point," Nasdatal said, "because I was the Master Adept in this area. The others V were using were merely trainees. However, I wanted nothing more to do with this project from which I foresaw nothing but disaster with or without my participation."

Zalkur nodded. "Once the wormhole was established, V planned to send through equipment that would both attract and coalesce the dark matter into the particles needed to build at least a new world. His ultimate plan was to create an entirely new universe from nothing."

"And again," Nasdatal responded, "the equipment needed in order to attract and coalesce proto-matter was based on techniques I had long ago achieved without external aid. I began to teach my techniques to my group of friends as we gathered with increased frequency to voice our concern over V's project. I was convinced that those techniques were our only hope for survival."

Zalkur nodded again. "X continually pointed out that the predominant weakness in the design was the delicate balance of maintaining a sufficiently powerful attractant force without it overpowering the wormhole stabilizers. If the balance were shifted but a fraction one way or the other, the materializing world could creep down the wormhole until it was sucked through the black hole. If that happened, the convergence of the two worlds would destroy them both."

"Yet," Nasdatal pointed out. "If V were successful in creating a fledgling universe and that crept down the wormhole, the moment that universe touched ours, there would be an implosion - a compression of matter down to an infinitely small size. The sheer energy created from compressing that much matter into such a small space would create an explosion of unimaginable proportions. Both universes would blink out of existence, and the magnitude of the explosion would hurl out the contents of both universes creating something entirely new. I sought the timelines as X spoke. The end results in almost all scenarios meant the destruction of our world as we knew it."

76

Giramusen, who had been sputtering from the sidelines, suddenly flamed. "I was so enraged that the government was ignoring all our warnings and allowing the project to proceed given such great odds. The fools!"

Emissary, who had joined them almost without being noticed, said, "The governing body listened almost entirely to the Master Science Seer, and he steadfastly supported the one probability that V's project would succeed as planned."

Nasdatal nodded. "And I finally accepted my Master's perceptions as Truth. It was now clear that the Science Seer's age had robbed him of his ability to view multiple timelines. Rather than admit that this was so, he chose to cling to his former glory by throwing all of his support behind his singular vision and his protégé.

"I decided to take one last stab at halting the project. I entered the Science University, found the Master Science Seer, and confronted him with my concerns. A flicker of fear crossed the antiquarian's face before being replaced by an arrogant sneer and much derision of my own Master Seer, who was certainly approaching his own demise at an even greater speed."

Nasdatal shook his head. "I couldn't believe the depths of the elder's madness and returned to the University of the Unseen to sit long in thought. If we couldn't stop the madness and the sure destruction of our world, then we needed some way of preserving a portion of our world in the universe to come. I locked myself in the tower room with the Visioning Sphere and sought the possibility of survival. When I finally emerged, I was gaunt but triumphant.

"I gathered my friends and Master and outlined my vision to them. In the quantum field where all possibilities existed simultaneously until one was chosen and the others collapsed into that choice, there was of course a time stream where our universe was destroyed. There was also one in which none of this ever happened, and every permutation in between. Because there were so many possible time streams carrying the destruction of our world, the weight of preponderance made that the most likely outcome.

"However, two options remained open. If we had a large enough group of people who believed as we did, that pursuing the project was too dangerous and must be dropped, we could literally cause the present time stream and its alternate to come into contact. With enough people focused on the alternate outcome at that choice point, we could cause our entire world to jump time streams and the disaster would be averted.

"But if we weren't able to gain enough supporters to create the jump at the choice point, then we needed to devise the means of preserving ourselves during the destruction and beyond," Nasdatal told them. "My friends voted to pursue both options at the same time and the race was on."

"We worked so hard," Marne said, "but we were only able to wrest 100 individuals away from the Science Seer's sway."

Nasdatal nodded. "With time running short and X having detected the fledgling universe's initiatory creep towards our own, I and my Master went deep beneath the University of the Unseen into the bowels of its great foundations. There, we created a chamber with a rectangular vat. Within it we built up a force, a protective shield and each of the one hundred lowered themselves into the force field every day.

"Over time the force field intermingled with our bodies until we all began to glow. Soon our bodies and the field would become one, and we would be part of the fabric of the stuff that made up the universe. As such, we would be outside its bounds and no longer subject to its destiny."

"And every day V's new universe edged closer to ours," Zalkur said. "To my dismay, I learned that V was well aware of the impending doom, only the two universes were so entangled by now and on such a great scale that change had become impossible and destruction was inevitable."

"And in spite of that, V refused to admit the truth to the government," Emissary said shaking his head sadly.

"I made one last effort to contact him and convince him to let the blackholes close and seal off the wormhole," Nasdatal said. "He refused and I fled my old friend, gathered the 100 and continued integrating our bodies with the field at a greater intensity. X kept a vigil over the project knowing that at the very last moment someone would have to give the word for us to enter the final procedure. My Seer had already agreed to stay behind and initiate the phase shift for us. He had been thoroughly ready to lay down the mantle of life before helping me try to stop V's project. He could think of no more fitting end than to help others escape the destruction."

"The day and moment of destruction finally arrived," Zalkur said. "X sounded the alarm and the 100 hastily converged on the vault, lowering themselves into the conversion chamber."

"I said one last good-bye to my Master," Nasdatal added, his eyes growing misty, "then I descended into the chamber myself. With the last of his strength and power, the Master Seer charged the chamber. As arcs
78

of power leapt about the vat and stood his thin, gray hair on end, glowing balls of light began to bob towards the surface

"Suddenly, one broke free and headed towards the stairs. Others popped out behind it and followed in a flowing line of golden, glowing spheres. The old Master held the portal open as long as he could, but not everyone was out yet. I saw his strength failing, climbed out of the vat and stepped into the portal just as he fell lifeless to the floor. I stepped into the gap though Marne implored me to let go. I held fast to the hope that all the others could make it through. Finally, I shook free a clone of myself to remain behind holding open the portal and collapsed myself into a glowing sphere to follow the others.

"I joined the others rocketing out of the University and headed straight for the wormhole. However, instead of traveling down along it, we found a thin crack between it and our universe's reality. We slipped through the crack and into the quantum foam.

"As the last sphere popped through the wormhole, the new universe touched the old and they ground together. Onlookers gasped in terror as the hole widened to become their whole horizon. And still it expanded until our world began tearing away chunk-by-chunk. The people tried to flee in terror, until an incredible weight forced down upon them. In the blink of an eye, their world was no more."

In the lecture hall, the two universes ground upon one another until all matter was sucked inwards then violently thrown outwards in an explosion akin to the Big Bang. Ginny sat there watching and shaking her head.

"This is all wrong," she muttered. "This view is from within their world. This view didn't come from outside of it or in the quantum foam."

"What do you mean?" Astara asked.

Suddenly, Ginny leapt up and headed toward Nasdatal. "I know where you left yourself," she cried breathlessly. "You didn't leave your clone behind! You left your core!"

CHAPTER 10 - GATHERING ALLIES

Nasdatal froze the hologram. Ginny moved around the lecture hall so she could get a better view. Enmarsikil appeared beside her floating in mid-air, while Astara stayed near her left elbow.

"Can you back it up a little?" Ginny called down to Nasdatal.

He moved his hand slightly and the scenes began playing in reverse.

"Stop!" Ginny called. "Go forward slowly."

Nasdatal moved his fingers as if waving in slow motion. The scenes inched forward.

"Almost there," Ginny said under her breath as the old Master Seer crumpled into a heap and Nasdatal took his place. "Just a little more."

Suddenly, they hit the spot where Nasdatal split and his clone appeared phase-shifted overlapping his body.

"Stop!" Ginny called again.

"I don't see any differences," Enmarsikil said with a pensive frown.

"There has to be," Astara insisted.

"Go slowly again," Ginny requested.

Nasdatal complied, and the scenes crept forward until the moment he jettisoned himself from the portal.

"There!" Ginny exclaimed. "Freeze that!"

The scene instantly froze in place. Ginny stared hard comparing one Nasdatal to the other.

"C'mon," she muttered. "I know there's a difference. Where is it?"

"A spark," Astara whispered.

"Spark?" Ginny asked squinting. "Where?"

Astara stretched forth her hand and pointed. "There. Around the heart of the one in the portal."

Enmarsikil was straining to see as well. "Yes! I see it! The one that jettisoned doesn't have a spark."

"Then that's it," Ginny confirmed. "That spark is his life force... his core."

"But it's tethered to the portal back in time," Astara remarked.

"Then that's where we have to go to get his core back," Ginny said as she threaded her way down to the floor.

The Multi-Dims let the holographic image fade. Marne mentally dismissed the hybrids, who rose and began filing out of the lecture hall. Ginny and Astara stood with Enmarsikil and the Multi-Dims watching the others leave. Young Astara stood at the top of the stairs wavering as to whether she should stay or leave. But Enmarsikil caught her eye and shook his head ever so slightly. The young woman slowly turned and disappeared out the door.

Nasdatal led the way down three steps, through a door and into an ante-room. The group gathered around a long conference table to talk.

"So, how should we go about traveling back in time to get Nasdatal's core?" Giramusen demanded at once.

"I'm not sure 'we' can," Marne admitted. "As multidimensional as we are, we might go back on all threads at once."

Her colleagues considered this soberly.

"I travel back on human timelines," Ginny ventured. "It's an old technique indigenous people have practiced for thousands of years."

Nasdatal considered her quietly. "The human timeline is a lot neater than ours."

"She traveled back on my timeline," Astara pointed out.

"And yours is tethered to hers, " Zalkur reminded her.

Astara sighed heavily.

"What if someone visioned and created a path for Ginny to follow?" Enmarsikil suggested.

Nasdatal shook his head. "I could not hold that vision on myself."

"I could," Enmarsikil said quietly. "You've taught me."

Nasdatal held the young man's gaze. "You have learned well, son, and your abilities are maturing, but...."

"I am good enough," Enmarsikil declared.

Ginny gently laid her hand on his arm. "There's a difference between ability and experience," she said quietly. "You have the ability...."

"But not the depth of experience," Nasdatal added.

Enmarsikil looked crestfallen.

Ginny studied him while tapping her fingers on the table. "You know, there is another way," she said after a while.

"Hm?" Nasdatal said raising an eyebrow.

"Ted can bring Enmarsikil through like I bring Astara through," Ginny said. "Not always as fully, but he can do it."

"And the older Enmarsikil would have both the ability and the experience," Astara said. "A lifetime of it."

Nasdatal considered the suggestion. "That would create and hold the vision but I doubt you would have sufficient strength and energy, even if Astara leant you hers."

Ginny knit her brows not yet ready to give up. "How about adding some of the First Gens?"

"I thought you said they were lost," Giramusen charged.

"They are," Ginny assured her. "They can't form a body like Astara can."

"Then how can they help?" Nasdatal wanted to know.

"Ted and I discovered that they exist on different planes and set up a beacon in our yard," Ginny explained. "Quite a few have found their way to it, and there's a handful who regularly interact with us. What if we brought them back here with us?" she suggested.

"But if they couldn't be seen here," Enmarsikil said, "what good would that do?"

"Join them with their younger selves," Astara said quietly. "That would give them physicality and the experiential base."

"That's if their younger selves even wanted to," Ginny pointed out. "Remember, they wouldn't just gain knowledge and experience. They'd remember losing themselves."

The room fell silent as the implications of the idea sank in.

"Who do you have in mind?" Nasdatal asked at last.

Ginny glanced at Astara.

"Well, Nita and Mamud," Astara said.

"Nita's partner, Barlumgeme," Ginny added, "and you can't forget

Satu. Of all of them, he's been the most physical in our world. He can move objects around the house."

Nasdatal nodded. "We should call them here...."

There was a sudden breeze and Ginny realized in looking around that Emissary was no longer amongst them.

"And we should tell them what has happened," Astara added.

"And...what they face," Ginny insisted.

In just a few minutes, there was a knock at the chamber door. It opened and the four individuals plus Emissary filed inside. Ginny couldn't help but stare. Their older selves had very infrequently broken through the barrier into her normal dimension, or she'd gotten a peek into theirs. She'd only ever gotten glimpses of them. Now, she was seeing their solid forms. Astara gave her a nudge, and Ginny cleared her throat while dropping her gaze.

The four individuals looked questioningly at Nasdatal.

"You know there has been considerable consternation lately," he began.

They nodded.

"The truth is that this is little Astara," he said gesturing, "only she's from your future, and she's here with a being the Anunnaki will create on another planet...Ki."

"Where Ea is going," Nita said.

Nasdatal nodded.

"Is this why the pairing process was stopped, and Ea's ship left without us?" Mamud asked.

"Yes. Ginny and Astara brought us news of your futures if we continued down our chosen path," Nasdatal concurred. "What they have shared with us was impossible to ignore. Changes had to be made to protect all of you."

"Then why are we here?" Satu wondered.

Nasdatal looked to Ginny. "Do you want to tell them?"

She took a deep breath and nodded. He gestured for her to pick up the thread.

Astara hastily spoke up. "You have to understand. On the timeline I've lived through, we all went to Ki."

"But Ea didn't realize how differently my planet's elements were attuned as compared to those on Nibiru. The entire First Generation was lost," Ginny explained.

"You said that in the lecture hall," Nita said.

"What exactly do you mean?" Barlumgeme asked.

"You got to Ki, dissolved into your elements and disappeared," Ginny replied.

The young women blanched.

"Did we never manage to come back together?" Nita whispered.

Ginny and Astara looked away and shook their heads. "No."

"But we are in the process of correcting mistakes now that can prevent that future timeline from playing out," Nasdatal assured them.

"Like not sending us to Ki now?" Satu asked.

"Precisely."

"So why are we here?" Mamud pressed.

"A little more background then we'll explain," Ginny said.

They eyed her expectantly.

"Before we faded, Ea, Teacher and Enmarsikil inserted our DNA into the human genome," Astara replied. "When I heard the signal Enmarsikil had set for us to awaken go off, I was actually now a part of Ginny."

"And I had to discover this part of myself," Ginny explained. "As I did, Astara came close enough to the surface so we could split periodically and act independently...like now."

"But our future selves are lost," Barlumgeme pointed out.

"Yeah, what does this have to do with us?" Satu wondered.

"You aren't entirely lost," Ginny said. "I found and married a man who was Enmarsikil's human counterpart and, together, we were able to create a beacon in our yard. Some First Gens have managed to follow it to us, though they're all on different dimensions."

Nita frowned. "Are you saying...you found us?"

Ginny nodded. "Actually there are others, but you four and a few others seem best able to interact with us."

Satu raised an eyebrow and Ginny chuckled.

"You in particular," she remarked. "You fly my cell phone all over the house even though you remain invisible."

"Then how do you know it's me?" he asked feigning innocence.

"Oh please," Mamud said. "That sounds just like you."

"Ok, you found us. Now what? Why are we here?" Nita pressed.

"To help us, we hope," Astara replied. "See, Teacher isn't all Teacher."

"What!?!" they chorused.

"At the end of his life story, it was really obvious that he jettisoned his clone," Ginny explained. "His core remains in the portal locked in time."

84

The four individuals gasped.

"That's horrible!" Barlumgeme cried.

"It's worse," Astara said. "The part of him that can accurately vision the future possibilities is the part that's stuck."

"So what can we do?" Satu asked.

"There is a way you may be able to help," Nasdatal replied. "Ginny knows how to traverse time as evidenced by her appearance here. She has proposed bringing Enmarsikil's older self back here and journeying to my core back along the timeline the older Enmarsikil visions."

Satu whistled appreciatively.

"The trouble is she won't have enough energy even with Astara to complete the mission," Nasdatal said.

"So you want us to help," Nita assumed.

"It's...a little more complicated than that," Ginny cautioned.

The foursome frowned.

"We need the experience of your older selves only they need to be physical," she explained.

They looked perplexed.

"We'd want you to let them merge with you," Astara told them.

The foursome's mouths dropped open in shock.

"This is the clincher and what you need to understand," Ginny said carefully. "You would gain their levels of achievement and experience but...you'd have their memories, too."

The foursome stood in stunned silence.

"I know...it's a lot to ask," Ginny said.

"We'd remember dissolving into nothing?" Barlumgeme whispered.

Satu shuddered.

"You'd remember dissolving into your elements," Astara insisted. "That's not nothing."

"But it's not form, either," Mamud said.

The little quartet looked solemn and troubled.

"Take time to think about this," Nasdatal offered.

"And 'No' can be a valid response," Ginny assured them.

"Wow!" Satu exclaimed under his breath as they left the chamber.

"Think they'll agree?" Astara wondered.

Ginny shrugged. "I'm not sure that I would if it were me."

"I can talk to them," Enmarsikil said beginning to rise.

Ginny placed her hand on his shoulder. "They have to figure this out for themselves. It's the only way to make things fair."

CHAPTER 11 - RESCUING NASDATAL

Nita, Barlumgeme, Satu and Mamud only made it as far as the front center row of seats in the lecture hall. They sank onto the chairs in stunned silence.

Nita shook his head. "It's too much...all of it."

"Knowing what happens to us," Barlumgeme whispered.

Satu rested his elbows on his knees and steepled his fingers. "Happened," he asserted, "on another timeline."

"True," Mamud said thoughtfully. "Given that on that timeline, we were on Ea's ship headed for Ki."

"And now, we're not," Satu added. "They've already changed things. We won't lose ourselves."

"But why do they still need to do this if the timeline has been shifted?" Barlumgeme wondered.

The chamber door opened, and Ginny and Astara entered the lecture hall. They slowly approached the little group. Ginny sat on the platform directly in front of them while Astara sat beside Mamud.

Nita glanced up at them. "Do you really understand what you're asking of us?"

Ginny looked down and shook her head. "I can only imagine; I don't really know."

"You've already changed the timeline," Satu pointed out. "Is this really necessary?"

"Yes, we didn't go with Ea," Barlumgeme protested. "Now we won't fade."

Astara sighed heavily. "There's so much more."

"Like what?" Nita pressed.

Astara wrung her hands nervously. "The way the Anunnaki treated us. When a Deluge threatened to wipe out life on Ki, they had us working to pack provisions for them. They made no plans for our survival."

Barlumgeme looked horrified.

"If Astara hadn't found Enmarsikil, and he hadn't pulled the hybrids in and organized them, they might have all faded then," Ginny told them.

"And then there was the war," Astara said. "They convinced our Ki to detonate an explosion that not only wiped out cities but sent a radiation cloud around the globe. Nearly a third of the Masters faded from radiation burns and wounds."

"And Ki only survived because Enmarsikil got to her in time to shield her with his own body," Ginny reminded her.

"After that things got so bad, I nearly forced my own fading," Astara said quietly. "A few First Gens had been found and helped by Ki's own elementals. You were one of them," she said looking up at Nita. "You saved my life."

He looked down between his knees unable to respond.

"Well, if we're not going to Ki, doesn't that change everything?" Mamud wondered.

Ginny shook her head. "Only one thing. It prevents your generation from fading."

"And what does getting Teacher back do?" Satu pressed.

"Think," Ginny responded. "You didn't go with Ea's ship, but...I'm still here. Astara's still here. Evidently, you all still go to Ki."

Satu's eyebrows raised.

"That didn't change the mission," Astara said. "And that brings in a second problem connected with Teacher. There was a pact he had the Anunnaki sign. Breaking it was supposed to be punishable by instant death, only Teacher could never infuse it with power. Instead, the Anunnaki took advantage of us, harmed us, did...." she looked away, "horrible things to us."

Nita and Satu glanced at each other, their faces ashen.

"It didn't end there, though," Ginny said. "Teacher entered your DNA into the human genome only, for our species, the experiences of our

88

ancestors get passed to us genetically as if they had been our own. By the time Enmarsikil's team was awakening in us, generations of our kind had passed these experiences on, and my generation drew mirror experiences to us in this lifetime."

Mamud held her head. "That's too much. How could that have possibly happened?"

"Because Teacher does not have his core integrated with his physical form," Enmarsikil's voice said from behind Ginny.

She jumped and spun around. "Lord, you were so quiet. I never heard you."

He merely gazed at her.

"But what if...what if we merge with our older selves...." Barlumgeme began.

"But we fade too?" Mamud finished, picking up on her thought.

"I can anchor your physical forms," Enmarsikil assured them. "I can maintain them and help you return to awareness of them."

"Because we're all derived from you," Nita surmised.

Enmarsikil nodded.

The foursome looked to one another. Nita wiped sweaty palms on his pants. Satu clapped his hands together.

"Well, I guess that's it," Satu said rising. "Seems we're the chosen few."

"I want to help, too," a clear voice called out.

Everyone turned and looked up into the stands. Young Astara stood resolutely on the stairs.

Enmarsikil went to move toward her but Ginny waved him back. Instead, she and the future Astara got up and climbed the stairs to where the young figure stood.

"I'm not too young," Astara declared firmly. "I can do whatever my elders do."

Ginny took her hand and pulled her over toward the seats. The three women sank onto the cushioned chairs.

"This isn't about age or ability," Ginny assured her.

"Then what?" young Astara wanted to know.

Her older counterpart took her hands. "Listen. I experienced a lot of horrible things. The whole idea for the other generations is to make it as if those experiences never happened."

"That's important to me," Ginny added, "because I'd like to stop attracting mirror experiences into my life. And I can only do that if you never have them or come into contact with them in any way."

Young Astara looked to her older self then to Ginny.

"We aren't asking anyone from any of the other generations to help," Astara assured her younger self.

Young Astara sighed heavily and nodded. She rose without another word, ran up the stairs and slipped out the door.

Ginny and the future Astara got up and headed back to where the others stood. The Multi-Dims had already returned to the lecture hall and stood expectantly waiting for Ginny.

"So, when do we begin?" Satu asked, quite eager to get the ordeal over with.

"I'll need to return to my time, call in your older selves and bring Ted up to speed. After that, it's a matter of setting a day and time around his work schedule," Ginny replied. "I'll work as quickly as possible."

Nasdatal nodded. "When you return, come to my suite. Enmarsikil will need my Visioning Sphere."

She nodded, took Astara's hand and they vanished into thin air.

The transit back to her healing circle then her body went quickly, and Ginny soon found herself lying on her bed. She got up and started thinking about how to get all of the pieces into place.

That evening after they cleared the supper dishes, Ginny and Ted sat out on their deck watching the sun set and the deer come in out of the field to investigate their apple trees.

"So, there's something big happening on the Guardian/Master front," she announced out of the blue.

Ted looked over at her. "Like what?"

"Astara and I have been traveling back in time. It's a long story so I'll let you read my journal," she replied handing him a vinyl covered notebook with several pages marked.

Ted pulled out his reading glasses from his shirt pocket, put them on and started reading. Fifteen minutes later, he glanced up and gazed thoughtfully at the pinks and purples painting the western horizon.

"So, how do we call them in?" he asked.

"I say we bring Enmarsikil and Astara forward, go to the Power Dome," their name for a very special garden they had created in their backyard, "and call them to the beacon."

Ted nodded, returned the journal to her and they went back inside.

"While we're thinking about this, when is going to be a good time to do this with your schedule?" Ginny asked.

Ted shrugged. "It's still early this evening. If they come in quickly, why not tonight?" he asked.

"Ok. Just let me do a few other preparations," Ginny suggested.

She entered the bedroom and set up candles at various points. She readied her iPod player, while Ted got down the crystal visioning sphere he had, an Eagle wand and a beautiful Tibetan singing bowl. Ginny set the candles and items around the room and lit the candles.

"You ready to bring them through?" she asked.

He nodded.

They each closed their eyes and consciously switched places with their counterparts. Enmarsikil and Astara opened their eyes, looking around them and picked up the items left for them. Enmarsikil solemnly led the way out the patio door and made sure they entered through the trellis arch. Once inside the Power Dome, they took up positions around the beacon lantern.

Enmarsikil called his siblings' names. Meanwhile, Astara watched carefully for them.

Soon, she caught a glimpse of Nita's ecru pants and dark jacket with his curly, shoulder length hair. Satu was close behind with his spiky hair and ever present, smart ass glint in his eyes. Barlumgeme coalesced out of a cloud above the garden while Mamud left her spot near the Elderflowers.

As quickly as possible, Astara explained what needed to be done and their part in it. The foursome were more than happy to be useful. On Enmarsikil's signal, they all moved back into the house, found spaces on the King bed and waited for Ginny's signal.

She turned on the double drumming CD, dropped a blindfold over her eyes and called out loud, "Nasdatal's suite."

In a whoosh of wind they were swept up and carried along a dark tunnel with purple streaks. Ted and Ginny held the orb between them while Enmarsikil used the Eagle wand for navigation. Before long, they slowed and emerged into Nasdatal's quarters.

The room was darkened as it frequently was when he used the Visioning Sphere. Points of light dotted the walls. A figure stepped into the beam of one light. The elder Enmarsikil and Ted turned toward the silhouette.

"That is my younger self," Enmarsikil said in a whisper.

Ted nodded then took a few steps in his direction. The young man moved out far enough to be visible. He studied Ted's form pensively, a glint of keen intelligence and curiosity in his eyes.

Ted extended his hand. "You are a fine, brave young man," he said.

The young Enmarsikil stared at Ted's hand then heard his own, though older voice, in his head.

Extend your hand as well. It is a human greeting of respect.

Young Enmarsikil's eyebrows raised but he extended his hand, and Ted grasped it warmly.

Ted stepped aside and the two ages of Enmarsikil faced each other.

"It is an honor to meet my new Teacher," the younger man said with a respectful bow of his head.

The older Enmarsikil nodded and placed his hand on the younger man's shoulder. "You already have a solid knowledge base," he assured him. "It's all in the application."

A door opened and bright light streamed in. Marne entered and stood looking with sight phase-shifted, as she studied the four First Gens.

"Truly this must be entirely prevented," she breathed. "But for now, we need you to merge with your younger selves."

Marne turned and led the way through the open door. Nita, Satu, Barlumgeme and Mamud waited nervously in the next room.

"This is it," Satu muttered under his breath and the others braced themselves.

The younger Enmarsikil stepped up behind them, touched each one on the back just behind their heart and pulled toward himself. A silver cord protruded from each individual's back for him to pull with his hands. He took the cords, placed his hand over his heart and pushed the cords into his chest.

"I have your forms anchored," he told his siblings. "I promise I won't let you fade."

Nita and Satu nodded in thanks then looked up.

Shimmering columns of cloud approached each of the siblings. As they neared, each individual put their hands up in front of them with palms facing out. Cool breeze touched their palms then pressure and the distinct sense of density entering their bodies. At first they resisted.

"Breathe," Enmarsikil urged from behind them. "Relax your bodies. Allow."

The foursome took a collective deep breath and their future selves slipped inside. Suddenly, a flurry of images assailed their minds, each one going further and further forward in time. All of a suddenly, they were stepping out onto Ki, and their physical forms in the room began to waiver.

"Steady them, Enmarsikil," Marne instructed.

Behind the foursome, Enmarsikil went deep inside himself. He found his own point of stability then began dropping down, down through his body. In front of him, his siblings' images solidified and they suddenly gasped, like coming up for air after a deep dive.

Satu felt his chest with his hands. Nita looked around, caught Astara's gaze and swallowed hard. The two girls looked at each other then down at their hands.

"It's been so long," Mamud breathed.

"I didn't think I'd ever feel real skin again," Barlumgeme concurred.

"I think you can let them go now," the older Enmarsikil remarked as he walked about each one.

His younger self gradually rose back up to waking consciousness, removed the silver cords from his heart and gently eased them back into the appropriate individuals.

Emissary poked his head in the door. "We're all gathered," he announced. "Nasdatal is ready."

The little group looked to one another. Satu clapped his hands and rubbed his palms together. The older Enmarsikil went over to Ted, and the two led the way into the Visioning Room beyond.

The elder Enmarsikil went straight to the Visioning Sphere, sat down and hovered over it. His younger self took up a position nearby where he could watch and learn. Nasdatal hovered in the air just opposite them.

"How do we want to do this?" Nita asked.

"Ginny knows how to travel through time," Astara said.

Ginny moved over to Nasdatal's side. "I'm going to touch your shoulder and make a connection," she told him.

He nodded his understanding.

She reached out her hand, placed it on his shoulder, and felt electricity zip up her arm.

"Ok. I'm going to lie down. If Enmarsikil would open the portal to the timeline, I'll journey back along it to the portal where Nasdatal got stuck. I'll provide the path for everyone else to follow," Ginny explained.

"Why don't Mamud and I stay here," Barlumgeme suggested. "We can provide the anchor to this time."

"And Satu and I can create an energetic slingshot to send Astara to the farthest reaches of space where the portal must be," Nita said.

Ted sat on the ground off to the side. "I'll hold space for the work you're doing."

To everyone's surprise, as soon as he dropped down within himself, a palpable sense of density and steady, humming energy permeated the room.

"I think we're ready," Ginny announced, stretching out on the floor. "Enmarsikil, open the way."

The elder Enmarsikil stretched out his hand toward the Visioning Sphere. A stream of charged particles shot from his fingertips toward the sphere. As the stream of energy hit its surface, a vortex swirled and a window like the shutter of a camera opened.

"It's open," he announced.

Barlumgeme and Nita held hands for a moment. When they disengaged, an energetic tether stretched between them. Mamud stood with her back to Barlumgeme. With one hand she drew the tether down and anchored it to the floor; with the other, she sent a whirlwind spinning around she and her sister.

Astara knelt beside Ginny. "Time to go," she whispered.

Ginny found a space inside where she could see and feel the portal Enmarsikil had opened. Holding Nasdatal's essence in her arms, she jumped into the opening and flew back along a ribbon of light. She closed her eyes and focused on the scene from his life story. Before long, she slowed to a stop and opened her eyes. She'd arrived at the point where he had just split himself.

In the Visioning Room, Astara got the image. "She's there," she announced.

Nita and Satu took Astara's arms, levitated and flew with her through the portal Enmarsikil held open. As Barlumgeme deployed the link between herself and Nita, the boys drew Astara up into the far reaches of space. When they reached the edge of what they could navigate, they created an energetic loop between them. Using it like a slingshot, they put Astara between them and shot her toward the edge of the universe.

Astara zipped along like a meteor streaking through the vacuum of space. A speck of light in the distance gradually grew larger until she found herself at the edge of a wormhole. In the middle of that wormhole stood a solitary figure braced against its sides while channeling his own energy into the space anomaly keeping it open and active.

"Nasdatal," Astara called.

His head turned toward her, and she could see starry sky in place of eyes.

"You need to come back now," Astara yelled. "Your people have all made it through and now your body needs your presence and energy."

94

He slowly shook his head. "I cannot disengage now. I've become part of the wormhole itself."

She chewed her lower lip. "Ok. We'll have to go back to when you took your Master's place."

"I cannot undo what I did," he replied.

"We'll find a way," she assured him.

The being in the wormhole considered this. "Then go," he said at last.

With that, Astara stretched out her inner senses. Immediately, she was sucked into the wormhole traveling to the other universe. With an abrupt halt, she found herself beside Ginny.

"Wouldn't let go?" Ginny asked.

"He can't," Astara replied.

"Then we need to shift his core and his clone," Ginny told her. "Nothing will happen to him if the clone disintegrates. It will just be reabsorbed."

Astara nodded.

Together, the two women carefully checked over the frozen-in-time Nasdatals.

"Look for that spark," Ginny instructed.

Astara squinted until at last she spotted it. "There."

"Ok, help me reposition these two," Ginny requested.

The women each grasped the shoulders of a different Nasdatal. Carefully, they pushed and shifted until the Nasdatal with the spark was the one jettisoning from the portal while the clone remained locked in. Creating an energetic lasso, Astara threw it around Nasdatal with the spark.

"Ok, I've got him," she announced.

Ginny took Astara's arm with one hand while holding the other in the air in front of her. "Looking for the parallel universe in which Nasdatal's core jettisons," she said.

Before them a swirling field opened.

"That's it!" Astara cried.

"Let's go," Ginny said.

Nita, Satu, pull us in, Astara called mentally.

A second later, she felt a hard tug then a long pull. Gradually, Nasdatal's core worked itself free of the portal, and they were flung forward through the wormhole. They gathered speed as they neared the figure bracing its sides. The girls held Nasdatal between them letting him slam into the figure and pulling a whole Nasdatal free.

As they swept through space, the wormhole collapsed behind them, the gateway between universes gone for good. The universe around them shifted like a huge grinding gear, and Nasdatal became like a rocket carrying them forward along his timeline.

Ginny was carefully monitoring their progress through time. "We're almost there. Somebody needs to help us put on the brakes or we'll overshoot."

Two blips appeared in the starry field, a web of energy held taught between them. The rocketing trio hit the energy net, and with effort they began to slow.

In the Visioning Room, the elder Enmarsikil sensed the difficulty beyond. "They need help," he said to his younger self. "You need to create a capture field."

The young man beside him began manipulating the dimensions, his hands moving faster and faster. Glowing wisps of purple and gold formed a ball between his palms. When it was ready, he directed it at the portal and sent it into the Visioning Sphere.

In space Astara, Ginny and Nasdatal suddenly shifted from rocketing through the vacuum to hovering in mid-flight with no sensation of change of air speed apparent. Nita and Satu flew over to the capture field, touched it and gently maneuvered it forward. In a blink, they all tumbled out into the Visioning Room, and the elder Enmarsikil snapped the portal closed. Astara and Ginny brought Nasdatal's core to his body, and the Multi-Dims began weaving it back into the fabric of his life.

At last, Nasdatal blinked his eyes open and looked around. Those gathered about him cheered. He was finally whole.

CHAPTER 12 - WHAT HAPPENS NOW?

For a while after his core returned, Nasdatal sat in his Visioning Room trying to take in the enormity of what happened. He was internally aware of different dimensions and timelines settling into place and waited patiently for the fullness to build indicating the integration process was complete. Finally, he took a deep breath, looked up and searched the faces of those around him. His gaze fell on Ginny, and he studied her

"You were right," he confirmed. "I was far from whole."

"What has to happen now?" Ginny wondered.

"We have to energize the process that has begun," he replied.

"What happens to us?" Barlumgeme asked.

"Yes, we still have memories of losing our form, yet you changed that," Nita pointed out.

"Our generation is still on Nibiru because Ea's ship left," Satu reminded him.

"Yet we still have memories of Ki and of finding Ted and Ginny," Mamud added.

"Does it just take time for the choice point to lock in?" Ginny wondered.

Nasdatal shook his head and floated over beside the Enmarsikils. "No, it takes an energy source; one I didn't possess when I chose to keep the hybrids on Nibiru rather than send them with Ea."

He stretched out his hand toward the Visioning Sphere, and a swirling vortex rose from its surface. As everyone watched, the eye of the vortex grew larger and larger. Soon they could all see a cramped council room and figures sitting around the table in the middle.

"You're going back again?" the elder Enmarsikil asked.

Nasdatal nodded. "I need to energize that Choice Point so the parallel universes can make a complete switch."

"But, will we still exist?" Barlumgeme fretted.

Nasdatal looked at the four individuals, presently a blend of young and ancient. He sighed. "The self that has endured millennia without form will be no more," he admitted, "because we will no longer be on that timeline. However, the self who is young, vibrant and has a long life ahead of them will remain."

Ginny gasped. "I know I knew this in my head, but when I go home...they'll all be gone?"

Nasdatal took in her distraught face. "As you said, you knew this intellectually."

Her eyes grew misty. "I guess I just never let myself really pay attention to that possibility," she admitted. "Their energy permeates our house, the yard, the field and woods out back, our...our lives. The emptiness is going to be staggering."

Nasdatal tilted his head to one side and considered her dilemma. "Perhaps," he said, "or perhaps not. It depends upon where their future missions take them, and what they choose to undertake."

Nita had been looking particularly distraught while listening to the conversation. Now he ran his hand through his long, curly dark hair. "May I...have a moment with Astara?" he asked hesitantly.

Nasdatal nodded and Ginny put her fingers over her mouth, tears near the surface. The others wore puzzled frowns except for the elder Enmarsikil who glanced away.

Taking Astara's hand, Nita led her to a darker section of the room out of earshot.

"I-I guess this is good-bye, for good," he said quietly.

Astara leaned her forehead against his chest and nodded. She raised her head till her eyes met his. "It will also be good-bye to a lot of pain."

Nita nodded then glanced at the elder Enmarsikil. "Does he know?"

Astara nodded. "I told him how you scooped me out of the water when I was trying to dissolve, how you built a cabin to shelter us, grew a

98

garden to feed us...."

"Does he know I helped you power up? Bonded with you even?" Nita pressed.

She nodded again. "He knows, Nita. How else could you have kept me alive or held form for so long?"

Nita took a deep breath. "I was never trying to...take his place. How did he take what you told him?"

"He was sad, Nita," Astara told him. "Enmarsikil bears so much deep sadness for all the times he couldn't help his siblings or me," she admitted. "He was forever grateful to you for keeping me safe and making me whole again."

Nita smiled grimly, took her hand and pressed her fingers to his lips. "I loved you then the very best that I could."

Astara reached up and pressed her lips to his cheek whispering in his ear. "I loved you, too. I wish I could say I'll always remember, but I know a place will always remain for you in my heart."

He wrapped his arms around her and gave Astara a long, deep hug. When he finally released her, tears dotted their lashes. Astara hastily flicked hers away. Nita took a deep breath, turned and led her back to the group huddled around the Visioning Sphere.

Satisfied that all was now in order, Nasdatal once again focused on the Visioning Sphere. *Hold the portal open for me*, he mentally told the Enmarsikils.

They each stretched their hand toward the Sphere and connected with the edges of the portal. When Nasdatal was certain, he let himself slip into the opening and followed the line back to that moment in time. Before he knew it, he was back in the secret conference room watching his former self pause time, step into himself sitting at the table and state the intention to keep the hybrids on Nibiru to help refine gold.

Nasdatal allowed himself to expand out into the universe yet intensify energetically in the conference room. Before long the table and chairs literally hummed. Anu and his people stared about them wide-eyed.

"What is happening?" he cried. "What are you doing?"

Nasdatal waited a moment as sparkles lit sections of the wall in the room. When they dissipated, the humming stopped.

"Whenever you come to a choice point like this," Nasdatal explained, "you are literally bringing two parallel universes together. We've been at this point before, and I chose poorly. The results were devastating. I've returned to choose again, but in the process one parallel universe must shift to a new trajectory, and the other must become congruent with this space and time."

"That was what we all just experienced," Emissary added. "Two parallel universes sliding by each other."

Anu blinked in confusion, shook his head to dislodge the uncomfortable feeling and carried on with the meeting as if nothing unusual had happened.

Nasdatal released his focus on that moment and slowly began tracing the timeline forward toward his Visioning Room. As he did so, the membranes of the two parallel universes touched and passed through one another, then one popped away and floated off while the new one settled into place. Satisfied with the results, he released his focus on the choice point, allowed his awareness to slip away and found himself back in his Visioning Room.

When Nasdatal opened his eyes, the four First Gens stood transfixed with fields of sparkles traversing up through their bodies. They stood blinking and glancing about wondering how they'd gotten there and what they'd been doing.

Ginny watched feeling a little sad. She turned to Ted. "They won't be back home to greet us when we return."

He gave her shoulders a squeeze. "It will feel emptier, that's for sure."

Nasdatal looked toward the human couple. "It can't be helped. This change spares their entire generation."

"I know. But I'll still miss them," Ginny replied.

Satu squinted as he looked at her. "Sorry, do I know you?" he asked. "It's the strangest feeling, but it feels like I should."

Ginny smiled wryly. "In another lifetime...once upon a time."

Satu frowned, perplexed.

Nasdatal turned to the befuddled young men and women. "I know you're not aware of your most recent actions, but that is because we changed a timeline that had disastrous outcomes for you and your siblings."

Barlumgeme squinted as she studied Astara. "You make me think of our babiest sister."

Ginny raised an eyebrow and glanced at her counterpart.

Astara cleared her throat. "I am Astara. This," she said gesturing to Enmarsikil, "is Enmarsikil's future self."

The two men stood side-by-side and the four young people stared in shock.

"We are from your future," the elder Enmarsikil told them as he reached for Astara's hand.

"Your future selves returned as well and both helped to restore my core self so I could be whole again as well as protected your generation and those that follow," Nasdatal elucidated.

"By not sending us on Ea's ship?" Mamud asked.

Nasdatal nodded.

"I feel strange," Nita murmured holding his head.

Nasdatal turned to Marne and Giramusen. "Take them to the infirmary and check them over," he requested. "I'm sure it's just the effects of time travel and parallel shifts."

"Better to be certain," Marne agreed.

The two women turned the foursome around and walked them across the room, out the door and to the infirmary.

Nasdatal turned back to the future Enmarsikil and Astara. "Where does that leave us now with the corrections."

"The pairing process," Ginny growled stepping forward. "So help me God, if you split up couples in love, I'll...."

Nasdatal raised an eyebrow. "Do what?"

"Apparently, I have a few hundred thousand years to think about it and the ability to travel back here till you get it right," she replied.

Ted put his hand on her shoulder and gently squeezed. She looked up at him knowing he was trying to calm her down.

"Seriously, you better than anyone else know the depth of sadness Enmarsikil carries, and I certainly know Astara's. Given that the entire Fourth Generation was badly mismatched, how can I calm down?"

Nasdatal cocked his head to one side and studied Ginny. "You care about my children that much?"

Ginny locked gazes with him, her blue eyes blazing. "Yes!"

"Are all your species like you?" he wondered.

"We're a mixed lot," Ted replied. "I'd hazard a guess that 80% to 90% of our people are generous and kind hearted. The leadership base is more of a problem."

"Problem?"

"Let's just say, the Anunnaki instituted kingship on Earth," Ginny replied, "and to this day, the leaders of countries around the world act more like puppets for a hidden regime than rulers."

"You have seen the factions of Anunnaki split and fight amongst themselves," Emissary suddenly whispered from near Nasdatal's ear. "You know their thirst for power."

Nasdatal frowned as he slowly nodded. "Yes. They may be

manipulating the humans they create to their own ends."

"If there really are that many good people, perhaps it would be worth seeing how they can be supported in independence from such influence," Zalkur commented.

"And there is still the gold to work with here and the hole in the atmosphere to heal," Nasdatal reminded them rising and appearing re-energized.

"Time to return?" Ginny asked looking up at Ted.

He glanced at the elder Enmarsikil who nodded.

Nasdatal saluted them as they all linked arms.

Ginny called out "Return!" and they disappeared in the blink of an eye.

"What do we do now?" Zalkur asked.

"First, we are the only ones on Nibiru who know the timeline has been changed," Nasdatal said. "Our children no longer expect to go to Ki with the Anunnaki."

"Then what goals do we set before them?" Emissary asked.

"I think," Nasdatal replied slowly, "it is time to offer them challenges and see just what solutions they devise."

CHAPTER 13 - NEW TRAJECTORY

When Ted, Ginny, Enmarsikil and Astara returned home, Ginny immediately leapt up and ran outdoors to their garden, the "Power Dome." She skidded to a stop with Ted pulling up abruptly behind her.

"The arch...the lantern," she cried. "They're gone!"

"Well, that proves they aren't lost on Earth anymore," Ted told her reassuringly. "Why need a lantern for a multidimensional beacon, if they are no longer lost?"

Ginny swallowed hard.

She stepped onto the white marble gravel path expecting to hear women's voices singing and the sound of Didi's flute playing. The dead silence stunned her. There was no brief glimpse out of the corner of her eye of Nita tending the elderberries. There was a dull nothing, or maybe that was normal space where magical space had always reigned supreme.

"It really does feel empty," Ted said, his feet crunching on the gravel behind her.

Ginny turned with tears trickling down her cheeks, and he reached out to hold her.

"You knew this would happen," Ted reminded her quietly.

She sniffed. "I know but the change is so profound, it's visceral."

Ted put this arm around her shoulders and led her back inside.

Over the next couple of weeks, Ginny grew withdrawn and sad.

"I don't think I realized how much their presence impacted me even when I wasn't interacting with them," she mourned to Astara.

Astara nodded sympathetically. "But if they aren't here...."

"It means they made it," Ginny acknowledged. "All of them."

"Wherever they are," Astara reminded her, "it means they've always been whole."

Ginny tried to smile.

"What I'd like to know," Astara continued, "is what other changes took place. Did they come to Earth at all?"

"They must have," Ginny replied. "You're still in my bloodline; Enmarsikil is still in Ted's."

"Good point," Astara acknowledged.

"So what now?" Ginny asked catching the inquisitive glint in her counterpart's eyes.

"Up for a journey?"

Ginny nodded.

"Let' see how things changed otherwise," Astara proposed.

"Follow your timeline again?" Ginny asked.

"It's all we've got," Astara said.

"True. Ok, Let's do this, and tonight would work perfectly," Ginny announced.

That evening, Ginny crawled into bed and got settled. Astara projected onto the bed beside her.

"Marne's house," Ginny declared.

Before they knew it, the two women were in the multidimensions and standing inside Marne's house of light. She was waiting for them in the entryway as if she'd been expecting them all along.

"Do you plan to jump into the time stream again?" she asked Ginny as she led them through her living room.

Ginny colored. "No, Ma'am. We just want to see how the changes are playing out now that Nasdatal's core self is back...."

"And the First Gens are safe," Astara hastily added.

They followed Marne toward her dimension viewing room.

"Do you think any of them have memories from the former timeline?" Ginny wondered as they entered the room and stood on the platform overlooking the skyfield holodeck.

"The majority will not," Marne replied. "If they were not actively engaging both timelines at the moment things were changed, when the old one drifted away to be completely replaced by the new timeline, all memories should have been replaced with those from the timeline they

104

now inhabit."

"What about Satu, Nita, Barlumgeme and Mamud?" Astara asked.

Marne nodded thoughtfully. "Their interactions were more personal and involved more than one timeline. I wouldn't doubt there will be some overlap for them somewhere."

"So, nobody else will know anything has happened?" Ginny pressed.

"Enmarsikil will," Astara said.

"Yes, he definitely will," Marne confirmed. "He was part of the entire process on multiple threads. Depending upon when you enter the current timeline to observe, he'll probably start by having memories, flashbacks from experiences he doesn't understand. As the timeline nears the point where you retrieved Nasdatal's core, he should start remembering both timelines more clearly."

Ginny nodded.

"Ready?" Marne asked Astara.

Astara took a deep breath and nodded.

"Then please take your place in the viewing arena," Marne instructed, "and remember, you will return different...changed."

"Because of how the timeline changes?" Astara clarified.

Marne nodded.

Astara took a deep breath. "Well, let's hope this time it's more pleasurable."

"Yes," Ginny agreed. "More pleasurable and less traumatic."

A twinkle lit Marne's eyes. "I don't believe you'll be disappointed."

The girls got themselves set.

"Ready?" Marne called.

"Ready," Astara called back.

In a blink, a starry universe-scape surrounded them, and Astara melted into the scene that began to play. Marne picked up the narration as before.

"As you remember, Astara was the baby of them all, born with an independent streak, strong empathic skills and a keen, observant mind. She would watch the older children attempt a skill, go off and practice it on her own then come back with a command of that skill having added her own tweaks and personal flare. This astonished some of her siblings yet irritated others. Only a few actually knew how hard she worked in secret to be like her elders.

"Her proclivity for learning things easily caught the attention of Emissary, who carefully watched her. Nasdatal gave her skills a passing glance mainly because everyone was so accustomed to how quickly she learned, many took it for granted it was her nature. Giramusen, though, got annoyed when Astara went off on her own and couldn't be found. However, Marne saw her spark of individuality and caring nature, traits that she chose to nurture."

Then word was whispered around that a special team was being auditioned. Enmarsikil, himself, would choose you to try out and, if you were good enough, you'd get special training. Astara had always looked up to the eldest brother. When he was demonstrating techniques for others, she watched him closely. A keen empath, she couldn't miss the loneliness in his eyes or the kindness of his actions. Now she wished she dared to dream he would choose her, but she was the youngest, and there were so many others older, more experienced and better than her at everything else that her chances were slim.

The scene shifted and it felt to Ginny as if she were in it. She was aware, in particular, of Astara's feelings. The girl was sitting in a lecture hall listening to Teacher's voice drone on. She was about to drift into one of her familiar daydreams when she felt a prickle up her neck. Whipping her head around, Astara was surprised to see Enmarsikil standing in the Lecture Hall doorway. He looked at her intently and suddenly the distance between them shrank.

"Follow me," he whispered, his voice echoing.

With a soft gasp, she snapped back to reality at her chair and shook her head to clear it. Slowly, with her heart pounding, Astara gathered her belongings, slipped out of her row and raced up the stairs. She met him in the corridor outside. As she began walking beside him towards the gymnasium, the walk took on the surreal quality of slow motion. Even the dust motes in the sunbeams seemed to slow almost to a stop in mid-air. The world of her dreams, the ones where she was chosen as an equal, and her real life were colliding. As they stepped inside the wooden-floored gym with its doubly high ceilings, things sped back up to normal.

Older siblings from the other generations were already gathered inside. They glanced their way as Enmarsikil led Astara inside. Whispers seemed to flutter about her like a thousand birds all flapping their wings at once. Immediately self-conscious, Astara shrank back against the far wall to avoid their taunts. But Enmarsikil's eyes and ears were sharp. He tolerated no disrespect on his team. One sharp glance about the room quelled any teasing. The group lined up to begin work, and Astara found a spot with the others. As she followed the others through Enmarsikil's drills, her confidence grew and she came out of her shell.

Marne's voice sounded as an overlay to the now swiftly passing scenes.

In that gymnasium, she found her true home. Every day she entered, Enmarsikil had a warm smile and an affectionate pat on the head for her. Every achievement she made, he cheered her on. It didn't matter that he praised all of the trainees' efforts; it was the fact that someone finally praised hers. She persisted through all of the trials making all of the cuts. After two shars of training, her proudest moment came the day when Enmarsikil named her to his final team. She beamed when he put the chain and medallion around her neck. She had a home, a place where she belonged and a purpose. No longer just the youngest; she was finally part of a group and accepted.

In council, Nasdatal and his colleagues sought new paths for their children.

"Since the eldest generation will soon be old enough to begin requiring power ups after they use their powers, the pairing should commence soon," he told them.

"Yes, but let's not forget Ginny's warning to make the process a joint effort with the generations now," Marne reminded him.

"But what if they choose a mate from another generation?" Giramusen wondered.

"Let them," Zalkur rumbled.

"As long as the pairing tests confirm their choice is healthy, there should be no harm," Emissary agreed.

"All right, " Nasdatal agreed noting their input. "On the other hand, even with Ea's ship preparing to leave and the eldest remaining here, they all need to be fully mature and ready to take action when the gold shipments begin arriving."

"We discussed using implants before," Marne pointed out.

"Did our data ever suggest harm came to the hybrids?" Giramusen asked.

Nasdatal shook his head. "As far as I know, the implants were fine."

"But perhaps there is some other way to attune their frequencies to Ki's," Marne proposed.

"All right. We'll table implants for now," Nasdatal agreed.

"And the maturational push?" Giramusen pressed

"That seemed to be the most beneficial and the least harmful," Nasdatal replied.

"Yes, Astara and Ginny said nothing of that being problematic," Emissary pointed out.

"Good," Nasdatal said. "We will continue with that as part of the path."

"You'd better let Enmarsikil know," Marne urged.

Nasdatal nodded in agreement.

"The one other thing Ginny mentioned," Emissary said, " was that Ea left admixture and notes hidden in Agade and his oldest son returned, found them and made beings of his own that he couldn't embody. They seem to have been huge problems for our children and still are for the humans."

"That's right," Zalkur said. "What do we do about that?"

Nasdatal sat in quiet contemplation for a moment. "The Anunnaki son will still create those lacking bodies," he said at last. "It would be better, however, if they were not of our genetic makeup. Our genetic components make them too powerful."

"Is there anything else equally as powerful that he could use with which to create beings?" Giramusen wondered.

Nasdatal shook his head slowly. "I don't know for certain, but my deepest sense is no...unless he used the stuff of the universe itself."

"Then let's deprive him of those notes and admixture," Zalkur said with a bang of his fist on a nearby stand.

"I agree. Would you and Giramusen go to Agade and take care of the matter?" Nasdatal requested.

The two stood immediately.

"It's as good as done," Zalkur replied and the couple vanished like smoke.

As the rest of the group broke up, Nasdatal left to seek out his eldest son. He found him standing on a portico watching the other hybrids socialize by generation and gender. Nasdatal eagerly explained the maturational process to him.

"Then what do I tell them about how fast their maturation is speeding up?" Enmarsikil asked, reading to round up his team.

"You don't," Teacher replied. "For their own good, they can know nothing of this and neither can Father Ea."

"But I cannot lie to them or Father Ea," Enmarsikil retorted, setting his jaw his eyes growing dark.

"We will be working with the hybrids as a whole," Teacher replied. "There is nothing to tell anyone about."

Enmarsikil began pacing. "I don't like to lie. My integrity is at stake."

"You will not have to lie, son. You will not tell Ea anything that is not the absolute truth. You just will not tell him everything."

"And when he asks me 'Is that all?' then what do I tell him?" Enmarsikil demanded, his eyes blazing.

"You tell him yes and inwardly think, 'That is all I can tell you for the safety of the others'."

Enmarsikil clenched and unclenched his fists. "Is that all I am good for? As a go between? The one who takes the chances first, so the others don't have to?" he demanded in a low growl. "Am I just the lab animal? I suppose you'll try to speed my maturation first to make certain it works before you risk the procedure on the others?"

Teacher blinked and took a step back. The words echoed those Marne had attacked him with when he first altered baby Enmarsikil's growth cycle.

"No, of course not!" Teacher sputtered.

"Really? Then why are there exactly 250 girls and 250 boys?" Enmarsikil challenged. "Why are they being tested, even now, for whom they will be paired with...for their mate? Why have I no mate?" Enmarsikil demanded, his body trembling with fury. "Unless I'm expendable, and they are not."

Somehow, his anger felt out of proportion even given the enormity of his situation. Enmarsikil had had dreams; dreams of struggling in isolation to build and work and set up instrumentation on a lonely world. Even as he stood before his Father shaking in fury, he felt an overwhelming loneliness that threatened to swallow him whole. He couldn't endure that again. Enmarsikil shook his head at the madness. *What again?* he wondered inwardly. And yet, he knew the raw, biting edge of that loneliness and shuddered.

Teacher stood before the distraught young man in shocked silence. "You are not expendable, son," he said huskily. "You are all I've got."

"Then why do you test everything on me first? Why do you teach everything to me first?" Enmarsikil cried, slapping his hands against his chest. "Why do you keep asking me to bear heavier and heavier burdens alone...always alone?"

Teacher backed up and sank onto a stool. Marne's words from cycles ago rang through his ears, and he groaned at the realization of their truth. *"You will sacrifice the one for the benefit of the many."*

"Oh my. What an error I've made," he groaned covering his face with one hand. "Despite my far-sighted vision, I was so focused on the mission we'd undertaken, that I didn't see the need in front of my face." He shook his head.

"That's it? That's all?"

Teacher raised his eyes to meet Enmarsikil. "I am so sorry. I have failed you, my only son."

"You can't do anything?" Enmarsikil pleaded, fear creeping into his heart.

"I will try," Teacher promised. "At this point, I don't know what I can do, but I will try."

With that he rose stiffly from the stool and slowly shuffled inside.

Enmarsikil spent long days in a darkness of spirit. By night he woke up sweating from nightmares. In one, he fought to survive a deluge of rain and flood alone except for shadowing beings who hovered about him but which he couldn't see clearly. When he reached out to touch them, they fled away like wisps of smoke. Another night, he suddenly found himself tumbling off a high cliff and bouncing down the rocky hill. Worn out, his life force exhausted, he lay battered and broken with no one to help him until his mother...could that be his mother? Enmarsikil squinted his eyes to see past the glare of the sun. Someone so very like his mother, he decided. She gently tended his wounds and restored his life force for yet a while longer. But the fear of his life force fading with no aid nearby lingered and deepened his dread.

By day the intensity of the dreams hung over him, weighing him down like some ominous, dark cloud. No one could reach or soothe him, not even his mother's hug. Almost, little Astara's smile touched him but it was as if even that bright ray of sunshine was no match for the darkness inside. At the same time, Teacher absented himself from everyone and everything. Enmarsikil felt more alone than he had ever felt. He was the solitary odd man out, Teacher had admitted it. All the others would be paired up to act out Teacher's dreams, and he would grow old in the gloom alone.

Several cycles went by. With little enthusiasm, Enmarsikil put his team of hybrids through their paces. One day, he spotted Teacher speaking with the other Multi-Dims on the portico outside the gymnasium. He
110

could only hope that their presence was a positive sign as he worked with his group.

On the portico Teacher discussed the results of his contemplations with his colleagues.

"There will be comings and goings between Nibiru and Ki," he told them.

"So, Enmarsikil will be needed on Ki," Emissary surmised.

Teacher nodded.

"But he can't be solitary!" Marne protested.

Teacher shook his head. "No, he of all our children cannot."

Giramusen, looking nervous, stepped forward. "Zalkur and I have taken a step that may aid the pairings."

Teacher looked quizzically to the most impetuous member of his comrades. "Oh?"

Zalkur put his arm around his mate's shoulders. "We found the admixture that Ea hadn't destroyed."

"We took it," Giramusen hastened. "We were going to destroy it as well, but when this dilemma of an odd number of hybrids to be paired arose, we...well...I'm carrying the last hybrid child."

Teacher's job dropped and Marne's face beamed bright.

"You'll need to pair Enmarsikil now so he has a mate to go with him to Ki," Giramusen pointed out.

"The hybrid left without a mate can stay behind with us until the child is of age," Zalkur added.

Teacher nodded, still too shocked to speak.

Marne placed her hand on his arm. "And Nasdatal...I-I may not have been wise."

Teacher glanced at his mate with one eyebrow raised in question.

"Well, when he would come to me and ask about pairing and mates, I-I got nostalgic and told him what it had been like for us," she explained hesitantly.

"So, he has a set of expectations?"

Marne made a face. "Perhaps."

"It may work out fine. We have already decided to allow the element of choice to enter the pairing process," Emissary pointed out.

Teacher nodded silently. He watched Enmarsikil's team end practice for the day. While the team members filed out of the gym, the other Multi-Dims left to see to upcoming lectures. Teacher waited quietly while Enmarsikil made his way out to the secluded porch. For a few minutes they stood side-by-side silently looking out over the courtyard.

Finally, Teacher cleared his throat.

"I have come to right a great error to the best of my ability," he said quietly.

Enmarsikil merely nodded stoically.

"I was so focused on keeping my vow from my own childhood to train my own son personally and keep him by my side that I ignored your other needs," Teacher confessed.

"I tried to tell you," Enmarsikil said.

"Yes, you did," Teacher acknowledge, "and I couldn't hear you."

Enmarsikil neither moved nor spoke.

"You were right in charging that I ask you to bear greater burdens without a companion to ease their weight," Teacher added. "You were right that there are exactly 250 girls and 250 boys, though that error may soon be remedied."

Enmarsikil glanced sideways at his father.

"I have seen that your siblings will most likely go to Ki of their own volition for different projects," Teacher continued. "When they do, you will be needed there with them."

"Then, how can I possibly do that without a mate?" Enmarsikil demanded.

"You can't," Teacher said. "Which is why we've decided not to include you in the regular pairings."

Enmarsikil spun to face him, mouth open to protest. Teacher raised his hand requesting one moment more.

"Study the girls in all the generations," Teacher continued. "If there is one female you feel particularly attracted to, we will arrange for you to get to know her. If she is equally attracted to you, then we would consider solidifying your pairing first. You will have first choice in the pairings. None will be paired until you have chosen."

Enmarsikil quickly snapped his mouth shut. "But...what if she rejects me?" he asked after a moment.

"When you choose for yourself, there is never a guarantee that your affections will be returned in kind," Teacher replied.

"Were you afraid when you asked mother?" Enmarsikil wondered.

"Son, it took me so many years to get up the nerve just to check the future lines for the probability that I would be in Marne's life, it's a wonder she didn't give up on me altogether," Teacher responded with a chuckle.

Enmarsikil cracked his first smile in cycles. "And had she given you any signs of interest?" he asked.

112

Teacher tilted his head back and laughed. "Not a cycle goes by that she doesn't remind me of exactly how much interest she showed that I was too scared to see."

Enmarsikil's smile grew. "Thank you, father. If I see someone I like and she returns my affections, I'll let you know."

CHAPTER 14 - PUSHING GROWTH

With Enmarsikil's status cleared, Teacher turned his attention to creating new goals at home. Knowing that Ea was nearing his lift off date to Ki, Teacher made a surprise trip to Agade to see him. Ea welcomed his old mentor, though he looked worried.

"I wish the hybrids were coming with me," he confessed to Teacher. "I would feel more confident of my ability to find gold with them."

Teacher pulled a device out from inside his robes. "That is why I prepared this," he said handing it to Ea. "One detection mode works in water, just set it to saline or fresh," he added demonstrating the settings. "Another mode works in soil and a third can do a scan from a distance."

Ea took the gift and studied it for a moment. At last he looked up. "Thank you. This will definitely give me an advantage. But what will the hybrids do now?"

"Exactly what we'd always planned for them to do," Teacher replied. "They will develop a processing center for the gold ore and will begin experimenting with such samples as we have from Nibiru to find the best way to refine it, inject it into the atmosphere and anchor it to Nibiru."

Ea placed his hand on his elder's shoulder and squeezed. "Perhaps we will be successful yet."

Teacher nodded. "Safe journeys, my friend." And with that, he turned and walked away fading from view as he went.

Emissary, who had waited nearby on another plane, shifted back through the multiverses until they were both back at the Academy. They found the others already briefed on the latest dilemma.

"We agreed to speed their growth," Zalkur put forth.

"What's the best way?" Marne wondered.

"We could transmit special frequencies via music that could act as carrier waves," Emissary proposed.

"But how do we get them all to listen to the same thing at the same time?" Giramusen fretted.

"A dance, remember?" Marne exclaimed. "We need them to mingle and we need to observe their social interactions to aid with the pairings. All of them under one roof listening to the same music at the same time would be perfect."

Teacher nodded. "We'll just have to safeguard Enmarsikil, since his maturation is complete, and the youngest generation, since the frequency will have the greatest impact on their growth."

The others nodded and hastened to make plans. The trainers spread word of a party and excitement grew within the Academy walls. The hour arrived and the hybrids hurried in. Lively music played and clusters of friends formed here and there. Teacher made certain to keep Enmarsikil apart from the others and made him wear specially filtered earplugs.

The night of the dance, Enmarsikil stood alone on a railed platform watching his unsuspecting siblings dance. After a while, he spotted the youngest, the girl from his special team. She stood apart from the others and scanned the crowd. His heart always went out to her when he saw her. She was exquisitely sensitive and highly intelligent and every bit the loner he was.

Now, she glanced up and headed toward the platform. Still apparently unaware of him, she climbed the steps, stood on tip toe and peered over the railing. Enmarsikil watched her intense focus on her siblings for a moment then walked over and bent near her ear.

"Don't you want to dance with the others?"

Astara shook her head. "Not right now."

"What are you so focused on?" he asked curiously.

"I must remember them," she murmured.

"You will never forget your brothers and sisters," Enmarsikil assured her.

"Marne said things have changed and there may come a day when the memory is too faded to recall. I must remember their energy," she explained.

He frowned. "Oh."

Astara continued to gaze at her siblings then pushed away from the railing, her pretty face very serious. Enmarsikil gave her a pat on the head and she smiled her thanks, her bright cheerfulness and sparkling blue eyes flying straight to his heart.

Too bad she's the youngest, he thought as she turned to descend the stairs. Yet, even as the thought registered, an image sprang to mind of little Astara magically transforming into a young woman before his eyes. He turned and watched as she began to descend the stairs.

Just as her foot hit the first step, the music changed and so did her body. Enmarsikil did a double take because with each step, she seemed to age a year or more. A wave of dizziness passed over him in spite of the earplugs and he grabbed the railing to steady himself.

I knew what happened before it happened, he thought. *How could that be? Where did that come from?*

When he looked back up, Astara hit the main floor, turned back toward him, smiled and waved. He swallowed hard for now she appeared to be 3-4 years older. Her previously flat chest had definitely been replaced by the curves of young womanhood. He had expected his siblings to age, but 3-4 years in less than a minute. He left the platform to find Teacher and interrogate him. Part of him was angry and concerned at how fast their growth was being pushed. Yet, another part of him held a speck of hope.

Several cycles after the growth enhancement treatments, the changes had slowed. For the older hybrids who had already been closer to maturity, the changes had stopped and their powers had stabilized. For the youngest generation, and especially Astara, the changes continued. Now closer to a 16 year old, she struggled with the magnitude of changes the growth treatments had brought.

Since the hybrids had often worked together only by generation and often only by gender, Teacher decided having them perform together for each other in mixed groups would be another excellent opportunity for he and his colleagues to observe their interactions. Everything from martial arts to healing, creating realities via harmonics to dance would be incorporated.

Astara took part all the way through but was dreading her final dance number with Marki. Of all the boys in her generation, he had the meanest temperament and had no musicality or sense of rhythm, yet they

116

were supposed to perform the courtship dance. That required all of the above and some measure of interpersonal chemistry.

To add to her problems, the stress of performing had caused further internal growth. She had felt it all day, so it came as no surprise to her when she went to put on her dance costume that it no longer fit and would have to be let out...again...in the bust and hips. However, when news came that Marki, her dance partner, had been injured in an earlier martial arts demonstration and was now in the infirmary, Astara first breathed a sigh of relief then dashed to the viewing stands to find Marne.

She crouched down and crawled to the edge of the viewing stand. Thankfully, Marne was seated close to the edge, and it wasn't hard to get her attention. Astara hastily whispered her dilemma to her then scrambled back to the dressing room to wait.

While Enmarsikil watched the choreographed dance his siblings were performing and the special combined field effects they produced, a sudden tingle of electricity jolted his spine. Thinking he'd heard Marne call him he turned only to see her bent toward the railing talking with a dancer. A moment later she turned, spotted him and beckoned him over.

"Astara's dance partner was injured in the sparring and she is supposed to present the finale," she whispered to him.

"What can I do?" he wondered naively.

"Be her partner."

"What?" he almost squeaked out loud.

"Quickly, go to the dressing rooms and get changed."

The suit isn't going to fit me, he fretted as he headed toward the staging area still somewhat in shock. *It should be silver*, he mused suddenly seeing streaks of fire against a metallic sheen.

Sure enough, when the girls inside put Marki's suit up against him, the size discrepancy was readily apparent. Frantically, they searched the wardrobe area for something longer and better fitting. Finally, they found a silver, one-piece jumpsuit with red flames streaking up the legs.

Unused to the chaos of open dorm living, Enmarsikil ducked behind a clothes rack, shed his clothes and struggled into the jumpsuit. Moments later, he reappeared feeling highly self-conscious in the body-hugging outfit. The girls appraised him with a critical eye. Aiya grabbed a long red scarf, wrapped it around his waist like a sash, and let the longer end drape down the front. Satisfied, she pushed him out the door toward the edge of the stage where Astara nervously waited.

As Enmarsikil hesitantly walked toward the edge of the stage, a whole scene played out in his mind. Hot, steamy, unbidden desires arose. He swallowed hard to regain his composure. He got to Astara side, looked down and gulped. In place of her usual leggings and tunic, she was wearing a body-revealing costume. A tight, short-waisted bodice of gold pushed her breasts together and up revealing deep cleavage. He stared for several moments before even noticing anything else, his pulse suddenly doing double time. Finally, his eyes traveled down along her exposed midriff to the low slung skirt of filmy gauze.

Feeling an uncomfortable tightening in the crotch of his costume, he tore his eyes away and watched the choreographed story-dance that was nearing completion.

"Mother says we're doing the courtship dance," he whispered near her ear.

Astara glanced up, saw who she was now partnered with and smiled broadly. "You just have to lead it," she told him as the other dancers took their bows and began to file off. "It's up to me to do the rest."

With his heart pounding in his ears, Enmarsikil let her lead him into the center of the smoothly paved courtyard. He drew her in close with one hand holding hers and the other cupping the bottom of her shoulder blade while she lightly rested her free hand on his shoulder. The music began and he swayed with her for a couple of measures getting the feel of how she moved her body. The tempo was slower, sensual and syncopated. Alone it was a very sensual piece of music; as part of a dance, it was designed to complement and augment the passion of the dancers' movements. Feeling woefully underprepared, Enmarsikil took a deep breath and began.

What he had intended to be a simple left side pass to an anchor point behind him, Astara turned into one of the most sensual moves he'd ever seen. She swayed her hips seductively as she passed by and rolled her body up from toe-to-head like a sinewy wave when she anchored. On the next pass by him, she hijacked the move when she was directly in front of him. She stopped, placed her hands on his upper thighs and rolled her hips in figure eights in front of him while leaning her upper shoulders and head against his chest.

Fire seemed to shoot through him from his groin spreading outwards. He felt a little dizzy, and it was all he could do to remain standing. He had never experienced the dance like this before. Then again, his mother had always been very modest while teaching it. Now, though, he was experiencing full, unbridled passion in all its throbbing glory. This petite young hybrid was making him feel things he hadn't
118

suspected were possible, and it was all he could do to keep his head straight enough to lead the dance.

On the next pass, he caught her back and whipped them around in a one-arm spin. She locked her gaze with his, and he swallowed hard. Desire blazed in her eyes and seared him through her touch. His mind spun wondering if she could be feeling the passion she was creating on the dance floor with him.

Hope, that dangerous emotion, caught hold of his heart much as the passion of the dance had taken over his libido. Enmarsikil's mind raced. *They're pushing her growth. Before long she'll be fully mature. We've always shared a close bond. I've always thought she was special.* He'd never thought about her for a mate because she was the "Little One." However, as she ran her fingers through his hair, over his shoulders, down his chest then shimmied down his legs, Enmarsikil knew there wasn't much little about her anymore. Images of them together in his garden, standing over a waterfall, frolicking in a mountain glade flooded his mind making his pulse pound.

He needed to catch his breath, gain a moment to straighten his thoughts. He spun her towards himself, caught her, wrapped his arm around her back and slow-danced. In response, Astara gazed lovingly up at him. Enmarsikil lowered his head towards hers memories colliding with reality. He hadn't kissed her; no he had. Her breath was hot against his face. Her rose red lips so close. With one quick, surreptitious move, he brushed his lips against hers and swallowed hard. Sweet, soft, firm, and pleading for more.

But the music shifted, intensified and he pressed her close to his body. His gazed locked with hers as they ground pelvis-against-pelvis in slow hip circles. She caught her lower lip in her upper teeth, her eyelids drooping languidly. He dipped her back, sweeping her long hair against the flagstones. Then he snapped her back up, and she wrapped one leg around his hip, crotch meeting crotch.

The pressure and the heat were exquisite and unlocked desires he'd kept tightly bottled. For a moment, he felt the urge to roll her to the ground and grind himself against her. But the music changed, and he snapped her into an intense pattern of movements across the courtyard during which their eyes rarely left each other's face. Moments later, he dropped down to one knee draping her back over it. The End! The onlookers applauded; they rose and took their bows. The dance was over.

Enmarsikil returned backstage with Astara. He peeled the silver jumpsuit off and slipped back into his own clothes. Astara hadn't had a chance to change yet; the other girls gathered around congratulating her on a sizzling performance. She spotted Enmarsikil, broke away from the others and caught his arm before he could leave. She reached her arms up around his neck, pressed herself against his chest and gave him a lingering kiss on the cheek. If she'd had any idea how little self-control he had left after that dance, she might have been less effusive. He kissed her back then hurriedly left.

Enmarsikil sped away to his research gardens trying to busy himself in the familiar. He dropped tools and kept bending down to pick them up with shaking hands. A twig snapped behind him, and he spun around to see Teacher coming toward him down the walk. He straightened fully to greet him.

"You saw?" Enmarsikil asked desperately trying to hide his eagerness.

Teacher nodded.

"What do you think" he pressed hardly daring to breathe.

"By all appearances it would look as if she were interested in you," Teacher conceded laying a hand on the young man's shoulder. "Just remember, she has undergone enormous changes in a very short time. She may have been reacting to them and not to you."

"But the way she looked at me...." Enmarsikil protested. *The way her lips felt*, he thought.

"Is the way she might look at any man right now given the acceleration of maturational factors," Teacher cautioned.

Enmarsikil's face fell and his shoulders drooped.

"You need more than that dance to go on," Teacher said squeezing the young man's shoulders.

"That's hard to come by when I spend so little time with the others," Enmarsikil mourned.

"We'll find a way," Teacher assured him. "I promised you this opportunity."

Enmarsikil nodded and watched his mentor leave. He set down his tools and made his way to his room. Large and spacious, he had filled it with books, apparatus of varying designs, specimens and seer's tools. However, he had what he called his dreaming corner. Here he would open a plane and transfer a memory he wanted to replay and relive. Then, at any time in the future, he only had to open that plane and step inside, and he could relive it as he wished.

Now, he opened a plane, transferred his memory of the dance and entered into it moving and feeling as he had earlier. He changed just one

120

thing, though. At the point where he'd brought Astara close and brushed her lips, this time he fully kissed her. The memory of those soft, luscious lips quivering against his made him groan aloud. He closed the bubble wondering if anything that wonderful would ever really happen for him.

It must. It had, he breathed silently.

"Not yet," an older voice cautioned.

Enmarsikil blinked and sat up fully. "Now I'm hearing voices?" he muttered glancing about his room.

"Only your own," the voice responded from a long ways away.

Unnerved, he sat staring at his memory bubbles alone with his fears.

CHAPTER 15 - CHANGES AND CHOICES

Astara took a good bit of teasing after the dance. It even followed her into the gymnasium where two boys from her generation started making remarks.

"Ooo, it's Astara. Are you still 'sizzling'?" Marki, the shorter, more muscular boy, goaded.

The other boy touched his hip with his hand, brought it up with the fingers on fire then slowly blew them out one-by-one.

"Their mouths haven't caught up to their bodies yet," Peenzermi, a homey, motherly sort, comforted her friend. "They're still 10 years old inside."

"Dip me, Enmarsikil," Marki said in a high falsetto while posturing with his friend.

The duo paired up and the friend swung Marki through an arc designed to mimic Astara with her hair sweeping the floor. Fighting back tears, she said nothing but started threading her way through the teams to find a quiet corner.

However, Enmarsikil had entered unnoticed as he often did, had observed the commotion and became visible directly beside the offending parties. Peenzermi caught hold of Astara while Aiya and Ki buttressed her other side. The three girls stood with her as Enmarsikil stared down her tormentors.

122

"Is there a problem?" he asked in a low, menacing voice.

Astara's face reddened further.

"Just talking about that dance," Marki said landing on his back on the floor where his partner unceremoniously dumped him. He sprang up and dusted himself off.

There was a wolf whistle from somewhere at the back of the room even as Enmarsikil blushed.

"You just wish you had those moves," Aiya yelled back.

Enmarsikil shot her a warning look. Returning his attention to Marki and company, he squared off to the two young men and held their gazes in turn.

"What is the fundamental requirement for all team members?" he demanded.

The boys cleared their throats. "Respect."

"Is this," Enmarsikil said gesturing toward Astara, "respect?"

"We didn't mean any harm," Marki complained.

His friend, however, looked contrite. "No, it wasn't respectful," he admitted. "Sorry, Astara," he said turning toward her.

She nodded her acknowledgement.

"See this doesn't happen again," Enmarsikil told the second boy before turning toward Marki. "On the other hand, you are dismissed from the team," he said in a low growl. "If you haven't learned that teasing others hurts them, therefore, harm has been done, you have no place on my team."

Marki threw down the towel he'd wrapped around his neck, shot Astara a hateful look and stomped out of the gymnasium. Enmarsikil sent Zalkur a mental message to be on the lookout for Marki then moved to the front of the room and began warm ups as if nothing had happened.

Silently, Astara was grateful. However, inwardly she couldn't help wondering why Enmarsikil had blushed. She was still puzzling out his reaction after the session as she took her seat in the big lecture hall. Now her curiosity was doubly piqued because all the Trainers were present, including Giramusen who was obviously pregnant. So she split her attention between the Trainers below and inwardly wondering about Enmarsikil, whom she'd developed a huge crush for.

Teacher stepped forward to begin the session. "As you know, Ea's ship took off for the planet Ki," he began. "Now is the time in your development to start considering how you want to apply your talents and powers."

Astara rested her elbow on the flip desk of her chair and set her chin in her hand.

"I foresee that Ea will find gold on Ki," Teacher continued, "so one challenge to consider is determining the best way to refine the ore and what method could be used to incorporate the gold with Nibiru's atmosphere to close the hole."

A number of siblings around the room who were particularly attuned to metals murmured interest at the thought of that challenge. Astara's mind drifted back to the dance, instead.

"I also see that the Anunnaki will build colonies on Ki while they mine the gold. Perhaps some of you will be adventurous enough to want to explore the planet," Teacher continued. "If so, we will not use Anunnaki transport. I am confident you are capable of devising much more suitable vehicles for coming and going."

This idea led to a split conversation between those eager for new vistas and those who never wanted to leave home. Astara furrowed her brow inwardly wondering where Enmarsikil would be and would he be there alone.

"For those who choose to remain entirely on Nibiru, we would ask that you devise ways to re-enliven the planet and better the lives of its people," Teacher concluded.

"This is a big task," Marne admitted from nearby. "As such we ask that you take several cycles to try different ideas and find what most closely resonates with you."

"Partner up with others," Zalkur urged, "and see how blending your talents and powers changes things."

Giramusen huffed as she stood up from where she sat, her belly rounded with the baby she carried. "You will not be permanently placed on either Nibiru or Ki," she told them. "You each have unique mixtures of talents, elements, and powers. Explore how blending them with others and applying them to create useful solutions works. This process is designed to be fluid and allow you to be self-determining."

"How about the pairings?" Barlumgeme asked from down near the front.

"As you start working with others, also consider who interests you and who you most resonate with while exploring your application options," Marne suggested.

Astara packed up her things and filed out of the lecture hall with her siblings, a million thoughts converging in her head. For one, no matter who teased her about it, the truth was that the dance with Enmarsikil had been a huge success. A lot of the girls were still congratulating her.

124

Their energy had blended in a perfect synergy; she'd felt it. The guys, particularly in her generation, were still uncomfortable with physicality.

But Enmarsikil's not, she thought.

Astara still remembered his intense gaze and the way he'd touched her body. Sizzle was a good word for that dance because it had lit fires in places she hadn't known were possible. Astara could still feel his hands on her bare skin, their bodies pressed close together. The moment he had brushed her lips with his had left her quivering, wanting and breathless. The physicality between them had ignited such heat and longing in her, it consumed her thoughts and dreams.

Marki brushed past her making a stray comment. Instantly, Astara snapped out of her reverie, blushed and dashed off with tears wetting her lashes. She climbed the courtyard wall facing the distant mountains and ran across the field parallel to the research facilities.

She spotted an old, gnarled tree up against the research walls. Its branches touched the ground and created a leafy screen. Putting up an invisibility field, she headed over and squeezed between it and the wall. Suddenly, her hand hit a woven reed door. Astara turned, studied it and, curiosity getting the better of her, pushed the door open.

She entered a magnificent garden filled with all types of trees, plants, birds and butterflies. Astara spun about trying to take everything in at once. She caught a flash of iridescent blue in a nearby treetop and took a step back to get a better view of the plumed bird trilling down at her. With the second step back, Astara stopped cold, or better yet, was stopped cold by a warm, upright body. Stifling a scream, she spun around to face Enmarsikil.

"Oh!" she cried bringing her hand up to her mouth. "I'm so sorry. I shouldn't be here." She backed toward the wicket door in the wall preparing to flee.

"No! No!" Enmarsikil countered quickly reaching out to stay her flight. "It's all right. You can stay. I'd love the company."

Astara stopped and studied him. Her heart skipped a beat when she saw the hopeful, soulful look in his eyes. The heat flushed to her cheeks and reddened her lips when she appraised his taut, chiseled body and full, slightly quivering lips.

Quickly, she inhaled a breath of fragrant air and tried to calm her racing pulse. "What do you do here?" she asked allowing him to slip his arm behind her, guiding her with a hand placed between her shoulder blades.

Enmarsikil glanced about the garden wondering in which direction

125

to take her. "I research different types of plants...try to create better strains."

"Why?"

"To make things grow under different conditions...produce better fruit...."

"What are these?" she asked, taking his hand and drawing him over to a nearby bush.

Dazed by her soft touch, he followed temporarily tongue-tied. "Um...that's...a-a new strain of fruit," he managed.

"And this?" Astara asked spinning toward a well-pruned tree.

Enmarsikil happily followed her about his garden answering her questions and describing his work.

Finally, they sat down under a tree out of breath with excitement.

"The Trainers were talking about us finding the ways we want to employ our powers," Astara said after a bit.

"Have any thoughts for yourself?" Enmarsikil asked.

"I'm already on your team," she replied.

"We won't always be busy," he assured her. "You'll have lots of time to pursue other things."

Astara glanced around the garden. "So far, what the Trainers have suggested sounds pretty dull. But your gardens," she gushed. "I've never seen anything so beautiful or felt so much life."

Enmarsikil nodded. "I like this. I do other things in the labs, but the gardens are my favorite."

Astara picked a multi-petaled white flower and studiously observed it. "The Trainers also said we may someday go to Ki where Ea has gone. Do you think you'd ever go there?" she asked glancing sideways.

He stared out toward the fish ponds beyond the low, arched bridge. "If any of the siblings go then I know I will go," he replied quietly.

Astara frowned and turned to look at him fully. "Why? You sound like you don't have a choice."

"If any siblings went, I would be needed as their liaison to the Anunnaki and to keep a watchful eye so they came to no harm," he explained.

"But the Trainers made it clear we're to be self-determining," Astara protested.

Enmarsikil's expression turned grim. "Five hundred hybrids will be self-determining. One...will be their shepherd."

"That...doesn't seem fair," Astara replied. "Do you want to be a shepherd?"

126

He shrugged. "My life hasn't been entirely fair. Some things I do because I'm meant to do them."

She reached out and touched his arm. "I'm sorry. I wish things were more fair for you."

Enmarsikil swallowed hard and gazed into her eyes. "Someday, if I'm lucky, maybe they'll get a little fairer."

He cupped his hand over hers and gave it a squeeze. Astara blushed and glanced away. She spotted the garden chronometer and took note of the time.

"I really should go now," she said. "I'm meeting with some friends to try to brainstorm."

Crestfallen, Enmarsikil refused to relinquish her hand though he helped her to her feet. "Will you come back?" he asked hesitantly.

Their feet crunched on the gravel of the path back to the wicket door.

"If you'll let me," Astara replied.

"You're welcome any time you're free," he replied stopping at the door in the wall.

Astara paused gazing up wistfully into his eyes, the memory of their lips touching at the end of the dance bringing heat and color to her cheeks. When he remained stoically beside her, she sighed, turned and slipped out the door. He waved as she took off across the field.

Enmarsikil went back to work on his latest flower, one he had been cross-pollinating when she had arrived. He worked for a while longer whistling and smiling, a dreamy look in his eyes.

Astara was out of breath by the time she found Aiya, Bilnammul, a strawberry blond with a bubbly personality, Ki, the solid, ground-attuned foundation sister, and Peenzermi. She only half listened to the conversation as they discussed their interests and if any of them could become a project. Aiya had to nudge her when it was Astara's turn.

"All I can think about are plants," she admitted. "We've never had a chance to really learn how they grow and what they like. But they take in water, so it would seem that might be something to explore."

"What good are plants?" Ki asked.

"We eat them," Bilnammul reminded her. "They use them for healing in the infirmary."

"Besides, they sing," Aiya said.

The others looked at her.

"I hear them...at night...."

"Ok, so we'll think about what we might do with plants and get back together," Astara suggested.

The other girls agreed and the huddle broke up.

After the next meal when most of the siblings were milling, Astara headed back to the door in the garden wall. She slipped inside and quietly made her way along the garden paths seeking Enmarsikil. She heard splashing and quickened her steps. Rounding a corner, she spotted him scooping leaves out of a fishpond. When the twig she stepped on snapped loudly, he dropped the skimming net and spun around.

"Sorry," she apologized. "I didn't mean to startle you."

"That's ok," he replied, picking the net back up and dumping out its contents on land. "I'm just glad to see you. I thought maybe you wouldn't come back."

"Oh no. I wasn't staying away on purpose," Astara quickly assured him. "I was trying out some group applications."

"Anything seem interesting to you?" he asked still focused on his fish.

"I think so...maybe," she replied. "We're just experimenting. Nobody really understands how to apply our skills or what to try them on."

"I'm sure it will become clearer over time," he assured her.

She laughed lightly and its music lifted his spirits. "That's what the Trainers keep saying."

Astara moved closer and peered into the water of the pond. "What's in here?"

Enmarsikil felt her shoulder brush his arm and warmth spread through his chest. "These are some fish I've been breeding. I've separated them into several ponds depending upon their gender and age."

"Kind of like a fish version of us hybrids," she remarked off hand.

He frowned at the analogy; the likeness was too close for comfort. Pushing the idea out of his mind, he led her from pond-to-pond showing her the different fish.

Coming to the pond with his best fish, he pointed out one with especially pretty markings. Astara leaned out over the edge of the bridge on which they stood attempting to get a better look. Suddenly, she wavered and started to fall forward.

In his mind, Enmarsikil saw her tumbling, reached out, grabbed her around the waist before she could totter forward. He leaned back and she fell against him with a soft thud. For a moment, they stood there her back to his front until he carefully turned her around.

His chest rose and fell heavily. "Are you all right?" Enmarsikil

128

asked, his voice husky with concern.

Still shaking from her near fall, Astara nodded breathlessly and gazed into his clear blue eyes. Enmarsikil's strong arms trembled as he held her. In response, she leaned more fully against his muscular chest.

All she could think was that this felt every bit as good as the dance. She had watched the other boys, particularly the older ones who hadn't picked on her much growing up. None of them made her catch her breath or made her heart sing and engendered the heat the Enmarsikil did. She bit her lower lip wishing he would kiss her and looked up at him through her long lashes.

Enmarsikil held her in his arms. He trembled with the effort to keep from sweeping her off her feet. He'd dreamed of this moment, wished for it, longed for it. But would she let him? He remembered the thrill of just brushing her lips, but now he gazed at her upturned face and full red lips and wanted more.

Hesitantly, Enmarsikil bent his head toward hers as time seemed to stand still. At last their lips touched and he felt like he could hardly breathe. He slipped his hand behind her head prolonging the moment any way he could and loathe to let her go. Finally, with a deep sigh of satisfaction, they pulled apart.

"Mm, that was...special," Astara remarked happily.

"Yes, just like you are," he replied.

"I'm special?" she asked, eyebrows raised in surprise.

He nodded. "You're sweet and kind and inquisitive," he said, inwardly thinking *and unbelievably sexy*. Enmarsikil smiled. "I appreciate your coming to see me."

"But I love coming to see you," Astara replied enthusiastically. "I love listening to you talk about your work. And I like spending time with you."

Hope took root and sent shoots into his heart. "I'm glad," he said. "I feel the same way about you."

Enmarsikil slipped his arm around her waist and led them over to a tall, spreading tree. They sat on a mossy patch with their backs against its trunk. He took her hand and held it in his, thrilled to know she at least liked him. While they chatted about inconsequential things, he periodically paused to christen her lips anew.

All too soon the garden chronometer showed that it was time for her to return to the Academy proper. Enmarsikil walked her back to the door in the wall but was loathe to let her go. He pulled her back for one last kiss molding his mouth over hers, listening to her quiet murmurs. She grabbed the edges of his tunic as loathe to leave as he was to let her go. Finally, their lips parted. With effort, Astara pulled away and he watched her squeeze outside and race across the field.

Enmarsikil watched her go with mixed feelings. On the one hand, his heart was singing and dancing a giddy jig to know that the attraction between them was mutual. If it led to love, Astara was all he could have hoped for. If she rejected him, though, he knew he would be crushed. He tried to only think about the hopeful possibilities and buried himself in his work.

Yet, somewhere inside the knowledge that she was already his welled up.

"My mate," he whispered, a shiver racing down his spine. "My... mate."

CHAPTER 16 - EMERGING PROJECTS

For several days, Astara worked with Aiya, Bilnammul, and two other girls trying to devise a project. When they took breaks, Astara slipped away and visited Enmarsikil. One day she watched as he took small seedlings out of a greenhouse and transplanted them into a larger bed. Suddenly, an idea struck her.

"Do you ever have any leftover seeds or seedlings?" she asked.

He glanced up at her. "Not often. Why?"

"I just got this idea how the group I'm in might be able to influence plant growth," she explained. "If you had anything you could spare, I'd like to try it out."

Enmarsikil gave it some thought and smiled. "Tell you what. I'll see what I have and bring a flew plants to the small lecture hall later."

Astara's smile broadened and his heart skipped a beat. He'd do anything to make her smile like that.

After she left, he perused his flats in the greenhouse and picked out some choice plants. He put them on a cart and wheeled them to the lecture hall that was designed for small groups. The girls were all waiting for him and jumped up immediately to see what he'd brought.

"These are all flowering herbs," Enmarsikil told them. "They can be used to heal people when they're sick."

"So, what do we do with them?" Aiya asked picking one up and looking it over.

"Here's what I was thinking," Astara replied. "We each take two plants. Half of us create a harmonic field around our living cubicle that would encourage the plants to grow. The other half won't do anything. After a cycle we'll compare our plants and see what happened."

As Enmarsikil listened to her speak, he had to admit he was impressed. Teacher had had to instruct him how to conduct experiments but Astara seemed to have an innate ability.

"Just let me know, too," he requested getting ready to leave. "I'm always looking for new ways to make plants grow."

Later, Astara snuck away to visit him again. He welcomed her, genuinely glad for such bright company. But he also strategically unveiled more and more aspects of himself as well.

While the others were preparing to lead self-determined lives, Enmarsikil knew his would never be like that. He had a different set of responsibilities because he was the oldest, and he knew Astara loved her freedom. Better she come to know the requirements of his life. This time he showed her the labs where he ran his experiments.

Astara looked around the pristine labs in awe. She'd never seen anything like them with their beakers and microscopes. Enmarsikil showed her the instruments he used and some of the assays that were ongoing. He particularly pointed out the control and experimental groups.

"Then I had the right idea!" she exclaimed.

He nodded. "You created a really good experimental model," he praised her.

When she left, Astara met with her group plants in hand. They compared them to each others'.

"Wow!" Ki said holding her non-field plant up against Aiya's. "There really is a difference."

"Cool!" was Aiya's only response.

"So do we want to continue like this?" Bilnammul asked.

Astara thought for a moment. "Let's try this. We want to able to show the growth difference, so let's keep one plant aside apiece. But let's swap what we're doing with our other plant and see if the growth affect is still there."

"So, put a bubble around one plant and create the field effect for the other," Ki clarified.

Astara nodded. "Let's see what happens. Will the non-field plants catch up in growth?"

"Will the ones that were in the field stay the same or lose growth?"

Bilnammul asked.

"Exactly," Astara replied.

The girls took their plants back to their cubicles then met again for a meal.

Afterward, Astara visited Enmarsikil again. This time, he took her into his most private space, his suite of rooms adjacent to the Research Facilities. This was where he slept and studied. As she approached the door to his room, a tingle flew up her spine. Somehow, his room felt... familiar. She tip-toed inside coming to an abrupt stop as she gazed about the spacious suite in awe. Here he kept everything from the sublime to the grotesque.

Astara stared in amazement at the sheer size of the rooms. How marvelous to have so much space all to yourself and not have to share it with a dozen other siblings. She scanned the bookshelves to see what tomes Enmarsikil read and referenced. There was one on male-female interactions including sex. Without thinking, she pulled it off the shelf and leafed through it. The page suddenly opened to the reproductive body parts, complete with illustrations. She stared at the page wide-eyed then, suddenly aware of his close presence, snapped the book shut. Enmarsikil had turned aside, glad she couldn't see his beet red face.

Recovering herself, Astara gazed at the large crystal orb set into a sunken retainer in the floor. She knelt down to get a closer look. Enmarsikil knelt beside her explaining how the Visioning Sphere work.

After a while, she moved on running her fingers lightly over a harp in beautiful harmonics. She turned the corner into a small alcove filled with shelves and a desk in front of an open window. On it was a telescope pointed skywards and she bent down to take a peek. Straightening up, she spun around and gave a sharp gasp because the shelves that lined the back of the alcove were filled with specimen jars of all types. With morbid curiosity, she checked out bugs, small animals, his collection of animal eyeballs that made her shudder, and a collection of parasitic worms she wished she'd never laid eyes on. Suddenly, she stopped and stared. There in a large jar was an unborn baby bobbing in fluid.

"What is that?" she asked.

"A fetus," Enmarsikil replied. "It's mother couldn't carry it to term, and it was too young to live on its own."

Astara reached toward the tiny fingers and toes. "Were we this small once?" she breathed.

He nodded. "We all come from embryos too tiny to see with the naked eye."

She puzzled over it for a while. "The baby gets inside after a couple join?" she asked.

"Y-yes," he stammered feeling the heat rise to his face.

"Like Giramusen?"

"Something like that," he replied.

She stopped and straightened up. "I wonder what it's like to have one inside. Will that happen to us when we're paired and we join?"

It was such an innocent question that it took him off guard. Yet, he was certain she wouldn't like the truth.

"We are hybrids, Astara," he began technically.

"Yes." She turned and looked up at him with big, innocent eyes.

"Hybrids are...sterile," he told her breaking into a mild sweat.

She knit her eyebrows. "What does that mean?"

Enmarsikil ran his hand through his hair. "Sterile means none of us can procreate."

Her face remained blank, and sweat beaded his brow.

"We cannot make babies," he finally said flat out. "Our bodies aren't able to."

Astara's face fell as she glanced back at the fetus. "Oh. I-I didn't know."

To take her mind off the tiny baby in his collection, he gently guided her to what looked like an empty corner of his room. A round, stepped up platform stood there, and the air above it was strangely viscous.

Astara frowned and stepped around it. "What is this?" she asked, her intense curiosity back in a flash.

"This is my dream corner," Enmarsikil explained. "If I have a memory I'm particularly fond of and I want to relive it, I create a plane for it here and store it. Later, I step back into it and re-experience it all over again."

"Really? Show me!" she urged.

Enmarsikil started with a fairly safe memory, the day he'd caught her on the bridge and they'd kissed. Her face beamed as she watched. Then he let that one go and opened another. In an instant, the dance began again, and she gave it her undivided attention, until one particular moment occurred.

Astara gasped. "I thought I dreamed that," she murmured. She pressed her fingertips to her lips still feeling the tentative touch of his lips against hers.

Enmarsikil had rivulets of sweat tracing paths down the sides of his face and was blushing heavily but there was no turning back. "I can alter the memory if I want to, and that one is pretty intensely imprinted."

"So, that was on purpose?" Astara asked wide-eyed. "You really wanted to kiss me?"

He nodded.

"You wanted to kiss me then?" she asked. "Y-you liked me even back then?" she probed.

He released that memory and brought up dozens more floating in air like giant bubbles. Astara studied them carefully then softly gasped.

"These all have me in them! Why?" she asked turning toward him half-hopeful, half-afraid.

Enmarsikil looked down at the floor for a moment struggling with what to say. "Please don't think me foolish," he said shyly looking back up at her. "But I always thought you were special. Your smile used to buoy my spirits even when you were little, and I kept a collection of your smiles and laughter."

Astara's eyes flew wide open. She glanced toward the collection shelf in the alcove then back at the bubbles of memories.

"When I would get lonely or feel down, I would open a bubble and relive your laughter," he continued. "It always seemed to flood my heart with sunshine."

Astara reached towards the bubbles hearing her own laughter. "I-I hardly know what to say," she whispered. "Everybody always told me you'd never pay any attention to me because I was too little."

"On the contrary," Enmarsikil replied. *You're the only one I ever paid attention to*, he breathed inwardly. *My eyes only ever saw you.*

"I only knew you made my heart sing and were easy to laugh with and smile around. I had no idea I meant anything to you. I'm so used to being the baby nobody wanted underfoot."

He took her hands, drew her close and kissed her forehead. "You've never been underfoot to me. You've always been my ray of sunshine."

After she left Enmarsikil, Astara felt like she was walking on sunshine. No one, not even Marki, could get to her. She had a secret; Enmarsikil had always liked her...her the baby. She was still on cloud nine the period when Enmarsikil's team met. However, a group of twenty men and women huddled near the front of the room waiting for him. Nita, Barlumgeme, Satu and Mamud were with them.

Astara frowned remembering she had seen them in the big lecture hall along with her future self and the being called Ginny. Pacing, she waited toward the front curious to hear what was going on.

Enmarsikil entered soon after, took in the waiting group and noted they were all First Gens. After instructing the rest of his team to begin warm ups, he joined the huddle.

"Is something wrong?" he asked.

"No, we just have a project we've been working on and wanted to ask you about," Nita replied.

Enmarsikil relaxed. "Go on."

"It's...a little strange," Nita prefaced.

Enmarsikil raised an eyebrow.

"We don't understand it," Barlumgeme confessed.

"Ea is on Ki," Mamud said, "yet, we have this strong pull to go there. I-I've even seen images of this world in my dreams."

A chill went down Enmarsikil's spine and a jolt. Images flashed through his mind of his older self and Teacher and strange new beings. There were his siblings and their older selves, and he was focusing with all his might on the Visioning Sphere to rescue his father. Suddenly, Enmarsikil's mind cleared and he knew. Time lines and crossovers and dreams. They finally all made sense. He looked at the twenty faces gazing at him knowing what they could not know; that on another timeline, they had actually traveled to this mysterious planet.

Clearing his throat, he proceeded with caution. "What would you propose to do there?"

"That's the thing," Nita said. "We've been working with Nibiru's elements. It never dawned on us that we might not be completely attuned to Ki's elements."

"But in working with Nibiru's elements," Barlumgeme added, "we realized that if we could be in dissonance with them here at home, if any of us went to Ki, they might be completely out of phase with the elements there."

Enmarsikil took this in, his heart pounding fast. "What would you propose to do?"

"We've been working with music to attune ourselves more closely to the elements and elementals here on Nibiru," Didi said holding up his reed flute.

"Has it been effective?" Enmarsikil wanted to know.

"We can easily get coherent with the elements here," Mamud replied.

"And when we do, Nibiru's elementals become really solid to us,"

Barlumgeme told him.

"And when we stay in the musical field long enough," Satu added, "we no longer have to think about maintaining the harmonic."

"Thing is," Nita confessed, "this feels really important. Like if we don't do this and our siblings go to Ki, something terrible could happen."

Enmarsikil paled, clearly shaken by their revelation. "Please see Teacher after the session," he told them. "He needs to hear this."

The group agreed and joined the team formation.

Enmarsikil took a moment to relay a mental message to his father and a bit longer to calm his nerves. When his heart stopped pounding in his throat, he turned back to his team and began to work.

CHAPTER 17 - FIRST PAIR

Before the time of cycles was up, Marne called everyone into the large lecture hall. Astara quickly noticed that all the Trainers except for Giramusen were present.

"We have a happy announcement to make," Teacher said. "As you know, Giramusen was pregnant with the last possible hybrid. She has just given birth to a baby girl."

"While the birth was difficult," Marne added, "she and the baby are in good health."

Cheers went up from the hybrids in the room. No one knew the child's significance; no one but Astara.

I'm not the baby anymore and now there are enough women so everyone will have a mate, she thought, and Enmarsikil's face instantly sprang to mind. Then she frowned. *Is that why he hasn't chosen a mate yet? He didn't want someone else to go without.*

When they were dismissed, Astara went straight to the gym for a team session. After warm ups, a First Generation man named Imgiri stepped forward to demonstrate an airblade technique. It was a high level technique by which anyone with a modicum of air element could extend a field of wind about themselves and spin it before giving it a sharp release as a cutting blade.

Her curiosity piqued, Astara found a corner and watched. After observing Imgiri for a while, she gave the idea a couple of tries. Before long, she had managed to extend a field of wind about herself.

"Astara's doing it again," someone yelled.

"How does she pick it up so fast?" came another voice.

"It's just easy for her," a third voice added. "Just ignore her and practice."

But by now all heads had turned to look at her, and Astara's cheeks burned bright.

"It would be nice if you had an original thought in your head," Imgiri's friend Lugulum, complained. "Copy cat to the end."

Before Enmarsikil could order a correction to the younger man, anger gripped the pit of her stomach. Without realizing what she was doing, Astara brought the wind field around her and a second later whipped an airblade across the room. Enmarsikil raised his hand halting it before it connected with anybody. But all eyes were wide as her teammates focused on her.

Enmarsikil made a motion with his hand and the airblade vanished. "When did you learn that?" he asked moving through the ranks toward her.

"I-I didn't," she stammered. "I just saw that for the first time."

"Then how?" he asked reaching her side and scrutinizing her.

"The same way I've learned everything else," she admitted. "I watch."

Enmarsikil studied her closely, and Astara shifted uncomfortably under his gaze. Yet, she felt a strange sensation from him and a new emotion flickered in his eyes.

She frowned slightly. *Is he proud?* she wondered inwardly. *Of me?*

"How long did it take you to master that, Imgiri?" Enmarsikil asked glancing back over his shoulder.

"About a shar," Imgiri replied coming up behind him. "But I've seen Astara do this sort of thing before...catching onto techniques no one has taught her."

Enmarsikil turned back to her. "And you figured it out from his demo?" he asked again.

"I watched and I felt what he felt as he did it," Astara explained.

Suddenly, Enmarsikil's eyes opened wide. "Your empathic skills! You're not picking up what others are doing. You're picking up how they feel when they're doing' it!"

Astara shrugged growing more uncomfortable at all the attention as the other team members gathered around her. "That's all I've ever done."

"But I never thought of using empathic skills," Enmarsikil insisted.

"Me neither," seconded Peenzermi.

Astara blushed and pulled back.

"You are quite the innovator," Enmarsikil said turning away to continue the training session.

For the remainder of the period, Astara only half heard what those around her said. *I'm an innovator*, kept ringing through her head.

When the others filed out, she remained standing in the gymnasium wondering at her newly found self.

I never thought what I did was so different, she mused. *But even Enmarsikil has never tried it. I'm not 'the baby.' I'm the innovator. I have an identity no one else gave me. I know who I am.*

Enmarsikil prepared to head out the door when he looked back and spotted her. He opened his mouth to speak only to watch her slowly rotate then spin faster and lift off the ground. It was a joyous moment. He could feel the happiness radiating from her. But he also knew she'd never tried this skill before, either. Remembering his own early attempts, he knew how quickly you could lose the energy.

Taking a few steps toward her, Enmarsikil spiraled up beside her. In moments, it was as if they had joined their vortexes. And when hers faltered, as he knew it would on a first attempt, he was there to catch her and gently lower her back to the ground. He landed softly beside her. She opened her eyelids and gazed up at him, her eyes bright.

"I finally know myself," she declared. "I know what I do and what I'm capable of."

Enmarsikil beamed at her wishing he could whisk her into his arms for a proper celebration. "Come by my gardens later. I have a surprise for you."

Astara cocked her head, curious as to what might be waiting for her.

He reached out and gently squeezed her shoulder. "I have a secret," he whispered. "Something I can only share with you."

Her eyes widened and she watched him walk away.

Astara returned to her bed in the dorm finding it in disarray as usual. Not her stuff, but everybody else's in the neighboring vicinity. Suddenly, she drew herself up to her full petite height. With flicks of her hands she sorted the things on her bed back to the beds of their owners and put the items on a return loop should said owners try to flip them back to her side again. Then she set up clear, energetic boundaries around her

140

space.

A place inside her had cracked open like an egg shell and was presently expanding at an exponential rate. She marveled at how the mere act of knowing who she was from the inside, not from the labels others had given her, could make her feel so different, so alive. But there it was and it wasn't stopping any time soon.

Her stomach growled and she hurried to the lunch room for a quick evening meal. While the others gathered together to discuss the announcement of Giramusen's baby, Astara felt she could withstand the suspense no longer. Drawing a cloaking plane about herself, she slipped from the halls and made her way to the wicket gate in the garden wall. She sought out the best friend she had ever had.

Astara once again crept inside the garden walls. Her stomach twisted into knots as she sought him out. She found Enmarsikil at the furthest fish ponds. He spun around sensing her presence and smiled. He knew what he had only once hoped. They would always be together.

"For a moment I thought you might not come," he said flinging the last handful of fish pellets over the water toward the hungry mouths that gaped above the surface.

He turned and moved toward her reaching out to wrap his arms around her. She put her arms up in front of her, blocking him. He frowned.

"Please...don't hug me...tell me," she begged. "I can't stand wondering what you have to say...what this secret could possibly be."

He slipped his arm around her back and led her to a nearby log bench. She sat with her hands folded in her lap not daring to look at him. The sudden thought that he might ask her never to come back to his gardens had crept into her heart.

"Is something wrong?" Enmarsikil asked.

She shook her head tensely.

Enmarsikil took her hands in his. "Do you care for me at all, Astara?" he asked. "Even the tiniest bit?"

She jerked her head up and gazed at him wide-eyed. "Yes. Of course. You're the best friend I've ever had."

He squeezed her hands then rose and pulled her to her feet. He put one arm around her shoulders and began leading her down the paths that wound between the fish ponds.

"Remember I have a secret," he reminded her. "Do you want to know what it is?"

Astara nodded. "Of course."

"When I was created, I was alone....the prototype," he began. "After me, 500 hybrids were created, 250 boys and 250 girls. There was no one for me."

She nodded. "I had thought about that. But Giramusen had the baby."

Enmarsikil squeezed her shoulders. "And father gave me the possibility to choose a mate before anyone else."

Astara held her breath waiting for him to continue.

"If I saw a woman from any of the generations I felt drawn to, and she returned my affections," he continued, his voice suddenly cracking and his mouth going dry, "I could choose that woman for myself and she could choose me in turn."

They stopped before a bush with beautiful, double petaled, red blooms. Astara stared at him, her heart pounding, and he could all but see the gears turning in her mind.

"You asked me if I care for you," she whispered.

He nodded.

"Does that mean you care for me, too?"

Enmarsikil bent down and picked up a pair of pruning shears. He clipped the largest, most fragrant bloom and held it in a his hand, steady and assured. He took a deep breath to ground himself then looked her squarely in the eye.

"Astara, you always had a spot in my heart from the day you were born and I was just a small boy," he began. "But I've watched you grow into such a beautiful, inspiring woman. I fell in love with you the moment our lips first touched, and that love has only grown stronger over time."

Her hand flew to her mouth, her eyes wide in disbelief.

"I've been given the power to choose my mate," Enmarsikil continued. "It would make me so happy if you were that woman. Will you be my mate, Astara?"

Her heart raced wildly, and for a moment she thought she'd hyperventilate, but when he extended the flower to her, Astara never hesitated.

"Yes," she whispered then suddenly found her voice, "Oh yes!"

Enmarsikil eagerly gathered her into his arms, his lips molded over hers. They lost themselves in that embrace for many long moments before finally parting with a soft, shared exhale.

Astara breathed deeply of the flower's scent. "I've never seen this flower in your garden before," she remarked.

Enmarsikil cupped her cheek in his hand, gently caressing her

142

skin with his thumb. "I created this flower to capture your beauty and sweetness just for this moment."

Her eyes glowed and her heart swelled in her chest.

Enmarsikil reached his arm around her shoulders and guided her towards the research building.

"Where are we going?" she asked noticing he was leading them straight through the labs and out to the Academy proper.

"If you're absolutely certain of your decision, I want to tell father and mother," Enmarsikil told her. "The sooner we tell them, the sooner they can begin the pairing process for everyone."

Almost as if walking in a blissful dream, Astara let him lead her to Teacher's quarters. She had never been inside anything but Marne's library before. Now, she gazed about at the instruments and Seer's tools in his main room. In a moment, both Teacher and Marne stepped inside from an adjacent porch.

Enmarsikil rubbed his suddenly sweaty palms on his tunic.

"That's a lovely flower," Marne observed.

Astara beamed and looked up at Enmarsikil.

"You...have something you wished to discuss?" Teacher prompted.

Enmarsikil nodded and put his hands on Astara's shoulders. "You promised that if I found a woman from any generation whom I liked and who returned my affections, I could choose her as my mate."

Teacher and Marne nodded in unison.

"I have chosen Astara," he announced.

"And I chose him back," she added with her usual spunk.

Teacher had to smile in spite of himself. She reminded him of a younger version of his own mate.

"I indeed made that promise," Teacher said, "and I am as good as my word. We will acknowledge yours as the first match."

"Even without going through all the tests?" Astara asked to make certain.

"Yes," Teacher replied. "You don't need to."

Marne caught a look in the young woman's eyes. "But do you want to?"

Astara looked up at Enmarsikil for a moment. "I don't need proof of our love, but I am curious...."

Enmarsikil looked to his parents. "Would the outcome change our pairing?" he asked.

Teacher shook his head. "No. The choice has been made. It is a permanent decision."

Enmarsikil thought for a few moment. "It could yield interesting results," he acknowledged.

"Then we will have you and Astara demonstrate the pairing tests at the next lecture," Marne agreed.

"For now, though, until we begin the pairing process with the others, you will continue to live in the dorm," Teacher insisted.

Astara nodded her understanding.

"But, you can visit Enmarsikil directly without using the wicket gate," Marne added.

Astara blushed; her secret was out.

When she and Enmarsikil parted for the day with a kiss at the research wing entrance, the startled onlookers watched in shocked silence as they kissed and hugged. Enmarsikil glanced up at the others, gave Astara a squeeze and his stunned siblings a wave of his hand before he disappeared inside the lab wing. Word spread quickly about their pairing, but Astara was in a world of her own.

When she got to her sleeping cubicle, she placed the flower Enmarsikil had given her in a clear glass vase, set it on her bed stand and created a breathable, domed shield to go over it so no one else could touch it. Then, in spite of the chatter around her mentioning her name, Astara laid down and slept with a smile on her face.

CHAPTER 18 - DEMONSTRATIONS OF POWER

Since Enmarsikil and Astara were now an official pair, word went out that they would demonstrate the pairing tests that would help confirm other pairings within the generations. On an announced day, Marne directed Astara to an anteroom on the lower level near the lecture hall to wait. Her heart thudded and her palms were sweaty. She had never demonstrated anything before, always preferring to observe and feel. Suddenly, she was going to be on the platform in the lecture hall well in front of everyone.

A click behind her startled her, and she spun to see Enmarsikil enter to join her. He gave her a quick hug before picking up his head to hear Teacher call the lecture to order.

"Are you nervous?" Astara asked.

Enmarsikil glanced down at her. "A few butterflies. You?"

She held out her hands, and he could clearly see them shaking.

"I've never been on the platform to demonstrate anything before," she told him anxiously.

He grimaced. "I've been up there way too often."

"'How do you do it," she asked. "Not get scared?"

"Sheer repetition, I suspect," he replied.

"I should never have said anything," Astara fretted wrapping her arms around herself.

Enmarsikil stopped listening to Teacher's voice from the lecture hall and observed her carefully. "This is no different than a lot of the 'games' we've played in my gardens or the techniques you've learned in training," he assured her. "Do what you always do."

"You mean, tune into you empathically?" she asked.

He nodded. "Focus on me. You won't notice the others."

She nodded her understanding as the door to the lecture hall opened, and Marne motioned them toward the platform.

As he ascended the stairs out of the anteroom, Enmarsikil contacted Teacher telepathically. *Put her back to the gallery if you can, father. She's shaking with fear and that won't help her abilities.*

Teacher nodded slightly in his son's direction and spun the instruments 180 degrees on the long table centered on the platform.

"I have explained the decision to give Enmarsikil choice," Teacher told the onlookers. "He and Astara, his chosen, have agreed to demonstrate the instruments for you."

Astara glanced up at the sea of faces watching her and wobbled. Enmarsikil took her arm to steady her, then placed her in front of the first instrument with her back to the gallery. She glanced up and smiled shakily.

"For this first test, please place your hands on the pads in front of you," Teacher instructed.

Each pad was split into segments like fingers and metal dots lined each finger. Marne helped them both line up their hands correctly.

She whispered in Astara's ear. "Breathe."

Astara took a quick gulp of air not even aware that she'd been holding her breath.

"As you watch the field above their heads, you will notice first the colors of their auras appearing," Teacher said.

As he spoke, yellows, oranges and indigos created an egg shape over Enmarsikil while the egg shape over Astara was orange with greens and blues.

"This is an interesting combination," Teacher commented. "Both share a strong sense of creativity, but where Enmarsikil's is guided by thought and intuition, Astara's is governed more by the heart and emotion."

A color spectrum then took the place of the auras.

"No two bandwidth spectrums are the same," Marne noted. "However, if you'll look, Enmarsikil's and Astara's personal bandwidths mesh well without much overlap. This is exactly the sort of completion
146

we're looking to see in a pair."

Astara sighed with relief and took her hands off the plates. She and Enmarsikil shuffled to the next instrument. This one had a glowing plate set in the center between them.

"Please clasp each others' hands directly over the plate," Marne instructed.

Enmarsikil reached out and Astara gratefully took his hands. She stared into his eyes seeing only him. In moments, the light from the disc turned to a deep pulsing red.

"The deeper the red and the more intense the pulsing, the better the interpersonal physical chemistry between individuals," Teacher announced.

Marne tapped Astara's shoulder, and she let go of Enmarsikil's hands. Together, they stepped to the next section of the table. Here they found metal balls, balance devices, hoops and more.

"This test is designed to see how well their powers mesh regardless of skill level," Teacher announced.

Astara frowned at the array. Nothing about this test was obvious to her.

Follow my lead, she heard echo in her head and snapped her eyes up to meet Enmarsikil's.

Taking a deep breath, Astara waited to see what would happen. In a moment, three colored metal balls rose off the table in a line. She glanced at Enmarsikil, noticed his focus and stared at the balls. Suddenly, to everyone's astonishment, they began juggling each other in mid-air.

Then to her right, Astara saw a balance set of two unevenly weighted metal balls dangling from a metal arm rise off the table. Setting a portion of her mental focus to continued the juggling, she turned to the balance set. Soon it was spinning around an unseen axis in mid-air.

Before she knew it, two hoops lifted off the table. She sent them back and forth over the other two tricks that were still in play.

"Well done," Teacher said.

Enmarsikil slowly lowered the items to the table.

"Your uses for the items don't have to duplicate theirs," Teacher continued. "It's a matter of being able to synchronize and harmonize your powers."

There were several more tests down the line, but after the first few Astara had grown in confidence and Enmarsikil had but to start whatever process they were challenged with, and she easily completed the requirements. When they had finished, both were shaking from exertion.

Marne turned them both to face the gallery while Teacher reviewed the results as holograms in front of him. Finally, he looked up.

"These are actually excellent results with both of you complementing each other well," he said. "It's a good match and typical of what we're hoping for."

He dismissed the couple and Marne showed them back to the anteroom. Once she closed the door on them, Astara fell into Enmarsikil's arms. He held her close as fine tremors ran throughout her body.

"I've never been so scared in my whole life," she breathed.

"You wouldn't have known it," Enmarsikil said rubbing her back. "You were a whiz out there. I could throw anything at you, and you were up for it."

"Only because it was you, and I could track you," Astara replied.

Enmarsikil pulled back and gazed into her eyes. "But that's the point. If it hadn't been me but someone else, the results wouldn't have been the same. That's why father and mother ultimately have the last say in the pairings, so really mismatched people don't wind up together and spend their lives miserable."

"Then I guess we got lucky," Astara commented.

He thought about it for a moment. "Maybe, but maybe not. I'm oldest...you were youngest...youngest of the generations at least. Alpha and Omega; beginnings and endings. Like bookends to bracket the others and anchor them."

Astara could only partially take in what he was saying. "Maybe later that will make sense to me," she said. "Right now, I'm starved."

"Want to eat with me today?" Enmarsikil asked leading her toward the outer door.

"Today and every day," she replied happily, hugging his arm as they left for his quarters.

As they left the anteroom, they heard Teacher address the others in the lecture hall.

"Now that you have seen how this works," Teacher told the hybrids in the gallery, "we would like anyone who has developed strong attractions to take these tests. They are the best indicators of compatibility that we have and will hopefully encourage happy pairings and prevent mismatched couples."

"If there are any hybrids who have made affectionate connections and wish to challenge the tests, please step down into the lecture well," Zalkur called. "The rest of you are dismissed.

"Just remember, we still have one more major assembly coming up," Marne called over the hubbub. "That one will give you the opportunity to demonstrate your group projects."

Half the hybrids in the lecture hall started filing down toward the well. The rest climbed the stairs and left through the upper doors.

Later, while Enmarsikil was busy in his labs and Astara was working with her group, Marne entered his suite and began shifting the space as only she could. Before long, an arch appeared on the left wall that opened into a large room off to the side of Enmarsikil's bed chamber. It was complete with its own large bed, wardrobe, bookshelves and large, bay window. When she was satisfied, Marne went in search of Astara whose group was just wrapping up. She caught Astara and guided her back to the dorm.

"It's time to move," Marne announced.

Astara frowned. "Where am I going?"

Marne busied herself in Astara's bed cubicle collecting clothes and draping them over the girl's arms. "You are now Enmarsikil's partner. You will live with him."

Astara's eyes widened but she dutifully followed her mentor out of the dorm, through the corridors, into the research wing and down the long hall to Enmarsikil's suite. Marne walked straight through Enmarsikil's bed chamber and into the large room beyond. In no time clothes had been hung, books shelved, plants arranged on a broad window sill, and Astara was gazing longingly at the large, sunken, freshwater pool near the windows.

She stood in the middle of the room slowly turning to take it all in. "This is all mine?" she asked incredulously.

"As is every room in the suite," Marne pointed out. "You now share it with Enmarsikil. It now belongs to both of you."

"Then, why do we have separate beds?" Astara wanted to know glancing first at hers then at the large bed she could see through the archway in Enmarsikil's chamber.

Marne sighed. "Astara, you have grown up your whole life surrounded by sisters in very close quarters. You barely know the meaning of personal space. Enmarsikil has had all of this space to himself for his whole life. He has never shared space with another. You may find the two of you mesh well or you may find you periodically need time in your own beds in order to acclimate to the new arrangements."

"Oh," Astara said, her mind working. "Are the other pairs going to get their own shared space, too?" she wondered.

Marne nodded. "Zalkur and Emissary are working right now building a new wing with apartments for the couples."

"I think," Astara said slowly, "that this is going to feel a little weird."

"You'll get used to it," Marne assured her as she left for other tasks.

Astara's back was to the door and she was humming as she arranged her things more to her liking. Suddenly, someone cleared their throat, and she spun around to see Enmarsikil taking it all in from the arch. She ran over to him with a big smile, encircled is neck with her arms and reached up for a long kiss.

"Mother said she helped you move in," he said shyly.

"Yes," she replied taking his hand and pulling him into the room. "I suddenly have this whole big room instead of the cubicle I used to live in."

"You have more than a room," Enmarsikil said sampling her lips again. "Whatever is mine is yours."

Their kiss turned steamy as he ran his hands up her back and cupped around the front of her bodice. Panting, she started pulling him toward the bed. Suddenly, he jerked his head up and froze.

"What?" Astara asked, frowning.

"I set an internal alarm for the next stage of an experiment," he replied.

"You have to leave now?" she asked incredulously.

"Just for a little," he promised giving her one last kiss. "I'll be back in a while."

He turned to leave, but Astara didn't let go so easily. When he finally extricated himself from her embrace, he had to dash out the door to their suite. Astara stared after him with her hands on her hips. While she waited for him to return, she finally gave into temptation. She slipped out of her clothes, tested the water in the sunken pool and sank in "dissolving" as she hit the water. A sensation filled the room of dispersed, sentient awareness. Time passed and the light outside the window dimmed, though during this long season of the shar cycle it never completely darkened, the awareness retreated to the pool, Astara rose up out of it and slowly dressed.

She checked Enmarsikil's bed chamber, his niche by the window, even the large bathroom. With him nowhere in sight, she found her way to the kitchen and ate alone. But when his absence stretched past bed time, she crawled into her big, new bed by herself. However, she found
150

it all too big, too new and too starched. She tossed and turned for a while then gave up on trying to sleep. She crawled out of bed and sauntered into Enmarsikil's bed chamber. Lying on his bed, she found the scent of his body on the sheet comforting and fell asleep clutching his pillow.

Sometime later, Enmarsikil staggered in from the lab. Too tired to eat, he didn't even bother turning on the light. He shed his clothes, climbed into bed and tried to locate his pillow. Finally finding it near the middle of the bed, he tried to move it to under his head but found it wouldn't budge. A couple more tugs and he heard a sleepy yawn. The pillow yanked free but there was something beyond it; something warm, soft and breathing.

Stunned, he illuminated his fingertips on one hand and looked into Astara's sleepy face. His brain, though weary, did some hasty mental back-tracking and novel calculations. When he had left for the lab earlier in the day, she had just moved her things in. He had distinctly seen a large bed in the other room, yet...she was...here.

"Everything ok?" she asked reaching out to caress his shoulder.

"Yes," he squeaked, cleared his throat and in a more normal tone replied, "Yes, fine."

"Did you want me to use the other bed?" she asked beginning to shift toward the far edge pulling all the covers with her.

Enmarsikil grabbed the retreating covers and held them firmly in place over his lower half. With the other hand, he reached for her arm.

"You don't have to go."

"You look...."

"Startled," he quickly finished. "I-I've never slept with anyone close by before. I'm just...startled."

He pulled her back toward him and slid down under the covers. Not certain what to expect, he waited for her. Astara scooted over beside him, wrapped her arms across his stomach and nestled her head against his shoulder. When nothing else happened, he encircled her shoulders with his arm.

"If I'd known you were going to sleep with me right away, I'd have cleaned up the bed," he commented.

Astara hugged him. "I'm glad you didn't."

"Why?"

"I tried to sleep in the other bed, but it was too new," she told him. "But your bed smelled like you. It was comforting."

Enmarsikil furrowed his brow. He was pretty certain his bed smelled like hours of sweat from work in gardens and the lab and then some, but if that suited her, he wasn't complaining.

She reached up, kissed his cheek then nestled back against him and was soon fast asleep.

The warmth from her body and gentle weight of her head were new sensations. Part of it soothed him to the core and made him feel content and drowsy. Another part, however, was going to be hard to ignore as his arousal awakened just as his brain shut off. He lay for a while smoothing her hair back from her face. At some point in time, he must have fallen asleep because another internal alarm suddenly went off.

Enmarsikil blinked his eyes open. He glanced beside him at the empty bed, squeezed his eyes shut and shook his head.

Must've been a dream, he thought swinging his legs out of bed and staggering into the foggy bathroom.

Suddenly, his eyes snapped wide open. "Foggy!"

At that moment, a slender hand reached out of the shower area, grabbed a hanging towel and stole it away. As Enmarsikil watched entranced, the door to the shower opened and a towel-wrapped Astara stepped out, her long slender legs dripping with water. He staggered back against the wall, another part of himself at full attention.

"Not a dream," he breathed.

She glanced up at him and smiled. "Hey. I wanted to get up so I could go with you to the lab today."

"Lab?" he managed.

"I wanted to see what kept you up so late last night."

For a moment nothing registered other than her barely covered body. Enmarsikil breathed hard thinking of other things he'd like to be doing right at that moment, none of them including the lab. Then he heard his internal alarm go off again.

He shook his head to clear it and stared as she made a motion to remove her towel. "Um...could I have the bathroom now?" he gasped.

Astara's eyebrows rose to peaks and she tucked the towel closer around her. "Sure...sorry."

Astara hurried toward the door gently brushing past him. He felt her bare legs and smelled the heavenly scent of some herbal scented shampoo. Once she was gone, he closed the door and leaned on it for a moment. Taking a deep breath, he turned and hastily rushed through his morning routine.

She came out of her room, dressed and ready, just in time to see him dash out the door.

"Wait!" she called then sighed.

Pacing, Astara vacillated between tears and the desire to scream. Finally, she took a deep breath and calmed herself. Closing her eyes, she dropped her awareness into her heart and felt for Enmarsikil. She latched onto that feeling and let it lead her out the door, down the hall and through the labs. Finally, she opened her eyes and spotted him bent low over a lab bench working with an array of specimens. Quietly, she moved toward a desk near the back and slid onto a stool to watch.

Lost in the midst of his latest assay, Enmarsikil worked without any sense of time. Suddenly, a beaker slipped out of his hand plummeting toward the floor. To his shock, it stopped in mid-air. Stunned, he slowly turned to see Astara manipulating a multi-dimensional grid to keep his beaker from smashing on the floor. He gratefully plucked it from the air, set it on the table and turned back toward her.

"Apparently, I can be useful," Astara quipped sliding off the stool and walking over. "Anything else I can do?"

"I-I never gave it any thought," he replied. "I've always done it all myself."

"Well, some of the things you're doing, I'm sure I could do," she told him. "I could wash beakers or do that squirt and count thing. You'd just have to show me how."

"You want to?" he asked, astonished.

"Right after you eat," she declared, grabbing his arm and dragging him toward the door. "Half the day has gone by."

"But...." he protested.

"I'll help...after."

That evening Enmarsikil came in late again. He stood in the doorway for a moment reminding himself that someone else now shared his space. Keeping the lights off, he shed his clothes but grabbed a comfy pair of sleep pants he'd set out and pulled them on. Then he carefully slipped under the covers trying not to jostle the bed too much."

He felt the warmth from her body and smelled her freshly washed hair. He took a deep breath and slowly let it out.

She's really going to sleep here every night, he thought.

As Enmarsikil sank down into the mattress and lay his head onto the pillow, Astara eased over until her back was tucked close to his front. His heart beat faster wondering if she'd awakened. He touched her arm, but she merely murmured in her sleep. He gently brushed the hair back from her face, kissed her neck and shoulder then slipped his arm over her side. Hugging her close, he drifted off to sleep.

CHAPTER 19 - PROJECTS ON DISPLAY

The next morning Enmarsikil and Astara collided in the bathroom again. She had a meeting with her project group before the big demonstration in the lecture hall that day, and he had some quick lab work before observing the groups' projects. As Astara began shedding her clothes to step into the shower, Enmarsikil nearly tripped over his own feet in a mad scramble to leave the bathroom. Frowning, she hurried through her shower and found him pacing outside the door when she came out.

She studied him anxiously. "You really aren't comfortable with my presence, are you?"

Enmarsikil stopped pacing, took a deep breath and looked at her, his expression pleading for understanding. "Sweet, I've been alone my whole life. I have just never had to share space with anyone before, let alone a-a...."

"Woman?" she asked cocking her head to one side.

He nodded. "I do want you here," Enmarsikil insisted putting his hands on her bare shoulders. "I-I just need time to adjust."

Astara reached up, kissed his cheek then slipped away to her own room to dress. By the time she had finished dressing, dried her hair and gathered her plants, he was long gone. She took a look around his room.

"Maybe I am coming on too strong," she fretted noticing how much of her things seemed to be draped everywhere.

154

Her clothes were hung over the backs of chairs and the bed, her books were piled here and there with his belongings barely peeking out from underneath. Astara sighed. She remembered how much she had disliked having her sisters' belongings cluttering her dorm cubicle.

With a decisive nod, she put her plants out in the hall then scurried about his room scooping up her clothes and books. She dumped her things on her bed, changed the sheets on his bed and carefully separated their toiletries and towels in the bathroom. Giving his chamber a quick once over, Astara grabbed her plants and dashed to the main lecture hall.

Guess I should have listened to Marne, she thought as she jogged along. *Tonight I'll sleep in my own bed.*

Astara skidded to a stop in front of the lecture hall doors, squeezed through and searched for her group. Peenzermi spotted her and waved, and Astara dodged around mingling siblings to plunk down on a seat beside the others. Moments later, the Multi-Dims entered the well below, and the groups scrambled for their seats.

Teacher took a step up onto the platform. "Welcome back after your hiatus," his voice boomed. "We hope you have used this time well. I and my colleagues are waiting in anticipation to see the ways you have devised to use your attributes and the projects you have applied them to."

"Elemental Harmonics has volunteered to go first," Emissary announced.

Nita, Barlumgeme, Satu and Mamud stood up, each carrying containers, and made their way to the platform in the well. A table was levitated into place, and they set their containers on it taking a few minutes to remove items and put together an equipment system. Finally ready, Nita stepped in front while Satu managed the equipment.

"The four of us chose to experiment with Nibiru's natural elements," Nita opened.

"We went out into the wilderness surrounding the Academy and interacted with elements in the environment," Barlumgeme said.

"We found, to our surprise, that we didn't fully resonate with them," Satu added.

Mamud picked up a large chunk of rock and held it close to her body. Satu sampled her frequency and that of the rock. The two bandwidths were displayed overhead.

"As you can see," Nita said gesturing to the display, "we may have been born on Nibiru and attuned to its elements, but not nearly close enough."

"So we wondered if there were some way to resonate better with

Nibiru's elements," Barlumgeme said placing more rocks in a circle around Mamud.

"We tried a lot of things," Mamud admitted, "but in the end, toning was the most effective."

Satu set his instruments then stepped into place with the others. They began by humming low harmonics and watching the display. As Mamud's frequency altered till it was in closer resonance with the stones, the stones began to change shape. As they did so, squat beings rose up and joined in the song. Around the lecture hall, each person present could feel the effects in their own bodies.

Enmarsikil suddenly appeared in a seat directly behind Astara. He gently squeezed her shoulder to let her know he was there. Otherwise, his focus was entirely on the presentation.

The little group showed the effects of water, fire, air and metal in turn. The effects were not only visually confirmed but palpable to the audience. When they were done, Barlumgeme and Mamud packed up one set of elements while Nita talked.

"After that, we wondered what might happen to our people if any of us ever traveled to Ki," Nita remarked.

"Teacher put a request in to Ea, and he has promised to send back samples from the planet for us to work on when he sends to first shipment of gold," Satu added.

"This has haunted my dreams almost as memories of beings so different from Ki's elements, we couldn't hold form," Mamud admitted.

"If we can find the way to harmonize our frequencies with those of Ki's elements, we should be able to create a tuning device for us to wear while on the planet to help us maintain a balanced resonance," Nita concluded.

"Excellent concept," Teacher commended as the audience in the gallery clapped.

The foursome packed up their equipment and boxes and hurried off the stage.

"Next up, Plant Growth Enhancement," Emissary announced.

Ki, Peenzermi, Bilanammul, Aiya and Astara rose and carefully balanced their plants as they carried them down to the table. They arranged them then looked to Astara. Her hands and knees were shaking when she looked up into the gallery. She found Enmarsikil and stared at him exclusively.

"It took us a while to figure out what to work with, but I'd watched Enmarsikil plant seedlings and wondered if it were possible to influence

156

how they grow," Astara explained. "So, Enmarsikil leant us some seedlings."

"The first time we worked with them, half of us put a growth enhancing field around our plants and half didn't," Ki said.

"And the growth field was really obvious," Aiya said as Bilanammul put out the initial plants.

"These tall branchy plants grew like this during the same time as those short plants," Bilanammul said.

"The difference was lots of growth due to the harmonic resonance of the field effect," Aiya said.

"So we took a plant each and for only that plant reversed the effect," Astara said showing her two plants. "We took the plants that had grown a lot, and left them out of the field to continue growing normally. And we put the original control plants in the growth field. The controls plants sprouted past its counterpart and got bushy."

"But the real key came when I was finally able to hear the plants singing," Aiya remarked.

She had set up wiring on her plants that she strung to an amplifier. She flipped it on and continued raising the volume. Gradually, everyone in the room could literally hear the plants singing.

"Once we could hear the tones, Aiya was able to determine if the plants were missing notes in their harmonics," Ki added.

"When they were, we knew they weren't as healthy," Bilanammul explained.

"Then I taught the others how to tone the missing notes to the plants," Aiya said.

"And the plants grew lush and healthy," Astara concluded. "If we were to apply this concept throughout Nibiru, more healthy vibrant plants could be grown for food and medicine."

While those in the gallery clapped, the girls put their plants off to one side and returned to their seats in the gallery. Enmarsikil squeezed Astara's shoulder.

"Good job, ladies. I may have to employ your skills in my gardens," he whispered to them.

They smiled happily.

"The next group is the Gold Refin...." Emissary began, but a commotion from the gallery made him cut his announcement short.

Another group stood up off to his right.

"Elemental Protection," a tall, muscular young man named, Allanagalaabadgal, better known as Allanagal, called out in a booming bass voice.

Emissary acknowledged them and they began to wind their way down to the platform. Meanwhile, the Gold Refinement group scrambled up the stairs and out into the hall.

"We're not ready," Nindulur, a lean, athletic brunette woman, fretted.

"We need Marki," Mirsigmi, a freckled blond, insisted.

"No way," Izishub, a ginger haired, athletically built man, said firmly. "I will not have that mean, insulting brat in this group."

"Let me talk to him," Mirsigmi persisted.

"I don't know what good that'll do," Simugatibira growled, his squared jaw tense and his silvery eyes flashing.

"Just let me try," Mirsigmi pleaded.

Izishub and Simugatibira looked at each other, shrugged and turned back to Mirsigmi.

"All right," Izishub relented. "They'll probably break after this presentation."

"But he has to stop with the put downs and insults," Sagtibira declared tossing his long black bangs aside. "Either he grows up or one word from him, and he's out."

Mirsigmi nodded and the group quietly re-entered the lecture hall and returned to their seats. As they did, Allanagal was speaking.

"We set out and did some travel around Nibiru," he began. "What we discovered are a lot of areas that haven't recovered from the Great War. Their elementals are withering or even leaving the areas, and the land and people are suffering for their absence."

"We decided to figure out how to create safe havens for them around the planet where they could be nurtured and protected," Kienelil said. She was a shorter woman with a smart sense of style who loved bright colors.

"With Allanagal's strength and my ability to create comforting shade," Napalker added, "all they need from there on out are our own elemental protectors like Lilnasaru, Sahanasaru, Nunasaru and Mudinasaru to protect the air, land, sun and water."

"We create a structure from our blending," Girimush said. "I provide the foundational structure into which Allanagal can anchor."

"Then I create an umbrella effect arching overhead," Napalkugissupa said, "while Kienelil is the bond between them. Dariag creates a warming fire of energy and our guards protect the space."

"In the end, we create a strong enough imprint on the space that

158

the nature elementals not only return but are able to thrive once we leave," Allanagal concluded.

Teacher nodded as he stepped forward on the platform. "This would be a project that would mesh well with Elemental Harmonics," he noted. "I would be very interested in seeing a larger collaboration between your two groups."

Allanagal nodded to acknowledge the new assignment and his group filed off the platform.

As expected, Marne stepped forward. "The presentations so far have been excellent. You have been very creative about applying your talents. We will break for a meal and a short rest then meet back here. At that time the Gold Refinement Project will present."

While everyone else rose and began filing out of the lecture hall amidst the hubbub of animated conversation, Mirsigmi searched the stands for one individual. She finally spotted him and began weaving through the throng of siblings to get near him. Marki was already getting his food and eyeing a table in a quiet corner when she finally caught up to him.

"Marki," Mirsigmi called. "Wait up!"

He turned and glowered at her. "My food's getting cold."

She reached his side as he plunked his tray on the table and sat down. Mirsigmi sat on the chair next to him.

"Listen, Marki. We need your skills," she said breathlessly.

He took a stab at his meat, put a bite in his mouth and chewed. "You sure the group needs me? Or is it just you?"

Color rose to her cheeks, but Mirsigmi pressed on. "No, the project really needs you. We've developed everything except for the actual refiner."

"And I can do that?" he snarled shoveling more food in his mouth.

Mirsigmi put her hand on his arm but he roughly shook it off. "I've watched you build things, repair things, machines and stuff," she insisted. "This is exactly where your talents lie."

Marki considered this for a moment. "So what if it is? I guarantee you, you're the only one who wants me in the group."

Mirsigmi hung her head. "The others find you difficult to deal with. If you'd just stop with the insults, they'd have you in the group in a heartbeat."

Marki swallowed his juice and started packing up to leave. Finally, he braced his hands on the table and shoved his face close to hers. "See, this is me. If they can't accept it, then no deal."

He rose and turned away.

"I don't think that's you," Mirsigmi said distinctly yet quietly. "I think you're afraid to show the real you."

He stopped dead in his tracks, his back stiffening.

"I think you make people annoyed so they won't want to get close to you," Mirsigmi said rising to stand near him. "I'm not sure what you have to hide, but if you distracted people by showing them the amazing things you can do with your hands rather than hurling insults, no one would pay any attention to whatever else you thought was wrong with you."

Marki turned. "You think it's that simple?" he challenged.

"Standard magician's trick," Mirsigmi replied. "Make them focus so hard in one direction, no one even sees what's happening right under their own noses."

His eyes widened then narrowed. At last his shoulders relaxed. "Maybe you're right."

"Look, I've got to eat, but we're meeting right after the meal," Mirsigmi told him. "We really would welcome you."

"You mean, you would," he said snidely.

Mirsigmi didn't back down. "I know you think everybody hates you, but yes, I would welcome you in the group."

Marki smirked. "I'll think about it," he replied walking away.

Mirsigmi hurried to get a tray of food then searched for her group and sat down.

"Well?" Izishub asked.

"He's thinking about it," she replied between bites.

Later, as they entered a smaller lecture hall to go over the plans, Marki quietly walked in and sat down in the back of the room.

"Well, speaking of the devil," Izishub whispered.

"Call him down," Mirsigmi whispered back.

"You call him," came the reply.

"He's looking to be invited by you," Mirsigmi hissed.

Izishub sighed. "Ok, but I'm warning you."

"Just try," Mirsigmi pleaded.

Izishub looked up. "Nice of you to join us."

Marki nodded mutely.

"If you come down, we can show you where we're stuck," Izishub offered.

"Only if I'm on it," Marki replied. "Not wasting my time otherwise."

160

Izishub gritted his teeth but finally nodded.

Marki swung his feet down from the chair back in front of him, rose and meandered to where the team was working. One-by-one, they showed him how far they'd gotten with determining how to refine the gold and what each degree of refinement would achieve.

"And this is where we need the actual mechanics of how to refine the gold," Izishub pointed out, "but it's not in our talent pool."

Marki pulled a pencil out from behind his ear and began drawing on the table they stood around. The others watched in studious silence. Finally, he tucked his pencil back behind his ear.

"If you run it through here, melt it down here, separate the impurities here and crush and filter it to varying degrees here," he said pointing out different spots in the drawing, "you'll have your refining machine."

Izishub whistled appreciatively. "That's it all right. Think you can build it?"

"I know he can," Mirsigmi spoke up. "I've seen him build amazing things before."

Izishub extended his hand toward Marki. "Welcome to the group. Glad to have you onboard."

When the lecture hall gathering began again, Marki joined the others on the platform in the well. Izishub took center stage and described their project. One-by-one, the others shared their pieces. Sagtibira discussed how pure ore could be discerned from the impurities. Simugatibira described smithy techniques to use, and Izishub talked about intensities of flame to use in the refinement process. But when they stood back, and Marki brought up a holographic image of the refinement center he envisioned, everyone in the room started commenting creating a low hubbub.

Marki looked uncomfortably into the gallery and frowned. "I told you...nobody likes me. Now it's just on display," he said out of the corner of his mouth to Mirsigmi, who stood nearby helping him hold the hologram.

"The don't hate you," she countered. "I can hear them. They're amazed! Impressed! You wowed the whole Academy."

Shock registered on Marki's face, and his gaze swept his siblings' faces. Izishub came over and clapped him on the shoulder.

"Well done, brother," he told Marki.

Marki was still in shock after they returned to the gallery. He didn't sit with the others but snuck out the upper doors and stood staring out a window off to one side. A footstep caught his attention.

"How did you know?" he asked without turning.

Mirsigmi stopped. "Because I'd already seen what you can do, and I knew people would be amazed."

Marki turned slowly. "Why do you like me? I've never been pleasant."

Mirsigmi edged closer looking down at her feet. "I've seen times when you thought you were all alone. You looked so miserable. I knew something hurt you bad. But there have been other moments when you could get people to laugh."

Marki snorted softly. "So you thought you would reform me."

Mirsigmi looked up shaking her head. "You don't need to reform; you need to shine in your own realm."

Marki turned back toward the window. "And now's my chance. Only...I'll blow it."

"Why does that have to be the outcome?" Mirsigmi asked.

He laughed wryly. "Because it always is."

"Who are you so angry at, Marki?" Mirsigmi wanted to know. "Why do you take your anger out on all of us rather than confront the right person?"

Marki laughed harshly. "Because that person is bigger than us."

"So, you took it out on the rest of us, but you're older now, Marki," Mirsigmi pointed out. "Give it a shot now."

"Maybe."

"I'll go with you," she offered.

"If I gave you the chance, you'd go everywhere with me," he noted.

She blushed and nodded.

"You like me that much?"

Mirsigmi looked up and held his eye. "Even if you went to Ki, I'd find a way to get there, too."

Marki moved closer. "I really thought there was nobody for me," he said taking her hand. "Could I have been wrong about that too?"

She gazed up at him and nodded.

"Maybe I have been a bit of a fool," he whispered, his lips brushing hers.

"Next group is presenting," someone called out the door jarring them in the process.

The couple jumped, startled.

"Sit with me?" Marki asked.

162

Mirsigmi nodded.

The couple slipped inside the lecture hall and sat in two empty upper seats. Marki slid his arm around her shoulder and she leaned in closer preparing to watch the next presentation.

CHAPTER 20 - NEW WORLD OF EDUCATION

The final group to present was the Space Transport Project. Emissary announced the group, and eight men and women filed out of the stands and down into the well.

Kappashegara, named for his love of traveling to extreme realms, stepped forward on the platform. "The first thing we did was took a look at the ships and space vehicles the Anunnaki already possess."

Astara frowned as she listened and turned to Enmarsikil who sat beside her. "How could they find the Anunnaki's space vehicles?" she whispered.

"They're in Agade," he replied quietly, his eyes never leaving the demonstration platform.

"But, how did they know how to find them?" she pressed. "None of us have ever been to Agade."

Enmarsikil stoically stared straight ahead. "I have."

Astara's eyebrows shot straight up. "You took them?" she squeaked.

Heads turned and somebody shushed her.

"You took them?" she whispered loudly.

"They asked," was all Enmarsikil would say pointing her back to the presentation below.

She turned back to it in a huff.

"Their craft all seem very crude," Kappa continued, "and their propulsion systems are too slow."

"We brainstormed what we would do differently," Guranmulla chimed in. "For one, their vessels' hulls are too rigid. They are really designed more for travel in an atmosphere around a planet with gravity, not the vacuum of space. Then we heard about Sagtibira's work with refining gold. We started playing with different densities of gold. At its finest, powdery dust, we realized that gold has amazing quantum properties."

"And that made us curious about other metals," Muduabzu, the brother who had come to understand limitlessness, interjected. "We found that silver and copper also display quantum properties when they're refined to powdery dust."

"So, right away we knew we'd be building our transports out of entirely different materials at very fine densities," Kappa determined.

"Then we looked into propulsion systems and how to travel the vast distances of space," Guranmulla said, a perfect project for him since he was attuned to the starry space expanses themselves. "Traditional physics is not sufficient for the task. Scalar physics and beyond make it possible to precisely track a destination and transit with little to no loss of power."

"We also thought of how to map our course through space. Anunnaki apparently coordinate trajectories via star systems. We played with the idea of using interdimensional mapping and hopping point-to-point on the grid of life that underlies all," Zupaturabu, an adept in interdimensional sifting, added. "This appears to be the only way to make such distant travel possible, reasonable and not dependent upon any one planet's orbit around the sun."

"And in my visions," Namtare, a budding seer, added, "I do see a time when siblings will venture to Ki and perhaps beyond."

"Between Tumumuermshun and me, we have the navigational aspects in place," Gugbubulu, the natural born navigator, assured them as he spoke of himself and his sky messenger brother.

"It's the actual process of refining metals on a larger scale and building the vehicles where we could use help," Kappa acknowledged. "That and they would have to be self-sustaining meaning we would need to determine how to feed ourselves and recycle waste and create breathable air."

Teacher nodded, pleased by the presentation. He stood and moved toward the front of the platform. "This is all very promising. While I'd

165

like to see a scale model built soon, it sounds like cooperation between your group, Gold Refinement and Plant Growth groups would be mutually beneficial. Well done."

While the Space Transport group filed off the platform and headed for their seats in the gallery, Emissary spoke to the rest of the groups that had yet to present. "Now that you see what's possible to achieve, work on your chosen challenges and think of how your projects might mesh with those from other groups. As you've already observed, one group may have brilliant ideas but be unable to manifest them without the expertise of another group. Such intergroup cooperation is to be fostered. We highly encourage it. We will have more presentations over the next few cycles."

"Meanwhile," Teacher said, "those couples who have now identified themselves as pairs and have signed partnership contracts should remain here in the lecture hall as your siblings leave. As soon as they have exited the room, please make your way down front for further instructions sitting in pairs. The demonstration session is dismissed."

Enmarsikil and Astara sat still until the flow of bodies pushing past their row had thinned. Before she could stand, he was out of his seat and headed down to the platform to confer with the Multi-Dims.

Teacher looked up, surprised to see him coming. "Is something wrong?" he asked.

"No," Enmarsikil replied. "You usually call me up when you instruct the others."

"This instruction set is for all of you and will be new to you," Teacher replied. "You will need to sit in the gallery with your partner and the others."

Enmarsikil's face registered shock. "But you always instruct me first and in private," he protested.

Teacher worked with a moving holography machine. "Because there are now a number of you who are paired, this way is more efficient," he replied without glancing up.

Enmarsikil stood watching his father for a moment in speechless silence before stumbling backwards and turning toward the gallery.

Marne approached Nasdatal and touched his arm. "Perhaps you should have at least briefed him ahead of time," she murmured. "He isn't used to group instructional and this is a sensitive subject."

Teacher glanced up. "When his learning pace was ahead of theirs, it was manageable. Now, there are too many entering new territory. He will adjust."

With that, Teacher activated the holography machine, and a static

166

image arose in the middle of the platform. He turned to face the one hundred couples seated in the first few rows of the gallery.

"Now that we have a sizeable number of pairings," he began, "it is time to address powering up."

In his seat, Enmarsikil's body stiffened. He remembered a shar or so ago when his father had tried to explain the concept to him. It had been overwhelming and had left him mortally confused.

"For you, powering up is the way you will sustain and replenish your life force," Marne explained. "Once you hit the age of maturity, your bodies began dipping into your life force reserves to sustain you. Even now, you've begun to feel irritable, frustrated, periodically confused or hyper focused and inflexible."

Murmurs of agreement rippled through the small crowd.

"These are all signals your body uses to tell you you need to replenish yourselves...to power up," she summed up.

"The way you were designed," Teacher continued, "is to work in matched pairs. Very much like an electrical circuit, men hold a positive charge and women a negative charge. And just like both charges are needed to complete a circuit so electricity can flow, so one of each charge is needed between you in order to achieve power up."

Enmarsikil nodded to himself. *Yes, this makes sense,* he thought.

"But powering up isn't just about completing some circuit," Marne added. "There is a synergistic effect to powering up where the sum of the two is far greater than each alone. And the internal chemistry of powering up creates a bond between the pair, and the more often you join, the stronger and deeper your bond becomes."

At the word 'join,' Enmarsikil broke out into a cold sweat. When he hadn't understood his father's lesson, Nasdatal had given him a book on reproductive science. It was the very book Astara had picked off his shelf and had so innocently opened to the full color anatomical illustrations. He still remembered his embarrassment. He swallowed hard.

"So today," Teacher said taking up the thread, "we will show a holographic stream that you can go back to and view whenever you need to. This will demonstrate the techniques required to power up."

"And we'll explain the natural urges and sensations you've most likely already been experiencing," Marne hastily added.

With that, Teacher waved his hand in an arc and the streaming hologram began. "If you have yet to feel comfortable enough to be without clothes with your partner, these images are a good representation of average male and female bodies."

A moment later, the holograms projected out onto the platform looking like opaque models in mid-air.

"As you can see, a man's body has strong muscles underlying his structure, a more barrel chest and vestigial breasts complete with nipples," Teacher said touching points in mid-air to make the designated sections light up.

Enmarsikil caught a quick reaction from Astara out of the corner of his eye.

"Women, on the other hand, tend to have smoother muscles underlying large rounded breasts with darker areolas surrounding pert nipples," Teacher continued.

Enmarsikil blushed to see the woman's figure though he took note of each feature. He remembered the brief moment when he had touched Astara's breasts through her clothes. Given her reaction, he hadn't wanted to stop, but an experiment alarm had pulled him away.

"Now, note the difference between men and women lower down," Teacher continued.

The light illuminating the holograms glowed around the genitals leaving the upper body more in the dark.

"In most species, this would be called the reproductive anatomy," Teacher announced. "However, since you are hybrids and cannot procreate, we will designate this the power up anatomy."

A few muffled sobs were heard around the room as the reality of their design suddenly became known to the women in the room. Marne sent out a heart wave to the group in order to calm them. She would have to have a more intimate talk with the girls later.

Without noticing the group's female response, Teacher didn't miss a beat. "In the man, the power up anatomy is predominantly external. Between his legs he has the testes carried in the scrotum," he said using his fingers to create a concentrated light ray to point out the indicated parts, "and the penis. When he is not aroused, the penis is flaccid. When he is aroused, it becomes erect."

Enmarsikil squirmed in his seat. *Does he have to make all of this so obvious?* he moaned inwardly.

Next to him, though, Astara's eyes widened. The dance came swirling back into her mind and she suddenly knew what she'd felt and why. Her pulse raced and she forgot to breathe.

"Now, for the female, her power up organs are mostly hidden deep within her body. She is the receptacle, and her womb is the crucible in which your life forces will mingle. You will each contribute to the end
168

result - the energizing and sustaining of your individual life forces."

"And to begin this process you need to understand how your touch affects your partner. When you hug and kiss," Marne said watching the holographic figures demonstrate the stated actions, "pleasurable feelings flood your body and create the desire for more intimate touch."

"This is the point at which where and how you touch each other becomes important," Teacher noted. "Males are fairly easily stimulated. The easiest method begins with sight. Since they are visually stimulated, seeing their female partner in varying stages of undress is the perfect starting point."

Enmarsikil sucked in a hasty breath as the image of Astara's shower wet body wrapped in a mere towel suddenly flashed in front of him. He licked his suddenly dry lips.

In the hologram, the woman walked around the man slowly as she removed various items of clothing. Simultaneously, the male's body responded with a partial erection.

"Women are stimulated far more by touch. Kissing, caressing, cuddling, fondling the breasts...all of these are way to arouse a woman," Marne said.

Enmarsikil remembered the dance and the heat that had engendered between he and Astara. A moment later it was as if he were back in her room tentatively touching her breasts. The way she had clamped his hand over her breasts and hearing her breath come in soft pants had made him want something more...only then, he hadn't understood what more there was to be had.

"These are all the initial points toward power up," Teacher said. "We will let the hologram run now and will point out only a few things."

Enmarsikil gripped the arms of his seat. As the hologram played out, the models kissed, caressed and stimulated each other in ways he hadn't conceived of. At the point where each was most highly aroused, Teacher paused the motion.

"Note the glow in their abdomens. This is part one of what you're aiming for," he said. "This glow indicates that the life force of each individual has come forward ready to join with their partners' life force."

He let the hologram's motion continue and now the man entered the woman and began love making.

Enmarsikil ran his hands down his legs clenching and unclenching his fists. His heart beat a fast staccato in his chest, and he imagined it was he and Astara.

At the moment of climax, the glowing balls of energy united and lit the room in a giant explosion of light. When it died down, Teacher turned off the hologram.

"And that explosion is power up," he concluded. "That sharing of your life force and ultimate combining of your individual power creates an energy store for each of you greater than much of what can be created by technology. This, children, is why you are so special. This is what the Anunnaki cannot comprehend even though you also carry their DNA. Their consummation is merely physical. Yours could power the universe."

With that he stepped back from the edge. A young man up two rows to the left raised his hand and Teacher nodded.

"Won't we...hurt them if we do that?" he asked.

A chorus of murmurs accompanied his question.

"Gentlemen," Marne said kindly. "I guarantee you that if you've gotten your partner to the point of glow, even if it isn't brilliant glow... just a little, you will do anything but hurt her. You may even give her the greatest pleasure of her life."

The room around them felt charged. It was all Enmarsikil could do to stay present and then he saw it. Astara's hand shot up. Before he could grab it and yank her hand down, her mouth was moving. It was as if her mouth moved and the sound came out later.

"So, you're saying all the things we've been feeling when we cuddle in bed and the like...that's all because we want to do this?" she asked pointing toward the still hologram.

Marne nodded.

"If it's not like this for the Anunnaki, is it like this for you?" an intrepid woman in the highest row asked.

At that point, Enmarsikil couldn't sink low enough in his seat. He just let go, faded from view and left the auditorium. Once he'd gathered himself together, he reappeared in his gardens. He considered the video and what his father had said, how powerful they were once powered up. He considered his team and the groups that were coordinating their efforts on different projects. They were highly creative in their endeavors. But what would happen once partners powered up? How might that factor impact the projects? What synergy could multiple powered up pairs create? Electrical circuits and bright balls of light maneuvered through his brain as he considered the implications.

Meanwhile, in the lecture hall Marne and Teacher smiled at each other. "We could if we chose, but we are so multidimensional, a look will send a part of ourselves into the ethers to enjoy contact while we remain fully present here."

170

"We would encourage you to explore now that you know what your bodies' have been asking for," Marne said.

"And you can access this hologram at any time for private viewing," Teacher reminded them.

With that, the lecture was dismissed.

CHAPTER 21 - UPSCALED EXPERIMENTS

Enmarsikil stayed out in the gardens methodically pulling weeds that threatened to choke out prized experimental plants. The mindlessness of the task calmed the overwhelm he had felt and allowed him to do some mental gymnastics. He thought back to the days when the siblings' elemental powers were just breaking through and then were pushed by the Multi- Dims when they accelerated their maturity. The boost to their powers and the intensity had been exponential and even their instructors had been taken off guard. But if father was right in what he'd said in the lecture hall, and when they powered up as couples, they could create enough energy to power the universe, how could the Academy possibly contain one such couple let alone 251?

He picked up his gardening tools, arranged them in the bucket holder he'd made and sent them flying unassisted to the shed. The well's hand pump worked on its own as he held his hands under the cool stream of water to wash off the loamy soil. Still deep in thought, Enmarsikil grabbed the sack of fish food propped against the shed and headed down the path to the fish ponds. He fed his ever hungry fish giving them a cursory glance as they surfaced to assess their health.

He sat on a wooden bench for a while other thoughts creeping into his mind. His future self had talked about humans. Ginny and Ted had been representatives of the species. Confusing as that had been, it was clear that the Anunnaki had created and enslaved them. That meant, their creation and enslavement was still imminent in his timeline.

Ginny had presented a branch of science specific to humans called epigenetics. His curiosity was mounting by the minute. He needed to understand humans. But the only way he could learn about them was from his future self. Therefore, he was going to have to find a way to call to his future self, visit him, question him.

He rose, noticed how light the pellet bags were and spread the remaining pellets over the water of the pond holding his favorite fish. He yawned, his body finally acknowledging the challenges of the day. His mind quickly shifted to thoughts of sleep and Astara's warm body. With that, he walked back to the shed, hung the pellet bag on a peg and made his way into the labs. Following the well-worn path on autopilot, he made one deviation and showered first before bed.

As the grime and sweat of the day trickled down his body and swirled into the drain, something niggled at his brain. Something seemed out of place. He reached for his soap and shampoo and found them in their old, pre-Astara spots. A nagging feeling hit him and it took his sleepy brain a couple of seconds to realize that Astara's things were no longer to be found. Quickly finishing and drying off, he pulled on his sleep pants and headed into the bed chamber.

He illuminated his fingertips, not wanting to awaken her, and spotted a beautiful flower draped across his pillow. Enmarsikil smiled to think Astara had been so thoughtful and sweet. He called a vase from his shelves to come to him, and it floated through the air to his hands. He stuck the flower in that, set it on the nightstand and eagerly reached for her.

Enmarsikil suddenly stopped. The bed was cold, the sheets were fresh, and Astara was nowhere to be found. He climbed out of bed and headed for his nook thinking of how she loved to sit there viewing the stars through his telescope. But it was empty as was his memory corner when he checked.

With his heart pounding in his chest and panic rising by the minute, Enmarsikil thought hard. *She couldn't have left,* he moaned *I know I've been uncertain and clumsy, but please tell me she didn't leave.*

A moment later, he heard the rustle of sheets from the other room. He let out of sigh of relief. Tiptoeing under the arch, he crept toward the other bed. He put his hand on his chest when he spotted Astara in her own bed. Suddenly, the sheets swished back and a form, white against the dark, sat up.

"Enmarsikil?" Astara whispered turning on a light on her nightstand.

He stood beside her bed, his face ashen.

"Are you all right?" she asked crawling to the edge of the bed and reaching for him.

"Why?" he whispered. "Did I do something wrong?"

Astara shook her head. "No, I just thought maybe I was overwhelming you...that I was coming on too strong," she admitted. "I wanted to give you some space...let you come around in your own time."

He sighed heavily and sank onto the edge of the bed. "Oh, good. I thought I'd done something horribly wrong and you'd left."

Astara curled up close against him. "I'd never leave. My dreams all came true when you asked me to be yours."

Enmarsikil smiled. "And you're my dream come true. I-I just didn't know what to do with what I was feeling."

"Me, neither," she confessed.

Enmarsikil scooped her up in his arms and stood up. "Come with me to 'our' bed in 'our' bedchamber," he whispered sampling her lips. "We are one and we share all."

Astara threw her arms around his neck and let him carry her to the adjoining room and lay her on the bed. He turned out the light, slid into bed and they curled up in each others' arms fast asleep.

The next morning when she awoke, Enmarsikil was already up and out in the gardens. She went into her old room only to stop abruptly and stare. Gone was the stiff, starched bed. In its place stood a comfortable sitting arrangement.

Wow! He meant 'ours' for real! she thought getting her clothes and heading toward the shower.

Later, Astara met with a combined group as they tried to determine where they'd find garden space and collect plant samples. They weren't having much luck, and she wandered back toward the lab after the meeting adjourned. As she eased the door open and was about to announce her return, she suddenly realized that the lab lights were dimmed and a holographic movie was playing.

Astara tip-toed in, drew near then froze. Enmarsikil was playing over the power up video, stopping, reversing and replaying different segments. He studied it all with great care. It hit a point where the models were preparing to join, and Astara let out a low moan.

Enmarsikil jerked his head up, turned and caught the look of heat and desire in her eyes. A red collar crept up his neck while his heart leapt

174

into his throat.

"I-I was j-just...reviewing," he stammered.

Neither spoke for long moments. Finally, he closed down the viewer with a gesture of his hand. She walked over to him, wrapped her arms around his shoulders and laid her cheek against the top of his head.

"You don't have to be perfect," she murmured softly.

Enmarsikil reached up and took her hand. "I just want to be good enough."

Astara knelt before him and gazed up. "You're already good enough."

His eyes swept the lab. "Here where I do my science, yes. But interacting with you? Like this? I just want to get it right."

She took his hands wishing there was something she could do or say to make him feel better, more confident. He grimaced, squeezed her hand then tugged her to her feet and walked her into their suite.

When they entered the bed chamber, Astara headed off to the bathroom for a quick shower, and Enmarsikil slipped into his sleep pants. When she took longer than he'd expected, he summoned a book from his shelves, propped himself up in bed and flipped the book open with a slight movement of one finger. It bobbed in mid-air before him as he read.

Finished, Astara dried off and slipped into a nightie she had recently altered. It was shorter than her others and the neckline was a little more daring. She entered the bed chamber, crossed the room and climbed into bed. Astara noticed Enmarsikil's studious gaze at the book and his knit eyebrows. Then she caught sight of his tight, muscular chest from all his gardening work and nice flat abs.

She bit her lower lip as heat spread through her. Ever so gently, she reached out and caressed his chest. It felt so smooth and the muscles rippled under her fingertips when he moved his arms. She glanced up noticing his gaze had become less focused. Gathering her courage, Astara edged closer and just touched her lips to his chest. Though the book moved to one side so he could see past her head, his breathing quickened.

For his part, Enmarsikil had been trying to figure out the problem creating a road block in his latest experiment. As far as he could tell, he was doing everything correct, and yet the problem persisted. And then Astara had touched his chest with her cool fingertips, and he'd ended up reading the same line three times. Now that she was kissing his chest and, oh she just hooked his nipple with her tongue, there would certainly be no more reading this night. Even his levitation skill faltered. But when she started rubbing his abdomen in slow circles that kept moving lower, he suddenly dropped the tome on the floor.

"Oh, sorry," she apologized looking at him through her long lashes.

"Oh, no. It's...it's fine, great really," he replied licking his suddenly dry lips.

"You were just so close and I...I couldn't not touch," she admitted.

"And kiss and lick," he added rolling toward her.

Astara moved slightly and he was suddenly aware of her long, bare legs and her breasts peeking through the V-cut of her nightie. His nostrils flared thinking about the demo he'd been studying. Other parts were also paying close attention.

Swallowing hard with his heart pounding through his veins, he molded his lips over hers while keeping his outside hand tucked firmly against her side. Suddenly, he felt Astara move his hand up and cup it around her breast. His senses spun as he gently cupped and squeezed it listening to her breath come in short pants.

How soft yet firm it felt, warm and inviting. He eased her top aside and just sampled her nipple. She arched her back and grabbed the sheets. He rubbed a little harder, got a little more fervent with his mouth, and she suddenly yanked away.

Enmarsikil froze then edged back. "I'm sorry. I didn't mean to hurt you."

"Just don't use your teeth," she suggested moving back toward him. "It wasn't what you were doing. It was how."

"Guess I got excited," he explained sheepishly.

He started to approach her again when suddenly her words echoed through his head - *It wasn't what you were doing. It was how.*

He'd been doing everything right with his experiment but he hadn't looked at how he'd been doing the operations. Enmarsikil grabbed her, gave her an enthusiastic kiss and started climbing out of bed.

"Wait! Where are you going?" Astara cried watching him throw his day robe on.

"The lab," he replied belting the robe. "You just solved my problem for me."

"Now?" she protested. "But we were...you were making this feel so good. Please don't go now."

He crawled over and gave her another kiss. "I promise, if this works I'll be back in no time."

Before she could say another word, he dashed out the door. Astara lay back in a huff of frustration and desire.

"I have to get him out of that lab," she muttered through clenched teeth.

Then the conversation at the group meeting came back to mind. There wasn't enough lab space available in the Academy proper but Enmarsikil had multiple labs. And he had plenty of garden space. A plan started developing in her mind complete with a chat with Marne. How could he say no to helping his own siblings? And if she could go collect plant samples in the wild and bring him with her, he just might relax. She turned off the lamp on the nightstand, lay back and fell asleep wearing a mischievous grin.

The next morning Astara hurried to catch Marne in her library. She wrapped on the door first then pushed it open. Marne glanced up from her desk and motioned Astara to enter. Astara ducked inside, closed the library door and hurried over to the desk. She dropped breathlessly into a chair.

"I think I have an answer to the lack of lab and garden space," she poured out in one breath. "Enmarsikil's labs and gardens. He's got tons of lab space and, my group in particular, could find space in the gardens."

Marne studied her carefully noticing what she wasn't saying.

"Are you sure he won't mind?"

Astara shook her head, and Marne paid special attention to the color of her hair and its listlessness.

"If his siblings ask him, Enmarsikil will never say no to them," Astara replied. "He always helps them out."

"But what will he do while his labs and gardens are occupied?" Marne pressed.

"Come with me."

Marne's eyebrows arched. "And where would that be?"

"Someone needs to go collect wild plant specimens," Astara said matter-of-factly.

"And you mean to take him with you," Marne surmised.

Astara nodded.

Marne tapped her fingers on the desk. "He has only been to Agade, you know...never into the wilds."

"About time he went," Astara said bruskly, her irritation surfacing.

"Turn your head, dear," Marne requested.

Astara faced the door.

"Let me see the back of your head,'" Marne insisted.

Astara turned again.

"Where is the red?" Marne asked, concerned. "Your hair used to be red."

Astara swung around and sank back into the chair. "It's been fading out a little every day," she confessed.

Marne got up and came over to her. "My dear, when did you last power up?" she asked quietly.

Astara nearly burst into tears and shook her head. "Every time we try, an alarm goes off for an experiment or some responsibility takes him somewhere else."

"Ah. I see," Marne said deep in thought. "Come. We must sustain you."

Marne took Astara into her personal quarters, lay her on a sofa and drew energized water into a specialized chalice. She gave it to Astara and bade her drink.

"Now," Marne said rising. "I have another session to co-teach on powering up. I want you to lie here and rest until the irritation and fatigue subside."

But Marne didn't need to say anything. Astara's eyes were already closed and her head drooped to one side. Marne returned the chalice to its spot near the black marble basin and quietly left.

As she walked through the halls, she considered Astara's idea. Allowing a clone to step outside of herself, she sent it on its way to do her bidding.

CHAPTER 22 - WILD ADVENTURE

With his last experiment completed and wrapped up, Enmarsikil cloaked himself and meandered the halls of the Academy. Another power up instructional was just beginning. He stepped inside the lecture hall and slid into a seat near the door. He had cleaned up the last of the beakers that morning. He sat in the shadowy cool and half-listened to the lecture. As soon as the couples started asking questions, he got up, slipped out and headed back toward his lab. But when he opened the door, he was surprised to find 50 siblings crowded inside waiting for him.

Uneasy at so many bodies crowded into so little space, Enmarsikil entered and stood before them. "Can I help you?"

It was a mere formality. He had really already thought of a new experiment and was chafing to get underway.

"Actually," Nita said coming forward, "we were hoping you could."

Enmarsikil frowned. "What do you need?"

"Lab space," Satu said.

"Just for a cycle or so," Nita added hastily.

Enmarsikil put his hands up. "Now hold on a second. What about the Academy labs?"

"Full to the brim," Barlumgeme said. "We really could use the help."

Enmarsikil ran his hand through his hair. Well, he could give up his labs and work in his gardens. Finally, he nodded.

"You're right. Your experiments are important and the Academy is short on lab space. You're welcome to use my labs," he granted magnanimously. "Just one condition...."

The group, which had already started to disperse, paused.

"Look around you. When you finish using these labs, please return them to me in the same condition."

"Absolutely," Nita agreed, relieved to be using them at all.

A warhoop went up. "We've got lab space!" and group members suddenly swarmed all over.

Enmarsikil shook his head, walked through the labs and out into the gardens. For a moment he was oblivious to his surroundings, his mind still back on his labs. Then, he heard it - humming and toning. It seemed to be coming from further down the path. He took off at a quick jog and skidded around a corner to see Astara, Ki, Aiya and Bilnammul all harmonizing around a bed of freshly planted plants. He recognized them as the herbs he'd giving them for their project.

"Um, ladies," he called loudly in order to be heard. "What are you doing?"

They stopped and turned to look at him.

"We needed garden space to continue our project," Astara explained. "I remembered that you had just cleared this plot and weren't going to use it again. I...didn't think you'd mind."

Enmarsikil ran his hand through his hair. "Astara, I was going to leave it fallow for a season."

She looked up at him with big, innocent eyes. "Does that mean we can't use it?"

He sighed heavily. "No, you can use it. I'd just set the plot aside for different plants in another season...but it will be all right."

She reached up and gave him a quick kiss. "Thank you. I knew you'd help us out."

A sudden niggle at the back of his brain made him wonder. Enmarsikil narrowed his eyes and took her aside. "Did you engineer all of this?"

She looked at him in astonishment. "No...well not exactly. I just mentioned to Marne that you had space right now."

He looked around and realized that two other groups had also invaded his garden space.

"And if you're all here working, what am I supposed to do?" he demanded.

"Well," she said taking his hand and leading him along the path toward the wicket gate, "you could come with me."

Enmarsikil stopped and stared. "And where exactly do you think you're going?"

"The wilderness," she replied bluntly. "Someone has to collect wild plant species, and I know where they are."

"So this is a research trip?" he pressed.

She blushed but held her ground. "Partially."

"But....?" he urged.

"Well, maybe away from the lectures, and research and gardens and stuff, we'll finally power up."

Enmarsikil put his finger to his lips hushing her as he glanced around making sure nobody heard.

"Hey, I ended up in Marne's quarters with her giving me a treatment because we haven't yet," she snapped.

Enmarsikil stared at her in shock, the realization of the importance of powering up finally sinking in. Then he noticed it. Her hair. "What happened to the red?" he asked lifting a lock of hair near her face.

Astara looked down at the ground. "It's gone. It's been fading out of my hair a little each day," she replied quietly. "The blond will too according to Marne."

"Because we haven't powered up?" he asked dismayed.

She nodded.

"Ok. I'll go. I just need few things," he replied.

Astara went over to a bush and dragged out two packs. She plunked them at his feet.

"Ok, one thing. I promise I'll be right back," he said turning and jogging toward his shed.

He packed a water test kit then hurried back to her side. "Where to?" he asked following her to the wicket gate.

"We," she said pushing it open, "are off on a wild adventure."

Astara stepped through first. Enmarsikil slung the pack over his shoulder, ducked through the gateway and nearly ran into thorns.

"Careful," she warned. "They aren't poisonous, but they do scratch."

He gave them a cursory glance, waved his hands closing his fingers at the end, and the backside of the tree was suddenly free of thorns.

"Wait! How'd you do that?" Astara wondered mentally replaying the scene.

She gazed at a section of tree with thorns, made the same motion he had, and the thorns disappeared.

Enmarsikil smiled. "You always do catch on fast."

Astara returned his smile. "I just felt your annoyance at the thorns and desire to have them gone."

"So, lead on," he said gesturing.

Astara turned, edged past the tree and stepped out into the open. Enmarsikil followed her as she headed toward the wilderness facing wall. To his amazement, she scrambled up the side and straddled the top.

"C'mon," she called and dropped over the other side.

Enmarsikil followed slowly and stood to his full height when he topped the wall. His eyes took in the vast expanse of meadow leading to a meandering brook and mountains beyond. The breeze brushed his hair back from his shoulders. He took one look back at the Academy whose buildings suddenly appeared less formidable then down at Astara. With a smile, he dropped off the wall and floated down to the ground beside her.

"You've got that whole wind thing going for you," she teased grabbing his hand and bounding out into the meadow with him in tow.

"Where are we going?" he called to her.

"Places I've been," she yelled back.

Their legs swished through the tall grass, flowers dotted tall stems here and there and flutter-winged bugs darted out of their way.

"You've been out here before?" Enmarsikil panted reaching her side.

She nodded. "Sometimes for lectures about the elements, but lots of times on my own."

The grasses thinned out as they neared the stream bank. Astara found an animal trail, which they followed, and slid down to the water's edge. Enmarsikil knelt and dipped his hand in.

"It's cool, almost cold," he remarked.

Astara was hunting the rocks just beneath the surface. "It's melt water from high mountain snow."

Enmarsikil took his kit out of his pack, dipped a tube into the water, plugged it and tucked it back into his pack.

"Oo! Look what I found!" Astara cried.

He glanced up and could swear the curious young Astara was before him so excited was she and so changed was her countenance. Enmarsikil made his way to her side.

"See that right under there?" she asked pointing.

Sure enough, there were small crab-like creatures hiding under the rocks. He reached in to grab one and yanked his hand back with a loud "Yeouch!" A long red crustacean hung from his thumb, its pincher clamped down tight.

While Astara giggled at him, she came around the back of the critter, pressed on a place on either side and the pincher opened releasing Enmarsikil's thumb. She bent down, stuck the critter back under the rock and released it.

Enmarsikil was still sucking his sore thumb when she dropped the rock back over the critter.

"Stick your hand in the water. It will numb up soon," she instructed.

Enmarsikil did as he was told and the smarting soon eased.

Meanwhile, Astara found the stepping stones for them to cross. They leapt from one to another until they were on the other side. A plant with a deep pitcher-shaped flower caught her attention. "Would this work near the fish bridge in your garden?" she asked.

Enmarsikil assessed its ecosystem and decided it would fit. He knelt down and helped her carefully remove it from the moist ground. Astara put it into a bubble, and he affixed it to a tray of air.

"It's nice to have company," Astara said washing her hands in the stream.

As they moved on, he took her hand. "Why did you come out here alone?" he asked.

"The dorm used to get overwhelming," Astara replied. "I picked up everybody's emotions. Out here was the only place where I could discharge them."

"I never knew," he said.

"And you've never been anywhere else but the Academy and Agade?" she asked.

"That's it," he admitted.

"So you have no idea how beautiful Nibiru can be."

Enmarsikil shook his head and shrugged. "I'm clueless."

"Well, then, we have to remedy that right now," Astara said scrambling up the far bank of the creek with him close behind.

Hand-in-hand they walked on and had soon put the first hill between themselves and the Academy. She guided them down to the river in the valley, and they admired its silvery water as they followed its banks. After a while, the lazy current picked up speed, and the water frothed about boulders in its path. As they continued, a dull roar reached their ears gradually growing louder and deeper.

"What's making that noise?" Enmarsikil asked.

Astara peered through the trees and pointed. "See that rainbow?"

He followed her outstretched arm to where she indicated and nodded.

"That's the falls. C'mon." She hurried forward and he eagerly followed.

Soon a fine mist sprayed their faces. Astara looked for a particular spot in the vegetation then sat and slid down the bank. Enmarsikil quickly followed. She shook off her pack and handed it to him.

"Where are you going?" he yelled as she started climbing out onto the rocks at the top of the falls.

"Meet me below," she yelled. "Catch me if you can."

He frowned, perplexed, but in the next moment gasped. She reached mid-way in the stream, perched carefully on a boulder, launched herself out over the falls and dissolved into a fine spray of water.

Almost without thinking, Enmarsikil levitated off the ground on a cushion of air and whooshed out over the precipice. Not seeing her, he lowered himself down the face of the falls. When he neared the bottom, a sudden arc of wave threatened to soak him. Instead, it landed on his air cushion first as bare feet quickly covered by boots, then legs followed by leggings and on up Astara's body.

Enmarsikil swallowed hard as he watched. She was teasing him and it was working. When she was finally all back with him, he guided the pad of air to the bank and set them down.

"Good catch," she remarked reaching up to kiss him.

He leaned in for a deeper kiss. "Thank you," he murmured.

With a mischievous glint in her eye, Astara tugged his hand and headed toward an eddy pool.

"There are a couple of plants here I thought would be good for the collection," she said kneeling beside one with golden flowers.

Enmarsikil knelt beside her and helped her carefully scoop them out of the ground and package them in a bubble.

"And there's one more up there," she added pointing up to the rocks alongside the waterfall.

Midway up the side, a plant with a deep pink flower bobbed in the breeze created by the rushing water. Enmarsikil led the way and they had soon collected that as well. When they got back down to terra firma and had put that in a bubble as well, he attached them all to his air tray and sent it flying back in the direction of the Academy.

"They should get that soon," he told her slinging back on his pack.

184

"Will they know what to do with them?"

"Aiya will," Astara assured him pulling her pack on as well.

"So, where to now?" he asked.

"To my all time favorite place. You'll love it. I promise," she hinted mysteriously.

Enmarsikil cocked one eyebrow. "Oh? And why might that be?"

She reached up and whispered in his ear. "Have you ever seen a water nymph?"

His eyes popped open wide. "What's that?"

Astara giggled and started scrambling up the bank. "You'll have to wait and see."

"Can't you give me a clue?" he begged following her.

Astara chuckled. "Now who doesn't like suspense?"

CHAPTER 23 - OF NYMPHS AND LOVE

Enmarsikil and Astara walked and hiked over the foothills of the looming mountains. Periodically, they stopped to eat the food she had packed or to rest in the shade of a tree. With Astara nestled in his arms, Enmarsikil felt like these moments could last forever, and he would never grow tired of her. When she sat between his legs and leaned back, it wasn't long before his arousal became obvious. He caressed her kissing her ears and neck. Yet, there was this block he couldn't seem to move past. He knew she was frustrated; he was frustrated and confused. He was with the woman he loved more than life itself, and he was scared.

Pressing on, they hiked through a thick forest eventually stepping out from under its eaves into a hilly glade. A stream trickled through it, and Astara led him along its banks.

"There's a place that's very special to me that I want to take you to," she told him. "It's been my refuge and my playground. Come." Her eyes danced like the bubbling water at their feet.

The couple climbed higher until they crept under the eaves of an old growth forest. From the moment they entered its cool shade, a whole different sense pervaded the air about them. It felt like an awareness, like a living entity they hadn't encountered before.

Enmarsikil marveled at the peacefulness of the woods as his footfalls were hushed by the thick carpet of needles. He closely observed
186

Astara noticing the profound change that crept over her visage. Her features grew fluid and softer the further into the woods they moved.

They reached a series of small waterfalls. Enmarsikil paused to quickly take a water sample and looked up. Almost as if in a trance, Astara slipped off her pack and handed it back to him without looking. Her eyes were glued to the water almost as if it were calling to her.

"Take this with you to the pool above," she instructed in a dreamy voice and with a languid gesture of her hand.

"Where will you be?" Enmarsikil asked suddenly alarmed.

She moved toward the stream one foot already stepping into the water.

"Astara!" he called more urgently. "Where will you be?"

"In my element," she replied, her voice bubbling cheerily as she suddenly dissolved into the water before his eyes.

Enmarsikil stared in shock and fascination at the spot where she had last stood. He was facile in using all of the elements, air in particular, but she wasn't utilizing water and joining the frothy waves of the waterfall. She had become it.

A sleepy, dreamy quality hung on the air about him, and he distinctly heard Astara's laugh in the gurgle of the stream. Unseen hands seemed to pull him upstream as he sensed her awareness moving toward the spot she had designated for their meeting. Without taking his eyes off the creek, he scooped up her pack and stumbled along the bank as it angled higher. Where the water tumbled over a small series of falls, Astara's laughter grew in vibrancy. Light filtered through the trees and caught the rivulets, which sent it streaming back like a rainbow from a prism.

Finally, Enmarsikil clambered up a steeper bank and was greeted by a broad, calm pool at the base of a larger series of falls. He dropped their packs to the ground and stared at the clear surface in mesmerized silence. How long he stood entranced by the pool and the atmosphere around it, he never knew. Gradually, though, he became aware of a shift. The surface, which had been smooth and glassy, began to ripple in concentric circles from the banks toward the pool's center. Enmarsikil blinked his eyes as if newly awakening.

He watched in fascination as the water in the center began to bubble and churn. Though he couldn't see it, he could sense fingers of awareness being drawn up the creek from down below. Slowly, a large bubble formed on the surface and began to skate toward shore. Enmarsikil stumbled backwards as it began to rise up from the surface and move straight toward him.

He almost turned to flee until a water form began to take shape. Though transparent and fluid like the water of the forest pool, the water held together and began molding itself into Astara's form. He blinked, his breath slamming into his chest as her breasts rose up out of the water. This form had no clothes on and they were all Astara. He licked his suddenly dry lips.

His eyes never left the gently bouncing, swaying mounds of water that appeared slightly suspended in air. His heart thudded against his ribs, his mouth went dry and a flush of heat spread throughout his body. A tightness and pulsing in his groin made him keenly aware of the desires he'd been suppressing. Blue eyes opened to meet his gaze as Astara's hips rose out of the water. The closer she came to him, the more intense the heat within him grew. He could only stare at the droplets of water that smoothed over the curves of her breasts and hips.

Astara was closer to the edge now. Enmarsikil could see every curve of her form and every undulation of her body as every step brought her nearer. With one last movement, she lifted a slender leg just giving him a glimpse of the V in between and placed her foot on the bank. As her foot touched solid ground, her clothes began to reappear on her body as the water form returned to flesh and blood. She reached out for him touching his arm just as the transformation became complete.

"H-how do you do that?" Enmarsikil stammered as she pressed her body close to his.

Astara shrugged nonchalantly. "I feel the water and become what I feel. How do you like your water nymph?"

"Amazing...." was all he could murmur before her lips closed over his.

Enmarsikil drew her close, ran his hands down her back and up her sides as their kiss deepened and grew more passionate. When he brought his hands up her front and cupped her breasts, Astara moaned and began unfastening her tunic soon shedding it by the pool. He greedily cupped and squeezed her breasts leaving her panting and barely able to stand. Astara grabbed at his tunic whipping it open and pressed her breasts to his chest. His lips found hers again as he cupped her bottom pulling her close. His erection was throbbing and the press of its length against her tummy made her gasp.

"Please...please," she begged.

Enmarsikil broke the kiss for a moment glancing about the glade. Not far away, a moss cushioned mound rose between the trees. Quickly scooping up their packs with one hand and wrapping his free arm around Astara's waist, he guided them to the mound. Dropping the packs, he ripped one open, hauled out a tightly rolled, bright blanket and threw it toward the mound. It glided smoothly to the intended spot and fluttered into place.

He turned back to Astara and saw her bare breasts exposed for him in all their naked beauty. His nostrils flared, and he couldn't resist. Enmarsikil scooped her up wrapping her legs around his waist and suckled one pert nipple, enraptured by its sweet taste.

With a gasp for air, he set her back on the ground. Astara immediately kicked off her boots and slid off her leggings. Enmarsikil had barely managed to get his boots off. Astara yanked his tunic down his arms. He stood before her panting.

"You still have too much on," she complained.

Before he could protest or think, Astara undid his pants and slid them off his hips. Enmarsikil froze, his heart thudding in his chest. Astara stared at his erection, and he groaned inwardly, fearing the worst.

Then she reached out and just touched it with her fingertips. He swallowed hard and closed his eyes. Astara dropped to her knees, cradled his member in her hands and pressed it to her cheek. Enmarsikil moaned at the intimate touch, his eyes flying open wide when she pressed her lips to its base and gently worked her way up the shaft with kisses. But when she curled her tongue around the head, he was done for.

Quickly lifting her up, Enmarsikil dropped to his knees on the blanket. With one hand supporting her back and his lips firmly planted against hers, he lay her back and kicked his pants all the way off. There was nothing between them anymore. He lay over her, his skin touching hers, his mouth against her breasts and listening to her moan.

After a while, Enmarsikil shifted. When he glanced down, he could already see the glow in his abdomen. A cursory look at Astara's showed a faint light. She took his hand guiding it lower and showed him how to rub her and give her pleasure. Finally, she moved him again, this time bidding him to slip a finger inside.

He gulped as his finger edged inside the wettest, hottest, sweetest place he'd ever known. Though his own head was spinning and blood pounded through his veins, he fought to watch her and notice as the glow grew brighter. When he slipped a second finger inside with the first, the walls clenched at him, and Astara let out a low scream.

Enmarsikil slowly pulled his fingers out and rubbed her silky wetness on himself.

"Be in me," she pleaded. "Please, I've waited so long. Be in me."

Enmarsikil needed no further urging. He positioned himself over her and slowly pushed inside. In and out a couple of times and then her body welcomed him and something beyond him took over.

It was as if they alone existed inside this pulsing ball of light. All was silent within yet he could clearly hear Astara's cries of ecstasy and feel her move against him. He caught the sound of his own voice chanting her name. And suddenly, it hit; a tremendous upwelling of energy. He had no more control, and as he felt his own release near, the world around him exploded in a shower of light.

Long minutes passed before the light dimmed enough to see. Enmarsikil found himself propped on his elbows over Astara. He bent down and sampled her lips.

"We did it," she whispered when they came up for air.

He lifted his head to gaze into her eyes and caught a glimpse of strawberry blond hair. He froze.

"Your hair," he whispered.

He took a handful and held it up for her to see. Astara stared at it, tears squeezing out the corners of her eyes.

"I was so afraid it wouldn't come back," she confessed sniffling. "I thought maybe the red was gone for good."

Enmarsikil ran her hair through his fingers. "It must be an indicator for you...of when your energy is low." He gave her an anguished look. "I'm so sorry, Sweet. I didn't even notice. Please, please forgive me."

A mischievous twinkle lit her eyes. "Oh, I don't know. Promise not to miss it again?"

"Oh Sweet, never again," he promised.

"And...to do it again?" she added provocatively moving her hips under him.

Enmarsikil had forgotten where he was, but a couple of hip rolls, and he was throbbing hard again.

"Oh, I guarantee it," he relied wrapping one arm under her shoulders and the other under her hips to deepen his thrust inside her.

Though the climax was less dramatic, Enmarsikil was relieved to see that Astara's hair had darkened to its normal light auburn. Satisfied and sated, he slipped out of her, rolled onto his back while cradling her and pulled her with him. He grabbed the blanket, made a cocoon around them and Astara laid her head on his chest already asleep.

A while later, he awoke to a tickling sensation on his nose.

190

Enmarsikil batted it away not wanting to lose his amazing dream, but the tickle persisted. Finally, he swatted at it in earnest and opened his eyes. Astara's mischievous grin stared down at him as she held a long piece of grass over his face. He glared for a moment then tackled her tickling her sides. She giggled and shrieked and he let her go.

Drawing her close to him, Enmarsikil sat up and gazed down at the stream and the pool while noticing the bright glow emanating from them that lit up the glade. He sighed contentedly.

"No dream," he murmured happily.

Astara leaned her head on his shoulder. "Why was it so hard back at the Academy?"

Enmarsikil raised his eyebrows. "What?"

"To power up?"

He knit his brows and stared off into space. "All my life father kept me at his side," he began. "When I would ask to join the others, he'd insist he always meant to train me personally," Enmarsikil confessed.

Astara frowned and curled her feet under her. "You mean he never let you out of his sight?"

Enmarsikil shook his head. "Not until I was old enough to work in the labs by myself. The first time I really got to participate with any of you was when I was choosing and training my team."

"Even then you really weren't one of us," Astara pointed out. "You're our leader."

He nodded. "Being out here with no walls and no rules and no responsibilities...." Enmarsikil shook his head. "This is so new, so... freeing. I think I was afraid to go beyond what I'd always known and could count on."

"So it was good we came out here?"

He hugged her to his side and kissed the top of her head. "You broke me out of bondage, my love. I may never be the same again."

"I hope not," Astara replied. "I want you to be free."

He breathed deeply, a smile playing across his lips. "Happy," he murmured.

"Hm?" she asked gazing at him.

"I'm happy," Enmarsikil said simply.

Astara cocked her head to one side in question.

"All my life has been rules, responsibilities and obedience. I didn't know there could be anything else." He turned and gave her a quick kiss. "But with you, I'm happy."

Astara's face lit up and she leaned in for a sweet kiss. Before long, it sizzled and had them wrapped about each other all over again.

CHAPTER 24 - EFFECTS OF THE POWER UP

This time when Enmarsikil and Astara completed their joining, he got up and briefly explored the glade. He came back to his pack, pulled out his test kit and held out his hand to her. Astara took it, and he tugged her to her feet.

"What?" she asked, mildly curious.

Enmarsikil led her toward the pool. "I had this hunch when I listened to the power up lecture. Father said we'd be incredibly powerful once we powered up."

Astara nodded. "I remember that, too."

He pulled out his last empty vial. "I've been taking water samples along the way. I took one right before you became a water nymph," he told her. "Now that we've joined, I thought it might be interesting to have you enter the water and take another sample."

"Whole water nymph bit?" she asking, her eyes glinting.

Enmarsikil caught his breath. "Yeah, that, too. I'll never get tired of seeing that."

Astara laughed merrily, reached up and planted a kiss on his lips then turned and stepped into the water. She controlled her transformation becoming a water creature step-by-step. She turned in the center of the pool, smiled, pressed her fingers to her lips and dissolved.

Immediately, a bright ball of light hung beneath the surface and sent out bubbles of light to all corners. Enmarsikil shook off the mesmerizing effect long enough to dip the tube into the water. It was more of a struggle to get the cap back on. He sighed with relief when he returned it to the kit.

Moments later, Astara's head and arms rose above the surface of the pool. She motioned to him to join her. He stood on the edge and made a shallow dive out to her. When he surfaced, however, she was nowhere to be found until smooth, watery hands ran up his legs from his feet to his crotch. But when they enclosed all of his manhood and began moving on him, Enmarsikil nearly went under. Treading water took more and more concentration, and he was rapidly losing his. Astara's head surfaced near his.

"Gotta get my footing," he panted.

"Over there," she said pointing to a shallow ledge. "Don't worry. I am the water. I won't let you sink."

And as if to prove it, she once again dissolved only now he felt strong support under his back and the irresistible tease around the front. He made the ledge, leaned his elbows against it and soon felt her water body crawl up his while giving erotic attention he could never have dreamed of. At last her solid body clung around him, and he found he was already deep inside her.

"My turn to pleasure you," Astara whispered in his ear.

Before he knew it, her hips rolled and she rocked back and forth creating exquisite friction between them. He cupped and squeezed her breasts and her movements quickened until they were both moaning. When he sensed his release was near, he grasped her hips, thrust into her and exploded. She drooped forward over him.

"That...has to be...a first," he panted.

Astara smiled, her cheek against his throat.

When they'd finally caught their breath, Enmarsikil swam back to shore and she met him at the bank. He found a flat rock and fully unpacked his test kit.

"This will only give up rudimentary measures, but I'm kind of dying to see if my hypothesis is at all valid."

Astara watched closely as he opened the monitor unit and inserted the tubes. Lights in different colors turned on under each tube.

"What do the colors mean?" she asked.

"Brown means the water is energy depleted. These I took at the stream and the waterfall," he explained. "This one that's blue, I took below these falls before you...." And here he leaned forward to kiss her neck, "showed me what a water nymph is."

She laughed.

"This last sample is from after you entered the water just now."

"Why is it green?" Astara wondered.

"Well, the blue light indicates a healthy energy level," Enmarsikil explained. "The green light shows that the water after our power up became supercharged when you entered it."

Her eyebrows shot straight up. "Then what happens now when I try to sing to the plants, or the teams try to devise a propulsion system?"

Enmarsikil looked up at her, his eyes dancing. "We could be the propulsion system. Any pair that was powered up could do it."

Astara pressed her fingertips to her lips in awe. "That changes everything!"

Enmarsikil packed away the kit and drew the string taut around its protective bag. He glanced up at her and nodded. "I daresay that not even the Multi-Dims knew this would happen. It's up to us to discover the effects and how to apply them."

He got up and headed back to his pack.

"We're not going back to the Academy right away, are we?" Astara fretted.

"Not on your life," Enmarsikil replied tackling her to the ground. "I've only just begun to find the many ways to love a water nymph."

She giggled, stretched her hand up over her head, called to the water in the pond and flipped a wave at him.

Enmarsikil shook his head water flying off his hair in all directions. "Apparently, play has a prominent spot in water nymph life."

She smiled at him and pulled him down close. "Play of all kinds," she assured him with a kiss.

Later, Enmarsikil sat alone staring into the pool. Astara eased up behind him, sat down and dangled her feet in the water.

"What's wrong?" she asked wrapping her arm across his back and leaning her head on his shoulders.

He picked up a pebble and threw it into the water. "It's time to go back."

Astara nodded against his shoulder. "I know. Wish we could stay here forever."

Enmarsikil sighed heavily and stood up. He took one long look about the glade. "I wish I could always have this freedom."

Astara pulled her feet out of the water and stood beside him. "Enmarsikil, you have to find a way to make this freedom for yourself...be self-determining."

He shook his head. "It's not to be."

He made to head toward the hillock, but she grabbed his arm and held him back.

"You don't understand," Astara said earnestly.

"Understand what?"

"If you aren't self-determining, then none of us really are."

He stared at her for a moment, her words sinking in. With a shake of his head, Enmarsikil tore away and headed for their packs with Astara following.

"You don't understand," he all but shouted as he yanked his clothes out. "Father has expectations set for me...rules...responsibilities."

Astara grabbed his clothes and hid them behind her back. "What about expectations we have for our life together? What about your responsibilities to me as your mate? To our siblings?"

Enmarsikil sank to the ground. "You don't understand," he grimaced.

She sank to her knees beside him. "Then help me understand. Please."

"I tried to confront him once," he replied. "He was so hard...like a stone wall. I've never tried again."

Astara frowned and sat back on her heels. "You're afraid of this man you call 'Father.' That is not love, Enmarsikil. That is control."

"He's your father, too," he reminded her.

Astara shook her head and gently handed back his clothes. "No. None of us call him that. He has many names amongst the siblings, but father is never one of them."

Enmarsikil stared at her in shock as she rose, pulled her clothes from her pack and began dressing. In a daze, he slowly began to dress as well. He was buckling the belt around his tunic when Astara walked up to him and laid her hand on his shoulder turning him to face her.

"What ever happened in the past, my love, was when you were young and not yet ready for the challenge," she told him.

Enmarsikil finished buckling the belt and reached down to close up his pack. "And you think I'm ready now?"

She caught his gaze. "You have something you didn't have back then. You have a secret weapon."

He raised an eyebrow.

"You've got me," she announced proudly. "You have a friend to support you, an ally who's got your back, someone who is on your side."

196

For the second time that day, shock registered in his eyes. "I-I never thought of it that way. I never had anyone else to ally with."

Astara hugged him and gave him a dazzling smile. "Well, you do now and forever, so don't you forget it."

Enmarsikil took the first deep breath in a while and let it out. He slung on his pack, waited for Astara to get hers then held out his hand to her. Hand-in-hand they hiked out of the mountains back down toward the Academy.

Enmarsikil took them up over the walls on his air ski. He set them down outside the lab walls. As soon as the doors opened, Teacher caught him just inside the door.

"We need to talk," he demanded.

Enmarsikil glanced at Astara. She stood at her full height and shook her head.

"It will have to wait," Enmarsikil replied. "We need to clean up and eat."

He pushed past Teacher, and they headed into his suite.

Teacher, who had bristled at the rebuff, paced for a while then turned and stormed into the suite and inside their bed chamber.

"Now listen here," he rumbled. "You've been gone a considerable amount of time, and there are issues to attend to."

Enmarsikil heard the shower turn off. "This is not a good time," he reiterated firmly.

"I determine the timing," Teacher insisted.

"You used to," Enmarsikil tried again.

Suddenly, an ear piercing scream startled them both. In the open bathroom doorway stood Astara dripping wet without even a towel. She dashed back inside the bath, grabbed any towel she could find, wrapped it around her and charged back out the door, her eyes blazing.

"How dare you barge in like this!" she demanded loudly.

"This is Enmarsikil's suite," Teacher informed her. "It's where I always meet him."

"Well, not anymore," Astara insisted with authority. Drawing herself up to her full petite height, she glared at the older man. "We," she said pointing to herself and Enmarsikil, "are partners, mates, joined, powered up...whatever term strikes a chord. This suite now belongs to both of us. I live here. And you will never walk in on me ever again. Is-that-clear? The only man who gets to see me naked is him." She jabbed a finger in Enmarsikil's direction.

"Astara, it's all right," Enmarsikil soothed.

She spun toward him. "It's ok to you that he just saw me naked?"

"No, no Sweet."

She turned back to Teacher. "Please...leave...now. This is all the restraint I have left."

As she said that a breeze began to circulate in the room picking up speed and tossing loose items about.

"Forgive me," Teacher said with a mock bow. "I'll give you privacy."

As he turned, Astara grabbed the door and paused in the doorway. "Mockery will get you nowhere." Then she slammed it hard and locked it."

When she turned, Enmarsikil was just staring at her.

"I've never felt so violated in my life," she fumed. "And then he had the nerve to mock me."

"I don't know if it's even safe to live here anymore," Enmarsikil worried.

"I already sent Marne a mental message," Astara confessed. "I-I'm not sure I can calm the storm."

Enmarsikil looked at her, alarmed. "Hurricane."

She grimaced. "Wants to be. Sorry. You should go."

"Where to?" he wondered.

"Lab. Take test kit. Teams working there," she gasped out, her hair standing on end and books beginning to enter the vortex off the shelves.

Enmarsikil grabbed the test kit and opened the door. "Astara, will you be all right?"

"Just...go," she raged, her voice rising to a shriek above the howling wind.

Enmarsikil ducked out the door and it slammed shut behind him. *This really does change things*, he thought.

Hesitantly, he headed out into the lab. With a sigh of relief, he noticed Teacher wasn't there. Kappashegara and Zupatu came over to him.

"Uh, glad to see you back," Kappa said.

Enmarsikil nodded setting his test kit on a lab table.

"We're still struggling with fuel, payload and propulsion," Zupatu admitted.

Enmarsikil snapped open the kit, set up the monitor and showed them the results. "These were all pre-power up," he said pointing to the three tubes on the left. "And this is after power up."

198

The brothers eyed the tests with keen interest.

"But how do we use it?" Kappa asked.

"I have a theory," Astara said from behind them.

They jumped and spun around. Though her hair was still wild, her demeanor was calmer. Enmarsikil reached for her, his fingertips just touching hers.

"What if we did what my group's been doing with plants?" she suggested. "Why not sing to the them?"

"To water?" Zupatu asked.

"To the energy in the water," she replied. "What if singing releases trapped energy? Maybe that's what's making our plants grow?" she speculated.

"That actually sounds plausible," Enmarsikil remarked.

"But who would do it?" Kappa asked.

"Aiya does it best," Astara replied.

"Can we play with your test samples?" Kappa requested.

"Yeah, this may be the breakthrough we've been looking for," Zupatu seconded.

Enmarsikil nodded. "I can create charged water any time," he said with a sly glance at Astara.

She blushed.

CHAPTER 25 - THE ONES WHO JUDGE

Teacher made his way back to his quarters in an entirely foul mood. Enmarsikil wanted a mate so badly, he gave him one. Only Astara was crafty and rebellious and apparently hell bent on changing his long held rules.

He flung open his door with the sweep of his hand. "She will need to be put in her place, " he growled to himself.

Shutting the door behind him with a flick of his wrist, he made his way to the center of his room. As he did, his steps slowed and he felt the weight of four very strong wills bearing down on him. Nasdatal slowly turned and eyed the shadows.

"Who-is-there?" he demanded.

Lights outside of the circle shined on each figure in turn - Marne, Zalkur, Giramusen and Emissary.

"Did you barge in on Astara when she was unclothed?" Giramusen demanded bluntly.

"It would be the other way around," Nasdatal responded smoothly. "She chose to shower while I was meeting with Enmarsikil. If she forgot who was there, that is not my problem."

"Incorrect," Emissary remarked bruskly. "Your first encounter was with Enmarsikil in the lab. He and Astara requested privacy and left for their suite to clean up. You made the choice to go interrupt them."

"A technicality," Nasdatal said dismissively.

"No technicality," Zalkur rumbled. "For years we've observed the chokehold you've kept over Enmarsikil and over the others. We've not interfered but...."

"But this has gone too far," Marne said sharply. "After seeing one of my daughters nude in front of her mate, you then mocked her." Her voice rose dramatically. "You are not objective enough now to run this Academy."

"What do you plan to do about it?" Nasdatal demanded arrogantly.

In answer the other four suddenly held him in a stasis field. One-by-one, they neutralized his powers. Nasdatal went from hovering in mid-air to landing unceremoniously on the floor.

"We leave you with but one power, that of invisibility," Emissary declared.

"I just want to know...want to understand," Marne pleaded. "Why would you do this? Why would you treat anyone like this let alone our children?"

Nasdatal sighed heavily and seemed to shrink down to a heap of clothes on the floor.

"They are too powerful," he said at last, "and Enmarsikil most of all."

"Too powerful for what?" Emissary asked evenly.

"For us...for this place," Nasdatal replied gesturing toward the Academy walls, "for this world...this universe."

Marne frowned. "Who are you comparing their power to?"

"V," Zalkur surmised.

Nasdatal nodded.

"And you're afraid they'll destroy this universe so you bottle them up?" Giramusen queried, astonished.

"There is no other way," Nasdatal asserted. "The moment we lose control over them is the moment to despair."

His four comrades stared at him in shocked silence.

After a while, Emissary seemed to come to a determination. "We left you the cloak of invisibility so you could preserve your dignity," he stated. "I would encourage you to use it for another purpose. Observe our children unawares and see if such ambitions harbor within their hearts."

"They are not V," Zalkur stated. "He had great power fueled by his Seer's avarice. We have raised our children from infancy to know a purpose of serving a greater good."

"Until then and until such time as you see with your heart, we will leave you," Giramusen said turning toward the door with Zalkur.

Emissary quickly followed and Marne also moved past Nasdatal.

"You, too?" he asked watching his mate prepare to leave.

Marne turned and her visage was pale and cold. "You mocked a woman," she spat, "and not just any woman. Our son's own mate. That is unforgiveable."

With that she turned and fled the room. Nasdatal remained a limp heap of cloth on the floor.

In the labs a small group huddled around one table. The blue test tube stood on a stand in the middle of the table while Aiya slowly worked her way vocally up the scale and octaves. Suddenly, the super charged water in the tube began to pulse. Aiya took a deep breath and held the tone purifying its frequency as she sang. Without warning, a bright light exploded from within the test tube knocking everyone off their feet and sending equipment flying.

Out in the gardens, Enmarsikil heard the explosion and zipped inside in record time. He held up his hand, gritting his teeth against the magnitude of the blast, and slowed the flying people and equipment to a halt. With a slow twist of his hand, time reversed until the moment the light had shined its brilliance. With one had he held that in place while separating out his siblings and righting them on their feet with his other hand. He stared at the bright spark of light.

"This is amazing!" he exclaimed in a low voice.

The others gathered around him to see as well.

"It's...like a star in miniature," Kappa said in awe.

Enmarsikil nodded. "That is exactly what this is."

"Well, if we can harness the power of this 'star,' we can travel anywhere we want," Zupatu said thoughtfully.

"Good luck finding something that doesn't explode on you," Aiya quipped heading out the door for the gardens.

"Yeah, now there's a challenge," Kappa agreed.

"I'm sure somebody will have some ideas," Enmarsikil said releasing the spark.

It took off like a rocket, tore a hole through the ceiling and headed through the atmosphere into outer space. Kappa whistled appreciatively.

Enmarsikil rose, glanced around his now crowded, messy labs, and headed back out into the gardens. But here, too, every space seemed to be occupied by someone singing to or meditating with his plants. He looked closer; no, they were not all his plants.

202

Grabbing a bag of fish pellets, Enmarsikil headed toward his fish ponds. It was the one area he had insisted no one touch. However, as he drew closer, the sounds and sight of a couple in close embrace at pondside attracted his most irritated gaze. He cleared his throat politely. No response. He cleared his throat louder. Still no response.

"Excuse me!" Enmarsikil all but yelled.

The couple jumped in startled surprise, looked up, then scrambled to their feet. Without a word, they dashed down the path toward the research wing.

"Noise and people everywhere," Enmarsikil growled spreading pellets on the water for his fish. "There's no peace to be found anywhere."

Finally, he set the bag down, raised his hand and created a transparent barrier to keep them all out.

Not all, he thought altering the barrier's frequency to allow in Astara.

Then he stomped his way to the furthest fish pond, found a bench and sat facing away from the Academy in silence.

Back in the gardens, Astara had watched him walk by with his bag of fish pellets and had smiled to herself knowing his love for those fish. However, when the couple had come dashing through from that direction, she frowned. Minutes later, she detected a distinct change in the air, almost a sensation of tightening or compression.

Concerned, Astara left her group and made her way down the path toward the ponds. Suddenly, she found an area where the air felt dense, thick and jelly-like. Glancing up and down, Astara stretched out her hand, touched the barrier and let her hand pass through. A moment later, she pressed her whole body through.

Wearing a worried frown, she crossed the bridge where they'd first kissed and looked for Enmarsikil everywhere. When Astara finally found him, he was slumped forward, elbows on his knees and his head in his hands. She crept closer and reached out to touch his shoulder.

"Don't," Enmarsikil said flinching and pulling away.

"What's wrong?"

Enmarsikil shook his head. "The gardens, the labs, they're crawling with people and constant noise. I can't take it anymore."

Astara sat on the ground leaning against the bench. "I know how you feel. I'm about at that point, too."

"I can't go back there," he complained.

"Don't," she replied. "Stay here till it's out of your system."

"How do I get this out of my system?" he wanted to know.

"Do what I always do," she relied. "Pick an element and allow yourself to become it. Let the jangled sensation become part of that element and leave it behind when you return to form."

"In this state?" he queried dubiously.

"Particularly in this state," Astara told him. She rose and kissed the top of his head.

Turning, she left him there, but as she neared the gardens, Astara collected the groups working there, brought them into the labs and rounded up everybody there as well.

"Look, people. We're all really taxing Enmarsikil," she said standing on a table so she could be seen and heard. "He's used to quiet, space and order. And this," Astara said gesturing around her, "isn't it."

"What should we do?" someone piped up.

"How about we split up the groups into smaller units and work in shifts?" Ki suggested.

"That would definitely be better," Astara agreed. "As for the labs, not one more experiment until this place is cleaned."

With that, Astara jumped down and began collecting beakers and test tubes in a cart and moving them to the sink. Others joined in sweeping the floors, wiping down lab tables and packing away equipment no longer in use. Before long, the lab was once again spotless. Groups had divvied up tasks and had broken up into smaller units. They quietly went about their work in the gardens and the lab.

Astara sighed heavily and left for their suite. She entered, walked straight through the bed chamber and into her room. There she shed her clothes, slipped into the indoor pool and dissolved in a rush of water and bubbles.

Out in the gardens, Enmarsikil tried to think of any element he could resonate with at the moment. His nerves blocked his every attempt at finding solace. All he could think of were the waterfalls and the forest pool. He glanced up at the walls, stood up and created his air ski. In moments, he rose up and over the walls, shot out across the broad expanse of meadow and zipped along toward the falls. He set himself down on the rock Astara had launched herself from. Remembering back, he felt into Astara's transformation, closed his eyes and leapt off the rock and over the falls. In a moment of bliss, he dissolved into the fine spray blown off the tumbling waters and the wind carried his tense sigh far away.

Much later, he surfaced in the eddy pool, climbed out and shook himself off. Taking a deep breath and feeling more at ease, he again brought up his air ski, took off and headed back to his gardens. He landed just inside the barrier, pressed through it and walked up the path. A soothing sense of quiet with but a soft hum of toning reached his ears. He cocked his head and glanced about. Two people moved around plants in one garden to his left and a couple more further up the path in a garden to his right. He sighed with relief. Space seemed to open before him.

Enmarsikil entered the labs and stopped abruptly. All of the beakers and test tubes were sparkling clean and arranged in their holders. The lab tables were clear and the floors swept. A small group huddled around a far table talking quietly. The tension in his chest eased and he took another deep breath.

Happy to finally have space and quiet again, he headed toward their suite. Entering, Enmarsikil glanced about but didn't see Astara at first. He checked in the bathroom, the alcove and even his memory corner. Shaking his head, he ducked through the arch into her room. The water in the pool swished and she climbed up out dripping wet. He swallowed hard and felt the heat of his desires well up.

"You know you can't do that and not have me want you," he said in a low voice.

Astara glanced up and smiled.

Enmarsikil kicked off his boots and his bare feet padded on the tile floor as he moved toward her. He wrapped his arms around her dripping body and pulled her close. Kissing her, his erection pressed against her stomach.

"I'm pretty wet for bed," she murmured between kisses.

"So, I'll get wet with you," he offered pulling back and shedding his clothes.

With that, they slipped into her pool and set the room glowing.

CHAPTER 26 - MASTERS OF THE UNIVERSE

Enmarsikil sat for a while in his alcove while Astara napped. In his mind's eye, he saw the bright spark of the miniature star that had been created out of their super charged water and the pure tone provided by Aiya. He ran through an array of possibilities in his head of all the things they could do with that much power at their disposal. And it was so easy to create; just power up, dip into the element and sing to it.

Rising from his chair, he strode back across the room to the sunken bowl in his floor that held his Visioning Sphere. Enmarsikil was still gaining mastery over Seeing, but he was uncomfortable going to the man he'd called Father after their last exchange. He hovered before the sphere, mentally connected with it as Teacher had taught him and brought his question up in his mind.

"How many possibilities of great good showing up for using this power?" he whispered, his mind easing into its customary altered state.

Violet and lilac swirled over the otherwise deep purple and black surface. Wisps of lilac stretched out toward him, each a link to a possible future. He felt each link and chose a couple for which he had a strong resonance. A moment later, he split himself into several clones each easing into the future lines to sample the visions.

When he returned, Enmarsikil asked a different question. "How many possibilities of great evil showing up for using this power?"

He watched the swirls become a roiling mass and the wisps that stretched out to him were many. Concern etched his face as he observed the sheer number of possibilities. This time when he sent out his clones and they returned, he found Astara sitting beside him.

"Can anyone do that?" she asked inquisitively.

"Perhaps. Takes a lot of practice," he added.

She nodded. "Yes, it would. It resonates less with me."

Enmarsikil glanced sideways at her and chuckled. "I have a feeling that if you set your mind to it, you would figure out how to in half the time it took me."

She smiled and shrugged. "Maybe."

Loud shouts from the lab reached their ears. Together, Enmarsikil and Astara rose and shot out of their suite on cushions of air. Skidding to a halt in the lab entrance, they saw all of the Space Transport Team gathered, excitement lighting up their faces.

"We did it!" Kappa announced excitedly.

"Did what?" Enmarsikil asked afraid to find out.

"We found the right substances to create a vessel for the star spark," Sagtibira explained.

"We put it in our model and tried to launch it," Guranmulla announced.

"What!?!" Enmarsikil cried.

"Come see," Gugbubulu urged. "We put a tracker on it so we can see its progress."

"So far, it's headed for the star belt," Zupatu said.

Enmarsikil scrambled out the door into the garden and climbed to the top of the wall where their instruments stood. He bent over the tracking console watching the screen with growing excitement. Suddenly, it veered off course due to a star's gravitational pull, dove straight for it and smashed into the gaseous giant. Moments later, the star erupted with a huge solar flare.

While the team members around him whooped and hollered, Enmarsikil stared at the screen. In little time the collision of stars, big and little, caused a super nova. He sat back on his heels feeling the weight of the world on his shoulders.

"We have so much more power than we were led to believe," he muttered. "No one warned us."

A gentle hand on his shoulder made him turn. "Maybe they didn't know," Astara offered.

"Maybe," he conceded. "We were a literal experiment." *And then maybe not*, his thoughts added.

Enmarsikil rose. "Great job, guys. If you can add a working model with navigational aids and show me a controlled, returnable flight, I'd say we're ready to build our space vehicle."

A riot of exuberant shouts broke out. Enmarsikil took his leave, went back in through the labs to the Academy and sought out his mother. She welcomed him with open arms and offered him a seat.

"What brings you?" Marne asked bracing for comments about Nasdatal's intrusion into their lives.

"Mother, did any of you know how powerful we would be? I mean, we just created a miniature star from water we super charged after powering up and sang to. It flew into a normal star that went super nova from the collision. Mother, how much more powerful will we grow?" he asked breathlessly.

Marne put her hand to her mouth, sat back in her chair and sighed. "We knew all along, son," she replied quietly. "We've done our best to instill a sense of service and integrity into each of you."

"But the truth is, we could be a danger to this world...this universe," Enmarsikil said in amazement.

She nodded.

"How many of your people were even capable of grasping your message about 'V's' project?" he asked.

"Maybe one percent of the population," she conceded.

"What is the percentage of Anunnaki blood we carry?" he wanted to know.

"Depending upon abilities, between 30% and 50%," Marne informed him. "And because you are the prototype, you are 50% and your blood is purely royal blood."

Enmarsikil's eyes widened then narrowed as he thought. "Yes, Father Ea is a royal prince and Ninti is a royal princess."

"Ea was heir to the throne of Nibiru before his younger brother was born," Marne informed him.

Enmarsikil looked sober. "I feel I know you and your people well," he began. "I know the characteristics we have that we derive from you. However, I'm keenly aware of aspects that crop up in us that confuse me, and I can only assume they belie our Anunnaki blood."

Marne nodded again.

"Then I need to come to an understanding of that side of our heritage as well," he stated.

Marne nodded. It was a moment she had been bracing for. "With

Ea on Ki, the next in line to approach is your grandfather, King Anu."

"Is he...pleasant?" Enmarsikil wondered.

"He is a king who must constantly be wary," she explained. "Go to him as a grandson seeking knowledge of his heritage."

Enmarsikil nodded.

"And remember to sift the dimensions directly around his person for information about his true thoughts and feelings," she counseled him.

"Thank you, mother. That is an excellent suggestion," Enmarsikil said gratefully as he rose.

He closed himself in a cloaking dimension as he traversed back through the Academy to his suite. On the one hand, Enmarsikil's heart was heavy because he would have to leave Astara here. On the other hand, excitement coursed through him; he was finally going to learn the whole of who he and his siblings were.

He removed the cloaking shield in his suite. Astara wasn't there so he mentally called to her. Within minutes, she appeared in the doorway to their chamber.

"Is something wrong?" she asked with a worried frown.

Enmarsikil shook his head, gestured for her to come inside then sealed the door shut. Astara's eyebrows shot straight up.

"What's going on?" she demanded.

Enmarsikil held up one hand while slipping his arm around her shoulders and escorting her into her special room. He sealed the archway as well. "Sorry, I don't want Father to hear our conversation."

She tilted her head sideways, her brows knit. "What is going on?"

Nervously, Enmarsikil led her to the lounger he had created for her, drew her down onto the seat beside him and took both of her hands in his.

"Sweet, I'm going away for a few cycles," he announced cautiously.

Her mouth flew open. "But...where will you go?"

"Agade," he said at last. "I'm going to Agade to meet with Grandfather Anu."

She frowned. "But why? And why can't I come with you?"

"Astara, we created a mini-star. You and I, by powering up, created such a charge in the water that all Aiya had to do was sing to it, make it vibrate at the right frequency, and it burst to life," he explained.

She nodded. "Yes, I heard about that. But what does that have to do with King Anu?"

"I saw it!" he breathed, his eyes bright with wonder. "I saw it and when I released it, the mini-star sped into space, collided with a large star and caused it to go super nova."

Astara stared at his awestruck face trying to comprehend the enormity of what had happened.

"Sweet, you, me, all of them," Enmarsikil said with a sweeping gesture toward the walls, "are powerful enough to destroy worlds, perhaps even create worlds of our own."

Astara's eyes lit up. "Oh, wouldn't that be fun?"

"Would it?" Enmarsikil wondered soberly. "There are ethics involved with this sort of thing. Remember Father's story about 'V'."

She nodded growing solemn.

"Before we could ever consider such a thing, we need to understand the other half of our genetic makeup," he asserted.

"Anunnaki," Astara breathed.

He nodded.

"So that's why you're going to Agade," she surmised.

"Yes, and it is to be a secret from all but a few," Enmarsikil added. "Most of all, I don't want Father to know. Can you keep a secret?"

Astara gave him an anguished look. "Mostly."

He frowned. "What...is mostly?"

"I never tell everyone...just my closest sisters. We've kept each others' secrets since we were little," she explained.

"Sweet, this isn't just your secret," he impressed upon her. "It's mine as well."

Astara took a deep breath and gave him an anguished look. "I'll do my best, love. I promise to do my best."

He patted her hand and kissed her. "Your best is all I can ask for."

"But how will you leave without your absence being noticed?" Astara wondered.

"I have that figured out, too," he assured her. "The groups working with metal ores and mining actually need some experience with mining. I have found a couple of abandoned mines not far from Agade," Enmarsikil delineated.

"So, you'll go with them," Astara said catching on, "and if anyone asks, you're there."

He nodded.

She looked him over then said, "Stand up."

Not understanding why, Enmarsikil gamely complied.

Astara viewed his attired with a critical eye. "Is all you have to wear black?"

He blinked. "Except for my gardening browns. Why?"

210

"Sweet, you look like a young Teacher."

He shrugged.

"Does King Anu feel intimidated by Teacher?" Astara probed.

Enmarsikil gave it some thought. "Yes, I suppose he does."

"Then you can't dress like Teacher or you'll put King Anu on edge," she explained.

Enmarsikil considered this. "You're probably right, but what can I do? My entire wardrobe is black."

A mischievous twinkle lit her eyes. "Oh, don't worry about that detail," Astara assured him. "That I can deal with without blowing your cover."

"Ok. I'll leave wardrobe in your capable hands," he replied kissing the top of her head. "I need to round up the mining team."

With that, Enmarsikil dismissed the barriers. He hurried out to find the individuals he'd need to gather while Astara thoughtfully sought out Aiya, Kienelil and Bilnammul. When she found them, they immediately noticed the plan-hatching look on her face.

"Ok, what's up?" Aiya asked.

"Oh, just thoughts," Astara teased.

"We know that look. Tell us," Kienelil insisted.

"Well...have you ever noticed what Enmarsikil wears?" Astara asked.

"Black," Bilanammul said firmly.

"Either he has no imagination or he's trying to be Teacher's twin," Kienelil agreed.

Astara bit her lower lip and nodded. "But what would look good on him?"

"Blue...whatever it is, blue would bring out the color of his eyes," Kienelil said.

"And something closer to his body. He's hot," Aiya added.

The other girls glared at her.

"Well, he is," Aiya defended herself. "I have eyes. I can look."

"But, he has to dig in the garden," Astara reminded them, "and work in the labs. But if all this goes the directions we're planning, he may someday stand before Anunnaki royalty."

"Deep electric blue," Bilanammul said, "with fine embroidery in silver thread."

"Oo, his fish," Astara added.

"I'll style them and Kienelil can create the patterns," Aiya said.

"And I'll sew them," Bilanammul added.

"When do you need them by?" Aiya asked.

"Before the end of this cycle?" Astara asked wincing at the short time frame.

"There's something you're not telling us," Bilnammul noted.

Astara grimaced and nodded.

"Then we'll get them done," Aiya assured her, "as long as you tell us what's going on."

"When I can...I promise," Astara told her. "And thanks."

Enmarsikil rounded up the metal workers who proposed to work straight from ore. They sat in one of the small lecture halls in the Academy listening while he laid out his ideas.

"To work with ore, it might be best to see it in the mines first," he suggested.

"We don't even know what a mine looks like," Kumzubar countered.

Enmarsikil nodded. "I know. But I've located a couple of abandoned mines between here and Agade."

"If they were abandoned, there's nothing left in them," Simugatibira countered.

Marki shook his head. "There's ore. It's just too deep for them and they don't know how to find it."

"Exactly my thought," Enmarsikil agreed. "If we can learn how to locate and extract the ore ourselves, we'll discover even more about its properties."

His siblings nodded in agreement.

"When do we go?" Kumzubar asked.

"Beginning of next cycle," Enmarsikil replied.

"Are we taking our mates with us?" Izishub asked.

Enmarsikil shook his head. "We're all working on different projects and each one is important. We'll be back soon enough."

"Tell that to Mirsigmi, Marki retorted.

Enmarsikil nodded. He knew Astara was disappointed not to be going with him but for reasons the others didn't know.

When the meeting broke up, Marki stayed behind. Enmarsikil desperately wanted to leave, but something in Marki's demeanor told him this was important.

"What do you need, Marki?" he asked as evenly as possible.

"I was wondering if you remember anything from when we were born?"

212

Enmarsikil frowned. "You're in the Fourth Generation?"

Marki nodded.

At the moment, all Enmarsikil could remember was being a young boy around ten and walking into a nursery filled with more babies. He'd been infinitely bored and irritated that he would lose yet so much more of his mother's time. Then one baby had turned her head and spotted him. She had let out a squeal of delight. And the moment he had approached her cradle, she had giggled and laughed at his funny faces. The moment mother had pulled him away, she had cried.

A pang rose in Enmarsikil's heart. That was the moment he had fallen in love with little Astara. And he had hated to see her cry ever since. He had a feeling he'd have the opportunity soon enough.

Enmarsikil sighed. "I'm afraid at that age, all I remember is seeing another nursery filled with babies."

Marki chuckled then grew serious. "Do you remember if any of us were born...wrong?"

Enmarsikil gave him a puzzled frown. "No. We were all born in perfect health. Why?"

"Nothing wrong with any of our attributes?" Marki pressed.

Enmarsikil shook his head. "No, I remember mother and father being pleased that all the children had turned out just right."

Marki sagged, found a seat and sank onto it.

"What's this about?" Enmarsikil pressed.

Marki was shaking. "All my life I've had this image of Teacher staring down at me saying 'This one's doing poorly. He's not like the others,' and all my life, I thought he was talking about me. I was jealous of everyone else who'd managed to be born fine."

Enmarsikil pensively knit his brow and thought hard. "Now that you say that, I do remember that one of the Anunnaki babies was born sickly. At first they were worried about the siblings born with him, but he pulled through and you were all fine. You must remember father working on him before shifting you into this dimension."

Marki nodded, too stunned to speak.

"I'm glad I could help clear that up for you," Enmarsikil said turning to leave.

"Me, too," Marki mumbled. "Thanks."

Time flew by and soon Enmarsikil would be headed on his great adventure. He wondered at not having seen Teacher for a while, but his mind was filled with too many other things and he pushed that concern away. Marne had called him to her suite, and he knocked before entering. Inside, Astara stood with her friends, each of them holding an outfit for him.

"It would seem that your sisters have gifts for you," Marne beamed.

Kienelil held hers up first. "We took the browns and greens of your gardens and created this."

Enmarsikil took the outfit and looked it over. "It has lots of pockets," he said smiling.

"And a built in tool belt," Kienelil pointed out.

He checked. "Wow! It does. Thanks." He gave her a hug.

"And this is just to be comfortable in during the day," Bilnammul said thrusting another outfit of heather gray pants, white shirt and navy blue short jacket toward him.

"It's cut like Nita's," Astara pointed out.

Enmarsikil nodded and hugged Bilanammul.

"And I thought you needed this," Aiya said holding up an athletic outfit of slender, stretchy slacks and a form fitting top.

Enmarsikil glanced at Astara but the look in her eyes was all heat and suggestions for later. He swallowed hard and hugged Aiya.

Then Astara stepped forward. "Someday," she began, "you'll have to meet the Anunnaki. I...wanted you to look like a prince."

She held up an outfit of close fitting pants and a long coat in electric blue with silver embroidered fish to wear over top. "Try it on," she urged.

Enmarsikil shed his black cape and slid his arms into the sleeves of the coat as the girls held it up for him. They fastened it up the front and Marne turned him toward a mirror. The girls arranged his hair on his shoulders, and Enmarsikil stared at his new visage. He had never seen himself in a bright color or such regal garb.

Turning, he asked the women, "Do I look all right?"

Astara stood before him, her eyes dancing. "You look like I always knew you could look...handsome and noble."

Enmarsikil blushed but checked his image in the mirror one last time. "I do think I'm ready," he whispered to his reflection.

"*Your time is now*," he heard as Marne's voice echoed through his mind.

CHAPTER 27 - STATE VISIT

With final preparations underway and the adventure about to begin, Enmarsikil took his last hours with Astara. They curled up together on their bed making the most of the remaining time. Astara cried, which Enmarsikil had expected. What he hadn't been prepared for in all his excitement was how he would feel. And how he felt in that moment was like spiriting Astara away to the pool in the forest and never leaving.

"Will I hear from you at all?" Astara asked valiantly attempting to dry her tears as Enmarsikil reluctantly rose to dress.

He shook his head. "Probably not," he admitted remorsefully. "If I do, it will be telepathically when I'm alone."

She came over and helped him button his jacket though her hands trembled.

"I packed your 'regal suite'," she told him, her voice wavering. "King Anu can't help but notice how noble you look in that."

Enmarsikil swallowed hard. He had very distant memories of the King; mostly times as a young boy when Father Ea would introduce him to the Secret Council and show them his budding abilities.

"I'm sure you have outfitted me like a prince," he assured her.

"I found a couple of other items so you have other, less formal, things to wear," Astara added.

"And I'm sure I will find good use for all of them," he said checking his pack and quickly closing it up.

He picked it up and slung it over his shoulder. Astara stared at him wide-eyed and pale.

"You're really going," she whispered.

He drew her close with his free hand and rocked back and forth with her. "I will be back in no time. I promise."

Finally, he led her out the door, through the Academy and to the courtyard where the others had gathered. Nindulur stood in the center of their packs and equipment and held a round, flat form as the foundation of their transport. As others climbed on board, they added their powers until a complete transport ship was built. Astara hung back with the other mates who were to be left behind.

Enmarsikil included his pack in the luggage bin. Turning, he gave a thumbs up to Gugbubulu to chart a course for the mines he'd marked on a holographic map. Zupatu manned the controls and the vehicle slowly rose from the ground. Enmarsikil turned toward Astara, brought his fingers to his lips and whispered in her mind, *I love you.* Then the transport was gone like it had been shot from a cannon.

The others turned to head back inside but Astara remained staring at the horizon.

"They'll be back soon," Ki reminded her.

"Some sooner than others," Astara replied cryptically as she allowed her sister to lead her back inside.

With a limitless power system, it took no time for the transport to reach the mineral hills. Sagtibira carefully watched a piece of equipment he had designed to recognize metals deep in the ground. Soon they set down near an abandoned mine shaft.

While the others got equipment ready, Enmarsikil took Marki and Kumzubar aside.

"There is no telling how stable the mines are. That's where we'll need you to shore up the walls and ceilings. If need be Izishub can melt the rock to make it stronger."

The boys nodded then all three headed back over to join the others.

"Any idea what was mined from here?" Sagtibira asked.

"What little gold Nibiru had was in there and some silver," Enmarsikil replied. "And just to warn you, we might see guards from Agade. If there are any problems, I will go with them to Agade and settle the issue."

Marki frowned. "We'll all go with you."

Enmarsikil shook his head. "Conceal and send back any ore you

216

find, but do not follow me to Agade. I'm prepared to speak with King Anu."

Marki and Kumzubar looked at each other, their eyes narrowing.

"He planned to go there all along," Kumzubar realized.

"Apparently, he wants that kept quiet," Marki agreed.

For now everyone who could lit up their fingertips and led the way into the mine. There turned out to be work for Izishub, Marki and Kumzubar. The going was slow, but soon elementals attuned to the metals were sensing their presence. Collaborating, they discovered veins of ore, dug into them and were rewarded with silver in one location and flecks of gold in another. As soon as they went topside, they packaged the ore and shipped it back to the Academy.

"There's one more mine I saw," Enmarsikil told them.

This one, Marki and Kumzubar noted, was close enough to Agade for all of them to see the spires of the palace. When they opened the mine, they found a man-made cavern devoid of anything but dust. They took dust samples to analyze later.

By the time they arrived topside again and had shipped their packages back to the Academy, guards from Agade were churning into their territory on vehicles whose sharp whine preceded them.

Enmarsikil had everyone sit down and eat. When the guards were nearer, they circled the group, finally set down, and the commander approached.

"By whose authority are you here?" the commander demanded.

"By mine," Enmarsikil replied evenly.

"And just who would you be who could authorize an exploration into these closed mines?" the commander pressed.

Enmarsikil rose to his full height. "I am Enmarsikil, son of Prince Ea and Princess Ninti, grandson of King Anu."

The commander looked him over carefully. "I can't say I've ever heard of you. Let's see if the King knows your name," he said. "Come with me."

With no resistance, Enmarsikil grabbed his pack, slung it over his shoulders and followed the commander to his transport vehicle.

"Don't worry about me," he called back to the others. "I've been to Agade before. I'll be fine."

His siblings watched in dismay as the vehicle leapt skyward, turned and zipped away toward the gleaming city in the valley. The remaining guards stayed behind.

"We haven't done anything wrong," Kumzubar spoke up.

"You trespassed on royal property," a guard told them.

"Is this ground out here royal property?" Marki asked.

"No, inside the cave," was the reply.

"Then how do you know we were in the caves?" Marki challenged.

"We picked up heat signatures," came the reply.

"How about I show you where we went and then you can determine if we trespassed on royal ground," Marki offered.

"What are you doing?" Kumzubar hissed. "That place is a labyrinth."

"And I'll bet they've never been inside before," Mardi replied.

Kumzubar's eyes flashed. "Got it. Let's show them."

The two brothers rose, headed past the lieutenant who motioned his men forward and brought up the rear. Marki and Kumzubar led them further and further into the mine. The darkness closed in around them only broken by faint lights. The twists and turns made the guards lose any sense of direction. Suddenly, they found themselves with dying lights in pitch dark.

Top side, Marki and Kumzubar appeared without warning.

"Where did you leave them?" Zupatu asked.

"In a deep chamber. It will take them awhile to find their way out," Kumzubar told them.

"Meanwhile, get everything picked up and ready to go," Marki instructed. "When they come out, I want this place to look like we've never been here."

"Where will we be?" Izishub asked.

"On our way back to the Academy," Marki replied.

"But what about Enmarsikil?" Sagtibira asked. "We can't just leave him in Agade."

Kumzubar nodded. "That's exactly what we need to do. I think he knew we'd trip some alarm system and was prepared to go. He said he wanted to meet his grandfather."

The others looked shocked but did what Marki said. Before long, the transport headed back to the Academy slowly in case they needed to turn around and speed to Enmarsikil's rescue.

Neither the Commander nor Enmarsikil spoke during the flight to Agade. They passed over the city walls, headed straight for the Palace and landed in an outer courtyard. The Commander prodded Enmarsikil toward a side door. Enmarsikil hitched his pack further up his shoulder and took in his surroundings. Nothing looked familiar.

218

With a lump rising in his throat, Enmarsikil followed the Commander into the cavernous palace. They threaded their way through inner passages until they exited just outside the throne room. The guards at the entrance stood at attention and let them pass. The Commander smartly stepped inside; Enmarsikil followed but halted abruptly. He gazed about the awe-inspiring room with its high vaulted ceilings and precious gold trim. The floors shone as if back lit and rich tapestries and curtains hung from the walls. The Commander turned and barked a sharp order Enmarsikil barely heard, but he dragged himself away from the fabulous sights and dutifully followed.

They walked the very long length of a single stretch of carpet so plush, Enmarsikil couldn't hear his own feet fall. At the end of the length of carpet were a set of wide marble steps leading up to a marble dais with two thrones. At the moment only a man sat upon his. Enmarsikil squinted as he studied him. Yes, he bore a resemblance to the man Father Ea had introduced him to shars ago.

"What have you here?" the man on the throne asked.

The Commander stood at attention and saluted his king. "Your highness. I found this young man leading a small group of pillagers into your mines."

"The old ones?" the King wondered, his brow furrowed.

"Yes, your highness."

"And who does he say he is that he has a right to enter my mines?" the King asked, his voice taking on an edge.

"Your Highness," Enmarsikil said with a bow of his head. "I am Enmarsikil, son of Prince Ea and Princess Ninti."

The King's jaw worked hard. "Thank you, Commander. I'll deal with him from here."

The Commander saluted, spun on his heel and silently left the room. King Anu slowly rose from his throne, made his way down the wide stairs until he finally stood face-to-face with the young man.

"I have not seen Enmarsikil for...."

"Many shars, sir," came the respectful reply.

King Anu walked about him checking him from every angle. Enmarsikil stood perfectly still.

"I'm not sure I ever expected to see you again," the King said thoughtfully. "What brings you to my mines and to my court?"

"Sir, we are working on the challenge of the hole in your atmosphere as promised," Enmarsikil replied. "In order to understand the metals, we needed to see them in their natural setting to better comprehend their makeup."

"And did you find any?" King Anu asked.

"Mostly dust and flakes."

"What can you do with so little?" the King wondered.

"With our abilities, a little becomes much," Enmarsikil assured him.

"You certainly have Ea's sharp, inquisitive, scientific mind," Anu admitted. "And I see Ninmah's, as she is called now, profile in your face. You have her eyes."

"I do love science, but I also work with plants. I have siblings now who have devised ways of improving the plants of Nibiru to increase food production."

"And you're sure you can do that?" Anu queried.

"Absolutely," Enmarsikil insisted. "We have already chosen a few sectors of Nibiru and are bringing new life to fields and meadows as we speak."

Anu reached out and clapped Enmarsikil on the shoulder. "Son of my son, welcome home. For any son of double royal blood is a Prince of high order in my court."

Enmarsikil's shock was evident and he remembered Astara telling him she wanted Anu to see him as a noble prince.

Anu slipped his arm around the young man's shoulder and escorted him to a secluded porch where they could speak in private.

"You come with no Teacher and your father is now on Ki," Anu remarked.

"So I'd heard," Enmarsikil replied.

"Then why the surprise visit?" Anu asked getting to the point.

"Sir, many of my siblings feel that at some point they will seek adventure on Ki, possibly to partner with your people there. It dawned on me that we know nothing about one side of our heritage and perhaps too much about the other. Sire, my keen hope is that, as my grandfather, you would instruct me in the heritage I am missing so I may understand the Anunnaki that is within me."

"And you suppose I have the time?" Anu asked amused.

"I know you have excellent tutors and instructors. Perhaps they would enlighten me as you deal with matters of state," Enmarsikil responded.

"No, no. You are my grandson. And when my grandson comes to me asking to learn of our heritage, how can I deny him my personal attention?" Anu turned them around and headed back inside the castle.

"Come, you will rest after your journey and sup with me at dinner," Anu said pleasantly.

"I am honored, your highness," Enmarsikil replied with a bow of his head.

The King waved and snapped his fingers. Minutes later, a servant hurried toward them.

"Please escort my noble guest to the best guest suite in the royal wing," King Anu ordered.

The man bowed lower, took Enmarsikil's pack and scurried away with the young man following. Through a few twists and turns of polished, columned corridors, they arrived before a large carved door. The servant threw the door wide open, entered and placed Enmarsikil's pack on a stand. As Enmarsikil entered, female servants entered from a side door and immediately began opening the pack and pulling out his clothes. In a rush of energy, they had his clothes out, hung and stored away in a large wardrobe off to the right.

Another man entered the room and Enmarsikil spun to face him.

"King Anu has sent attire for dinner," he announced and several more individuals entered with pants, slippers, shirt and long coat.

One of the young women took Enmarsikil's arm. "Come, we will help you bathe and perfume yourself for this evening."

Enmarsikil sputtered. "I'm quite sure I can bathe myself," he protested as the women urged him toward a separate room.

He finally managed to convince them that where he was from everyone jolly-well bathed themselves. He let them draw his bath but firmly shooed them into the bed chamber, locked the door energetically and performed his own ablutions himself. He made certain to dry off thoroughly and pull on his own pants before opening the door and allowing anyone to help him with anything else. The young women seemed to take great delight in combing and fixing his hair. They rubbed fragrant oil on his back and chest and when they left, Enmarsikil was pretty certain he smelled as potently as did any of his prized flowers in his garden.

"I will come for you when it is time to dine," the servant Anu had assigned him in the throne room said. He bowed and backed out of the room shutting the door behind him.

Enmarsikil stood in the middle of the suddenly empty room. A huge bed stood against the wall opposite the door with comfortable chairs just to its right and large windows framing an arch to the balcony to its left. He walked over to the balcony and stood gazing out over the courtyards below and the city of Agade beyond. A pang of emptiness hit him.

Astara would so love this, he thought. *And that room. She'd dance through the whole thing.*

He took a deep breath. He'd sought this opportunity and it was now here. Time to put his mother's teachings to work and learn all he could. He remained on the balcony till the servant knocked on the door and came to escort him away.

CHAPTER 28 - ENHANCED AWARENESS

Back at the Academy, the mining team set down their craft in the large courtyard. As Nindulur released focus on the structure, it dissipated into the air. While all the other mates ran out to greet them, one was absent. Marki hugged Mirsigmi and gave her a quick kiss then hurried through the Academy.

He perused the labs and considered knocking on the door of Enmarsikil's suite, but his instincts told him to look elsewhere. Marki headed out into the gardens methodically checking every twisting path. Finally, as he neared the fish ponds, he spotted Astara standing on the bridge with her eyes red from crying. Marki tried to whistle so he wouldn't startle her.

Astara glanced up, spotted him and looked away.

"He didn't come back with us," Marki said, his boots crunching on the fine gravel leading up to the bridge.

Astara nodded.

"You knew, didn't you?" he asked stepping onto the bridge.

Astara looked back and sighed.

"Look, Astara," Marki said gently touching her shoulder. "There's something I need to tell you. It's important."

She frowned.

"I grew up thinking there was something wrong with me, that

Teacher had said I was born defective," Marki confessed. "Enmarsikil cleared that up for me before we left. The Anunnaki baby I was tethered to was born sick. It was him Teacher was talking about but I always thought it was me. I was so mean all these years because it seemed so unfair that everybody else got born normal, and I was a piece of garbage."

Astara's mouth flew open. "Garbage? Marki, you were never garbage."

He shrugged. "It's just how I felt."

"I'm so sorry, Marki. I never knew."

"No," he said getting down on bent knee, "I'm the one who is sorry. I was mean to everybody but I was particularly harsh with you." He took her hand. "I beg your forgiveness, and I swear that the rest of your life, I'll be in your service. Whatever you ask me to do, I'll do."

"Marki, you're forgiven," Astara replied, stunned. "But you have a mate. You don't need to be in my service."

Marki nodded vehemently. "Oh yes I do. You have no idea how it feels in here," he said holding his closed fist to his chest. "My heart hurts every time I remember how I treated you. I have to repair that damage, make things right."

Astara considered this for a moment. "Why me?" she asked simply.

Marki rose to his feet. "Because I liked you."

Astara's eyes opened wide. "That's how you treat someone you like?"

"You have to understand," he replied. "I thought I was defective. And you were so perfect. I couldn't take the chance you'd ever like me back and end up bearing my defect, too."

Astara put her hand on his shoulder. "Well, in your own twisted way, you were trying to protect me...and it worked really well."

He nodded, his eyes downcast. "I know. Just tell me something I can do to make you happier."

"Ha!" Astara laughed cynically. "That's a tall order."

"Anything," Marki pleaded.

"Marki, the only thing I want right now is to see Enmarsikil come walking down that path," she said pointing toward the labs. "That is the only thing I want."

Marki drew a deep breath. "Then I'll do everything I can to make certain that happens soon."

Meanwhile, inside the Academy Marne paced outside Nasdatal's

224

door. It had been many cycles since she and the other Multi-Dims had confronted him. He had closeted himself away and had not come out, and now she was concerned. She stared at the door, once or twice stretching out to it, only to pull her hand back. Finally, she touched the door and opened it.

Gliding inside, Marne adjusted her vision to the dim light. She spotted a dark heap of clothes on the floor before the Visioning Sphere. With a sigh, she drew closer.

"I cannot see a thing in my sphere," Nasdatal said in a low, quiet voice. "I barely remember a time of not seeing. I am reduced to the state of a child."

Marne stopped where she was. "There are other ways to vision and other sights to see," she responded evenly.

"But this...this is what I gave my life for," Nasdatal countered.

"And it consumed you," she replied. "Your visions consumed you to the point where you could no longer see the reality in front of you."

"Then what is left?"

"Put on your cloak of invisibility," she told him. "Wrap it about you and come see the wonders unfolding at your very doorstep."

He sighed. "Where is my son?"

"He is visiting Agade," Marne told him.

The figure on the floor turned rapidly. "Alone? How could you let him go alone? I always protected him from the dulling influences of Anunnaki minds."

"He is a man, Nasdatal," Marne said firmly. "He needs to experience that dullness and learn to block it for himself. Some day, he will need to teach his siblings about that dullness and how to remain clear. You cannot protect him forever."

"But...Agade," Nasdatal moaned.

"Emissary shadows him," Marne let slip.

The dark figure straightened. "Everywhere? All the time?"

She nodded.

Nasdatal sighed with relief. "Good. Good. He will learn what he needs to but he won't come to great harm."

"He will learn how to extricate himself," Marne countered.

"I still feel better knowing Emissary shadows him."

Marne turned to leave.

"You...must still care," Nasdatal all but whispered.

Marne stopped. "A heart that loves can never stop caring."

"Then...why do you shun me?" Nasdatal asked.

"When you mocked Astara, it felt as if you had mocked me," she admitted. "Remember where she gets her empathic nature from."

Nasdatal slowly rose to his feet.

"Why?" Marne asked simply.

He shook his head though she could not see him. "I was losing control of everything. I had never meant for them to be self-determining. I had always intended to direct their paths. And then Astara's future self came back and ruined everything. I could not show my anger and displeasure."

"So you took it out on young Astara? Would you rather have taken it out on me?" Marne demanded turning to look at him.

"I would rather that Astara, all of her, would have stayed in her appropriate place and followed the rules."

"You were losing power and authority and you were too insecure in your own ability to instruct them to let them become who they were meant to be," she countered.

"They will be ruined as will the entire universe," he replied.

"Do you hear yourself, Nasdatal?" Marne asked. "Because of Astara's bravery and that of her human, all of our children still live. ALL OF THEM. They are not slaves to the Anunnaki. They have a chance for a better life. If we had followed your original path, so many would have been lost, so many harmed. How could you think your way was better... more protective...for them?

Marne spun around and sped toward the door. She paused in the doorway.

"Come out of this dank, dark hole, stop looking for possible futures and see what actually is," she said bruskly then left slamming the door after her.

For a while, Nasdatal stood there staring at the closed door. Finally, he took slow steps toward it and opened the door. Light streamed inside, and he threw his hands up to shield his face. At last, he stretched out one hand, sampled the dimensions and found that he really could still sense them, still manipulate them. Nasdatal connected with one, wrapped it about himself and stepped out into the light.

At the palace in Agade, Enmarsikil had been watching people below, adjusting his vision, tapping into their intent, practicing for the real event. It was difficult not to be awestruck by the palace, and he was sure that was the intent behind the design. He paced on the balcony reminding himself of his purpose in his grandfather's court.

A sharp knock at the door startled him. He turned as the servant entered the room.

"If you will follow me," the servant said with a bow of his head.

As Enmarsikil approached the man from the balcony, he shifted his sight.

Hm, he is pleased to have such a high position in court, Enmarsikil noticed. *He can feed his family, give them good quarters, afford a few luxuries.* Then Enmarsikil frowned. *He is always afraid of losing his position, always has an eye out for lesser servants wanting his job and for higher servants who might make an error leaving room for an upward move.*

Enmarsikil shook his head. If that was just the mind of a servant, he could only imagine how tortured the minds of nobility must be.

Having reached the servant, he quickly followed him to a stately dining room. Panels in the ceiling had been pulled back allowing natural light to shine through. The table itself was made of a warm red-brown wood, its legs intricately carved as were the backs of the chairs placed around it. Fine china graced each setting as well as tall, fluted glasses.

King Anu spotted him and stood waving him over. "Come, come. Sit at my right hand. You have the place of honor this meal."

Enmarsikil made his way to his grandfather's side. Bowing his head he said, "Thank you for this honor."

The servant seated him, tucked a large napkin about him almost like a bib and whispered in his ear, "Eat and drink nothing till the King takes the first sip and bite."

Enmarsikil nodded his understanding, grateful for the instruction. He did not have to wait long, though, for savants and councilmen were already being seated, and the wine was being poured. Once the King's cup bearer tasted the wine and certified it to be poison free, the King raised his glass in a toast.

"To the appearance of my grandson at a time most needed when both my sons are light years away. Comfort in my old age has come in my time of need."

Enmarsikil watched the others at the table following their manners for the toast, and the meal was officially open. Wine flowed freely, though he merely sipped his, and the food was rich, delicious and plentiful.

Enmarsikil listened attentively to conversations around the table. A savant across the table directed his attention to the young man after a while.

"The king says you are a scientist like your father."

Around the man Enmarsikil could see woven patterns for distrust and a need for testing truth.

Enmarsikil nodded. "Yes, I have studied biology, chemistry, horticulture, animal husbandry, quantum and scalar physics and have operated my own labs for several shars now."

Buzz went around the table at this list of accomplishments. As Enmarsikil studied the interacting fields between them, he could tell his answer pleased them, particularly the King.

"Yes," replied the savant across from him, "that is much the same path your father, Ea, took. Have you also studied genetics?"

"Some," Enmarsikil replied. "Mostly as it applies to fish and fowl."

Again the patterns in the field about those at the table suggested the answer pleased them.

"But, are you trained in combat, in martial arts?" Anu wondered.

Enmarsikil paused before replying sensing a need for caution. "We do indeed train in martial arts but not with weapons such as I suppose you use. I have worked for several shars teaching these skills as well."

Anu narrowed his eyes appraising him. "It would seem you are well rounded in your talents."

Enmarsikil detected a pattern of fear and uncertainty.

"And surely such a fine, handsome young man as yourself does not have an empty bed," said the man at his right elbow.

Enmarsikil frowned. "It was just recently that I took a mate."

"Just one?" someone else asked further down the table and out of his line of sight.

"One is plenty for me," Enmarsikil replied.

That seemed to tickle their fancy and jokes were bantered about that made his cheeks burn.

Noticing his discomfort, Anu came to his rescue. "He is young. He has more than enough years to learn the pleasure of many women. For now, I am pleased to hear you have a spouse," he said directing his attention toward Enmarsikil.

The young man breathed a sigh of relief and no more was said for the evening.

As the dinner party broke, the servant again came for Enmarsikil. He guided him to his suite and left him at the door. Once inside, Enmarsikil shed his borrowed clothes and went to slip into his sleep pants, the efforts to screen those he conversed with beginning to take their toll. As he grabbed his sleep pants, a slip of paper fell out and drifted toward

228

the floor. He bent and quickly snatched it up.

My love,
How I miss you even as I write this and slip it into your pack. I
know you'll do well in court, and I'm certain you'll garner the King's
favor. You can't help but do this given your intelligence and quiet charm.
Beware of making agreements against your nature and purpose.
Only you know your upbringing, our purpose and those back home who
rely on your calm clarity to guide them. And I for one would be lost
without you.
Keep your heart open and your head clear. And never forget the
arms of your Water Nymph waiting to welcome you home.

Forever yours,
Astara

His eyes misted and heat rose in his body. How he missed her,
too. Yet, she had reached out to give him solace in his own loneliness,
when he'd neglected to leave anything for her so focused had he been on
preparations. Enmarsikil kissed the note and slipped it into a pocket.

With his head spinning from all the events of the day, Enmarsikil
crawled into bed. He lay in the large, unfamiliar bed with no soft warm
body to cuddle close to. For a long while he stared at the ceiling. Finally,
he turned his mind to his bed chamber back home, the bed and Astara
lying in it. A part of himself slid out and stretched back toward the
Academy. He curled up on the bed behind her, actually smelling her
freshly washed hair. His aching arms stretched out, wrapped themselves
around her soft, warm body and pulled her close. With that comfort for
them both, he drifted off to sleep.

CHAPTER 29 - ROYAL MACHINATIONS

At the Academy, Astara blinked open her sleepy eyes. For a moment, she lay quiet in Enmarsikil's arms savoring his strong body curled protectively about her own, and his warm breath on her ear. Suddenly, her eyes flew wide open and she looked down. A transparent arm wrapped protectively over her side. She slid her fingers between his feeling the physicality of his form. With her other hand she felt up to his shoulder and down along his side.

Tears welled in her eyes spilling over her lashes. He had found a way to do more than contact her. Her beloved had found a way to be with her keeping her warm and safe in his embrace. Afraid to move lest the apparition disappear, Astara closed her eyes and sighed contentedly. In no time she fell into a peaceful deep sleep.

In other parts of the Academy, Nasdatal watched the teams work. Their exuberance and energy were running high. Marne joined him on his cloaking plane.

"Their creativity has simply exploded," she remarked.

"They are discovering they can literally do anything they want," Nasdatal fretted.

"And yet, look at their joy," Marne countered. "Their self discovery and collaborations have given them confidence and created strong bonds."

"We did things so differently, always a Teacher to guide the instructed," Nasdatal mourned.

"Given how easily 'V' was manipulated and influenced," Zalkur said showing up, "time is ripe for a new model."

"But what happens when experiments go wrong?" Nasdatal wondered.

"So far, Enmarsikil has done a consummate job of stopping and releasing explosions and moderating their focus. He is a good Shepherd," Giramusen added, as she eased into the plane with the others.

"Where is Kisikilturkusa," Zalkur asked.

"I left the child with Astara hoping the baby would distract her from her loneliness and worry," Giramusen replied.

"Should we be worried as well?" Zalkur asked.

"There is no doubt he is going to face challenges with Anu," Marne replied. "But I am certain he is ready for them."

And in Agade, Enmarsikil was waking to a new line of activities. He lingered longer in bed hoping Astara would feel his kisses on her cheek. At last, a knock at the door brought him fully present. For a moment, he forgot about his personal servant and the fact he'd put an energetic lock on his door for privacy. With a flick of his wrist, he removed the lock.

His servant entered with two more who pushed in carts laden with food. They arranged trays across his bed and in minutes Enmarsikil was again treated to a sumptuous meal.

The young women again entered and drew his bath water, and Enmarsikil made it clear he would bathe alone. He chose one of the alternate tunic and slack outfits that Astara had packed for him. Though they were in his traditional black, iridescent maroon threads had been woven in and provided a glowing effect whenever he moved.

Enmarsikil was escorted to an ante room just outside the court. Within minutes Anu wrapped up his last petitioner and entered the room. He greeted Enmarsikil by an arm salute then motioned him to follow.

With an entourage around them, Anu took Enmarsikil on a tour of the city's planning facilities, to the armory, space transport and control rooms. Enmarsikil observed quietly taking in everything he saw and that Anu told him. Then Anu led him to the quarters of the royal harem where his concubines were housed.

"Whose wives are they?" Enmarsikil asked innocently.

"Antu is my official wife and queen," Anu explained. "But law says I can have many wives. These are my concubines."

Though he colored, Enmarsikil had to ask. "You have sex with all of them?"

Anu nodded proudly. "You will have your own harem some day."

Enmarsikil sputtered. "I'm quite happy with my mate, thank you."

Anu clapped him on the shoulder. "Oh, I'm certain you are. Young, newlywed, in the throes of passion. But that will grow dull, my son. And when it does, another darling in your bed will change all that."

Enmarsikil frowned saying nothing. He sampled the patterns around his grandfather discovering the older man believed his words to be truth.

"Plus," Anu continued leading Enmarsikil out of the harem and down winding paths to another, lower building, "having many concubines shows your power, your wealth and your virility. Why, I've nearly rebuilt the population of Agade all on my own."

Enmarsikil's head spun. Naive to politics, the many threads in Nibiru's highest office were completely out of character with anything he had experienced to date. He methodically and purposefully filed away this information. Obviously, understanding the motivations of the Anunnaki would be important in dealing with them in the future.

"This is the Archives," Anu announced as they entered the building, traversed its narrow corridors and approached the only gold decorated door seen to date. "In here is housed the Book of Generations."

They entered the room and Anu headed straight for the pedestal on which the tome stood. When he stepped onto the stone before the pedestal, a light came on overhead.

Anu opened the book carefully turning its ancient pages. "It was in this book, before Alalu overthrew Lahma, that I discovered my name."

The King found the page, let his finger travel down the lines and stopped.

"I am the son of King An's youngest son. Both of my parents had royal blood making me double royal. While Alalu claimed royal parentage, because his mother was a concubine and his father was not in direct line to the throne, his name and birth were not recorded."

Enmarsikil frowned. "Then is Father Ea's name recorded?"

Anu turned the page and pointed. "Ea's name was recorded because he was my firstborn, Ninmah my second born, and Enlil, my youngest. Until Enlil's birth, Ea was in direct line for the throne, so his name had to be recorded."

232

"I'm sorry, grandfather. I'm confused. Ea is the eldest but is no longer in line for the throne."

Anu sighed. "When the north and south ceased their war and became but one nation, the Law of Succession stated only that the eldest son inherited the throne. But there were so few men left after the war that keeping concubines became legal in order to provide for the many widows left behind."

"Ah, I see," Enmarsikil replied.

"However, if a concubine's son was the elder but a younger son was born of the union between king and queen, it was deemed that the son with double royal blood should take precedence," Anu explained.

"So, you're saying that Father Ea was born to a concubine but Enlil...."

"Was born to my queen," Anu said nodding.

Curiosity got the better of him. "Am I in this book?" Enmarsikil asked.

Anu turned the page and read. "Yes, there are actually several royal children recorded in your generation. Ea had a son, Marduk, by Damkina, Alalu's daughter. Ninmah had a son, Ninurta, through Enlil. He is just a little older than you. And yes, here you are," Anu said looking up at him. "Your name is included in the Book of Generations, and you have double royal blood."

Enmarsikil noticed the patterns around Anu showed that he took great pleasure at the fact but also there was a measure of conniving involved as well.

Anu gently closed the book and stepped off the stone. The light dimmed and the two men left the Archives. Anu was particularly quiet on his way back to his suite. He invited Enmarsikil inside and had his servants bring them refreshment.

He sighed heavily as he gazed at the young man before him. His grandson was so unencumbered by the trappings of power and wealth. Almost he wished he could join him. Instead, Anu knew he needed him.

"Son, I have a proposal for you," the King announced quietly.

Enmarsikil paused in cutting his meat, set down his utensils and gazed directly at his elder, patiently waiting. Anu raised an eyebrow in wonder certain he had never had anyone's undivided attention before.

"I have it in mind to make you my heir to the throne of Nibiru," Anu said.

Enmarsikil's heart raced and sweat beaded on his brow. He sifted the patterns around Anu, but the offer was genuine.

"I-I'm not certain I could accept," the young man replied.

"Hear me out," Anu cautioned. "Nibiru must remain united at all costs. The Great War decimated the population and nearly destroyed the planet."

Enmarsikil frowned. "Is another war eminent?"

Anu nodded. "I fear it is. The discord between Ea and Enlil has grown. I think Ea could have been appeased with the offer of Ninmah as his spouse. They were even betrothed. But once her affair with Enlil was exposed, and she bore him a son, there was no amount of appeasement on the planet to assuage Ea's feelings. I even sent him to Ki to give him territory over which to rule."

"Does he still rule Ki now that Enlil is there?" Enmarsikil queried.

Anu shook his head. "When Ea wasn't quick enough in discovering sufficient sources of gold, Enlil drew supporters. Together, they would have overthrown me. So, I sent Enlil to Ki to oversee the gold operations and gave Ea a new title, Enki."

"But Ea...I mean Enki, has no real power now, so that's a hollow title," Enmarsikil said bluntly.

Anu's eyebrows raised at hearing such a naked reply with no manipulative intent behind it. As he regarded his grandson, he realized this was both Enmarsikil's strength and weakness. *Time spent in court will cure that*, he thought.

"This is true," Anu said aloud. "And the next generation, though just children, are proving to be as competitive as their elders. I have every intention of assigning Marduk and Ninurta to positions off of Nibiru as soon as they are of age."

Enmarsikil frowned thinking back to the Book of Generations. "But who will be left to inherit your throne?"

Anu leaned forward. "You, dear boy. You are my last male descendent of double royal blood."

Enmarsikil sat back in his chair and pushed his plate away having suddenly lost his appetite.

"Obviously, you will need training in politics and matters of court," Anu continued. "I would install you in a lesser position in court, let you work your way up through the ranks...learn the ropes."

Enmarsikil's heart sank. "I would have to live here, in Agade?"

"But of course," Anu said.

"And...what of my mate?" Enmarsikil asked, Astara's face springing to mind.

"Of course she could live here as well," Anu said smoothly.

234

Enmarsikil looked at him noticing the patterns around the man had taken on an oily quality.

"But you will also need a wife of royal blood," Anu insisted. "In fact, I have just the woman in mind and have scheduled for you to meet her in my private garden in just a while."

Enmarsikil felt like the walls and the ceiling of the room were closing in on him. He couldn't breathe. None of this was part of his agenda.

"I will need time to consider your...generous offer," he gasped out.

Anu waved for a servant to guide the young man back to his suite. "Take all the time you need," he called after him his smile growing more devious by the minute.

Enmarsikil entered his suite feeling quite shaken. He dismissed the servant, put an energetic lock on the door and sank into a chair. He turned his eyes upward wondering how he could possibly meet another woman with the intentions of marriage and keep his vow to Astara intact.

I only have to meet her, he told himself rising to bathe and change. *No one said I had to propose*.

With that, he begrudgingly rose to his feet, took a hasty bath and stood in front of the open wardrobe. The "princely" suit of blue Astara had personally given him caught his eye. He touched it then pulled his hand back.

How could I wear that in order to meet another? Enmarsikil chastised himself.

Yet, no matter how many other outfits he looked at, this one seemed to call to him. In the end, he had no choice. He pulled it out and carefully put it on. Enmarsikil stood before a large framed mirror watching himself as he fastened the royal blue long coat. His hands trembled, and in his mind's eye he saw Astara fastening it, her own hands trembling when she'd given it to him.

Did she know? he wondered. *But how could she? I'm the only one who has been to court...unless...is that what future Astara told her? Was she somehow prepared for this?*

The thought gave Enmarsikil little comfort. He was preparing himself to do something that went against his very nature. He rolled his shoulders back, shook out his arms and held his head high. He would not disappoint Anu, but he was certain this was the only time he would see this young woman.

The servant knocked at his door, and Enmarsikil took off the lock. As soon as the door opened, Enmarsikil stepped up and prepared to follow the man. As he walked through the doorway, he could swear the long coat gave him...a hug.

The servant led him back to Anu's wing. They headed down a broad, wooden staircase to the lower level, through a brightly lit vestibule and out onto a rounded portico. Down a short flight of steps stretched the most beautiful, well-manicured garden Enmarsikil had ever seen. For a moment, he was so caught up with the forms of the beds and identifying the plants therein, he nearly missed the beautiful young woman sitting on a white marble bench obviously waiting for him.

Enmarsikil spotted her then took a second look at the young woman and swallowed hard. His Astara was beautiful but rarely wore a dress. The last time he'd seen her in one was when they'd performed the dance, and then she'd been quite exposed. This woman was almost as exposed he realized.

She was dressed in a form-fitting, cropped top of a rich, scarlet material that formed over her breasts like a second skin but scalloped away to show deep cleavage. Enmarsikil inhaled sharply. Apparently, Astara's breasts weren't the only ones capable of arousing him. The woman's midriff was bare and her long skirt was slung low revealing a flat stomach and rounded hips. The skirt itself hugged tightly to her legs and walking was only permitted by a slit in one side that showed, and here Enmarsikil again swallowed hard as parts of him stood at attention, her whole shapely leg.

A movement behind him broke the spell, and Anu placed his hand on his grandson's shoulder.

"Beautiful, is she not?" he asked.

Enmarsikil could only nod helplessly.

"Come, I will make the introduction," Anu offered wrapping his arm around Enmarsikil's shoulder and leading him off the portico.

As King and suitor approached, the young woman rose and bowed low to her sovereign showing much of her ample bosom. Enmarsikil wanted to drag his eyes away, but they had developed a mind of their own and were intent on admiring the view. She rose and Anu took her hand and placed it in Enmarsikil's.

"Grandson, meet Sud, one of Ninmah's younger nurses. Healing may not be the science you're accustomed to but...."

"Science and the healing arts lend much to one another," Enmarsikil added, never once taking his eyes off the young woman.

She smiled and batted lashes that were as dark as night.

"Sud also excels in the Art of Love," Anu added. "She is

considered a consummate seductress."

Somewhere in Enmarsikil's brain, an alarm was sounding. Instinctively, he knew she was playing on his innocence and naivety to the hilt. But another part of himself had gotten the bit between its teeth, had grabbed the reins and was wholly in control.

"I can see you two are enamored of each other," Anu said smoothly. "I will leave you to explore my garden and...perhaps...each other."

His chuckle turned sinister by the time he reached his door. For a moment a dark cloud passed overhead only to clear out as soon as he was gone.

Sud slipped her arm into Enmarsikil's and began leading him along the paths. Bright, fragrant flowers bloomed at intervals creating a heady scent. Somewhere he heard the faint sound of bubbling water. He ached to find it, but for now his whole being was focused solely on the woman at his side.

"I understand that Ninmah is your mother," Sud opened in a languid, musical voice.

Enmarsikil blinked. "Uh...yes, she is."

"What was she like when you were a child?" Sud asked.

"I'm afraid I didn't know her well. I...uh...grew up...."

And here it seemed his windpipe closed as a voice not his own whispered in his ear, *Do not betray the others.*

Enmarsikil coughed and his throat cleared.

"Go on," Sud encouraged. "You grew up...?"

"At an Academy," Enmarsikil replied hastily. "At a private Academy where I received... uh...specialized training. I saw Father Ea much more."

"So, that is why I have never seen you before," Sud surmised. "No wonder the king thinks so highly of you. He must have invested a lot in your preparation."

Enmarsikil looked startled for a moment and frowned.

"Did you know that King Anu is sending Ninmah to Ki?" Sud asked.

Enmarsikil stared at her. Somewhere in the back of his mind, he felt as if he should know that. "I'm afraid I hadn't heard," he admitted.

The bubbling sound of a fountain was louder now. He glanced about hoping to spot it.

One more bed away, he thought but Sud stopped there.

She leaned against him turning her eyes upward to look at him through her long lashes. Her breasts were pressed tight against his side and Enmarsikil was finding it hard to breathe.

"Ninmah wants to take all of her nurses to Ki with her," Sud told him, "even me. But I would much prefer to stay on Nibiru...with...you."

Her voice was a whisper, her eyes imploring and her lips set in a perfect, kissable pout. Enmarsikil found himself bending forward, their lips brushing.

All of a sudden, it was as if the world stopped and he was in a bubble. He felt her body, her warm breath and noticed a peculiar scent. A breeze tossed the branches of a nearby bush giving him a glimpse of the nearby fountain whose waters tumbled into a basin below. Rising up from the basin was his very own water nymph, her eyes penetrating his own.

Without warning, the spell was broken and he snapped back to reality. Enmarsikil looked at Sud's lips and face. Suddenly, the patterns she had woven about herself were very clear, and he pulled back.

"You, my lady, are wearing a very potent mix of pheromones," Enmarsikil declared, his clinical brain kicking into high gear. "The flowers in these gardens are prized because their scents, particularly in combination, create a heady aphrodisiac."

"Why else do you think they call it seduction?" she demanded, her pleasing persona rapidly devolving.

"You are angry," he stated.

"I-am-humiliated," she growled.

"How so?" Enmarsikil asked.

"The King doesn't see me as a potential mate for either of his sons or his other two grandsons," she stormed, "so he sicks me on you, some bumbling innocent from who knows where who claims to be his grandson but can't even remember his own mother. There has to be a reason you were sent away and locked up all these years."

"My name is in the Book of Generations," Enmarsikil told her. "Anu showed me himself."

"He's so desperate for an heir that won't tear the kingdom apart, it wouldn't surprise me if he put your name in there himself," Sud fumed.

Enmarsikil shrugged.

Sud started crying, which made Enmarsikil frown with confusion. He reached out to comfort her, but she tore away in a huff.

"I am worthy of greatness," she declared, crying harder. "But all Anu sees is someone worthy of scraps."

Enmarsikil folded his arms across his chest. "You really are insecure, aren't you?" he challenged. "That's why you use this whole seduction game."

She glared at him through tear-stained eyes, dark makeup running down her cheeks. "And how would you know what I'm like?"

Enmarsikil adjusted his vision. "For one, you must care about the suffering of others. Otherwise, why become a nurse? You are quite beautiful as well."

He led her to the fountain, found a piece of cloth in his pocket, which he dipped into the water, and carefully wiped away her makeup. Where the water pooled on the ground, she could see her visage.

"You are beautiful just as you are," he said simply.

Sud sighed and sank onto the edge surrounding the basin. She shook her head. "I wish it were so simple," she mourned. "That men saw the beauty of women and loved them for that."

Enmarsikil sighed. "Where I was raised, it is that simple."

Sud looked up at him all pretense gone. "I wish I could join you there."

He took her hand and helped her to her feet. "Entry is highly exclusive, even for me."

Sud nodded.

They began walking back toward the palace.

"You know, I had this all planned," she told him.

"What do you mean?" Enmarsikil asked.

"I only saw two options," she replied. "I would either seduce you to my bed or claim you had taken me by force if you refused."

Enmarsikil's face registered alarm. "Whatever for?"

"To pursue my goal of marrying royalty."

"You are that desperate?" Enmarsikil required.

"Was," she replied smiling. "I think a trip to Ki to get away from this place is just what the doctor ordered."

Enmarsikil smiled and nodded. "Safe journeys then," he replied giving her a warm hug.

They parted in the vestibule and Enmarsikil watched her leave through a side door before facing his grandfather.

"So, what do you think?" Anu asked eagerly, nearly wringing his hands with glee.

"She is a beautiful, intelligent, caring woman," Enmarsikil answered truthfully.

"And...?" the King pressed.

The wheels in Enmarsikil's head were rapidly spinning as he sought the means to extricate himself from his grandfather's web.

"There is one last place you have yet to show me," Enmarsikil stated.

Anu frowned wondering what was left.

"Show me Father Enki's old research labs," Enmarsikil requested, "even those kept secret. Then I will give you my decision."

Anu blanched and swallowed hard. *He knows...too much.*

CHAPTER 30 - ESCAPE

Anu sighed heavily. "You truly are like your father...all labs and science."

Enmarsikil nodded but stood resolutely. "I have observed everything you offered to show me," he said evenly. "To see my father's research labs is my only request."

Anu nodded. "You're right. You're right. Most people who approach me have a much longer list. All right. I'll have a servant...."

"It would be a great honor if you would show me in person," Enmarsikil countered. "Besides, a servant knows no secrets."

Anu knew he was backed into a corner. Still, he was certain he could find a way around his grandson's request and save the day.

"Follow me," he invited leaving his residential wing.

Enmarsikil followed him to areas behind the palace to a string of two-story buildings.

"Herein lies the research facilities and the private medical wing," Anu announced as they strode through the doors.

While Anu would have liked to rush through the labs, Enmarsikil's keen interest drew him from one to another. Inside one lab, he suddenly felt light-headed and quickly glanced about. Technicians were opening sealed boxes of materials, and Enmarsikil could tell by how they made him feel that they weren't from Nibiru.

"What is in those boxes?" he asked Anu, struggling to get his breath.

"Materials from Ki that Enki sent to test for valuable components," Anu replied.

Enmarsikil left the lab quickly and leaned against the wall in the corridor outside. *So that is what the First Gens experienced before Astara traveled back in time to warn us*, he thought.

Anu studied him carefully. "Are you all right?"

Enmarsikil nodded and began walking again. "This whole experience has been a bit overwhelming," he told his elder.

Anu frowned but asked no more. Inwardly, he marked Enmarsikil's reaction at the same time the technician opened the package.

"I really just want to see Father Enki's lab," Enmarsikil insisted.

Anu led the young man up a flight of stairs, down a long hall and into a darkened room. He flipped on a light switch, and Enmarsikil took in the large holoprojector stand in the center along with banks of equipment and high powered microscopes lining the walls. He walked slowly around the room peering closely at everything.

"Yes, genetics," Enmarsikil breathed. "I remember some of this equipment from when Father Ea...Enki taught me to manipulate the DNA in fowl and fish."

"He taught you!?!" Anu asked, his face darkening.

Enmarsikil glanced up at him. "Before he had to start preparing for his mission to Ki."

"I never authorized that," Anu fumed.

Enmarsikil turned back to a console. "Probably not."

He flipped a switch on the console, punched some buttons and suddenly the room lights dimmed while an image was projected onto the platform in 3D. Enmarsikil walked all around it gazing at it in wonder.

"Do you know what this is, grandfather?" he asked.

"No. That is beyond me," Anu grumbled.

"That, grandfather, is the DNA sequence that led to me." Enmarsikil stared a little longer. "My life began in this very room."

Anu was less impressed and far more nervous. It was he for whom the walls were closing in now. "Come, there are a couple of others places for you to see," he announced.

Enmarsikil turned off the machine, the lights came back up and he followed Anu out of the room.

"I suppose you'd like to see the private medical wing," Anu muttered.

242

"Yes."

Against his better judgment, Anu led him through the halls to a door with his official seal. He removed it, opened the doors and turned on the lights.

Enmarsikil entered, chills running down his spine. In his mind's eye he saw himself at differing stages of childhood tiptoeing through the ward to see the next batch of babies.

"Here!" he exclaimed softly. "I and the others were born here."

So many memories swirled about him every where he looked. He could hardly shut them off. Finally, he turned to Anu.

"Thank you. I needed to connect with my origins again."

Anu nodded glumly and followed his grandson out the door. Enmarsikil stood statue-like staring around him.

"This part of the facility is familiar to me," he said and took off down a hall with Anu puffing behind him trying to keep up.

"Both Father Ea and Teacher used to bring me here," Enmarsikil said excitedly. "I remember a room somewhere right around here."

He suddenly spotted a mark on a wall, reached out and touched it before Anu could warn him. A portion of the wall slid back and Enmarsikil hurried inside. He ran his hands over the backs of the chairs around a conference table while Anu hastily shut the door.

"You always sat at the head of the table," Enmarsikil said pointing. "Won't you sit there now?"

His face was so innocent and childlike in that moment that Anu complied without question.

"And I would stand about...here," Enmarsikil said glancing down as if looking for a mark, "and I would perform my tricks for you and the council."

A pencil hovered in mid-air. Anu started to sweat.

"Then I learned more and I could do this," Enmarsikil said lighting his fingertips. "But these are mere parlor tricks, grandfather. I can do so much more now."

Recalling Astara's air blade trick, he called one up and kept it spinning about his waist. "You wanted to know what martial arts I know. Observe."

In seconds, he brought the air blade to his hands, aimed and released it. It sliced through the air past Anu's head and ripped a hole in the wall behind him.

"I'm sure you can imagine why we have no need of your weapons,'" Enmarsikil said sitting.

"That was certainly an impressive demonstration," Anu admitted studying the gash not far from his head.

He turned and watched Enmarsikil's movements with utter curiosity. At first a planet would form in the palm of his right hand. He'd release it and create a star that blinded Anu then release that. Next was a swirling galaxy. Anu stretched out his hand to touch it. Enmarsikil suddenly clamped his hand over the man's arm and held him with amazing strength.

"I wouldn't do that," Enmarsikil warned. "Each thing I bring up actually exists. This solar system is our own. To disrupt this means to possibly destroy ourselves."

Enmarsikil released it and Anu's arm.

"Ok, so you can do some pretty powerful stuff. All the more reason you're the man to hold the union together," Anu pointed out.

Enmarsikil was still filled with memories. "I still remember the day Teacher promised we'd be the tools to heal the hole in your atmosphere."

"Yes, well, the goal changed when I had to send Enki to Ki," Anu replied.

"No," Enmarsikil countered. "It never changed. Teacher maintained his promise and we are on the verge of being able to provide your planet's salvation right now. Which do you want more - salvation for Nibiru or for your throne?"

Anu's face reflected his inner struggle.

"See, I can't forget that promise," Enmarsikil told him, " nor can I forget my siblings. They are each capable of creating a small world, and when powered up, their own sun. They've already created a small star in the lab. Consider the mischief and destruction if no one is there to shepherd their decisions."

Anu clenched the arms of his chair till his knuckles were white.

"I understand your political predicament, grandfather, more than you may realize," Enmarsikil told him, "but I cannot be your solution. I was created....literally created in a test tube for another purpose. And the time for me to fulfill that purpose is now."

Enmarsikil rose to leave and heard the ring of metal behind him.

"Turn around and sit down," Anu growled. "I have no intention of allowing you to leave Agade."

Enmarsikil kept his back to the man. "And just what do you think would have happened if my air blade had connected with your neck? No grandfather, I am leaving now, and if I don't return soon, my siblings will
244

worry about me and come for me. And they can ALL create air blades and far greater than that."

With that, Enmarsikil held up his left hand with his fingers splayed. He waved it side-to-side twice before a bright blast of light filled the room. When it dimmed, Anu had just enough time to spot Enmarsikil exiting the secret chamber. Anu threw his sword like a javelin only to quickly duck for cover as it hit an invisible barrier and hurtled back at him. His hopes and dreams of maintaining Nibiru's unity was getting away.

At the Academy, Marki had left Astara and had swiftly returned to the courtyard where he and the mining team had landed.

"We've got to go back!" he yelled as the group started dispersing.

The others stopped and turned to watch him approach.

"Astara thinks he's in trouble," Marki said as he neared. "We've got to go back."

His comrades gave their mates a quick kiss and hurried to the center of the courtyard where Nindulur was already building up the base of their craft.

"What do we do?" Kumzubar asked, as the others built the rest of the craft around them.

"Get to Agade as fast as we can," Marki replied, "get to the palace and get Enmarsikil out of there."

Zupatu and Gugbubulu came dashing towards them.

"Wait for us," they called as the vehicle started levitating off the ground.

They leapt and Sagtibira caught them. They added their components to the craft.

"We'll sift the dimensions," Zupatu said, "and get you there faster."

The others hung on as Zupatu accessed the web of dimensions. One moment the vehicle was there; the next moment it was but a star on the horizon.

In the research facilities Enmarsikil ran through the halls, down a flight of stairs and counted the doors on his left until he found the right one. He quickly wrapped an invisible envelope around his face, pushed the door open and dashed inside. He went down the line of sealed boxes checking designations on them. One stood out, and he picked it up. Teacher's insignia was on top. Enmarsikil tucked the box under his arm and started threading his way toward the door.

"Hey! You can't take that," a technician yelled. "That's a special delivery."

"I know," Enmarsikil called over his shoulder, "and I'm the courier."

He thrust open the door just as the technician hit the security alarm and klaxons went off. Enmarsikil spotted Anu coming down the stairs to his right and guards charging down the hall directly across from the door. They brandished weapons and shouted the moment they spotted him.

Enmarsikil dashed to his left leading a merry chase through another building. Anu yelled, "Stop him!" and the guard yelled, "Halt!"

Enmarsikil remembered a side door that led to a courtyard near the closest city gate. He grit his teeth, threw his weight against the door and tumbled outside. Hastily scrambling to his feet, Enmarsikil took off again. Anu charged close at his heels while more guards circled round in an attempt to cut off his escape through the gate.

Suddenly, Enmarsikil spotted an object flying low over Agade. To his immense surprise and relief, he recognized his siblings on it. He sent out a telepathic distress signal and careened toward a flat area used as parade grounds. In an instant, the craft changed direction, sped towards him and began lowering to the ground.

"Stop him!" Anu yelled again.

Several guards skidded to a halt and raised their weapons commencing fire.

Anu waved his arms and ran toward the guards. "Stop! Stop!" But his voice was drowned out by the weapon fire.

"Hurry!" Marki yelled as Enmarsikil ran full tilt toward them.

He ducked a volley of weapon fire, made one last effort and leapt at the vehicle. Marki and Kumzubar grabbed his arms and hauled him aboard. Zupatu and Sagtibira stood ready to return fire.

"Don't fire! Don't fire!" Enmarsikil yelled. "Shields only!"

The brothers shifted to shields and the weapon fire began bouncing back.

"We're too heavy," Nindulur shouted. "What's in the box?"

"Not the box," Enmarsikil replied balancing it on his fingertips.

Suddenly, a stray shot from an unprotected side caught Enmarsikil in the left arm and side. The box tumbled off his fingertips but Marki caught it before it fell too far. Enmarsikil clutched his arm, which he held close to his side, the pain sharp and biting.

"We've got to get out of here!" Marki insisted.

"I can't," Nindulur replied. "It's as if there's a whole other person

246

on board. I can't get lift."

Enmarsikil spotted Anu and the guards closing in. Gritting his teeth against the pain, he maneuvered his right hand toward the thrusters and injected the last of his energy into them. The craft suddenly leapt into the sky then shot over the horizon.

Anu skidded to a halt watching the retreating star with his mouth hanging agape.

With Gugbubulu navigating and Zupatu sifting the dimensions, it was no time before they were setting down in the courtyard of the Academy. Marki helped Enmarsikil to his feet. Kumzubar reached for the box.

"Don't...touch it," Enmarsikil gasped out. "For Teacher...only."

As if by magic Emissary appeared, retrieved the box and left for Teacher's lab.

"We've got to get you to the infirmary," Marki insisted slinging Enmarsikil's good arm over his shoulder.

Enmarsikil shook his head. "Astara...please."

Marki looked at Kumzubar, who shrugged.

"Can you make it?" Marki asked.

Enmarsikil grit his teeth, nodded and staggered to his feet.

"You've got quite a gash in your side," Nindulur announced.

Enmarsikil waved her away. "Astara," was all he would say.

So, with Marki supporting his weight, the rag tag group helped him limp through the Academy, past his lab tables and out into his gardens.

"Where will she be?" Nindulur wondered.

"On the pond bridge," Marki panted.

"I'll go on ahead," Nindulur told them and dashed off down the path.

Within minutes, the two girls came racing back. Astara spotted Enmarsikil, gave a little scream and covered the distance to his side in the blink of an eye. Enmarsikil sagged to his knees on the ground, and Astara dropped to her knees beside him.

"I brought him back," Marki huffed.

Astara glanced up, took his hand, and squeezed it in thanks. Then she turned her full attention back to Enmarsikil.

"You're injured."

"Not too bad," he replied until the next movement made him cry out in pain.

"We need to get him to the infirmary," Nindulur insisted.

Astara shook her head, put her fingers to her temple and mentally called. In minutes, Aiya, Ki and Bilnammul raced toward them. They helped Astara lay Enmarsikil on the ground then the four women held hands and began to sing. As they sang, the air over his body produced an image of his wounds totally healed. Changes in pitch and harmonics brought the overlay down onto his body. One more vocal shift, and the healing was complete.

Enmarsikil gasped, opened his eyes and reached over toward his side and arm. He moved the arm and, when he felt no more pain, gingerly sat up. He reached for Astara wrapping his arms around her as their siblings cheered wildly. He had escaped Agade and now he was home.

CHAPTER 31 - WELCOME HOME

The little group broke up, everyone happy to finally be able to reunite with their mates. Enmarsikil wrapped his arm around Astara's shoulders, gave her a squeeze and kissed her.

"I think we need somewhere more private," she admonished breathlessly.

"I know. I just don't want to stop," he murmured in her ear.

She poked his ribs on his good side, ducked out from under his arm and skipped away down the path. She turned, blew him kisses and took off toward the labs.

Enmarsikil stood for a moment watching her go, a huge smile stretched across his face. *This is why I come home*, he thought happily, his heart too full for words. He took off down the path after her, caught up to her just inside the lab, scooped her up in his arms and carried her to their suite.

After a slight fumble with the door, Enmarsikil carried Astara inside, shut the door with his heel and set her feet on the floor. She reached up to kiss him then examined his long coat and the large gashes in the sleeve and side.

"I suppose it's ruined," he mourned as Astara carefully unbuttoned it.

She helped him slip out of it, and laid it on the bed. "Hm. Maybe,

maybe not," she replied. "Kienelil or Bilnammul may be able to fix it."

Astara looked back over her shoulder. "Did you see the water nymph?"

"You mean in the fountain?" he asked.

Astara chuckled. "Well, there, too."

She moved the material and embroidered in silver thread across the chest piece over his heart was a water nymph.

"She deflected this blast to your side," Astara pointed out.

Enmarsikil ran his fingers over the figure.

"I tried to instill some of my energy into it, make it come alive," Astara explained.

"Oh, it did," Enmarsikil assured her, "at the most important moments."

Astara smiled and reached for another kiss.

"I need a shower," he complained.

"Let me help you," she suggested slyly.

Enmarsikil's nostrils flared at the thought and, before he knew it, she had shed her clothes and was helping him out of his slippers and pants. His need was self-evident and he required no further encouragement. In moments they stood beneath the hot water soaping each others' bodies in all the right places.

"I can't wait," he moaned as Astara slid soapy hands over his erection.

"Better rinse off," she admonished biting her lower lip as he ran soapy hands over her breasts and nipples.

"You're really making it difficult," he complained turning around so the water got his front while she pressed her soapy breasts to his back.

"Me? What about you?"

"I don't care who," Enmarsikil declared. "I need you...now."

He yanked open the shower door, grabbed a towel and threw it on the floor. In one swift move, he swept her out from under the water and onto her back on the towel. He knelt between her legs, scooped inside her and found quick release.

"Sorry," he apologized kissing her neck. "I've been saving that for a while, and you're just too good."

"We can take our time in bed," she whispered squeezing his buttocks with her hands.

"Absolutely and right now," he agreed.

Enmarsikil pushed to his feet, took her hand and pulled her up then carried her to the bed. He didn't even wait to pull down the covers but

250

began passionately loving every inch of her luscious body until her moans filled the room. This time when he came, she did too, and the glow of their union filled every nook and cranny of the room.

Afterwards Astara lay on the bed half asleep. She felt Enmarsikil get up, heard his bare feet slap against the stone floor towards his Dream Corner and then silence. She grabbed the edge of the comforter, brought it up over herself and snuggled into its warmth.

Later when she awakened, Enmarsikil was gone. She slid out of bed, grabbed her tunic and tugged it on. Astara noticed that his Dream Corner was still activated. Curious, she wandered over, climbed the steps, and sat cross-legged on the circular platform. The face of a woman stared out from a bubble. Astara frowned; the woman was not one of them.

With her gut beginning to churn, she reached out and touched the bubble. It immediately opened and played out Enmarsikil's meeting with Sud. She saw him lean in to kiss her and stopped the playback. Tears brimmed her lashes and her chest heaved.

Suddenly, the bed chamber door sprang open and Enmarsikil entered. Astara leapt off the platform, her fists clenched.

"How could you?" she demanded. "How could you go there and see another woman then come back to me?"

Enmarsikil shut and sealed the door then hurried forward. He lunged for her as Astara tried to pull away and caught her before she could fall. She opened her mouth again but he put his finger to her lips.

"Hear me," he said in his most commanding, authoritative voice. "This isn't what you think, and I mean to show it both to you and our siblings."

Tears trickled down her cheeks as Astara pulled her head back. "How could you plan to humiliate me like this?" she cried.

Enmarsikil shook his head. "Not humiliate you, Sweet. You know I would never do that. Educate you and the others. That woman was weaving a spell and our meeting was set up by the King."

Astara stared at him then relaxed in his arms.

"Come, I need to show you this," Enmarsikil insisted.

She turned her head away.

"I need to show you so that you feel what I felt and see what I saw," Enmarsikil said. "I promise, my vow to you remains intact, and you will see how differently women are treated in the Anunnaki world."

Astara slowly turned back toward him. "You promise nothing happened between you?"

Enmarsikil smiled reassuringly. "I guarantee it. A certain water

251

nymph showed up and broke the spell."

Her eyes widened and her face softened. "Ok."

Astara let him lead her to his Dream Corner. He sat down with his legs outstretched and nestled her between them with her back to his chest.

"Now," he whispered in her ear, "I'm going to show you this. Tap into me and join my experience."

Astara held his free arm tightly around her waist while he reached out with the other and started the sequence from the beginning.

At first, she laughed. "All those beds and flowers. I'm surprised you didn't run straight past her."

"Just watch," he admonished.

Now Astara noticed the woman's attire or lack thereof and Enmarsikil's natural attraction. When Sud bowed, Astara felt very uncomfortable.

"I honestly wanted to look away," Enmarsikil confessed, "but my body developed a mind of its own."

"Why?" Astara wondered.

"Given the size of Anu's harem, which are all the women he's taken as wives besides his queen, I suspect the Anunnaki part of me is wired quite differently from the Multi-Dims for sex and arousal."

Astara frowned. "Oh."

"Now, watch the area just off to the side of her around her head," he instructed. "The dimensions around her get very muddy."

Astara knit her brows and pursed her lips as she watched. "What is that that keeps reaching out to you?"

"Sud was wearing a very potent mix of pheromones guaranteed to cause male arousal and make a man forget himself," Enmarsikil explained.

"How dare she!" Astara cried indignantly.

"She was trained," he told her. "This behavior and sex with the designated man was expected of her."

Astara's mouth dropped open in shock. "But why?"

"She is a lesser royal who would like to marry someone of pure royal blood in order to gain status," Enmarsikil replied. "Status means a lot to the Anunnaki, particularly the women, because it dictates for them the amount of personal freedom and self-determination they are afforded. But for Sud, in order to achieve that, she needed to garner King Anu's favor, and this is what he required her to do."

"By manipulating you?" Astara asked incredulously.

"Actually, the idea was for her to seduce me in order to force me into a royal marriage," he replied.

252

"But...you already have a mate!" she protested.

"Something I reminded him repeatedly," Enmarsikil assured her. "Now, watch."

As they viewed the continuing drama, the bushes between Enmarsikil and the fountain tossed about and the branches parted. The fountain came clearly into view at which point he paused the playback.

"You see what's coming out of that basin?"

Astara nodded, her eyes tearing. "My water nymph."

"She broke the spell over me and the seduction ended."

He closed the bubble.

"So why do the others need to see this?" Astara wanted to know.

Enmarsikil wrapped his arms around her. "Because I discovered that there are sides to the Anunnaki nature that reside in us that we haven't yet explored. We are naive to those aspects of ourselves and are ripe for manipulation by the Anunnaki. It was hard work keeping my wits about me while I was at the palace," he confessed. "I was too inexperienced, too ignorant of their ways and I felt very vulnerable and naive. "

"So how did you fight it?" Astara asked.

"With knowledge," he replied. "Mother had taught me how to sift the dimensions around people to learn their thoughts and true intentions."

Astara turned sideways and gazed up at him. "I never had anything to worry about, did I?"

Enmarsikil smiled and shook his head. "Now, her dress on the other hand reminded me of what you wore for the dance. I'm still not sure if I was reacting to Sud or remembering you."

Astara bit her lower lip. "Would you show me how you felt at the dance so I can experience it?"

Enmarsikil smiled, drew her back against him and opened up one of his favorite bubbles. She gasped when she realized he'd stared down her cleavage. And she'd never realized how desperately aroused he was when they'd done the crotch grind. As it was, his hands were presently wandering over her breasts again.

"D-do you like feeling like that and seeing me like that?" she asked, gasping as he hit a good spot.

"Oh yes," he moaned low in her ear. "When I see your breasts, I want to fondle them, and seeing your body attired so fetchingly makes me ache for you."

"We'd spend more time in here than anywhere else," she protested lightly.

"I have yet to hear you complain," he replied, turning her so she faced him. "Put me in you. We'll make a memory bubble together right here."

She didn't have to be asked twice though later when they finally got dressed, Astara kept turning the dress concept over and over in her mind.

"Hm, maybe," she murmured picking up his long coat to go see if her sisters could help repair it.

Refreshed and invigorated, Enmarsikil headed out to his gardens and fish ponds. He spotted Aiya and Bilnammul working in one of their experimental beds. A small, blond-haired toddler was with them examining bugs in the soil and on the leaves. He caught his breath for a moment remembering Astara's long ago question about babies and pregnancy. For a moment he felt a pang knowing how much she would enjoy such a little one of her own. For that matter, the sisters seemed equally engaged with their youngest sibling.

Enmarsikil walked on finally coming to the bridge. He first noted the stray leaves floating on the surface of the pond and scooped them out onto dry land. After that, it was easy to spot the fish from the bridge. He spread a handful of pellets over the water and watched as they surfaced to feed.

He moved from pond-to-pond noting the fish he would soon have to move. Once they were all fed, Enmarsikil sat on his favorite bench and gazed out over the water allowing his thoughts to flow like the stream that fed the ponds.

The image of the little girl flashed into his mind as well as the humans the future Astara and Enmarsikil had brought with them. He knit his brows pensively realizing as hybrids they might not bear children, but it was obvious that the Anunnaki would overcome the issue of sterile hybrids so the humans could reproduce. He had never gotten that far in his genetic studies with Father Enki. That made him all the more curious.

He also recalled that Ginny's whole reason for traveling back in time to save the First Gens and to rescue Teacher's core. Because they were genetically capable of passing experiences to their offspring through changes in their DNA, he wondered if Father Enki was aware of that. What was apparent to Enmarsikil is that he and his siblings had two choices: to withdraw their genetic input from the human bloodline or to continue that project no matter what else the siblings chose to do.

He needed to find a way to have a conversation with his future self. Cycles ago, Enmarsikil had decided that none of them were venturing to
254

Ki without having a clear understanding of what they would face there. His elder self had experiences that he was ignorant of, but they were important and could guide them all. Though Enmarsikil was unsure how he would stretch forward in time to do that, he sensed Astara might be more attuned to her future self and she could be the key.

Rising to his feet, he headed back toward the labs and went to their suite. At first, he didn't see Astara anywhere and was ready leave for the Academy proper to seek her. The sudden swish of fabric from the other room made Enmarsikil pause. He walked to the archway and stopped in his tracks, his pulse pounding. Astara stood before her mirror in a dress.

It wasn't just any dress. Her sisters had actually wanted to have it ready for her to greet Enmarsikil on his return from Agade. It had a dark blue bodice that molded to the curves of her breasts and showed deep cleavage. Her midriff was bare, and his fingers itched to touch the exposed flesh. A low slung skirt of flimsy material sat just on her hips, its pattern mimicking the play of water. At the moment, Astara cast a dubious look at it until she caught sight of Enmarsikil's face behind her.

She turned slowly. "You like?"

He moved forward running his fingers along the scalloped front and down into her cleavage. He kissed her while he squeezed her breasts. When she came up for air, she whispered, "I'm not wearing anything under the skirt."

He was hard in an instant.

"I think I need a closer look at your attire," he murmured.

"On or off?" she asked slyly.

"Oh, both," he said grinning and squeezing her breasts.

"You're enjoying this way too much," she chuckled lightly.

"I plan to right now. Just do me one favor," he proposed.

"Hm?"

"Just walk away from me and come back."

Astara tilted her head to one side for a moment, then did as he'd asked. He watched as her hips rolled smoothly while she walked away from him, the filmy skirt swishing out around her feet. When she turned, it flowed around her legs outlining them in fabric. She sashayed back to him, her breasts swaying and bouncing with each step.

Enmarsikil licked his lips. "Ok, I know I was looking for you to tell you something, but I'd say you've made me completely forget anything except...wow...your hips, your breasts. You, woman, have the power to bring me to my knees."

At this, he dropped to his knees and mouthed over the exposed parts of her breasts and her stomach.

Astara held his head between her hands enjoying the attention.

"I will desperately try to remember what I was actually going to tell you," Enmarsikil promised, "but for now...oh Sweet...I need you."

With that, he rose, scooped her up and carried her to the bed reveling in her sensual beauty.

CHAPTER 32 - LAST PUZZLE PIECE

When Enmarsikil and Astara climbed out of bed this time, she purposely wore a gray tunic over black leggings, pulled on her boots and braided her hair down her back. He watched as he also dressed.

"On purpose?" he quipped as she turned toward him.

Astara nodded. "I'd like you to remember what you wanted to tell me."

He nodded and chuckled. "Let's see. I'd finished feeding the fish."

She held out her hand to him. "Why don't we take a walk."

Enmarsikil gladly took her hand, left the Research Wing and wandered through the gardens with her. None of the sisters were about now but he paused at one bed with his brows knit. He pointed at thin air, tilted his head up to look at the treetops and continued walking. Astara watched him as she followed. They crossed the bridge, got to the bench overlooking the last pond, and Enmarsikil sat down. All of a sudden his eyes widened and he jumped right back up.

"You remembered?" she asked.

"Yes. Yes I did. I want to contact my future self," Enmarsikil explained. "I'm rather foggy on how it happened before. I was hoping you'd remember."

Astara brightened. "My future self told me how to contact her.

I've been repeating the instructions to myself for ages so I wouldn't forget."

"Oh good! I knew I could count on you. What do we do?" he asked.

"Well, we can sit on the bench and get comfortable," Astara suggested. "After that it's what I do."

He nodded. "Ok. Are you up for trying it?"

Astara nodded, took a seat and patted the bench beside her. He sat down and she took his hand.

"Just close your eyes and relax," she instructed. "I'm going to call her and, either we'll go there or she'll come here."

Enmarsikil nodded and closed his eyes.

"Future me, future me, future me," Astara chanted softly.

The wind tossed their hair and the world quieted around them. Suddenly, a portal seemed to open before them, and they felt themselves be sucked in and hurled down a long tunnel whose sides were streaked with electric blue and green. Before they knew it, the motion stopped abruptly.

Astara opened her eyes to find them standing under a trellis covered with red climbing roses. They faced a circular garden with a lantern in its center and a wrought iron bench off to their right. Bushes swept along the right side in an arc while four flower beds made up the interior around the white gravel walkway.

"Where are we?" she wondered.

Enmarsikil immediately brought up a protective bubble around each of them. "My guess is you brought us to Ki."

"Yes, but where?"

As they turned around, they spotted a house behind them, and Astara's eyes lifted up to the deck above. Her fact lit up with recognition.

"It's Ginny!" she cried and headed toward the deck.

Enmarsikil followed a little more slowly.

When Ginny spotted them, she called inside the house. Moments later, Ted walked out onto the deck to join them.

"I don't think I actually thought you'd visit," Ginny said.

"We didn't know we were going to," Astara confessed. "I just did what my future self told me to do."

"But is this after Teacher's core was retrieved?" Enmarsikil pressed to make certain.

Ginny and Ted both nodded affirmatively.

Enmarsikil glanced back into the house. "Is my older self here?"

"They both are," Ginny replied. "We'll let them come forward."

Ginny and Ted closed their eyes and in seconds their countenances changed. Then the familiar forms of Astara and Enmarsikil stepped out of their human counterparts and stood off to one side. Ginny and Ted opened their eyes again.

Younger Enmarsikil looked straight at his older self. "I need to know what went wrong here on Ki," he told him. "What do you wish you had done differently?"

The elder Enmarsikil studied his younger self for a moment. "You are so different from how I remember myself. Is Teacher here with you?"

Astara shook her head. "We haven't seen him for many cycles now. But we've all been so busy designing projects, we haven't paid attention."

Older Enmarsikil frowned. "Projects?"

"Things like how to refine the gold for the atmosphere, how to use our powers to create transport vehicles," younger Enmarsikil described. "We're even working on a space transport vehicle."

"And he even went to King Anu to learn about our Anunnaki heritage," Astara piped up.

The older couples' eyes widened in surprise.

"The changes have really started taking place," Older Astara breathed.

"Yes, but how are you retaining form here?" Older Enmarsikil asked.

"I put up special biofields around each of us," younger Enmarsikil replied.

Older Enmarsikil nodded. "There are some things I do wish I'd done differently."

The younger couple leaned forward, eager to hear what he had to say.

The older Enmarsikil stood quietly for a while searching his memories. Finally, he took a seat in a chair beside Ted.

"One priority is the Pact Teacher made with the Anunnaki," he began. "It never seemed to work as intended especially where Enki's son, Marduk, was concerned."

The younger Enmarsikil furrowed his brow. "King Anu did tell me he plans to send both Marduk and Ninurta to Ki as soon as they are of age because of how competitive they are."

"Yes, well, their competition gets way worse down here," the older Astara said. "Ninurta is respectful but Marduk will stop at nothing in

259

order to gain an edge over the Enlilites."

"Indeed," the older Enmarsikil agreed. "After he abducted our siblings on several occasions, I was forced to confront him."

His younger self's eyebrows raised sharply in alarm.

"I made him allergic to our kind and shortened his telomeres thereby shortening his life," the older Enmarsikil said. "He died on Ki."

The older Astara shook her head. "If the Pact were to be believed, the first time he tried to harm one of us, he should have died instantly. Instead, so much harm was done to so many and he suffered no consequences."

"That's where a lot of negative experiences began that altered human DNA when your genetics were entered into our bloodline. The memories of these experiences were passed to us," Ginny explained.

"So, if Teacher cannot guarantee the lethal clause of the Pact, pretend it doesn't exist and watch the Anunnaki closely," the elder Enmarsikil admonished.

"Should we even come to Ki at all then?" the younger Enmarsikil wondered.

His elder self glanced at Ted and Ginny. "At this point, major changes in your timeline have already occurred. You've already experienced so much that we never did."

"You're together...and happy," older Astara said, her eyes misting. "We were never either of those things."

The younger Enmarsikil reached for his mate's hand and held it firmly

"But it's one thing to change your own trajectory, and quite another to change that of a whole other species," his elder self pointed out. "You will have to Vision and see how the two choice paths play out. But I suspect that if our kind never chooses to aid the humans, they will never break free of the Anunnaki's hold over them."

"There's also the fact that these humans," older Astara said gesturing to Ted and Ginny, "saved the First Generation. To abandon them to the Anunnaki would be a poor way to repay them for their efforts."

The younger Enmarsikil's face grew troubled as he listened. "Then, how should we approach coming to Ki? And for what purpose other than to incorporate our DNA with that of humans?" he asked.

"Offer your expertise in different matters on a contractual base," his older self said. "If the Anunnaki break the contract, stop working with that group and move on."

"And live in groups in your own towns," the older Astara said.

260

"Don't rely on the Anunnaki for anything. And whatever you do, you two live close to the other siblings so you can help them when they need it."

"When the time comes to add your DNA to the human gene pool and rest in the Facility, make sure to lead the chosen humans to remote areas and teach them how to free themselves from Anunnaki control before you leave," the elder Enmarsikil instructed.

"Facility?" his younger self asked.

"Teacher hasn't told you?"

The younger Enmarsikil shook his head.

"We don't die like other species," older Astara explained, "but we can deplete even the energy we gain from powering up. Then we need to rest in a special Facility while our reserves rebuild."

"Ki is not a good place for it," the elder Enmarsikil added. "In this present era, humans have the capacity to find and destroy it and us with them. That's something we never thought was possible."

The younger couple sat back in their chairs, the wind knocked out of them. Then Enmarsikil started coughing and realized the biofilms were breaking down and leaking.

"We've got to go...now," he stated.

Astara tightened her grip on his hand. "Return now!" she declared, and they left Earth in a blink.

They found themselves sitting on the bench outdoors, a light breeze rustling their hair. They opened their eyes and sighed with relief glad to be back by Enmarsikil's fish ponds.

"That was weighty information," Astara remarked rising from her seat.

Enmarsikil looked troubled. "Father hasn't spoken about a Pact or the need for a Facility."

Astara looked out across the ponds. "I wonder how much else he hasn't spoken about that he planned to spring on you at the last minute."

"You sound so distrustful," he pointed out.

She put her hands on her hips and turned toward him. "Do you trust a man who leaves out important information and expects you to follow him blindly?" she countered.

Enmarsikil put his head in his hands resting his elbows on his knees. "It's as if everything I've known since childhood has been turned upside down."

Astara knelt beside him and wrapped her arms around him. "I'm truly sorry."

He took a deep breath and slowly rose to his feet. "C'mon. We should see how the others are faring."

He gave her a hand up and put his arm around her waist starting down the path toward the Research Wing. Suddenly, they heard footsteps behind them, turned and gasped. Their future selves as well as Ginny and Ted were following them.

"I was concerned about how much you weren't aware of," the future Enmarsikil said once they all caught up to the pair. "I thought it might be wise to find out what's going on."

The younger man nodded appreciatively, and the group moved on together. As they neared the lab entrance, Zupatu and Gugbubulu came dashing out the door. They skidded to a halt in front of them.

"We did it!" they cried in unison before registering the future pair and Ginny and Ted.

"Did what?" the younger Enmarsikil asked.

"Who...what?" Zupatu asked looking from the elder pair to the humans and back.

"I'll explain later," Enmarsikil assured them. "Now, what have you done?"

"Built a space vehicle," Gugbubulu said excitedly.

"Functioning?" Enmarsikil asked, his interest building.

"Absolutely," Zupatu affirmed.

"Now, this I've got to see," Enmarsikil said leading his small posse after the brothers.

They wound their way through the Academy exiting into the large courtyard at the center of the main buildings. In the middle of the courtyard stood a large, smooth surfaced, rounded, dish shaped craft that rose to the height of the upper floors of the dorms. The two Enmarsikils gazed at it with much the same amazed expression while the Astaras ran forward to check it out.

Younger Enmarsikil walked forward, stretched out his hand and touched the side of the shiny silver disc. A door in the upper part of its side opened and a ramp extended down to the ground.

"C'mon in," Nindulur invited from the doorway.

While Ginny and Ted stayed on the ground, the Enmarsikils and Astaras ascended the ramp and cautiously entered the spacious interior. Nindulur showed them the main control center for navigating and piloting the ship. Zupatu took them through the interior, and the Astaras checked out the spacious living quarters and galley.

"What is the propulsion?" Enmarsikil asked.

The brothers took them to the engine room to show him the

containment field.

"We trapped a star," the brothers declared proudly.

"But...where did it come from?" the elder Enmarsikil asked perplexed.

"It's the byproduct of powering up," Zupatu said.

"Yes, all we need are several mated pairs on board, and we have a continual energy supply," Gugbubulu added.

The elder Enmarsikil staggered back. "I never imagined we were capable of so much."

"And to think, if we'd known, we would never have had to be crammed into Anunnaki transports," the older Astara mourned.

"Want to be part of her first flight?" Nindulur asked.

The two couples nodded and made their way back to the control center. Nindulur and Gugbubulu worked together and fired up the engines. The craft slowly rose off the ground. They made a couple of adjustments, and the craft suddenly leapt into the sky, passed through the atmosphere and was soon hovering miles above the planet.

"We really did it," Enmarsikil breathed then frowned. "Take us down," he requested. "It's time to call everybody together."

The jubilant crew took the craft once around the planet before landing in the courtyard.

Inside the Academy, Teacher heard the roar of engines slowly growing louder. Around his unseen form, the siblings raced toward the courtyard. Weary without his energy-sustaining connection to his own people, he turned back toward his suite and hauled himself inside. With a heavy sigh, he collapsed onto the floor in front of his Visioning Sphere.

As the door to the craft opened, enthusiastic cheers came from their siblings waiting on the ground. They were finally ready to soar.

CHAPTER 33 - MANY PATHS TO CHOOSE

"Gather all the siblings into the Great Lecture Hall," Enmarsikil yelled above the cheers.

The siblings slowly stopped applauding and started filing inside the Academy.

"What are you planning?" his elder self asked.

Enmarsikil put his hands on his hips and studied the ground for a moment. "All of the projects are divergent. Teacher had wanted them to intersect, but there is no plan, no guiding theme to them." He raised his head. "I think it is time they know about humans, that they know about their Anunnaki heritage, that we develop a unifying theme that includes all talents and abilities."

"That is good and necessary," his elder self replied, "but it concerns me that Teacher has told you so little and has been absent for so long."

Astara frowned. "His absence hasn't been unpleasant," she remarked.

"Perhaps," the elder Enmarsikil replied, "but it is abnormal."

"So, what do we do?" his younger self asked.

"Take Ted and Ginny with you and address the siblings. Find out about their projects," the elder Enmarsikil replied. "Stall for as long as you can. My Astara and I will see what has happened to Teacher."

The younger man nodded and led the two humans plus his Astara inside.

"What do you think happened?" the older Astara asked.

"I don't know," her Enmarsikil replied taking her hand, "but we're going to find out."

They jogged off together entering the Academy and heading toward Teacher's quarters. While nothing and no one moved in the corridor outside his door, a strange sensation or perhaps lack of sensation made them pause. With a worried glance at each other, they hurried forward and knocked on Teacher's door. When they got no reply, they cautiously pushed it open and tip-toed in. They almost missed the huddle of black robes on the floor beside the Visioning Orb. Astara pointed and they rushed forward.

Enmarsikil knelt down and put his hand on one shoulder. "Father?"

The head turned, dark rimmed eyes peering out from a pale face framed by dark, stringy black hair. "They have forsaken me."

Enmarsikil looked at Astara, concern etched across his brow. "We must help him or it will be too late."

In the Great Lecture Hall, the siblings were all gathered. The younger Enmarsikil led his Astara, Ted and Ginny in through a lower door. They approached the platform in the well and hesitantly walked forward.

Enmarsikil gazed up at the animated faces of his siblings and swallowed hard. He'd demonstrated so many things for them on that very platform, but he'd never pretended to be their leader. Now, he had no choice. He took a deep breath, put his fingers between his teeth and whistled loudly. The hubbub died off as his siblings turned to look at him.

"Uh, hi. We haven't all gotten together in quite awhile," Enmarsikil began. "I just took a ride in a space vehicle."

Those gathered oohed.

"I figure if those teams are that far along, some of the rest of you must be pretty far along on your projects, too."

"Where's Teacher?" Satu yelled from a middle row seat.

"I don't exactly know," Enmarsikil confessed. "But we're working at finding out. In the meantime, what have the teams developed?"

For a few moments, a low buzz filled the auditorium. Finally, a group stood to talk about their project then another. Astara took notes for later reference while Enmarsikil glanced uneasily toward the doors.

At the rate they're going through this stuff, it won't be much longer till they're done, he thought.

Stall, came his elder self's reply inside his head. *Tell them about Agade.*

The younger Enmarsikil nodded to himself, confident he had quite the adventure and hard-earned knowledge to share with the others.

Back in Teacher's quarters, the older Enmarsikil knelt beside the huddled figure. He placed one hand over Teacher's heart and the other over his forehead. He dropped deep into himself then let his own energy flow into the older man. At last, the crouched figure straightened up, and Enmarsikil removed his hands. He studied the man's face intently.

"You said 'they' have forsaken you," Enmarsikil said. "Who are you speaking of?"

Nasdatal took a deep, unsteady breath. "My people."

Enmarsikil frowned. "The siblings?"

"Well, them too," came the terse reply.

"Who else?" Enmarsikil pressed. "The Multi-Dims?"

Nasdatal nodded.

Enmarsikil's eyes widened. "But why?"

Nasdatal sighed heavily. "It seems I've been too controlling, too heavy handed...and now our children run amok without guidance."

Enmarsikil sat on his heels. "Really? You think so little of them... of us?"

"Did you know they've created a spacecraft better than anything the Anunnaki devised?" Astara queried.

"We took its first flight," Enmarsikil concurred. "Powered by paired mates...a nearly endless supply of energy."

Nasdatal looked up at him, stunned. "They did that? On their own?"

Enmarsikil nodded.

"And his younger self went to Agade to learn from King Anu," Astara continued.

"He brought back some key insights that, if I'd only known them," Enmarsikil mourned, "so much suffering could have been avoided. Our people could have fared so much better."

Nasdatal studied his countenance, remorse darkening his own features.

"You ought to hear what the siblings have created, what young Enmarsikil learned," Astara urged.

"How? I was stripped of all but my powers of invisibility and they

266

have forsaken me," Nasdatal said collapsing inward again.

As they sat there, four faint lights began glowing brighter in an arc around them. Gradually, Marne, Emissary, Zalkur and Giramusen came into view.

"We have been with you all the time," Emissary said.

Nasdatal glanced up. "But...I couldn't feel you, sense you. You were dead to me."

Emissary stretched out his hand sending a wave of silver light toward him. Zalkur sent him a brown wave while Giramusen's was orange red.

Nasdatal breathed deeply. "Ah, now I feel you again. All but...." and he turned, "Marne. Are you still so angry?"

Clearly, the internal battle that waged inside her was visible on her face. "I will reconsider once you seek forgiveness."

Nasdatal hung his head sorrowfully.

Enmarsikil hooked one hand under Nasdatal's left arm while Astara grabbed the right.

"Come, we shall take you with us in a cloaking plane so you can see and hear for yourself," Enmarsikil told him.

The Multi-Dims stepped forward, enclosed them all in a bubble and instantly transported them to the Great Lecture Hall where they remained invisible while they watched and listened.

The young Enmarsikil stood out prominently in the well orchestrating the wonders his siblings' projects had created. His elder self and Astara's faded into view standing beside Ted and Ginny, who listened with rapt attention.

"Ok, so let me get this straight," Enmarsikil said. "Zupatu, you and your group have a luxury space vehicle ready for intergalactic travel."

Zupatu nodded.

"Kumzubar and Marki's group have already begun tests of their gold dust on the hole in the atmosphere."

"This patch probably won't hold," Marki admitted. "Next pass near the sun, it'll get burned off. But we think we know what's needed to fix that. The next patch will hold indefinitely."

"And Latakuses you think you've found a planet that can be terraformed," Enmarsikil read from Astara's notes.

"We have a test grid initiated now," Latakuses replied. "As long as we keep a biofilm over ourselves, we can work there."

"What's the goal?" Enmarsikil queried.

"Nothing short of a planet of our own," Latakuses replied.

"But what about Ki?" Nita asked. "Have any element samples been found and can we adjust to them?"

"I brought back the samples Father Ea had sent," Enmarsikil assured them. "I just don't know what phase of testing they're in."

"Why do we want to bother with Ki?" one disgruntled person asked.

Enmarsikil glanced back at Ted and Ginny. "There are some things that have happened you have yet to hear about," he told them. "Adventures and a people who might change your mind."

The elder Enmarsikil stepped forward. "I am from a possible future. What I know and what has changed already will surprise you."

"I think, once you hear the whole story, we can find a way to dovetail all of your projects into something more cohesive," the younger Enmarsikil announced. "And along the way we can pay a debt of gratitude."

Murmurs ran around the room.

In the invisibility bubble, Nasdatal watched the proceedings becoming more impressed all the time. "I would never have imagined they were capable of achieving so much," he remarked.

"And if you had maintained such strict control over them, they never would have created so much with the skill of geniuses," Emissary replied.

"And my son," Nasdatal remarked in awe, "he is so confident and alive. He's a leader without the need for control, and the vitality that just radiates from him...."

"Is due to his mate," Marne said quietly.

Nasdatal's face softened. "I thought she would make him wild and irresponsible. Instead, she has infused him with a sense of himself I could never give him."

"She believes in him and his ability to achieve what others can only dream of," Giramusen stated.

The younger Enmarsikil glanced at his future self. "Where do I begin?"

"Tell them about Agade and their plans for Ki," his future self encouraged.

Enmarsikil put his hands on his hips, his head down and his brows knit. Finally, he turned toward his siblings and raised his head to look at

268

them.

"There is so much to tell you," he began. "It's hard to know where to start. As excited as I've been to see your projects grow and develop, there have been things I was keen to investigate as well."

He paused for a moment to collect his thoughts.

"We've grown up here at the Academy," he said gesturing toward the walls. "We've been quite sheltered actually. And our caregivers and teachers have all been Multi-Dims. I know we've heard the story of our origins before, but I got to see the very lab in which my own DNA sequence was created and the hospital nursery that was once lined with basinets filled with hybrid babies."

Surprised murmurs rippled about the large hall like waves.

"Remember, brothers and sisters, we have two sets of parents. Half our DNA is Multi-Dim but the other half is Anunnaki. We know and understand our Multi-Dim natures well but, with Father Ea...uh, Enki now...with him on Ki and his brother, Enlil, as well, I realized our opportunity to understand the drives and motivations gifted us by the royal Anunnaki blood remained a mystery to us. But with some of you talking about terraforming worlds and others eager to see Ki, I knew I had to find a way to gain a more intimate knowledge of our Anunnaki heritage," Enmarsikil concluded.

"Your lives and the lives of beings not yet developed may very well depend upon how well we comprehend these latent drives and ambitions," the elder Enmarsikil seconded.

A solemn hush fell over the room.

"I went to Agade," Enmarsikil confessed, "alone. And I approached King Anu as his grandson, for so I am. I respectfully asked him to educate me in the ways of the Anunnaki and to teach me their heritage. I nearly didn't find a way to return. But I learned a lot, and what I discovered is important as we create a cohesive goal for our efforts. Let me share my adventure with you."

There was a general shuffle around the room as siblings leaned forward prepared to hang on his every word.

"Their world and culture is nothing like ours," Enmarsikil warned them. "And if we're smart, we'll keep it that way."

"It's a little hard to talk about my experiences," Enmarsikil admitted to his siblings. "Once we were paired, I began to sense where there were differences between ourselves and our Multi-Dim parents. I had been forewarned that the Anunnaki might prove to be dangerous. More on that later. For now, given that we have Anunnaki genes as well

269

as those from the Multi-Dims, I decided to go to Agade while the metal workers were examining ore in the closed mines close to the city."

He brought up a large, holographic field and initiated a holovideo.

"I had the feeling sensors in the mines would alert the Anunnaki to our presence," Enmarsikil continued. "But I never imagined that Agade would send armed guards."

Everyone watched the guards surround the small mining group training their weapons on the unarmed party.

"I was hopeful that I could jam their weapons, so I went with them," he continued. "It was the only way I knew I was going to get to see King Anu. I approached him as a grandson desiring to learn of his wisdom, and he was cordial and welcoming at the outset."

The scenes continued at a quickened pace.

"What I learned from him were the mind and heart of the Anunnaki," Enmarsikil said turning off the holovideo. "Power is their primary objective. There are levels of power with King Anu at the very top. Everyone beneath him either wants his position of power or to be in a position of power close to him. He must be prepared to fight, even his owns sons, in order to keep his kingship. He has chosen not to fight them, but to send Father Enki and his brother, Enlil, to Ki. Even their sons are eager to compete for power, and they are less than a shar older than me. The King told me that when they are of age, he will send them to Ki as well to prevent another civil war on Nibiru."

Confused murmurs rippled around the hall.

"I don't understand," Barlumgeme finally called out. "What makes kingship so special?"

"Power," Enmarsikil replied. "The power to make laws and have say over the lives of others. Then there are the trappings of luxury that must be maintained in order to appear powerful. Rich furnishings in lavish palaces, the finest clothes and food. Servants, slaves to maintain the premises. And in the King's case, he keeps hundreds of women as concubines, essentially secondary wives."

A cry went up from the women in the room.

"How does he manage to power up with all those women?" Satu asked.

"Or bond with them?" Bilnammul wondered.

"Anunnaki don't power up," Enmarsikil explained. "They produce children, in King Anu's case enough to repopulate Agade with almost nothing but his own progeny. And the women aren't seeking a bond. They seek status because then they will be better cared for."

270

"This is outrageous!" Kienelil fumed.

"Yes," Enmarsikil said simply. "It is. And the women are taught special measures to take to seduce men in order to marry better and have better lives. The King had a lesser royal woman attempt to seduce me."

A general uproar erupted. When it subsided, Enmarsikil continued.

"The most important thing to them, however, is bloodlines. I learned that though Father Enki is older and initially born the heir to the throne, because his mother was only a concubine when Enlil was born to the queen, his bloodline contained double royal blood and was pure. Thus, Enlil became the heir in Father Enki's place. With all of the men closest to the throne off world, I found myself in a predicament. My bloodline is pure since Enki and Ninmah are royal siblings. King Anu was prepared to use force to keep me at the palace as his new heir."

At this the hubbub exploded and almost refused to die down.

"How could he do that?" Peenzermi cried in outrage.

"With guards and a watcher with me all the time," Enmarsikil replied. "It wasn't until I convinced him to take me to Father Enki's old lab where I showed him my DNA sequence that I was able to formulate a plan to escape. Still, if Nindulur, Marki and the others hadn't returned for me, I might still be there under lock and key."

"This highlights some important things," the elder Enmarsikil said stepping forward.

"Why is he here?" Nita yelled down.

"Patience. We will explain soon," the contemporary Enmarsikil soothed.

"What is more important to remember," his elder self began again, "is that the Anunnaki are not to be trusted implicitly. Power and status are their driving motivations. Offer to help them attain power, and they'll accept. But you have to be on guard against them enslaving you once they know what you can do. They think nothing of using force to get their way, and women are second class citizens to them."

"We inherited their genes and some of their makeup," the younger Enmarsikil reminded them, "but we must neither allow ourselves to become like them nor be bound to them. Where their culture is hierarchical, we must maintain the cooperative nature of our beings."

"So, let's leave Nibiru and never go to Ki," Pukisimar of the Teraforming project suggested.

Nita stood. "I, for one, know I must go to Ki as do the others in my project group."

An argument immediately broke out between the Teraformers and

Nita's group. In response, the Enmarsikils sank into deep internal spaces finally establishing a calming field they expanded throughout the room. In minutes the argument died down.

"It's in this next piece that I will explain why my future self and Astara's are here and introduce you to another Anunnaki-hybridized race. This younger race has already risked much to help us even though their kind are now in grave danger," the younger Enmarsikil said.

Silence fell over the room.

"Let us tell you how Time has been rewound," the elder Enmarsikil said. "This is where our friends and descendents, as it were, are pivotal."

The elder Astara brought Ted and Ginny forward to stand beside her Enmarsikil.

"By now, Ninmah has traveled to Ki to set up medical facilities for the Anunnaki," she told them. "At some point in the future, she will accept Enki's offer to help him in his lands. There they will develop a slave race by creating a hybrid from an existing hominid species and their own."

"Enki forever dabbled with this new hybrid until the species was as intelligent as the Anunnaki and able to procreate," the older Enmarsikil related. "But they were also given a gene that created a slave mentality in this species so they would remain loyal to their Anunnaki overlords. The Anunnaki stopped mining for themselves, raising food for themselves and even warring on their own behalf. Instead, they had this new species do the mining, gardening, hunting and even armed and trained them so they could fight wars on their behalf."

"Originally, Teacher switched our primary mission from healing the hole in Nibiru's atmosphere to helping the Anunnaki with their endeavors on Ki. As such, different generations were designated to work with specific royal Anunnaki. However, there was also a second mission," the elder Astara said. "At some point when all our energy became too low, we would enter a secure Facility to rest and recharge. The idea was that those on Enmarsikil's team would awaken at a future point to complete this second mission - that of freeing the human species from Anunnaki mind control and restoring their original heritage to them."

"But Teacher saw the probability that the Facility on Ki might be breached and our lives destroyed, so he, Enki and I gathered humans from all parts of the globe and entered the DNA sequence of each sibling into the human race. The idea was they would lie dormant in humans until a time of need when our genetics would push to the surface."

"Ted and Ginny are those humans in whom our bloodline has

finally awakened," Astara said. "But there's a problem with the process on a number of levels."

"We had nothing to really inherit from our genetic parents," the elder Enmarsikil stated. "No past experiences from anyone to impact our own genetic expression."

"But it's different for humans," his Astara said. She turned and nodded to Ginny.

"For us," Ginny said gesturing toward Ted and herself, "the experiences of our parents, grandparents, and even ancient relatives leave an imprint on our genes. This means that as your peoples' DNA awakens in us, their experiences impact us. Generally, they seem to draw mirror experiences into our own lifetimes. When your peoples' awareness awakens in us, it is to people who are traumatized and damaged and not able to fully express their potential, let alone yours."

"Yes, but how is this important to us?" Mudu demanded.

The future Astara took a deep breath. "From our timeline our First Generation was entirely lost because they went with Ea to Ki before anyone realized our attunement to Ki's elements was off. They couldn't hold form and dissipated into their elemental base as soon as they landed on Ki. For the rest of us, what was supposed to be a partnership relationship with the Anunnaki became a near slave state, particularly for the women. And when Enki's oldest son learned of our uniqueness, he sought to understand our differences to exploit for his own purposes...generally through abducting siblings and experimentation. The experiences were horrific."

"And those experiences have translated to us," Ginny told them. "Few of us are capable of being effective. Yet, we need to be more now than ever because it would appear the Anunnaki are the masters behind the political puppets around the world and the game is about set for another world war. Any way you look at it, we humans lose."

"So, how does this explain how present and future are together here in the same room?" Satu challenged.

"Choice points," the younger Enmarsikil replied. "We were told of poor choices that Teacher once made that set up the life circumstances they experienced." He pointed to the future couple.

"Ginny was the one who knew a way to travel back in time," the elder Astara said. "We watched as Teacher shared his story, and she discovered a pivotal clue. Teacher ejected a clone from his universe, not his core, and without that his Visioning was clouded, his decisions were ineffective and he was unable to energize choice points. As a result, we suffered. I, along with four siblings, retrieved Teacher's core."

"Once Teacher had his core back, he was able to go back in time to major choice points, decide differently, and energize those moments so the parallel universe with the defective decision was jettisoned and the new parallel locked into place," the elder Enmarsikil explained.

"Because of that first act," his Astara continued, "the First Generation did not go to Ki with Father Ea. You are whole, safe, and here."

"And back on Earth," Ted spoke up, "the presence you'd had in our lives has changed. We'd built a sanctuary to attract any First Gens still capable of interacting even in elemental form. We could always feel their presence, but now...that space is empty and your presence is sorely missed."

"Particularly Satu's pranks," Ginny added. "The physical pranks helped us know your presence was real and not just something our imaginations conjured up."

Satu's' face registered shock.

"So the future Enmarsikil and Astara are here because...?" Nita pressed.

"We are closing in on another pivotal choice point," the older Enmarsikil replied. "In this case there are a lot of factors involved, but we hope that the end results mean we are personally changed and the nightmares of our experiences are finally gone."

"And we hope to repay the humans for the risk they took to aid us while freeing them from the slave mentality imposed on them by the Anunnaki," his Astara added.

"But...how?" Marki wondered.

"By choosing differently," the elder Enmarsikil said. "And that will be your personal responsibility. We can only await the outcome."

He turned to his younger self. "Are you ready?"

The young man drew a deep breath and nodded.

"Good luck then," he replied.

Then the human couple and the future couple huddled together. Ginny called out "Return" and they vanished in a blink.

Enmarsikil took a few minutes to collect his thoughts and give this latest information time to sink in. Finally, he clasped his hands together.

"I've listened very closely to the goals and accomplishments for each of your groups. But as I carefully consider them, I think it is possible to create a common goal and plan that will weave in all these disparate things and create cohesion amongst us. And given what I saw amongst the

274

Anunnaki, I prize our ability to cooperate and cross pollinate ideas with equal excitement about more than anything."

"I think we'd like to hear your ideas," Mudizi called from the top row.

"Then I will do my best to bring all of these pieces together," Enmarsikil agreed.

In the concealing plane, Nasdatal shook his head. "I just never imagined. I am speechless."

"They are our children," Zalkur remarked. "How could they be any different?"

CHAPTER 34 - EVICTED

Enmarsikil stood in the well of the Great Lecture Hall and scanned the shocked, tired faces in the tiers above him. At that moment, a weariness hit him and he sagged where he stood. He shook his head to clear it.

"We need rest," he announced quietly. "You've heard a lot that is disquieting and I, for one, am weary. Let's disband for the moment and come back together in a while."

He turned toward Astara while his siblings slowly rose and made their way toward the exits. The couple made their way to the Research Wing and their suite, and Enmarsikil immediately started removing his tunic once inside.

"What do you feel like?" Astara asked.

"A long, hot shower and...you...or a nap...or both," he replied mischievously.

Astara joined him in disrobing as they maneuvered their way into the bathroom. A short time later they were soaping up under a steady, soothing stream.

Enmarsikil held her soapy body close to his. "It never ceases to amaze me," he said sampling her lips, "that no matter how tired I am, one look at you and I am so turned on."

She grabbed his buttocks and squeezed, and his manhood pulsed against her tummy fully hard.

"Maybe we should take this elsewhere," she murmured.

"Oh, I'm sure we should," he replied moving so the water washed the soap away.

They stepped out and began drying off. Astara knelt down and took his erection between her breasts. Enmarsikil gritted his teeth.

"'You don't want to make it to the bed, do you?" he groaned.

"Perhaps not," she purred standing and pressing her breasts against his chest.

She lifted up one leg maneuvering into the crotch press from the now famous dance. But without clothes between them, the heat was exquisite and he could feel her increasing wetness.

Enmarsikil hooked his arm under her leg, cupped her buttocks and lifted her up. Then he slowly lowered Astara straight down onto his erection. Staggering to a nearby wall, he leaned her against it as he thrust. Before long, their abdomens were glowing and his release was near.

Panting, he set Astara on the floor and they made their way to the bed. After some special ministration from her, he was ready again, and this time their union lit up the room. The last thing Enmarsikil remembered before drifting off to sleep was being bathed in a soft, pastel pink and yellow light.

The sound of pounding entered his dream. In a dark, windowless room, Enmarsikil sought to discover the source of the noise. Suddenly, awareness came back to him in a rush of sound and light. He sprang upright in bed with a gasp.

The pounding came again from near at hand. This time a voice yelled his name. Rubbing his hand across his eyes, Enmarsikil leapt out of bed, grabbed his slacks, jammed his feet into the legs and hobbled to the door.

"Who is it?" he yelled watching Astara throw on her tunic out of the corner of his eye.

"It's Satu, man. Hurry up! There's an army coming."

Enmarsikil glanced at Astara who wore a concerned frown.

"We'll be right out," he assured Satu.

"What is an army?" Astara asked sliding into her leggings and pulling on her boots, "and why are they coming here?"

Enmarsikil grabbed a fresh tunic, yanked it over his head, drew the belt around his waist then jammed his feet into the boots.

"An army is soldiers with weapons," he explained.

"Has Anu come after you?" Astara worried.

"I don't know, but we're going to find out," he replied grabbing her hand and yanking the door open.

"They're approaching from Agade," Satu said as they jogged to the entrance to the Academy."

Nita and several others joined them.

"Marki and his men had been out in the field and spotted them," Nita said. "They rushed back to spread the word."

"Ok, here's where my team comes into play," Enmarsikil said thinking aloud as he ran. "Gather the team and those they're responsible for. Have them all meet on the plain before the Academy. Remember, defensive only unless I signal otherwise."

Satu and Nita nodded and the small group headed off in different directions to get their charges together. Enmarsikil and Astara hurried down the main corridor, out the front door, across the broad courtyard and through the main gate. They stood on a hillock from which they could see the sky darkening with the incoming, airborne army.

"Do you have any idea what they want?" Astara wondered.

"Not yet."

"Aren't you anxious?"

Enmarsikil shook his head. "He's vulnerable out here. He just brought the fight to me, and that was his mistake."

As they spoke, they could hear the thud of feet behind them as siblings filed into place. While they watched, the army set down and soldiers poured out with their weapons drawn and took up firing positions.

"Shields," Enmarsikil called, and his team created transparent interlocking shields to protect the others.

A smaller transport hovered toward the front. King Anu stepped off followed by a Sage, a Councilman and personal guards.

"King Anu," Enmarsikil called. "You've pursued me a long ways. State the nature of your business."

"It would seem you stole something from my research labs before you left the palace," Anu said evenly. "If you return it, I will waive punishment."

"I took a box with Teacher's mark upon it," Enmarsikil countered. "I stole nothing."

"Show me!" Anu demanded.

Enmarsikil glanced around. "Wish I still had it," he muttered.

From out of nowhere, Emissary appeared at his side with the box in hand. Enmarsikil took it gratefully. He turned and handed the box to Anu.

278

"As you can see, that is Teacher's specific mark on the box and the accompanying note is written from Father Enki directly to Teacher detailing the contents. It would seem your people were withholding it on purpose. I merely offered to make the designated delivery."

Anu showed the Sage and the Councilman. They turned it over and read the note muttering between themselves.

"It is as he says," the Councilman announced. "All charges are dismissed."

"Very well," Anu grumbled. "That issue is cleared up. But there is the issue where I had offered Sud's father a marriage pact between you and she," he stated looking straight at Enmarsikil. "You left without fulfilling that pact."

Astara stepped even with Enmarsikil and squared her shoulders.

"And who would this be?" Anu asked snidely.

"I would be his spouse," Astara replied evenly. "His.Only.Spouse. We marry for life and only take one mate."

"We had already signed our marriage contract and had been joined for several cycles," Enmarsikil added.

Emissary produced their marriage pact and handed it to the King. Again the Sage and the Councilman scrutinized the document carefully. Finally, they rolled it up and handed it back to Enmarsikil.

"It is dated much earlier than the proposal you made on his behalf and is airtight. It cannot be broken. It supersedes your offer to Sud's father by several cycles making yours null and void," the Sage told the King.

Anu stared at the ground, a vein in his neck pulsing. Finally, he looked up, his eyes narrowing. "There is one other matter," he said at last in a low growl. "The lease on this military base is up and I've come to reclaim it."

Worried cries sounded throughout the crowd of gathered hybrids, and Enmarsikil frowned anxiously.

"That contract was not made with me," he replied.

"No, it was not," Anu sneered. "It was made before your time... boy."

Invisible standing nearby, Teacher turned to Marne. "I beg of you. Return my last power and free me to help our children."

Marne hesitated for a moment then blew her breath across the palm of her hand. Blue and silver sparkles showered Teacher, and his stature grew until he was once again full size. In a blink, he became visible at

Enmarsikil's left side. Enmarsikil sighed with relief.

"I believe I am the one who made that contract with you," Teacher said evenly.

Emissary passed a scroll to his hand. Teacher read it and handed it to Anu.

"In my version it says the contract is for in perpetuity. That was defined to mean for the life of its inhabitants," Teacher stated.

"That contract was only ratified by a small sub-committee and not the full Council," the Councilman interposed. "The Council has voted to nullify the contract."

"You...are hereby evicted," Anu gloated.

Enmarsikil stood for a moment with the breeze tossing his hair. He could feel the panic and grief of his siblings. He could feel Astara's deep sadness.

"And where would you have us go?" he demanded.

"Anywhere," Anu replied with an expansive gesture.

Enmarsikil froze. It couldn't be simpler. He bit back a smile. A chortle bubbled up into his throat and he swallowed hard to suppress it.

"Please define 'anywhere'," Enmarsikil pressed in a loud voice.

Anu squared off to him, his nose nearly in his face. "Anywhere but here," he yelled pointing toward the Academy.

"Very well," Enmarsikil replied calmly. "Give us a cycle to pack and we shall be gone."

"You aren't giving up, are you?" Aiya cried.

Enmarsikil held up his hand for silence. "Follow me back into the Academy. We have much work to do but I assure you, where I am taking you, we'll be well cared for."

For the next few days all clothes and personal belongings were packed into bins. Any ripe fruit or vegetables were harvested and stowed. Experiments and results were placed in suspended animation.

On the last day, Astara found Enmarsikil in the garden. He was carefully digging up seedlings of her flower to take with him.

"What about your fish?" she asked watching him work.

"I have harvested their fertilized eggs and have done the same with the fowl. I will be able to reconstitute them later."

"Where are we going?" Astara whispered. "This is the only home any of us has known."

Enmarsikil acknowledged her concern. "The truth is, we've been severely overcrowded since the pairing and the projects."

Astara nodded. "It's true. It was too much trying to turn dorms into apartments."

"Where we're headed, that won't be a problem."

"And you won't tell me?" she begged.

"I will tell all of the siblings once we're out of the range of Anu's guards," Enmarsikil replied. "I don't want to take the chance of anyone following us."

Astara conceded with a sigh.

Enmarsikil carefully packed the seedlings with the rest of his research specimens, put their cases and their personal belongings on an air skid and maneuvered it out of the research wing toward the main courtyard. There, Nindulur and other foundational hybrids were building a craft layer-by-layer. The hold levels were complete and already being loaded. Enmarsikil added their belongings to those being stowed on board.

He stood with his hands on his hips observing the progress. *This won't be the only time we do this,* he sighed inwardly.

The upper decks were rising quickly and by the time the hold was completely packed, the siblings were boarding. It was a somber procession up the gangway with many crying as they went.

Enmarsikil put his arm comfortingly around Astara's shoulders. "It's going to be all right," he whispered. "I promise."

Teacher approached and beckoned to him. Enmarsikil gave Astara a squeeze then turned and followed.

"You know where you're going," Teacher surmised.

Enmarsikil gave him a sly grin. "The last place Anu would think of."

Teacher studied him a moment breaking out into a grin. "You've gotten wily in my absence. Good," he said nodding. "Keep your wits about you. You'll need them."

"What about you and the others?" Enmarsikil wondered.

"Emissary will be with you," Teacher explained. "We'll stay behind for a little. Once Anu and his men settle into the Academy, we'll release our presence."

Enmarsikil frowned. "What will that do?"

"We built the Academy the same way you build your transports," Teacher replied.

"So, once you release your presence...." Enmarsikil said starting to catch on.

"It reverts back to the original ruin we began with," Teacher confirmed.

"Who's wily now?" Enmarsikil ribbed.

Teacher smiled conspiratorially. "Better get going. We'll join you as soon as we're done here."

Enmarsikil nodded and turned toward the transport where Astara waited for him. He took her hand, led her up the gangway and ducked inside. The gangway retracted, the door lowered locking into place and the enormous silver ball slowly rose from the ground.

As the craft hovered over the courtyard, Enmarsikil wound his way to the command deck.

"Where to?" Gugbubulu asked as Enmarsikil stepped on deck.

Enmarsikil rubbed his hands together gleefully. "Can I communicate with everyone simultaneously from here?"

"I built in a communications link here," Nindulur told him pointing to a hologram suspended in mid-air.

Enmarsikil strode over, put his hand up to one side of the hologram to activate it and listened to the crackle in the air.

"Listen up, everyone," he announced. "While I know leaving our home is a difficult choice, and we aren't headed for a permanent home yet, I promise we'll be taken care of. When I visited King Anu, he showed me my name written in the royal annals. By their standards, I am a Royal Prince. He wanted to keep me captive in the palace. So, I've decided to oblige him and bring my siblings with me. We...my brothers and sisters... are heading to Agade's royal palace."

He turned to Gugbubulu and Zupatu. "Hit it boys. Dimension shift us straight to the palace courtyard."

In the field before the Academy, Anu looked up at the hovering craft shielding his eyes from the wind and dust kicked up by the thrusters. He watched with great satisfaction as the craft began rising higher in the air.

I'll finally be done with this giant fiasco, he thought.

A moment later, the craft shot towards the horizon disappearing in a bright flash of light.

CHAPTER 35 - THE HIGH LIFE

In but the blink of an eye, navigator and pilot brought the hybrids' transport vehicle within range of the palace courtyard in Agade.

"We're just going to fit," Nindulur commented as she watched their landing progress through the command center windows.

Enmarsikil took one last look before heading toward the holographic communications link. He touched his hand to it in order to speak.

"My team, assemble on the exit level. Everyone with metal attractant traits in the front line. Fire and lava behind them," he instructed.

"We in for a fight?" Zupatu asked.

"I plan to disarm and stun," Enmarsikil replied heading out of the room and down toward the disembarkment zone. Astara met him in the corridor.

"Stay behind the others," he instructed. "If we can't disarm them, we'll need your air blade."

Astara nodded and held back with the others possessing battle skills. Meanwhile, Enmarsikil made his way to the front of his team and stood near the door.

"Ok, folks. These soldiers are trained to shoot first and not bother with formalities," Enmarsikil explained. "Metal attractants, disarm the soldiers and pile up their weapons. If need be, I'll stun them. Fire and lava, melt the weapons in the piles and render them useless."

His team members nodded the affirmative. Suddenly, they felt the transport jolt as it set down and the thrusters died quickly.

"Get ready!" he cried.

They heard the whine of the gangway being extended.

"Opening exit door," Nindulur announced over the speaker system. The team braced for action.

Even as the door began sliding up, shots were fired through the narrow opening. Everyone flattened against the walls. The air quickly became hot and charged then the metal attractants leapt out, hands held before them palms out. To the shock of the palace guard, their weapons were ripped from them by an unseen force.

As fast as the metal attractants piled up the weapons, the fire and lava attuned hybrids set them on fire. Soon smoldering heaps of twisted, molten metal lay along the edges of the courtyard. A couple of soldiers tried to charge using hand-to-hand combat, but Enmarsikil stunned them with an invisible force field. They lay unconscious on the ground.

Suddenly, an air blade went screaming over Enmarsikil's head and he ducked. A quick glance up showed him backup military transports now headed groundward leaving trails of thick smoke. He looked back over his shoulder, spotted Astara and gave her a quick salute.

"Metal attractants. Incoming!" he yelled. "Marki, Kimkukala and Uribira with me. The rest, take care of these new soldiers. Kumzubar, follow us and keep those weapons hot. Mudizi, behind him. Put out the fires so the palace itself remains safe. Boys! Follow me!"

The five brothers plus Astara leapt to his side. Nita and Satu already waited near the palace entrance. They threw up a shield before them with the three metal attractants directly behind them. Enmarsikil and Astara brought up the rear checking side corridors for hidden guards. Weapons flew overhead piling up in front of the corridors and instantly exploded on fire as Kumzubar passed.

"Where are we headed?" Satu called back over his shoulder.

"Throne room...this corridor to the third right...up two flights," Enmarsikil yelled back.

For a moment the world seemed to pause around him as Ushumgal sent a telepathic message.

All guards captured. All weapons melted.

Enmarsikil put his fingers to his temple. *Gather everyone and follow our path in. Meet in the throne room.*

Understood, Ushumgal replied.

The world suddenly moved forward at normal speed again.

The group turned the corner entering the broad main corridor, marched toward the grand staircase proceeding as they had. Numerous piles of weapons were now on fire behind them but were carefully dowsed by Mudizi as he brought up the rear. In no time they faced the barred throne room doors.

Enmarsikil pushed forward, put his hands on the doors and felt the wood and metal they were comprised of. To the shock and horror of everyone inside the throne room, the bars slid out of place and the doors whooshed open slamming back against the walls.

For a moment Enmarsikil experienced that same sensation of awe at the filigree gold trim on the walls and columns but quickly snapped himself out of the trance. Guards who tried to stop them lost their weapons left and right and were overwhelmed by the ranks of hybrids whose numbers swelled the great hall.

Enmarsikil marched forward hand-in-hand with Astara, his intent focused on but one aim - the throne of King Anu itself. None opposed him for long and before he knew it, they were mounting the steps of the dais.

"You'd make a beautiful queen," Enmarsikil quipped to Astara as they took the ornate seats.

A flustered vizier approached. "Sire, who are all these people?"

"Sir, this is my spouse, Astara."

"Ah, the princess," he said bowing.

"We don't use those ter....." she began but Enmarsikil quickly cut her off.

"And the others are my siblings," he announced with a sweep of his hand.

"You will need accommodations," the vizier assumed feeling faint.

"Yes, indeed. Rooms for 251. Each mated pair gets their own space," Enmarsikil instructed.

"And your room?" the vizier asked.

"I am here because King Anu is away on extended business. His suite would work well for my spouse and myself," Enmarsikil replied.

The vizier's face paled. "As you wish," he said bowing and backing from the room.

"What do we do now?" several siblings asked from nearby.

"Rooms are being prepared now for each couple," Enmarsikil announced loudly. "Settle in then get to work. Sagtibira, Simugatibira, Izishub, Nindulur, Marki and Mirsigmi, as soon as you're settled in, retrieve your project materials and find the sages and scientists working on healing that atmospheric hole. Our whole reason for existing has depended upon us healing that thing. Let's keep that promise and make it so."

The Project Group huddled together and moved to one side, where servants quickly found them and whisked them away with their spouses to sumptuous rooms they'd never even dreamed of seeing.

"Healers and herbalists, once you're settled in, make your way through the palace and the town and help as many sick or injured as you can. Builders, refresh the structures of Agade but come to me for explicit instructions before you head out," Enmarsikil said. "I want to leave the palace and the city better off than what we found."

The builders pressed closer in for a quick huddle with Enmarsikil.

"Here's the deal," Enmarsikil told them in a low voice. "I want you to feel down into the quantum levels of every single structure except for the Archive. In the spaces between, plant a quantum explosive attuned to me. We won't have promises and contracts disregarded anymore," he told them. "Repair around the explosives and give the people the best structures you can."

They nodded their understanding then took off to find their rooms and begin their assigned tasks.

Group-by-group, the siblings were led to fine quarters, fed rich food and drank sparkling water. The vizier led Enmarsikil and Astara to the King's suite. The large, multi-room apartment was filled with furniture but virtually empty of people.

"Where is the queen?" Astara whispered to Enmarsikil.

The vizier cleared his throat. "Our queen has her own suite."

Astara blinked then frowned up at Enmarsikil.

"Will you be sleeping in the royal bed?" the vizier asked.

"Is there a guest room?" Enmarsikil asked.

"This way," the vizier replied leading them to another room with a carved double door. He opened the doors wide and led them inside. "Family and high-ranking officials from the north often stay in this room," the vizier explained.

Enmarsikil took in the large, ornate bed, comfortable seating arrangements and sunken tub. "This will be fine," he told him.

The vizier nodded.

At that moment, a train of servants entered with steaming dishes of food. Before she knew what was happening, Astara was seated at a table with more choices of menu than she had ever seen. Enmarsikil was already mounding spoonfuls on his plate.

286

"Try this," he suggested passing a bowl of stewed fruit to her. "It's really good."

Cautiously, Astara tried a spoonful of everything and gingerly took a bite of each to see what they tasted like. She got to the stewed fruit, set it on her tongue and closed her eyes in rapture.

"Good? Yes?" Enmarsikil asked watching her face.

She nodded as she savored the mouthful. He plopped another spoonful on her plate, and she dug in.

A servant brought a cart of delicate pastries. Astara glanced at them curiously but Enmarsikil waved them away.

"Sorry. I have an agenda while we're here," he told her pushing his chair back from the table. "I don't know how much time the Multi-Dims can buy us, but I want to accomplish a few things before we leave."

"Do they know?" Astara asked rising and following him.

"Mother knows. She'll alert the others," he explained.

He took her hand and guided her out of Anu's suite.

"Where to?" she wondered.

"The Archives," he replied. "But I'm sifting to save time."

One moment they stood in the palace; the next moment they stood on a golden grid in a dark vacuum. Enmarsikil stretched out his hand, envisioned the Archives and an intersection point lit up. As if suction were suddenly turned on, he and Astara were drawn directly to that point. He let go of the dimensions and they found themselves standing before an ornate gold door.

Enmarsikil reached out and eased the door open gently pulling Astara in after him. Lights came on starting dim and gradually growing brighter.

"What's in here?" Astara asked following him to a stand upon which a thick tome reposed.

"This," Enmarsikil replied stepping onto the stone before the stand. which triggered reading lights to come on.

"What is it?" she asked watching as he carefully turned the pages.

"It is the Book of Generations," he replied. "Anu showed me my name written in here making me a legitimate heir in the eyes of the Anunnaki. Sud suggested he was desperate enough for an heir that he might have put my name in himself."

"So you want to determine the truth," Astara surmised.

"Yes, I do."

He turned another page, ran his finger down the columns and noted the names. "Father Ea had a different name at birth," he noticed.

"Even the name, Ea, sounds more like a title," Astara remarked.

"Yes, but his birth name was his original name." He paused then gave a soft exclamation. "Here it is!"

Astara peered over his shoulder. "Well, unless he's been logging all of those other names and changes, too, I'd say this was written in here by an archivist."

"The royal archivist," a deep bass voice from behind them concurred.

They spun around coming face-to-face with an elderly man in gold trimmed robes.

"You're the royal archivist?" Astara asked descending off the step. "Did you write Enmarsikil's name in the book?"

The man nodded. "Indeed I did."

Enmarsikil stepped down, shock registering on his face. "Then this is real."

"Yes," the elderly man replied. "You have a legitimate claim to the throne of Nibiru, if you chose to take it."

"If I chose to," Enmarsikil echoed idly.

The archivist saw them out the door.

"You aren't planning on making yourself their king, are you?" Astara asked as they walked through the narrow corridors.

"I hadn't even given it a thought," Enmarsikil conceded. "I wanted to prove the legitimacy of my name in the book because, in all honesty, it's the only proof that any of us hybrids exist. They would only record the first born not all the rest of you."

"So, we won't be staying in Agade?" Astara pressed.

"It all depends upon the positive futures," he replied leading her outside. "Could I prevent the slavery and wars on Ki by taking the throne and guiding the future differently?"

"Or would you forever be fighting off rivals for power?" Astara wondered.

"There is that," he conceded, "and I'm not interested in fighting."

"C'mon. Show me that seductive garden," she said taking his hand and leading him into the streets back toward the palace.

Enmarsikil followed along, his mind working furiously on lines of possibilities. After a while, he shook his head to clear it, sifted the dimensions and in a blink, they stood at the entrance to Anu's private gardens.

"Wow!" Astara breathed. "No offense, but this even outdoes your gardens."

288

"No offense taken," Enmarsikil replied. "Mine were more for research, but these are for pleasure."

He held out his hand to her, she slipped her hand in his, and they strolled along the paths. Some were fine gravel, others fitted, cut stone and yet others smooth cobblestone.

"I never thought about creating a design and forming each bed so it fitted into the design like puzzle pieces," Enmarsikil commented stopping at the intersection of three paths and observing the specific plan of each bed.

Astara glanced at them then searched down the long, gravel path they had been walking. "Where are these scented flowers you talked about?" she asked.

"Hm?" He looked up from where he was squatting beside an ornate edging. "Oh. Up here," he said pointing.

Astara took his hand and tugged. With an affable smile, Enmarsikil got up and joined her.

"You want to see if their effect is real?" he asked mischievously.

"Yes, I do. C'mon."

They hastened their footsteps down the path, their boots crunching on the gravel. Soon, however, they slowed their pace as the heady scent of flowers reached their nostrils. Large pink blooms to their right produced an odor that could almost be seen like waves of heat rising from hot pavement. A purple and black butterfly-like insect had parked itself in the center of one bloom and lazily opened and closed its wings. Enmarsikil stepped closer for a whiff and mental analysis.

"Whoa!" he exclaimed reeling back. "That is one potent aphrodisiac in that scent."

Astara studied his flushed face and dilated pupils. "Hm. Must be like the herb that drives male felines crazy," she commented.

"Yeah, could be," was all he said as he slowly continued on.

In the next bed stood a bush with delicate yellow flowers, each striped with a narrow band of orange down their petals. Their bell-shape pointed out towards the path.

"That's hypnotic," Astara remarked after taking a whiff.

Enmarsikil took a step back and pulled her back beside him. "And if you stand right here, the hypnotic scent mixed with the aphrodisiac scent suggests only one thing."

"If you're male," Astara countered.

He glanced around them then pointed at a clump of long, narrow mushrooms growing up out of leaf mold under a tree, each with a bulbous 'head.' "Oh, I don't know," he remarked slurring. "They look pretty suggestive to me."

Astara crept over ducking between the two beds. She knelt beside the mushrooms and ran her hand up the side of one. The puff of spores hit her in the face. She tried to wipe them off.

"Ok. I agree," she giggled.

Looking just beyond the tree, she spotted a secluded nook and waved him over.

"Thinking what I'm thinking?" she asked.

"I'm certain I am," Enmarsikil replied leading the way to a foliage enshrouded arbor that hid a comfortable lounger inside.

He sat down on the lounger, pulled her toward him and she fell against him pushing him flat on his back. He kissed her hungrily as she straddled him.

"Sud could never have gotten me in here," he whispered, "and you wouldn't be able to keep me out."

With that, they threw caution to the wind and enjoyed what the hypnotic scents compelled them to do. It was some time before they finally crawled back out. Astara spotted the fountain, hurried over and splashed water on her face to wash off the lingering mushroom spores.

Enmarsikil sat beside her and gazed all around. "Guess it was worth a trip back here."

Astara giggled still heavily under the influence of the floral scents.

"Your water nymph rose up right here," he commented pointing to a spot in the water. "Saved me from making a terrible mistake."

Astara sobered. "We should sift back."

"Yeah, I agree. The scent is really becoming overwhelming."

They got up and Enmarsikil again sifted the dimensions. Before they knew it, they were standing inside their room in the King's suite.

"I suggest we shed these clothes and bathe to get the pollen off us," he suggested.

Astara studied the pollen a moment. "I'll bet this is what the seductress used in the potion she wore."

"Probably," Enmarsikil replied shedding his tunic. "But I've got to get my head back on straight. I want to know how the plant teams are doing on the surrounding farmlands."

They slipped into the water of the sunken tub, bathed hastily and were already dressing when they heard a knock on the outside door. A butler suddenly appeared out of nowhere and opened it.

"We're the Atmosphere team," Uribira announced.

Enmarsikil walked out into the vestibule still buttoning up his more royal looking long robe. "What's wrong?"

"Nothing," Uribira replied. "We're ready to close that hole in the atmosphere for good. Thought you'd want to see."

Enmarsikil came alive at the news. "Give Astara another second, and we'll all sift to the site."

She came out in a silk sari of gold-trimmed scarlet.

"Ready?" he asked.

"Yes," she replied taking his arm.

"And here we go," Enmarsikil announced.

To the surprise of the butler, the three individuals disappeared before his eyes.

CHAPTER 36 - PROMISES FULFILLED

At the Academy King Anu, his Sage and his Councilman turned from watching the horizon where the transport had disappeared and faced the imposing structures before them.

"So, they took it from a rambled ruin and created this?" the Sage mused.

"Yes, and now it is ours again," Anu replied smugly.

He led the way into the main courtyard and looked about at the quadrant of buildings, most of them dorms, with the main training and educational facility directly in front of them. A raw breeze made him hug his thick cape up closer around his shoulders. Whispers around the yard made him nervous. When he glanced up into the windows of the dorms, ghostly faces peered down at him suddenly flitting away into the shadows. The hair on the nape of his neck stood on end.

"He said they were all gone," Anu muttered under his breath.

"I counted them as they boarded their transport," the Council man assured him. "They are all gone."

"Well, I just saw someone up there," Anu replied pointing. "Guards, search these buildings from top to bottom. Find whoever's in there."

His captains saluted, shouted orders to their troops and several groups split off entering different buildings.

292

"Come, they can take care of the stragglers," the Sage said. "I'm eager to see the training and educational facilities."

He moved forward quickly toward the main building, opened the door and disappeared inside. The Councilman glanced at Anu who set his jaw and moved forward as well. They entered the tall building whose main corridor was flanked by vast gymnasiums still filled with the remnants of strange equipment. The Sage walked trancelike across the floor of one, stopped in front of an odd fixture on the wall and slowly reached out to touch it.

Instantly, laser bolts fired in a sequence of patterns, and they all ducked. When the firing ceased, the King and his Councilman hurried to the side of the Sage who cowered in a heap on the floor.

"I'd say 'Don't touch anything'," Anu quipped, "but it's apparently too late for that."

The men helped the Sage to his feet, guided him back out into the corridors and closed the gymnasium door.

"I'll have the Brigadier of Armaments check these out," Anu said raising his arm to his mouth and speaking into a round, multi-rayed communications device strapped to his wrist. He spoke in clipped tones then turned back to the others. "He and his squad will be here in less than a cycle. They'll sort this nonsense out."

"I wouldn't call it nonsense," the Councilman argued. "If you ask me, these people are well versed in the arts of war and self-defense."

The Sage frowned pensively. "Well, if that's true, why did they give up without a fight?"

Something gnawed at Anu's brain. "Enmarsikil wouldn't let them," he finally said. "It was the same when he left the palace. Even though my guards were firing on them, he wouldn't let those who rescued him return fire...not even after he was injured."

"Perhaps their martial abilities aren't very strong," the Sage postulated.

The memory of the air blade whizzing past his head and slicing a gash in the secret council room wall instantly sprang to Anu's mind. He shook his head. "No, I've seen what he can do. Strength is not their limitation. Neither is skill."

"And yet, they seem to choose to avoid a fight," the Councilman mused.

At that moment, the door behind them opened and the tromp of booted feet echoed down the corridor. Anu turned and waited for his captains to reach his side.

"Well?" he asked. "Who was there?"

The first captain shook his head. "No one, sire. We searched from attic to basement, checked every room and broom closet."

"We even looked for hidden rooms and secret passages," the second captain added.

"All is in order Sire, " the first captain declared.

Anu studied them for a moment then sighed. "Must be light playing tricks with me," he muttered.

From somewhere nearby, they all heard a woman's deep laughter.

"Well, someone is still here," the Councilman acknowledged.

Anu looked at his captains. "Bring your men inside and search this building systematically. Do NOT under any circumstances touch the equipment on the walls of the gymnasiums. They're dangerous training devices. The Brigadier of Armament is coming in less than a cycle to dismantle them."

The Captains saluted, spun on their heels, and marched back out the door to their waiting men.

Anu gazed about him even studying the windows near the peak. *What trap did you set for me, Enmarsikil?* he wondered inwardly. *What game are you playing?*

Resolutely, the King set his will and moved forward. By the determined set of his jaw, the Sage and Councilman knew he was prepared to rip the buildings apart stone-by-stone to find whoever was toying with them.

"Where is Teacher?" the Sage asked as they came to a circular tower holding the lecture halls.

Anu's eyes narrowed. "Ye-es," he growled. "Where is he?"

"I would say he is the one least happy with this breach of contract," the Councilman suggested.

"And he and his people are not to be toyed with," the Sage warned. "Why, I remember that day in the Secret Council when...."

"Yes, yes," Anu snapped irritably. "We all remember that incident."

The King stood under the dome in the center of the tower, cupped his hands around his mouth and yelled. "Teacher! Come out! Show yourself! Quit with these childish games!"

His voice echoed back for a moment dying off into eerie silence.

"I don't much like this," the Councilman said.

Anu's face was red with rage. "I will not let him get the best of me. Come on. Let's check this tower."

294

With that, he marched straight forward and through the doors into the Great Lecture Hall. The Sage and the Councilman looked at each other nervously.

"These games of cat and mouse are fine for the military," the Sage said.

"Yes, but we're not that," the Councilman pointed out.

"Shall we?" the Sage asked pointing to a cushioned window seat overlooking gardens below.

"Yes, definitely," the Councilman agreed.

The two men ambled over, got comfortable and prepared to watch the show.

Back in Agade, Enmarsikil, Astara and Uribira suddenly appeared on the vast plain below the city. Quite a throng of onlookers had gathered as well as scientists and sages. Enmarsikil ignored them all and immediately met with the Atmosphere Team.

"All right. Lay this out in steps for me. I want to double check the future probabilities before we implement it," he told them.

"Ok, first I will open a portal in the atmosphere to access points in multiple dimensions," Radarkumita said.

"I'll ready the multi-dimensional rockets," Uribira said.

"And I will lift them into sky positions near the portals," their bird man, Uabilla, added.

"On their signal, I will dimensionally shift the gold dust mesh expelled from the rockets through the dimensional portals," Zupatu said.

They paused watching as Enmarsikil held his hand out in front of him testing invisible parameters. Finally, he nodded.

"I will be working to create anchor points on the ground," Girimush said.

"Gishmugal and I will coordinate with him to create matching anchor points in the sky," Annisiga added.

Enmarsikil busily checked the probabilities and waved them on.

"When the anchor points are set," Kienelil continued, "I will weave an interlocking pattern through the gold dust mesh and between the sky and ground anchors."

"Once they're finished," Adusenga said, "I will set up a continual renewal feedback loop distributed by fresh rain that will lock the atmospheric patch in place for good."

"Frankly, the rest of the atmosphere might blow away, but our patch would still be standing," Uribira said proudly.

Enmarsikil's eyes were closed and his brow furrowed in concentration. At last, he let out a sigh of relief and opened his eyes nodding his head in affirmation.

"This will indeed fix that hole for good," he told them smiling. "Let's get this done."

The Team hurried away to take up their positions. Enmarsikil waved his hand overhead to signal their start. In what seemed like a whirlwind to the onlookers below, the sky above peeled back revealing a dark vacuum crisscrossed by a golden grid. Rockets suddenly fired off from stands at intervals across the plain. As they approached the vacuum, they exploded sending out fine sparkling golden mesh. The mesh stretched across the sky in multiple layers and threads attached to intersections on the golden grid in the vacuum.

Meanwhile, Gishmugal and Annisiga streaked across the sky creating anchor points that mirrored those Girimush was installing on the ground. Once those three stopped, Uabilla went over the Kienelil and lifted her skyward as she wove the anchoring threads between dimensions, mesh and anchor points all the way down to the ground. Adusenga waited till Uabilla set Kienelil down then closed the sky over the vacuum portal and caused a gentle rain to fall. The microscopic lines shimmered briefly then disappeared entirely signaling that the work was complete.

The Team gathered back on the platform with Enmarsikil and Astara, and the throng cheered. The scientists checked and rechecked their instrument readings at last confirming what the hybrids already knew. The hole in the atmosphere was gone. Nibiru was saved.

A small, hovering platform behind where Enmarsikil stood held two women who had keenly watched the work on the atmosphere. Now, the older woman with regal bearing motioned with her hand and her younger attendant turned the platform around heading toward the palace.

Meanwhile, Enmarsikil turned away from the crowd, put his arm around Astara and instantly vanished from sight. Moments later, they reappeared on the dais. Enmarsikil sank onto the throne and ran a hand over his face.

"We did it," he said quietly.

"Healed the hole in the atmosphere?" Astara asked taking a seat.

He nodded suddenly looking both relieved and exhausted. "That was the entire reason any of us were created...to heal that hole and anchor it to Nibiru so it would be permanent."

"And now we have."

"Yes, finally. That burden is off my shoulders," he replied sighing.

Astara frowned. "I never realized how important that was to you."

He leaned his head back against the seat and nodded. "I've fixated on that problem wondering how we would ever achieve it. Until we did, we were never really free as a people. We always owed a debt."

"A debt?" Astara queried.

"We were indebted to Teacher because he made a promise and created us to fulfill it," Enmarsikil explained. "And we were indebted to the people of Nibiru to whom the promise had been made."

"So, what will we do now?" Astara wondered.

"Become our own people with our own goals and objectives with no indebtedness to anyone but each other," he declared.

At that moment, the door at the far end of the hall opened and a lone woman entered approaching them down the carpet leading to the dais. When she was near, she stopped and bowed her head.

"How may we help you?" Enmarsikil asked, curious as to her intentions.

"My mistress, the queen, requests your presence in her suite. She has watched you and longs to speak with you," the woman announced.

Enmarsikil's eyebrows raised and he looked at Astara. She gave a little shrug and nodded. He took her hand and they descended the dais following the woman out of the throne room and through the corridors. Soon, they stopped before an ornately carved door, which a butler opened for them. The woman stepped aside allowing the couple free entry.

The older woman from the hovering platform stood with her back to them as she gazed out an open window.

"You wished to see us, Ma'am," Enmarsikil said.

The woman turned studying them with a keen eye. "Most people call me, Your Highness."

Enmarsikil nodded. "We don't use those terms."

"What do you call the King?" she wondered.

Enmarsikil smiled. "Grandfather."

She smiled in return and shook her head. "So different from us are your people."

"Yes and no," Enmarsikil replied. "While we collaborate freely as equals, we crave family and connections."

Antu nodded. "The former seems foreign to us, but the latter is familiar."

"Did you have something specific in mind for this meeting?" Enmarsikil asked.

"Yes, actually, I did," Antu replied motioning two servants to her side. "I have watched you on both visits and you are a very worthy heir. But most of all, I wish to express thanks for saving Nibiru. I would like you each to have these."

The servants stepped forward, snapped open the boxes and held out circlets of gold to each of them. Enmarsikil picked his up, studied it turning it over and over in his hands. Astara touched hers with her fingertips feeling the craftsmanship.

Enmarsikil set his back in the box. "I'm sorry, Ma'am. These are beautiful but they are what the princes wear."

"And so you are," she pointed out.

He shook his head. "No, not like that. Yes, according to my blood and the records in the Archive, but not as someone better than others. Frankly, the Team who healed that hole figured out how to do something that had stumped me for ages. All I actually did was double check future probabilities to be certain of their success. They designed and implemented the entire plan themselves."

Enmarsikil and Astara shut the boxes returning them to the servants.

"How...unusual," Antu remarked. "Marduk and Ninurta could barely wait till they came of age and received their circlets."

"I am not them," Enmarsikil replied simply.

"No, you are not in some very good ways." Antu motioned for two other servants to come forward. She stepped closer to Astara, and the servant held up a beautiful dress of blues and silver. "This was Ninmah's coming out dress. She left it for you."

Astara touched the dress feeling the gossamer fine silk. She looked to Enmarsikil whose countenance revealed his inner conflict.

"Try it on," Antu suggested.

Astara held it up to herself, bit her lower lip in thought then followed the servant into another room. In a few minutes a door opened and a vision in sparkling blue entered. Enmarsikil couldn't take his eyes off her as she spun around to give him the full effect.

"It's...amazing," he croaked out.

"Then may I assume you'll accept this gift from your mother?" Antu asked

Enmarsikil nodded slowly.

"There is a suit as well from your father, Ea. He was very determined that you have it," Antu added.

A servant whisked him into the other room, and he soon returned with his new suit on looking regal.

298

"Now, make sure you wear these," Antu admonished. "Anu will not stay away forever. When he returns, he may not be in a good mood. But he has special memories attached to these clothes. He will remember you are family, not foe."

Enmarsikil bowed his head to her. "Thank you, Ma'am."

"Call me grandmother," Antu replied reaching out to hug and kiss each of them. "For so I am."

CHAPTER 37 - OUT MANEUVERED

Anu entered the Great Lecture Hall from the top tier and angrily began stomping his way down an aisle of steps. Without warning, the doors at the top of the hall banged shut. He jumped and spun around. On every level, door after door slammed shut till he was left in the dark with the echoes.

"Show yourself!" he shouted sweat trickling down his back.

Five figures suddenly appeared in different locations around the lecture hall, each figure illumined in a bright mist.

"Your contract is up," Anu declared. "It is time you vacate the premises."

"There was never to be an eviction," Teacher reminded him from where his image appeared in the well.

"That was before we needed more training facilities and accommodations for our own personnel," Anu responded. "Much more financially feasible to recover what was ours to begin with than to start anew."

"Do you," Giramusen began seeming to float closer, "have any measure of integrity?"

"And what is that supposed to mean?" Anu demanded.

"You make pacts; you break pacts when they become inconvenient to you. You sign contracts; you break contracts when it suits you,"

Emissary said from off to the left. "It would seem that your word is not to be trusted, even when it's signed on paper."

"Every pact and contract must be ratified by the full Council," Anu told him. "These were not, so they are not binding."

"Ah...your words never have to bind you to your actions. How... novel," Giramusen mused ominously.

"We plan to occupy this facility this evening and every day henceforth," Anu stated.

"Very well," Teacher replied with an edge of threat to his tone and delivery. "By all means...stay."

One of the figures disappeared from the hall while the other four continued their conversation with Anu. Out in the lounge near the upper door, Marne appeared and approached the Sage and the Councilman.

"We have no desire to join him," the Sage emphatically stated as soon as he saw her.

"I don't want you to," Marne replied. "I believe it would be safer for you elsewhere."

"Safer sounds good to me," the Councilman added rising.

"Yes, Anu seems determined to tempt fate," the Sage added joining them and quickly heading downstairs and out the main door.

Marne took them beyond the main gates to their flying transports. "Find a way to get comfortable here. You'll be safe."

"From what?" the Sage wondered.

"You'll see in the morning," Marne responded cryptically and disappeared.

Meanwhile, the soldiers dragged their packs into the dorms, chose beds and crawled in for the night after eating cold rations.

The Multi-Dims gathered physically in the main courtyard enjoying a brief chuckle over Anu arguing with their holographic replicants in the Great Lecture Hall.

"Where shall we begin?" Zalkur asked.

"Take it from the top down," Teacher suggested. "That way if they have the good fortune to awaken, they will have time to run."

The five beings rose to the height of the roof. They closed their eyes and breathed. Slowly, then picking up speed, shingles and tiles disintegrated into dust followed by the joists and rafters. The buildings began to creak and whistle as the structures destabilized and wind passed through widening cracks. Since no one woke up, the Multi-Dims picked up the speed of their work. The roof over the upper floors vanished, then the ceilings of the upper floors. The soldiers sat bolt upright just in time for the floor beneath their beds to disappear from under them. Their screams were heard as they tumbled down crashing through the floors below and ultimately ending up in the dank basements.

In the transport where they cowered, the Sage and the Councilman heard the screams and the thud of rubble hitting the ground. While Nibiru was in its growing twilight phase and the light was but a dim gray, though still sufficient to illuminate the surroundings, the men remained in the transport. Finally, when the light began to grow again and the dust had cleared, they ventured forth from hiding. They crept to the entrance of the outer courtyard and stood with their mouths agape.

"Th-there's nothing left of the Academy," the Sage stammered.

"This is all ruin," the Councilman agreed.

"It's-it's just like it was before we turned the property over to them," the Sage gasped in realization.

Vague figures stumbled through the ruins in shock. Some dug away debris to free their comrades.

"Where's the King?" the Sage wondered.

"Oh my! The King!" the Councilman exclaimed and launched himself toward where the lecture hall tower had once stood, the Sage close on his heels.

They skidded to a halt at the edge of a deep pit peering in at the tumble of stones and beams.

"King Anu," the Councilman called cupping his hands around his mouth. "Can-you-hear-me?"

For a moment they heard no reply. Then the faint sound of stone knocking against rock reached their ears.

"He's alive!" the Sage cried with relief.

The Councilman turned and flagged down a few soldiers. "The King's trapped down there. Help us get him out."

Quickly, the men retrieved what gear they had managed to salvage and soon rappelled into the deep hole.

"Keep knocking," the Councilman yelled.

Pretty soon the soldiers located the King and managed to push beams out of the way and move boulder sized rocks until they finally spotted a hand waving above the mess. Grasping his hand, they pulled him free of the lucky pocket he had been crouched in and soon handed him up topside. Once there, he dusted himself off and started toward the transports. The Multi-Dims blocked the exit to the courtyard.

"What do you want since you managed to break your end of the contract," Anu fumed.

302

Teacher shook his head. "No, we followed the contract to the exact letter of the law. According to it," he said taking the scroll Emissary handed him and unrolling it, "we were instructed to 'return the base in as good a condition as it was when we received it'."

"This is the way it was when we handed it over to you," Anu pointed out.

"With some improvements," Marne added. "Fish ponds and gardens outside the former research wing."

"But how could all of that," Anu asked turning and looking at where stalwart buildings had stood, "just disappear?"

"We anchored our building materials to our observations and our presence," Zalkur said.

"Once we removed our focus and presence," Giramusen said, "what we built disintegrated into nothing and returned to the quantum foam."

"So, we shall leave," Teacher concluded. "Enjoy building anew," he added in parting as the Multi-Dims turned, began walking and disappeared into the mist.

Anu stood with his hands on his hips watching them go.

"Well, they held to the letter of the contract," the Councilman noted.

"Bah!" Anu grumbled. "Round up what you can salvage. We need to return to Agade."

It took some time but the transports were eventually loaded. Even they seemed to be affected by the Multi-Dims' actions and limped slowly toward their distant destination.

In Agade, Nindulur landed her personal transport in the outer courtyard and ran toward the throne room. She dashed straight for the dais where Enmarsikil and Astara sat on the thrones.

Enmarsikil leaned forward, concerned.

"Incoming," she panted.

"The King?"

Nindulur nodded.

"Spread the word, everyone to the throne room, except Ushumgal, Erumgal and Kumzubar. They're to remove and melt their weapons and escort the king to me."

Nindulur nodded and hurried off to attend to business. Enmarsikil paused with his hand to his temple sending a personal call back to his siblings with urgency.

"So what happens now?" Astara asked.

"I have a plan," Enmarsikil replied. "I have an offer for the King that he can't refuse."

At that moment, Queen Antu's lady-in-waiting entered from a side door carrying the circlet boxes.

"I thought you said we didn't want them," Astara reminded him.

"We do for the time being," Enmarsikil replied opening his box and adjusting the circlet on his brow. "It's all part of my plan."

He handed Astara's circlet to her and she slipped it on as well. Then they sat back to wait.

Before long all but three of the hybrids were gathered inside the throne room. The two pan-elementals and Kumzubar awaited Anu and his soldiers in the courtyard outside. They didn't have long to wait. And as the transports set down in the courtyard, Ushumgal and Erumgal made short work of removing weaponry from the soldiers and piling it up. Kumzubar rather gleefully set it all on fire.

With the soldiers rounded up and their weapons melted, Anu had no choice but to march through familiar halls between the two pan-elementals. They turned the corner into the processional corridor, mounted the stairs and entered the throne room.

Anu cast astonished eyes about the packed room. There was no space not occupied by a hybrid. As he stepped onto the lush carpet strip leading toward the throne, the hybrids parted to let him pass. But what he saw on the dais made Anu freeze. His throne was his no more. A prod from behind forced him to move forward, and he made the long walk down the carpet with leaden feet. When he reached the base of the stairs, he knelt and bowed his head.

"Your humble servant," Anu said quietly.

"Don't bow down to me," Enmarsikil said. "We don't do that amongst my people."

Anu stiffly rose to his feet and gazed upwards taking in the clothes Enmarsikil and Astara wore and the circlets. *Even Antu has endorsed him,* he thought. *Ea and Ninmah were to wear that garb when they became regents for the child I'd hoped they'd have. But, Enmarsikil is their child.*

"I see you came straight to the palace," Anu said aloud.

Enmarsikil crossed his right ankle over his left knee and leaned back. "Where else was I to go, grandfather?" he asked. "The Academy was all we really knew, and you assured me I had a right to be in the palace." He gestured to the ceilings and the walls. "I double checked at the royal archives when I first arrived to make sure."

304

"Well, yes, you have the right," Anu agreed, "but not all of these," he said with a sweeping gesture toward the other hybrids.

"They are blood of my blood, DNA shared alike," Enmarsikil responded. "Why wouldn't they also belong here. And where else was there space enough to fit them all? I had to provide for my people."

Anu raised his hands. "All right, you took care of them. There's more to ruling than caring for your own. Are you prepared to fight to keep your throne?"

Enmarsikil gave him an amused grin. "Did we have to fight you when you landed? It only took three of us against your hand picked guard, and no shots were fired."

"There is that," Anu conceded. "But what about fire power from a military vessel? You don't seem inclined to fight."

"Oh, I'm not, but let us demonstrate to you why we choose not to," Enmarsikil said. He nodded to a group of hybrids off to his right.

The others parted to give Anu a clear view.

"Don't hold back," Enmarsikil instructed in a loud voice.

In the midst of the throne room stood a large statue made of the hardest stone found on Nibiru. Enmarsikil particularly hated this statue because it depicted a man subduing a woman to his bidding. He gave the signal for its destruction.

A wind elemental immediately took off the head of the man with an air blade never having to physically touch it. A fire elemental burned a hole through the chest. A water elemental melted the torso till the hard stone ran like mud over the sides of the female and onto the throne room floor. On and on they went taking the statue apart like so much butter until nothing remained but a molten heap of rock. Anu watched with chills trickling down his spine.

"My people haven't even broken a sweat and they have never had to physically touch that object," Enmarsikil pointed out. "Where would your soldiers and fighting machines be now?"

"Dead and destroyed," Anu stated in a voice that cracked.

"And this is why we choose not to fight. We don't need to," Enmarsikil replied. "And we have no desire to inflict unnecessary damage."

"Then how about my people," Anu demanded gathering what was left of his courage. "How have they fared under your rulership?"

"Quite well," Enmarsikil remarked as scientists entered from the left side. "We healed that hole in Nibiru's atmosphere and anchored it to the planet...just as had been promised."

"We have all the instrumental proof of what we saw with our own eyes," the Scientists concurred presenting the printouts to Anu.

Anu staggered back. He had never believed that promise was true.

"Someone get him a chair and some water," Enmarsikil called.

The hybrids sprang into action and in no time eased Anu into a comfortable seat and handed him a goblet of the purest water. He drank and breathed hard trying to recover from his own shock.

"We have done a lot more than just heal your atmosphere," Enmarsikil continued. "I sent my people throughout the palace and the city restoring buildings and infrastructure wherever they went. From the palace to the lowliest stable, every structure is as good as new. I also sent our healers throughout the palace and Agade to heal and restore anyone who was ailing. As it was, one of your concubines was in the midst of a difficult birth and both child and woman would have been lost. Instead, our healers saved both child and mother."

A young woman clothed in finest silk entered bearing an infant in her arms. She knelt before Anu and presented his child to him. Anu touched the baby's head, sighed deeply and nodded. She rose and melted back into the crowd.

"It seems you have done a lot," he conceded.

"Oh, we didn't stop there," Enmarsikil said. "Our plant specialists went out into your fields, studied your crops and invigorated both soil and plant. We reestablished rains and have given your farmers the hope of a bountiful harvest. Others of our people visited your dormant volcanoes, so important for the maintenance of Nibiru's atmosphere. After removing long standing plugs and energizing their fires, the volcanoes rumble and belch smoke once more. The planet is waking up."

Anu seemed to shrink in the chair. "I could never have done those things for my people," he admitted. "It has been tried for shars by some of our most gifted sages and scientists. And in a blink of time, your people have accomplished what mine could not."

"I know," Enmarsikil said.

Anu took a deep breath and forced himself to stand. "I still want my throne back."

"You would fight for your throne?" Enmarsikil asked shrewdly.

Anu shook his head. "Nay. There is no withstanding your people."

"Then how would you propose to get your throne back?" Enmarsikil asked.

Anu thought hard. "I removed you from your only home. You

306

have nowhere else to go. Would territory of your own be sufficient?"

Enmarsikil seemed to mull over this offer. "Only if it is territory we determine, both the where and the amount."

"But we agree it's away from Agade," Anu confirmed.

Enmarsikil nodded then spread out his hands bringing up a holographic topographical map between he and Anu. It showed a vast territory that spanned rivers, streams, valleys, mountains, rocks and desert. "This would suit us."

Anu studied the map. "I am unfamiliar with this territory," he said at last.

"I have traveled it," Enmarsikil said. "It has every ecosystem my people need in order to thrive."

"How much territory?" Anu asked.

"Fifty thousand two hundred square miles," Enmarsikil replied. "One hundred square miles of territory per person."

"That's a hefty amount of land," Anu countered.

Enmarsikil settled back into the throne. "And I'm very comfortable right here."

Anu looked up at him and narrowed his eyes. Enmarsikil held all the cards, and he knew it.

"Very well," Anu replied. "So shall it be."

"The contract for this land will stipulate that it be ours forever. No citizen of Nibiru is to walk on it, float down its rivers, fly over it, dig under it or in any way disturb this territory whatsoever," Enmarsikil stated forcefully. "And it shall be ratified by your full Council and made valid, even to you."

Anu's nostrils flared. His grandson had learned his game and was no longer willing to play. He nodded. "As you wish it," he replied.

At that moment, all fifty Council members filed into the already crowded throne room.

"We are prepared to draw up and ratify this contract right now," the Chairman said.

"But this isn't in the actual council chambers," Anu argued. "It still wouldn't be valid."

"If the fifty of us vote that it is valid when drawn up and ratified in this great hall," the Chairman said stiffly, "then it is so. Please give a show of hands as to the contract's validity."

All fifty hands were raised high.

"It is the price you pay for your throne," the Chairman told him.

Anu nodded and hung his head.

Within minutes the official scrolls had been prepared and the official council seal was placed upon them. One went to Anu and the other to Enmarsikil. Enmarsikil and Astara took off their circlets and Anu sighed with relief. He made to ascend the dais to his throne, but Enmarsikil put his arm around the older man's shoulders.

"Please, grandfather. It would mean much to me if you would see me and my siblings off," Enmarsikil said cordially.

"Very well," Anu agreed.

They waited patiently while the other hybrids began filing out of the throne room to the transport that was building even as they stood. As they walked through the throne room, out the door and down the corridors, Enmarsikil kept a tight grip on Anu's shoulder. When they reached the first side hall, Enmarsikil pulled him aside into it and kept the man close.

"Here is the thing," Enmarsikil said in a low voice. "I've seen your deception at work first hand, and I don't trust you."

Anu squirmed but there was no freeing himself from the young man's grip.

"When my builders went through the palace and the city, they placed quantum explosives between the atoms of the structures. Explosives that are linked to me, and me alone. All that needs to remain of me in this universe is one strand of DNA and those explosives can be triggered. If they are triggered, every building will turn to dust and blow away...every building save one."

"Which one?" Anu croaked.

"The Archives," Enmarsikil replied. "That building has been restored in such a way that your most potent military weapons could never destroy."

"Why?" Anu wondered uncomfortably.

"Because, in that building rests a book and in that book my name is written. It is the only official record that we exist. And for that reason, I will spare that building," Enmarsikil told him.

"So why destroy the palace and Agade?" Anu wondered.

"Oh I won't," Enmarsikil responded, "unless you renege on this contract," he said waving the scroll under the King's nose. "Should you or your people deviate from this contract in any way, you will lose what you are so proud of. And then, we'll be even."

Anu swallowed hard. "I underestimated you," he admitted. "I thought you to be naive and a simpleton. You've proven to be very astute."

"I am not naive, grandfather," Enmarsikil replied, "just innocent.
308

I do not have the years of conniving you have developed. I do not have desire for power and status and wealth. And therein lie your greatest weaknesses to be exploited by everyone who desires your throne."

With that, Enmarsikil guided Anu back into the corridor and out into the courtyard. There the transport was complete, everyone was onboard, and it was time to go. Enmarsikil gave Anu a hug, released him, climbed the entry ramp and reached the doorway. He turned, waved the contract high in the air, then ducked inside, the door closing behind him. Moments later, the transport lifted off from the courtyard, floated over the palace walls then shot away toward the horizon like a blazing star. They were homeward bound.

CHAPTER 38 - HOME OF THEIR OWN

Enmarsikil quickly made his way through the transport to the control room. He immediately brought up the holographic map of their new territory and fed it into the navigational system.

"Where exactly?" Zupatu asked. "That's a lot of ground to cover."

Enmarsikil touched the hologram, enlarged one section and zeroed in on a target placing a marker.

"There's fresh water and shelter in this area," he told Zupatu. "From there we can decide our next steps."

Zupatu brought the image to a screen near him, connected the marker to his controls and the transport veered to the right. Knowing they were headed in the correct direction, Enmarsikil left for the more open living areas of the vehicle. A large lounge had been constructed on a mid-level deck where most of the siblings were presently milling.

He scanned the sea of familiar faces, spotting Astara off to the right sitting with Bilnammul, Kienelil, Ki, Aiya and Barlumgeme. He caught her eye and her face flushed.

"Are you going to leave us already?" Aiya asked.

"He'll survive without you while we all catch up," Ki remarked.

Astara nodded.

"You have been rather glued to his side," Bilnammul added.

"What happened to your independent streak?" Kienelil wondered.

"I know," Astara admitted. "I used to feel like I had to prove myself all the time. I had to accomplish more to be taken seriously. But I don't have to prove anything to Enmarsikil. He saw it in me all along."

"So, what will you focus on when we get to our land?" Barlumgeme asked.

"Him," Astara replied simply. "He used to tell me how much responsibility he had to shoulder as the oldest, trying to make sure the rest of us are ok and provided for. Now that I've seen that burden in person, I realize how much he carried without saying a word. While he's busy making our lives safe and pleasant, someone has to support him."

"That actually sounds like a bigger job than getting plants to grow," Bilnammul remarked.

Astara shrugged.

"He's waving to you," Ki said pointing.

"I'll see you later," Astara said rising and scampering across the room to Enmarsikil's side.

He gave her a quick hug then whistled for everyone's attention. "Just so you know, we really are headed home, to a new home, one that won't be taken from us. I've guaranteed it."

The siblings broke out in whoops and cheers.

"Where we'll land is on a large plain with a river on one side, foothills and forest on the other. Not far away from the plain, the river feeds into another that flows toward a steep waterfall," he continued.

Astara looked up at him wide-eyed with recognition. He smiled and nodded.

"The first thing we'll need to build is shelter," Enmarsikil told them. "I suggest we maintain the lower decks for storage until we have things better sorted. Meanwhile, get with your partners and friends. Let's dream up a home, a real home, one that truly suits us. Then let's build that."

While the others cheered, Enmarsikil waved over some of the architects, engineers and builders he had sent out into the palace and city.

"What did you learn from the layout of Agade?" he asked.

"How to do it better," Marki said winking.

"That's my brothers, always one step ahead," Enmarsikil commended. "You all will need to get the lay of the land and help the visions of the others come together cohesively."

This new team nodded and drifted away melting into the crowd.

Nita and Satu approached.

"What about going off world?" Satu pressed.

"I haven't forgotten," Enmarsikil promised. "But we have to get everyone settled here and safe first, and there is still the matter of the dissonance between Ki's elements and our systems. That has to be resolved before anyone goes anywhere."

Nita nodded.

"That really happened?" Satu wondered.

Enmarsikil nodded solemnly. "I saw you when you had no physical form. I'm not letting that happen this time."

"So what do we do in the meantime?" Nita asked.

"Consider this training for going off world," Enmarsikil replied. "Help set up a settlement. Figure out how to tweak it. Take that know-how to Ki with you."

"Sounds good," Satu replied.

Before too long, they all felt the transport slowing till it hovered in place gradually lowering to the ground. A slight jiggle was all that let them know the trip was over.

"They improved the landing," Enmarsikil remarked leading the way toward the exit door.

Once down the gangway and outdoors, the siblings looked around.

"This somehow looks familiar," Ki said.

"We did that one cycle of element training out around here when we were kids," Aiya reminded her.

While the others worked to set up large, subdivided tents, Enmarsikil stood off to one side watching, his brow knit. Six individuals faded into view around him. The youngest, Kisikilturkusa, a sunny twelve year old with golden blond hair, happily skipped away to help her older siblings. Enmarsikil watched her go.

"Pushing her growth, too?"

"Yes," Teacher replied from his left, "but much more slowly."

Enmarsikil nodded absently.

"That was a fine job you did in Agade," Teacher commended. "You kept your wits about you."

"Hmph!" Zalkur snorted. "He showed up the King ten times over."

"Thanks, but it doesn't matter now except we start a home of our own from scratch," Enmarsikil replied.

"Where will you build?" Giramusen wondered.

"It's not up to me," Enmarsikil replied. "It's up to them."

"Let us help," Marne offered.

Enmarsikil glanced sideways at her. "It has to be their vision. And with some of them wanting to go off world, they need the practice now,

312

here, where it's safe."

Teacher nodded. "May I set up a lab again? I think I was close to figuring out the Ki elements and their attunement to you."

Enmarsikil sighed with relief. "I'd welcome that, since I don't dare work on them myself."

"You're going to Ki someday?" Marne asked.

Enmarsikil watched Astara help her sisters. "Maybe."

"You know. Once they have the design and building begins, we could speed up the process," Zalkur proposed.

"They will still integrate the knowledge and experience only at a much faster pace," Giramusen explained.

Enmarsikil stared at the ground with his hands on his hips. "That might be useful. Somehow time seems of the essence."

The Multi-Dims nodded.

For now, they stood and watched as living quarters were raised and some supplies were brought off the transport.

"I think the one really necessary thing is a meeting hall that's centrally located and large enough to house all of us," Enmarsikil said at last.

He headed down toward the plain where the tent city was rising. He caught a couple of builders, shared his vision and made it a priority. Within days, the meeting hall was built in the center of the plain. Meanwhile, cobbled streets spread out from the center with homes of all sorts taking shape.

Some of the ground attuned hybrids moved out from the town center and were digging holes into the foothills carving out comfortable, well-insulated homes underground. Some of the air attuned moved higher up in elevation and raised glorious, elaborate treehouses high in the tops of the elder trees of the forest. Long spans of bridges linked the homes and trees together. In town, the homes were two and three story cozy buildings. And out along the river above the roaring falls, other hybrids built a series of homes with open filigree work so the roar of the falls constantly permeated the air and the mist drifted in on the breeze.

In the town Astara helped Aiya as she furnished and decorated her new home. It had three stories, the bottom two with high ceilings braced with hand hewn timbers. She watched as Aiya carefully arranged tables, chairs, sitting space and added splashes of color here and there with flowers.

"What do you think?" Aiya asked whirling around to face Astara.

Astara couldn't help but notice her friend's glowing face and bright eyes. "Everything is so well placed," she gushed. "It's so cozy...like you could move in, curl up by the fire and never leave."

Aiya promptly dropped into a chair in front of the fireplace. "How about you? Where are you and Enmarsikil building?"

Astara's face paled.

Aiya sat up straight and narrowed her eyes. "You are building, aren't you?"

Astara swallowed hard. "H-he hasn't mentioned it yet."

"You have a tongue. Have you mentioned it?" Aiya asked pointedly.

Astara shook her head.

Aiya frowned. "Are you...afraid?"

"I-I don't know, Aiya. Ever since he went to Agade, Enmarsikil's been different. Before, it was a lot about us. Now, he's got this mission fixation. It didn't help that Anu kicked us out of the Academy," Astara replied.

"Best thing that ever happened to us if you ask me," Aiya said gazing around her home.

"It is unless you feel like you're responsible for making sure 500 siblings are ok," Astara replied.

Aiya shook her head. "That doesn't matter. You've got to make him hear you. You have as much right as we do to be happy."

Astara mulled over what her sister had said and nodded. "You're right. I do."

"Well, just make sure you tell him," Aiya insisted as Astara stepped out onto the street.

She visited Bilnammul, whose house was done in bright colors befitting a fire elemental. Ki's was earthy and strong, while Kienelil's home was filled with light and color. She had even painted the walls and had woven brightly colored fabric for the windows and chairs.

As Astara left the last house and set part of her mind on locating Enmarsikil, for the first time in many cycles, she let herself dream. But nothing new came to mind. What filled her heart with the most longing were all the little details that had been so familiar about the Academy.

For his own part, Enmarsikil stood on a hillside overlooking the town so he could take in its full effect. He shook his head and marveled at how well his siblings had risen to the challenge of creating a home for themselves from scratch after Anu had set them in such disarray.

A twig snapped and he turned to see Astara approaching. She

walked toward him with a dreamy look in her eyes.

"I've just been visiting Aiya, Bilnammul, Ki and Kienelil. Their new homes are so vibrant. I could walk in and easily tell who lived in each just by how they're designed and decorated. They're all so happy. When will we build?" she asked.

"I thought we could create something small in town. Practical. Near everyone else. Just a couple of rooms. We don't have many needs," Enmarsikil proposed and knew in an instant his idea was a fail.

Astara's lashes instantly brimmed with tears and her face fell. "Just a couple of rooms? Crammed in somewhere like an afterthought?" she asked incredulously. "When everyone else has been planning and dreaming and building, and they're so happy?"

He sighed. "I thought a couple of rooms would be easier to take care of if we're coming and going."

Astara's eyes narrowed. "Coming and going where?"

"Ki, Astara," he said quietly. "There is a Mission to Ki already in the works that Satu and Nita have been designing for cycles. And we have a debt to pay to the humans, Ginny and Ted."

Astara stiffened, her face paled and she looked away. "So, while everyone else creates their dream, we sacrifice to live like rats in a hole?" she whispered sniffling. "Is that how it's going to work in the new settlement? Everyone else gets to dream big but us?"

Enmarsikil sighed again and went to put his hands on her shoulders, but she pulled away. "I just thought it would be less effort, something easy to come home to."

"Well, if Satu and Nita are going to Ki, they've built like they're putting roots down here, and Barlumgeme and Mamud have decorated to perfection. And we're the only ones even considering a hole in the wall."

Enmarsikil heard the note of hurt and deep disappointment in her voice. "I'm sorry, Astara. I've just been trying to weigh the time we may spend off world against the time we'll be here."

Astara frowned and folded her arms across her chest. "So it's already decided. You have a plan and I'm just going to march in step with it. Where would we go? What if I don't want to leave Nibiru?" she asked whirling to face him. "What if I want to set down roots of my own. Real roots, a real home, created by us?"

Sweat beaded on his brow. "Are you saying you don't ever want to go to Ki?"

"I won't even consider it while I have no place here to call home. I'm not a nomad. I want a place where I belong. And I spent all my life crowded into those hideous dorms," Astara reminded him. "I can't stand the thought of being cramped into two rooms. If everyone else got to dream and build, why can't we, too?" she pleaded

"But Astara, who will care for our place when we're gone?" he countered.

"Satu and Nita don't seem worried about that," she countered. "Why am I being asked to sacrifice my dreams and happiness when I'm the only one?"

Enmarsikil ran his hand through his hair tapping into the ache in her heart. "This really is a big deal for you?"

"It's huge, Enmarsikil. I don't get how it can't be for you, too," Astara said. "You came back from Agade a really different person. Everyone has your attention but me. Everything you do is to keep promises to this person and that person and to make sure everyone is happy. Everyone. But. Me," she added, her voice rising. "Why are my dreams so unimportant? Why aren't we supposed to be happy, too? We're siblings. I'm a sibling!"

Enmarsikil breathed hard listening to her. *Have I really changed that much*? he wondered inwardly. "I guess, after seeing how everything Anu does is geared toward impressing others and focusing on his own comfort, I wanted to be the sort of leader that thought about the welfare of his people instead."

"Then why is my happiness and welfare last?" Astara challenged.

"I thought you understood how I felt," Enmarsikil replied quietly.

"Without ever telling me anything, I'm supposed to pick this up by osmosis?"

Enmarsikil shook his head. "No. No you're not. So you want a dream?"

"I already have my dream," Astara declared.

"Ok, what do you want to build?" he asked.

"You sure you want to know?" she asked uncertainly.

Enmarsikil nodded emphatically. "I want to know. You've made your point. I've ignored you and now it's time to make that right."

Astara took a deep breath, her face turning dreamy. "Your bedroom with its indentation for the sphere and the memory bubbles. The shelves of books, the window and the telescope, my wardrobe and my sunken pool," she said breathlessly. "That can be on one side of the house connected to a great kitchen by a columned, vaulted-ceiling hall. And in the center of those two wings, a great hall for eating and holding dances."

Enmarsikil swallowed hard. "I had no idea you've been dreaming

316

so big."

She put her hand up. "I want a tree house that overlooks water, and we have to have a garden like your old one. We met in your garden. We kissed for the first time on the bridge while watching your fish. We pledged our love beside the flower bush. Please Enmarsikil. It's all got to be there...and a place for my water nymph. Something familiar and I'll feel at home."

"But if we only come back to it now and then...." Enmarsikil protested.

"Everyone else has built homes they dreamed into existence and they're happy," Astara reminded him. "I'm not sacrificing my dreams and happiness over these missions you obsess over. Why are you asking me to be the only one who is miserable?"

With that, she stormed off up the hill and Enmarsikil watched her go. She was moving at speed away from the town, from him, from their siblings. Before long, she disappeared into the deep forest and was gone.

He sighed. "She's right. I always made sacrifices because it was expected of me. Maybe I've asked her to sacrifice too much."

He scanned the valley wondering where to build. The near side of the river was already becoming crowded, but the far bank was still fairly open. He could see the long, low building of Teacher's new labs, and several large fields were already producing crops. A little ways upstream there was a more secluded location with large weeping trees near the river. Nodding to himself, Enmarsikil headed down into the town to find Marki and his team of builders.

CHAPTER 39 - FINDING BALANCE

Enmarsikil opted for his air skid to quicken his pace and rode it down the main street of the town looking for signs of his builder brothers. He finally found them in the Meeting Hall doing some finishing work on the interior. Marki looked up when he heard Enmarsikil enter. He laid down his tools and headed over.

"What do you think?" Marki asked.

Enmarsikil gazed about the hall with its stadium seating leading down into a large well that was centrally situated. "Reminds me a bit of the Academy but more functional and less educational."

"We added some touches to the holographic projector, and there's a build table we can raise in the middle of the floor," Marki told him. "Plus, we can project a hologram of any known astrobody into midair to study."

Enmarsikil nodded appreciatively. "I'm impressed."

Marki studied him from the corner of his eyes. "You sound surprised like you didn't expect us to achieve so much."

Enmarsikil looked stunned. "Well, no...not exactly. I thought everyone was in shock after Anu's edict."

"Well, yes...till we saw Agade," Marki admitted. "When we saw what we were capable of achieving when we applied our technology, the Academy felt too small. Trust me. No one wanted to go back."

Enmarsikil's eyebrows shot up in surprise. "So, no one's

homesick?"

"Look around at the town, brother," Marki challenged. "Do we look homesick?"

"I-I'll do that," Enmarsikil replied still processing this new information.

"So, you have your place built yet?" Marki asked leading Enmarsikil down into the well to demonstrate the new technological features.

"Uh, no," Enmarsikil replied. "It's what I was coming to talk to you about."

"We'll be another cycle finishing up here, but I could get a Team to your build site to get things started," Marki replied. He brought the build table up from the floor and locked it into place. "Know what you want?"

"I know what Astara wants," Enmarsikil replied beginning to bring up the individual features she had mentioned.

Marki studied the model that was developing before him. He could feel Astara's longings in each feature.

"Mind if I make tweaks here and there?" he asked.

"No, please do. I'm afraid I was amiss in waiting so long," Enmarsikil replied quietly.

Marki cast him a sidelong glance, his eyes narrowing. "Astara is hurt to the core, isn't she?"

Enmarsikil flinched but said nothing.

"I have lots of experience in inflicting that kind of pain. But after shars of tormenting her, I vowed I would spend the rest of my life doing whatever it takes to make her happy," Marki stated forcefully. "You leave this to me. This will be beyond her dreams. Now, where's the location."

"Across the river," Enmarsikil said feeling uncomfortably chastised.

"Shidim! Kiderin!" Marki yelled. "We have another build to design."

Two men popped their heads up from the top gallery, floated down towards the well and landed beside the build table. Marki talked fast and rearranged elements even faster. Pretty soon all three men were molding and shaping the model. Finally, they stepped back.

"Does this look like what she described?" Marki asked.

Enmarsikil studied the model carefully. "The garden needs a high wall around it to maintain an even temperature inside. The bridge looked more like this," he said modeling it more carefully. He studied the layout of the garden, and his face lit up. "I want to change how the garden is laid out." He quickly rearranged beds and walkways until the final design looked like a rose from above. "That will do well."

"Let's see the location," Marki proposed.

They headed outside, hopped onto Enmarsikil's air skid and were soon well across the river.

"I thought those large weeping trees along the river banks would be a good spot to build beside," Enmarsikil said.

Marki, Shidim and Kiderin levitated and swept around the area marking out the walls for buildings and gardens on the ground. Marki finally landed back beside Enmarsikil.

"Shidim will get the plans finalized," Marki said. "Kiderin will grab our stone mason, Kabsar, and determine what we need of wood and stone to build. We may be able to get Nindulur to lay the foundations. As soon as the guys finish the meeting hall, we'll have them out here building."

"Thanks, Marki."

"If Astara's around, Latesh and Gadug could help her decide how to furnish and decorate," Marki added.

Enmarsikil swallowed hard and turned away. "She's not around at the moment."

Marki frowned but said nothing as he watched the Elder Brother trudge away.

"Not a good sign," Shidim said coming up behind Marki.

"Can you blame her?" Latesh asked. "Being the last to build?"

Marki just shook his head. "C'mon boys. We have a special build on our hands."

While Marki's Team started on Astara's dream, Enmarsikil took a long walk. Approaching Teacher's labs, he stopped and stared at the front door. Finally, curiosity got the better of him, and he went in. Once inside, he followed a hallway to a glass viewing area. Peering through the transparent wall, he watched Teacher work with the element samples from Ki. Enmarsikil took great interest in the swabs of material Teacher took from each sample and the cultures he set up using the swabs. Before long, Teacher left his benches, stepped into an airlock to strip out of his lab cloak and reset his personal frequency, and walked out into the viewing area where Enmarsikil waited.

"What are you culturing?" Enmarsikil asked.

"Bacterial samples," Teacher replied leading him back down the hall and outdoors. "I'm having Zalkur and Marne gather similar samples from Nibiru for me to test."

320

Enmarsikil tilted his head to one side. "Why?"

"Because I have found a bacterium on the Ki samples that seems to thrive in many different ecosystems adapting easily to each one. I'm wondering if we have a similar bacterium on Nibiru."

"What do you suspect?" Enmarsikil asked, intrigued.

"That the one on Nibiru may be more static, which is what allows you and the others to hold form here and anchor changes to Nibiru," Teacher replied.

"But the one of Ki may change to fit its new element and ecosystem thereby making it harder for us to hold to one form, the physical body. And that's why we would dissolve into our dominant element," Enmarsikil finished, his excitement growing.

Teacher nodded. "That's the hypothesis I'm testing now. I'm also testing microbial samples from some hybrid volunteers. If I have a match in their systems to the bacterium in the Nibiru samples, I may be able to devise a plan for your safety on Ki."

Enmarsikil's eyes were shining. "This is amazing, Father. I would never have thought to look at bacteria."

Teacher paused in their walk and gazed at him. "Father. You... acknowledge me again. I wasn't certain that would ever happen."

Enmarsikil looked down, nodded then raised his eyes to meet Teacher's. "I guess trying to be a leader," he said with a sweeping gesture of the town, "and being 'King' for a time taught me how hard this job really is and how easy it is to make mistakes even though you mean well."

"Oh?" Teacher asked.

Enmarsikil grimaced pausing while he tried to put his thoughts together. "I saw all the splendor of Agade and how everything was designed to make Anu look magnificent. Yet, my Teams found people living in squalor. I thought it better to put others first and deny my own happiness, live simply."

"And?" Teacher pressed.

"Well, I could do it, but Astara was absolutely crushed. She saw her sisters making their dreams come true and couldn't understand why we weren't also dreaming away," Enmarsikil admitted.

Teacher put his hand on Enmarsikil's shoulder. "No leader should deny themselves. That just depletes you. Your fellows thrive at your expense. Neither should a leader make ostentatious dreams their personal reality at the expense of their fellows. Then everyone resents them. No, it's a matter of balance, Enmarsikil. Your needs are no less real than those of your siblings. You can make certain they're provided for as you provide for yourself."

"Balance," Enmarsikil echoed. "I guess I lost that somewhere along the way."

"Easily regained," Teacher told him with a clap on the shoulder. "Easily regained."

They parted there, Teacher turning to inspect the fields of crops while Enmarsikil slid down the riverbank and took the stepping stones across like he and Astara had so long ago now. He stood on a large boulder in mid-stream reliving that memory when she had led him on a wild adventure. He could hear her laughter in his mind. A sudden pang clenched his chest.

Her laughter, he thought. *How long has it been since I've heard her laugh? Ah, Astara. How oppressive I've become that even your laughter has died.*

Enmarsikil continued across and up the other bank. He strolled the streets and alleys of their new town greeting siblings and feeling the jubilance in the air. Astara and Marki were right. No one here was homesick or lost in sadness. They were creative, energetic, vibrant. The move had given them all new life.

He entered the Meeting Hall and sat in the gallery watching the workmen craft the interior. Before long, Marki slid into a seat beside him.

"Aren't you worried about where she went?" he asked watching some ornamentation being raised for the ceiling.

Enmarsikil shook his head. "I know exactly where she is," he remarked.

"Think she'll come back?" Marki pressed.

"When I apologize. I'm waiting to have something to show her to make the apology mean something," Enmarsikil replied.

"That's why I'm here. To come get you. See what we've done so far. Make changes," Marki said.

Enmarsikil was out of his seat in a flash. "Let's go."

They took his air skid across the river. Enmarsikil marveled at the fact the garden walls were up and he could see the main buildings rising beyond them. He took the skid up over the walls and studied the work from above.

"The garden design is coming along well," he commented. "The waterfall needs less height, more stepped and the pool below needs to be deeper and broader. I like that the exit feeds the ponds beyond."

"You don't have any more fish to put in them," Marki pointed out.

Enmarsikil raised his finger. "Oh, but I do. I just need to hatch them out."

They quickly went through the house then Enmarsikil left for Teacher's labs. He found him sitting on the riverbank outside.

"Any chance you have a lab room I could use?" Enmarsikil asked sitting beside him.

"How big?"

"Large enough to set up a flow tank and hatch fish eggs," Enmarsikil replied.

"I've got just the spot," Teacher replied rising. "Let me get it set up for you."

"And I'll go get those eggs," Enmarsikil said, a note of excitement in his voice.

He took off across the city toward the Meeting Hall. Inside, up a narrow staircase, were two rooms. He opened one that held his equipment and samples from the Academy. Grabbing the case of his best fish eggs, he closed the door. Hesitantly, he opened the other. He'd been sleeping there nightly on a bed that took up the whole room. He thought of the cozy homes he'd seen in town with neighbor calling to neighbor out the windows. He shook his head and closed the door. *What was I thinking*? he wondered.

He hurried down the stairs and out the door heading straight back to the labs where Teacher awaited with a gravel bed in a tank with lightly flowing water. Enmarsikil added the eggs, spreading them over the surface of the gravel, and Teacher added a growth medium. In hours several hundred fish fry hatched out.

"Mind if I accelerate their growth?" Teacher asked.

Enmarsikil shook his head.

"We should be able to get them big enough to go in the ponds. They just may not have started to turn color," Teacher explained.

"Doesn't matter as long as they're there," Enmarsikil replied leaving.

With one glance back at the home in progress, he knew it was time to fly and find Astara. He hopped on his air skid and took off toward the mountains. He landed just outside the forest and slowly followed the gurgling creek up under the forest eaves.

Enmarsikil kept climbing up into the mountains until at last he could clearly detect a presence in the woods. However, rather than surrounding him and filling the air with gaiety, it retreated upstream. Slowly, he followed. When he reached the falls below the forest pool, a clear, determined pressure against him forced him to halt. It was impossible to move forward.

"Astara!" he called. "It's me! Enmarsikil!"

The pressure relented a little and allowed him to edge forward. He climbed over boulders until he finally stood on the bank of the pool. Glancing about, the forest seemed dark and foreboding. When he studied the clear water, it appeared empty.

"Astara, I came to apologize," he said kicking off his boots and pulling his tunic over his head. "I kept thinking everybody was in shock and homesick." Enmarsikil shed his pants and carefully stepped into the water. "But you were right," he admitted. "Everyone is happy, jubilant."

Enmarsikil slowly waded out into the middle of the pool. He sensed a presence watching him from above but coming no nearer.

"Astara, I'm sorry. I wasn't trying to make you miserable. I just became so focused on what I thought must be happening that I lost sight of what was really occurring. I lost perspective...balance," he concluded.

The presence hovered near though still remaining out of reach.

"Sweet, I miss you. I miss your laughter. More than anything I want you to be happy," Enmarsikil confessed. "I haven't heard your laughter in so long. Please give me a chance to bring it back."

Now, Enmarsikil sensed movement flowing toward him in the water. A breath shifted the tree limbs and the leaves fluttered. The water tumbling over the upper falls began to glow. It flowed into the pool and circled his legs spiraling upward. He gasped as her awareness touched him becoming more form-like though not fully physical. A head with deep wells of blue for eyes rose from the surface, and slender arms snaked up about him.

"You always take my breath away," he murmured. "I looked for you in the King's fountain. Something told me you'd be there."

A smile caressed her lips, and she began drawing him toward the shore. As she stepped onto the bank, Astara's physical form returned. She wrapped her arms around him.

"I missed you, too," she whispered.

He held her close wondering when the last time had been that their embrace had been so intimate and knowing it had been way too long.

"I have a surprise waiting for you," he told her.

"Our home?" she asked hopefully.

He nodded. "That and a lot more."

She pulled him in close.

"All of your favorite things," he whispered, "and a few additional touches."

324

Her smile lit her face, and she kissed his cheek. Enmarsikil didn't let her leave but turned his head and molded his lips over hers. Heat rose between them and the kiss deepened quickly.

"Shouldn't we find some place more comfortable?" he asked.

"Our moss bed is still here," Astara replied breaking away and leading him into the glade.

They got to the mossy bed that topped a low hillock, and he pulled her down beside him.

"I forgot how much I need you," he murmured sampling her lips again and caressing her breasts. "Not just this but your radiant smiles, your bubbling laughter. I must have that in my life. And your sense of play."

Astara ran her hands down his back and squeezed his buttocks, a mischievous gleam in her eyes.

"I need you to pull me back when I've lost my focus, my balance," Enmarsikil admitted. "You are my anchor, my change agent, my mate."

She kissed him and wrapped her legs around him reminding him of all the other wonderful things she was as well. And in a while, the glade glowed brilliantly.

They slept in each others' arms a while until a chilly breeze picked up.

"Brr. I need my clothes," Enmarsikil said sitting up and looking for where he had left them.

Astara retrieved hers and started dressing. "So, tell me about the house," she requested.

A mischievous gleam hit Enmarsikil's eyes. "Now, I can't give away all the secrets."

"You're going to make me wait?" she asked pouting.

He chuckled.

"You know I hate suspense," she reminded him.

"Which is why I'm taking you straight there on my air skid."

She sighed happily. "Oh good!"

He took her hand leading her down out of the mountains. When he found a wide opening, he initiated his air skid, they hopped on board and took off headed toward the town. Enmarsikil skirted the town, crossed the river and brought the air skid down to a few feet off the ground as they whisked past fields of crops and Teacher's labs.

"We'd better pull up," Astara called over her shoulder. "If we don't, we'll hit that wall."

Enmarsikil smiled to himself, butterflies dancing a jig in his stomach. He slowed to a halt right before the wall, reached over her shoulders and covered her eyes. Then he brought the air skid slowly up to the height of the wall. As he eased it forward, he slowly removed his hands.

"What do you think?" he asked.

Astara's eyes grew wide and her jaw dropped. Tears beaded on her lashes as she took in the gardens. To her left, a stepped waterfall splashed into a deep pool so like her favorite mountain haven. Some water siphoned off feeding a shallow creek that supplied long fish ponds. A small, arched bridge linked the path on the near side to the path on the far side. Beyond the ponds lay a well-manicured garden. As she studied it, she recognized the layout as the design of her flower. At the center of the garden she could just make out a lone bush.

Enmarsikil eased the air skid to the ground and let it go. Astara ran to the waterfall pool first almost diving in. He hurried after her grabbing her shoulders and holding her back.

"We have others here," he said nodding up the path toward a tree-shrouded building where Marki and his team waited.

Astara pulled back from the water's edge but dipped her hand in letting the water drip from her fingertips back into the pool. She rose and headed toward the bridge. She stood against the railing gazing into the water.

"Oh! There's fish!" she cried as several small fish swam out from under the bridge bright markings just beginning to emerge from the drab brown.

Astara glanced up at Enmarsikil wiping tears from her cheeks with her fingertips. "It's so much like home!"

She took his hand and led him down the other side of the bridge to the path that wound through the formal garden. Enmarsikil once again found himself tugged and pulled this way and that, happy memories of Astara's visits to his old gardens bubbling up. She led him all the way back to the center bed where a young bush with one dark red bud stood.

"Is it my flower?" Astara asked. "The one you made for me?"

"Yes, Sweet. That is your flower. I took a sapling with me."

Astara threw her arms around him then let go, bent down and pressed her lips to the bud.

Enmarsikil took her hand. "Don't you want to see our home?"

She looked up nodding.

Putting his arm around her shoulders, he led her toward the main path. As they approached the front door, Marki and his builders lined each

326

side of the path.

"Welcome to your home, Astara," he announced and thrust open the doors.

Astara tiptoed inside and gasped. The entry way opened to the long hall with the vaulted ceiling she had requested.   Up near the ceiling stained glass windows caught the light and cast colored designs on the floor.

"This makes me think of the long hall in the Academy," she breathed. "It's gorgeous."

Marki hurried to open the door straight across from the main entrance. Astara peered inside, clapped her hands with glee and danced her way inside.

"Oh, there's enough room for everyone! And the floor is amazing!" she exclaimed.

Enmarsikil gestured for her to come back out, and she twirled over into his arms. Marki led them to the right and into the great kitchen she had requested. Then they marched down the hall to the other end where Marki opened the door to their bedroom suite.

Astara put her hands over her mouth and started crying in earnest. "It's just like back home," she kept repeating as she flitted from the Visioning Sphere sunk into the floor, to the alcove and window with the telescope to the circular Memory Corner and lastly, her wardrobe. She finally sank onto the edge of the bed sobbing.

Marki frowned worriedly as Enmarsikil knelt beside her.

"Sweet, is something wrong?" he asked.

Astara emphatically shook her head no.

"Then, why are you crying, my love?" he asked, perplexed.

In between sobs, Astara managed to tell him. "I was so homesick," she sobbed. "No place felt comforting and...we weren't even together. But this is home! This is home! I'm finally home!"

Enmarsikil put his arms around her letting her cry on his shoulder. "You must have been terribly homesick," he murmured.

She nodded against his neck.

"I picked it up as if it were from everyone."

"No," she replied shaking her head.

Marki hesitated. "There is one more thing to show you."

Astara glanced up. He beckoned and she rose. Marki led them back to the dance hall and out a back door to a path that meandered down to a grove of large trees on the river bank. Suddenly, Astara spotted the treehouse nestled in the branches, squealed with delight and ran on ahead.

She reached the circular staircase that wound around a particularly straight tree and was soon waving to them from the deck above.

"You did an amazing job, Marki," Enmarsikil said huskily.

Marki cleared his throat and rubbed his eyes. "I told you I swore to do anything I could to make her happy."

"I'd say...mission accomplished," Enmarsikil replied.

"Hurry up, guys! You have to see this," Astara yelled down to them.

She disappeared into the foliage and Enmarsikil and Marki hurried up the stairs to the treehouse. They found her lounging in a swinging basket reminiscent of a bird's nest from which she watched the river flow by and the birds fly between the tree branches. As they approached, she grabbed both of the men and tugged them onto the swing beside her.

"Thank you, both of you," she said squeezing their hands. "You for conveying my dream so well," Astara said to Enmarsikil, "and you for creating it," she added giving Marki's cheek a kiss. "This is everything I could have hoped for."

Marki got up. "I'm going to leave you two to enjoy. Oh, and Teacher was by earlier about some research. He'll be back tomorrow."

Enmarsikil waved as Marki left the treehouse then snuggled back with Astara nestled in his arms. If Teacher had the news he hoped to hear, they might all finally have a way forward.

CHAPTER 40 - WAY FORWARD

Enmarsikil and Astara remained in the treehouse until the deep twilight fell. Nibiru was still too far out from the bright yellow sun at the center of the solar system, but it was on its approach toward its fellow planets and the sun. Soon twilight would be replaced by dusk then a growing light, and the days would grow hotter. For now, they left the chill of the tree branches and hurried inside to their new bedroom.

As Astara climbed into bed, she gazed about them. "You mean to tell me, you didn't miss any of this?" she asked.

Enmarsikil slipped under the covers beside her. "Now that we're here, I can feel how much this would have been comforting. But I was so focused that a closet was sufficient."

"You didn't even miss me?" she asked hesitantly.

He started to answer, opened his mouth, held his breath, held up one finger then clamped his mouth shut again. Finally, he exhaled and shook his head. "There is no good way to respond to that."

Astara's face registered her hurt.

"Sweet," Enmarsikil soothed reaching for her and drawing her closer. "I was so focused, so busy...I didn't even know how I felt. I pushed everything aside because it felt to me like everyone was drowning in shock and homesickness. I was driven to make things better."

"But the feeling grew stronger, didn't it?"

He nodded.

"Because it was me," she surmised.

"You and...well, perhaps as an empath, you drew to yourself the homesickness everyone else had felt as well," Enmarsikil hypothesized. "That way, the majority could move forward."

"Well, I'm not interested in moving," Astara remarked curling up against him. "I'm just interested in sleeping deeply for a long time."

Within minutes she was fast asleep, and he was close behind.

Awakening long before her, Enmarsikil gently slid out of bed and tucked the covers around her. He dressed quietly and left the house, meandering through the garden and feeding the fish as he used to. He stood looking around and realized how much he had missed the familiar routine.

The gate in the wall swung open, and he glanced over. Seeing Teacher, Enmarsikil set down his seed bag and pond skimmer and hurried to greet him.

"A little bit of the Academy here," Teacher noticed appreciatively.

"Astara was homesick but, truth be told, I think we all were a little," Enmarsikil replied. "It's just that she felt it for all of us."

He guided them to the rose garden paths, and they meandered through it slowly.

"So, Marki says you have news," Enmarsikil said.

"Confirmation," Teacher replied smiling. "Not only was my hypothesis about the bacteria correct, but I have devised a solution that a few volunteers have tried with great success."

Enmarsikil stopped, his feet crunching on the gravel. "Wait, why didn't you come to me?"

"Because you, son, have been the unwilling volunteer for too many trials. It was time for others to take the risks."

"Who?" Enmarsikil demanded.

"Satu and Nita were first," Teacher replied.

Enmarsikil nodded.

"Then their spouses and, when that was successful, their entire team," Teacher explained.

"How did you test your solution?" Enmarsikil wondered. "We have but small samples of Ki materials."

"I appropriated cast off materials from Agade and received further samples from Enki," Teacher replied. "I have entire rooms set up in the labs as Ecosystems mimicking Ki."

"And they didn't dissolve into their elements?" Enmarsikil pressed.

330

"They had a little difficulty at first, but we found foods and drink that help populate the inner microbiome. And those bacteria seem capable of communicating with the bacteria from Nibiru. They co-exist happily so far."

"I want to try this process," Enmarsikil said firmly. "I need to understand its nature for myself. It's time to gather the siblings to the Meeting Hall."

At that moment, they heard laughter and splashing.

Enmarsikil glanced about nervously. "Astara's in, um, water nymph mode I'm afraid."

Teacher turned toward the nearby garden wall, waved his hand and a wicket gate appeared. "I'll just let myself out here," he said with a wink.

Enmarsikil put his hands on his hips and nodded. It all felt like home. He hurried back through the gardens and across the bridge and had soon joined Astara in the Waterfall Pool. He stayed with Astara in the pool for a while, but turned more serious at last.

"Astara," he called out trying to dodge her nearly invisible, tickling fingers. "Sweet, I need to talk to you for a moment."

He tried to climb out, and she tried to hold him back.

"C'mon," Enmarsikil urged. "We'll play some more later."

With a mock pout, Astara let him go and pulled herself out of the pool. They grabbed their clothes and headed for the house.

"What's wrong?" she asked tugging her tunic over her head.

Enmarsikil shook his head. "Nothing's wrong. It's what has gone right. Teacher has devised a way for us to hold form on Ki."

Astara glanced up at him. "You want to go, don't you?"

Enmarsikil opened their front door. "I'll have to go to establish the Pact there. And Nita, Satu and their team are really hot to be there. I-I'd at least have to travel back and forth to make sure they're ok."

Astara stepped into the house and headed toward the bedroom. She quickly pulled out a fresh change of clothes and got dressed. "You want me to go, too, don't you?" she asked after a while.

Enmarsikil who had also pulled on fresh clothes sat on the edge of their bed. "I have no idea how long the journey is to Ki and back," he admitted. "But even a short time away from you seems too long."

She ambled over, sat next to him and put her head on his shoulder. "I'm having trouble wrapping my head around the idea," she confessed.

"It's ok," he assured her. "I want you to stay here the first time I go. I don't know what we'll come up against."

"You want me to be safe," she surmised.

He kissed her then wrapped his arms around her for a deeper kiss. "And I want to maintain my focus. You really do make it hard."

Astara smiled and chuckled lightly. "I don't do anything."

Enmarsikil smothered her in another kiss. "You don't have to. You're the honey and I'm the fly."

"Ok, I'll think about Ki," she replied.

"Thanks. Now, I want to see what Teacher has at the lab," he said rising and heading out the door.

Once on the patio, he mentally connected with Satu and Nita. *Meet me at Teacher's lab.*

Give us a little while," he heard Satu respond.

Enmarsikil went back inside their home, grabbed a bite to eat in the kitchen and headed back through the garden toward the main gate. Astara stood on the bridge watching the fish.

"Going somewhere?" she asked.

"The lab," Enmarsikil replied.

She smiled. "This feels like old times."

He smiled, waved and ducked out the main gate. As quickly as he could, Enmarsikil made the transit to the lab. Satu and Nita were just coming up the road from town. They met him outside and the three brothers walked in together.

"So, this treatment works?" Enmarsikil pressed. "You felt alright in Teacher's ecosystems?"

"We're still here, aren't we?" Satu challenged.

"The first couple of times were unpleasant," Nita admitted. "After you have enough of the Ki bacteria in your system, you almost don't notice the difference."

"I want to try this for myself," Enmarsikil insisted.

"Maybe," Nita responded, "but I'd do the culture first and feed it and wait till you have a high enough concentration in your system before entering the ecosystem."

Enmarsikil's face fell. "I wanted to call a Gathering in the Meeting Hall today. I wanted to be able to report on the process."

Satu stopped him. "You don't have to do everything first anymore. We've already done it. Let us give the report."

Enmarsikil chafed at the idea but finally acknowledged Satu's offer as his only way forward. Moments later, Teacher spotted them and exited a nearby lab.

"I have the culture ready for you," Teacher told Enmarsikil. "But I'd let it develop in your system first."

332

Enmarsikil nodded. "I've already been warned," he replied nodding toward Nita.

They followed Teacher into a lab, and he pulled a bottle from an area he kept cooled. He shook it and swirled the liquid inside a bit then handed it to Enmarsikil who eyed it suspiciously.

"What's it like?" he asked the brothers.

"Kind of like sour milk," Nita said.

"With a side order of chalk," Satu added. "Gulp it fast."

"Yeah, don't let it linger," Nita advised.

Enmarsikil held up the bottle, took a deep breath, tilted his head back and gulped it down. He coughed and gagged on the stuff, tears squeezing out the corners of his eyes, but he got it down.

"Flavoring," he sputtered. "Doesn't anyone believe in flavoring? Ack!"

Teacher handed him a goblet. "I promise this tastes far better. I didn't flavor the culture because I was concerned about killing off some of the bacteria."

Enmarsikil took the goblet. "What about killing us off?"

"You're made of tougher stuff than that," Teacher assured him.

Enmarsikil took a sip from the goblet. "Oh, much better." He gulped that down as well to chase away the hideous aftertaste.

"How long does it take for the bacteria to colonize?" he wanted to know.

"If you eat the foods Nita will show you and drink a goblet of this each day, I'd say you'd be ready to try an Ecosystem in a cycle," Teacher replied.

Enmarsikil nodded. "I plan to hold a gathering in the Meeting Hall."

"Do you want us there?" Teacher asked meaning he and the rest of the Multi-Dims.

Enmarsikil nodded. "Have you given any thought to that pact?"

Teacher's face turned dark. "Oh, I know exactly what will be in that pact and exactly how I will empower it."

"Good," Enmarsikil replied then turned to the brothers. "Would you mind helping me move my Visioning Sphere?"

They looked at each other then nodded.

The three brothers headed back to the new house whistling appreciatively at the gardens but stopping just inside the front door to stare at the long hall.

"Wow! I'd say some of the Academy sprang up again," Satu

remarked.

Nita turned around studying the stained glass higher up. "I always thought Astara was trying to escape the Academy."

"Not toward the end," Enmarsikil replied. "Let me see if she's about."

He checked the rooms but she was nowhere to be found. He led the brothers through the dance hall and out the back door.

"Where are we going?" Satu wondered.

Enmarsikil pointed up. The brothers followed the line of his outstretched hand. "C'mon. I'll show you the treehouse."

They climbed the spiral stairs finding Astara curled up in the basket swing admiring the river. She glanced up when she heard footsteps.

"What do you think?" she asked the brothers.

"Reminds me of home," Nita replied diplomatically.

"I like this up here better," Satu said.

"Well, right now we have to get the Visioning Sphere," Enmarsikil told them.

"Where is it going?" Astara wondered.

"Gathering at the Meeting Hall," Enmarsikil said. "Do you know where that special drape is you had made for it?"

Astara reached out her hand, he took it and pulled her to her feet. She nimbly headed down the steps with the brothers following. They filed into the dance hall, and Satu bowed with a sweeping gesture.

"One dance?" he asked Astara.

She giggled and took his outstretched hand. They waltzed awkwardly about the hall with Satu badly humming a tune.

"We need Didi and his flute," Nita remarked loudly.

The dancing pair stopped breathlessly alongside Enmarsikil.

"Maybe we could invite everybody over after the Gathering for a dance," she suggested, her eyes sparkling.

Enmarsikil nodded. "It would be nice to hear music and laughter again. But for now, I need that drape."

Astara headed toward their room. While the brothers helped Enmarsikil levitate the sphere out of its hollow, Astara ducked into her wardrobe, opened a drawer and pulled out a large, black silk cloth. She threw it over and around the sphere, and it was ready to transport.

"Sifting," Enmarsikil warned.

They quickly transited from the house to the Meeting House. The brothers lowered the sphere into place then Enmarsikil went to ring the bell on top of the building. Soon the seats would be full, and he would
334

outline the intent for the next phase of their lives.

When Enmarsikil returned to the meeting hall proper, his siblings were filing in and taking seats. It was an old, familiar routine. Before long, he stood down in the well ready to address them.

"The town!" Enmarsikil began exuberantly. "So well constructed, so well laid out. Each home unique. The hill homes, the tree homes and those along the river, solidly crafted yet artistically designed. And the crops; well done all! We have created our own world here, our own homes, our own comfort. Give yourselves a hand."

The hall rang with applause as the siblings celebrated this major milestone.

"Now that we've created a home of our own," Enmarsikil said once the applause died down, "it is time to look to the future. We fulfilled the promise we were literally created in order to keep. Our teams healed the hole in Nibiru's atmosphere. We were tossed from our childhood home and landed solidly on our own feet. However, if you will remember, two members of a new race on Ki both aided us and have asked for our aid in return."

Murmurs rippled around the room.

Enmarsikil held up his hand for quiet. "I do not expect that everyone will desire to travel to Ki. That's fine. We need to maintain a solid presence on Nibiru. However, there are teams who have already been preparing for the journey. As my elder self warned, the First Generation once lost their ability to hold form on Ki. As we know in our world, the past can be changed, timelines can be altered, and doing so impacts the future. And so today we still have our First Generation with us. We owe a great debt to that race that warned us of danger. And to this end, Teacher has researched and devised a treatment that will allow us to be in the presence of Ki's elements and maintain our physical form."

"But have you tried it?" someone yelled.

"I've only taken the first treatment," Enmarsikil admitted. "But Satu and Nita have completed the process."

Enmarsikil turned aside allowing his brothers to step forward along with Teacher.

"It all boils down to a simple, highly adaptable bacterium," Teacher informed them. "The Ulud, the Ancient of Days, is a bacterium that may even have begun time. It appears to inhabit every environment, adapts easily to the harshest conditions, and even resides in your bodies. There are a couple of fundamental differences between the species on Ki and the one on Nibiru, but when given the opportunity, they co-exist nicely and give the host perfect control over their physical form."

"Just drink Teacher's culture, feed the bacteria specific foods to cultivate them and within a cycle you can handle and be surrounded by Ki elements just as if they originated from Nibiru," Nita explained.

"And that was the last impediment to our traveling off world," Enmarsikil confirmed. "Only this isn't a straight shot. It will be done in stages for those who wish to take up the mission."

Teacher walked up beside him.

"First and foremost Teacher will establish a Pact with Anu, one that guarantees our safety and equality with the Anunnaki. One that metes out consequences should the Pact be acted against or broken in any way. Never again will our people live in subjugation to the Anunnaki as high class servants, which was our fate on the previous timeline. We aim to partner with them and at times accept work for a contract," Enmarsikil declared.

"Yes, and this Pact will extend from Anu to his sons, grandsons and any other Anunnaki leaders," Teacher said. "Should any of them deny the Pact and refuse to sign it, they will immediately be sucked into a null universe. If he or she doesn't quickly agree to sign it, they will die. This Pact shall be binding on all who possess DNA from Nibiru. And this time I and Enmarsikil shall join together to empower it."

"So, the first mission will be to establish the Pact with Anu here on Nibiru," Enmarsikil said. "The second will be a trip to Ki for Teacher and me to bring the Pact to Enki and Enlil and any other leaders in power. A small team of explorers will search for a suitable location for us to establish a colony."

"Once the Pact is in place," Enmarsikil continued, "we will take the experience of building this town and settlement and apply it to building our own settlement on Ki. Those who know terraforming and the raising of crops will be very important then as well."

"What is the final goal?" someone else called out.

"To find these humans, draw them out of Anunnaki slavery and teach them how to be free and remain free," Satu replied from nearby.

"Hopefully, if neither they nor us experience victimhood, it won't get passed down through human bloodlines," Nita added.

"May this cycle be broken," Enmarsikil agreed.

"When do we begin?" a brother half way down asked.

"I have the Pact ready," Teacher announced.

"Then I would say, right away," Enmarsikil replied. "While Teacher and I make our way to Agade and confront Anu, those teams intent on going off world need to gather and join together in creating a comprehensive plan."

"We'll facilitate this part," Satu offered.

Enmarsikil nodded and the meeting was over.

CHAPTER 41 - PREPARING THE WAY

When the meeting broke up and everyone was filing out of the Meeting Hall, Enmarsikil stayed behind to confer with Satu and Nita.

"For these first two missions, we won't need many," Enmarsikil said. "Teacher and I will tackle Anu on our own. And I can't think about traveling to Ki until I can enter the lab ecosystems safely."

The brothers nodded.

"The first mission to Ki will be sparse as well," Enmarsikil continued. "Our Space Transport Team and a Scout team to look for a settlement will be the only personnel besides Teacher and myself."

"It's the missions afterwards where more will be needed," Nita surmised.

Enmarsikil nodded. "Once the Pact has been established with Enki and Enlil, we will establish a colony, then contact the humans, then lead a select group of humans to establish a far flung colony and, lastly, inoculate humans with our DNA."

"You still need to consider a Facility in which to rest when you fade," Teacher remarked from nearby.

Enmarsikil glanced toward him. "I've been giving thought to that as well," he replied. "Given the spread of humans on Ki in the future and the wars the Anunnaki engender, locating a Facility on the planet is no longer a viable suggestion."

338

"Then what?" Satu challenged. "We aren't all coming back here."

Enmarsikil shook his head.

"We need something...a place," Nita began, his mind churning. "We need a way to be dimensionally close yet out of the time stream."

The three brothers looked at each other and chorused, "A pocket universe!"

"Or several," Nita said.

Enmarsikil gazed up as he mulled over the idea. "Yes. We could set everything up on Ki, get everything in readiness then step into an alternate dimension of no time. It would be but the blink of an eye to us when our DNA was fully awakening in humans."

"But when would we know it was time to step out? What would open the portals?" Satu wondered.

"World events?" Nita proposed.

"If I may offer a suggestion...." Teacher interjected.

The three men looked to him.

"You need to be brought out of your pocket universes by the awakened humans themselves. Humans who have gone through the process of discovering this extra aspect of themselves and who are actively recovering their lineage and history," Teacher explained. "Humans and Anunnaki will engender many world events. Nibiru's periodic near passes will perturb all the inner planets. There will be cyclic patterns of catastrophes. No, you must wait till you have living connections. The power, the force that engenders these connections will call to you. That is when you will know the time is right."

Enmarsikil looked to his brothers. They nodded in full agreement.

"Then we know what needs to be done," Enmarsikil said.

The brothers nodded again and the small group split up.

Enmarsikil headed up the levels with Teacher. Astara waited for him in the doorway. He stopped and studied her face.

"I'll see you at the lab," Teacher said and left.

"You don't look happy," Enmarsikil remarked.

Astara let out a heavy sigh. "All of this is going so fast, and you're talking about plans like they're all a done deal," she complained. "I can't even engage them. I've just found my way home again."

They walked out into the streets of their town listening to the sounds of the bustling nearby market where siblings exchanged goods and services.

"I'm just not ready to be uprooted yet," she said flatly.

Enmarsikil put his arm around her shoulders. "I guess I get caught up in Nita's and Satu's vision. They're driving to get to Ki."

"Do you think they still have some lasting effects from the other time line?" Astara wondered.

He nodded. "That's been my suspicion for a while now. And for me, having met myself on that timeline, interacted with him, even visited the humans...makes going to Ki feel imperative."

Astara's face fell. "It doesn't hit me that way at all. I feel like staying far away."

Enmarsikil frowned but said nothing.

"Then again, my future self and Ginny told me they didn't want me to have any of the bad experiences to pass along. When they said that, I just shut down."

"Ah," he replied comprehension dawning on his face. "I see. Well, we're going to have to figure a way to work this out. We can't be apart indefinitely."

Astara shook her head. "No, we already know what happens to me when we wait too long to power up."

Enmarsikil glanced at her hair, relieved to see it was still her normal light auburn. "You're right," he agreed hugging her to his side, "we can't let that happen again. We'll make it work out somehow."

She gave him a tight smile.

"For now, I need another dose of Teacher's culture," he told her.

"Ok. Then I'm going to the market," she said.

Enmarsikil gave her a quick kiss then headed over the bridge. Astara spun around, turned back toward the market and was soon engaged in spirited conversations with her friends.

Enmarsikil soon reached Teacher's labs, went inside and braced himself for the horrible tasting concoction.

"Seriously," he groaned handing the bottle back to Teacher, "you will not get many to take enough of that to make a difference."

Teacher proffered the goblet, which Enmarsikil gratefully accepted and swigged down the liquid. Then Teacher handed him a bowl filled with dark, leafy vegetables and berries. When he finished that, Teacher pulled a rock from Ki out of his robe..

"Want to try holding it?" he asked.

Enmarsikil didn't even need to get close to feel the effects from it. He shook his head. "Not yet."

Teacher tucked it back into his robes. "Ok. Maybe after the next dose of culture."

Enmarsikil shook himself like a wet dog stepping out of a pond

340

and hurried to leave the lab. He all but ran down the road to their new home, took up his pond skimmer and fish pellets and was soon lost in one of his old, familiar routines. He spent a long time mindlessly skimming leaves off the pond. Then he stood on the bridge and threw out pellets onto the water. Finally, he found a spot on the bank, sat down and watched the fish surface and the water boil as they ate.

Astara had a good idea building this place, he conceded inwardly. *I have to confess, I really missed all of this.*

A tingle flew up his spine, and he glanced up to spot her on the bridge watching the fish eat. Enmarsikil got to his feet, ambled over and stood on the bridge beside her.

"One of the happiest memories of my life happened on a bridge like this one," Astara murmured dreamily.

"When we kissed," he said smiling.

She nodded and leaned her head against his arm. "I stand on this bridge and relive that memory all over again."

"But it's in a bubble in my memory corner," Enmarsikil protested.

Astara shook her head. "It doesn't feel the same. Something about the physicality of the bridge and the fish and the gardens...just makes it feel more real to me."

He took her hand and led her up the path to their home. Once inside, they continued straight to the bed chamber. Astara stopped in the doorway taking in the large room.

"I remember the first time you showed me your room," she said quietly. "I was so awestruck. After having lived in a cubicle all my life to see such space." They moved inside the door. "There was your sphere in the floor," she said pointing to the empty spot since he'd recently moved it. "There were the bookshelves filled with tomes," she added sweeping her hand over the backs of books on the shelves. "There was the alcove with the desk and telescope." Astara walked over to where the new one stood, bent down and peered into the lens. "Your collection of oddities," she added spinning around to the shelves behind her. "Musical instruments... just all sorts of stuff that you were curious about and occupied your time."

Enmarsikil quietly followed her, the memory of that day warming his heart

Astara stopped at the circular, stepped memory corner. "But this was the best," she murmured. "Seeing all those memory bubbles." She reached her hand forward and bubbles popped up. One-by-one she touched them and laughter filled the room. "You know what's sad?"

Enmarsikil shook his head.

"This is the last bubble," she said opening the one of them making love upon his return from Agade. "After this, you stopped saving memories."

"We haven't exactly been in one place for a long time and a lot was happening," Enmarsikil pointed out.

She nodded in agreement. "But we are now."

He tilted his head to one side. "I wonder if you could learn to create memory bubbles," he mused. "Maybe the reason they don't feel as real to you is that they're my memories from my perspective."

"Or I need something physical to stimulate the memory," she suggested. "What do you do to create them?"

"Well, there's the element of water but a lot of air and electricity and...." he began.

"That has already gone beyond my elements," Astara pointed out.

Enmarsikil sighed. "I guess you're right. Nobody else seems to have created these."

"Probably because nobody else has as complete a set of elements and facility with them as you do," she said.

Still, he stood staring at the bubbles thinking there might be some other way something similar could be useful. Astara got a playful gleam in her eye, reached out and touched her favorite. The dance started playing all over again.

"You really like that one," Enmarsikil murmured pulling her close.

She grinned like a fiend. "Oh yes. I love the outcome."

He chuckled and began the dance with her in their room. As they got to different segments, Astara strategically removed an item of clothing. Not to be outdone, Enmarsikil began playing along. Soon, the floor was littered with clothes, the bubble was still playing but they were much too busy in bed to notice.

Enmarsikil and Astara curled up around each other and drifted off to sleep. After a while, images and ideas began swirling through his dreams. He shifted on the bed and murmured in his sleep. His eyes fluttered open and he ran his hand over his face.

There may be some good, alternate possibilities, he thought. *Need to test them out.*

Carefully sliding out of bed and quietly dressing, Enmarsikil sifted the dimensions straight into the heart of the Meeting Hall in town. Raising his hand, he darkened all the windows and closed and locked the doors. In moments, he hovered before his Visioning Sphere checking various possibilities. After a bit, he let the lines of possibility go and set his feet
342

back on the ground.

"If I make Nita and Satu my official representatives," Enmarsikil muttered while pacing. "Minor princes...something the Anunnaki would understand."

"That would work," Teacher's voice said from the shadows.

Enmarsikil stopped and spun to face him.

"Delegation of authority is a strategy employed by great leaders," Teacher affirmed.

"It just feels like I should be there, but I can't force Astara to move," Enmarsikil confessed.

Teacher rose and approached him. "I'm afraid I'm responsible for your need to be first, out in the forefront. It is not a true need, son. It's a habit I conditioned into you."

Enmarsikil crossed his arms in front of him and considered his father's confession. "Do you think the Anunnaki will accept my brothers as my equals? As my voice of authority in my absence?"

"You have learned how they structure status and authority," Teacher replied. "Use what you learned in Agade to your advantage."

Enmarsikil nodded thoughtfully. "Thanks. I will."

With a wave good-bye, Enmarsikil sifted back to his home and found Astara in the kitchen. He took her hands, drew her over to the table and pulled her down onto a chair beside him.

Still cupping her hands in his, he held her gaze. "I think I may have discovered a possible solution to the Ki dilemma," he announced.

Astara tilted her head to one side and raised her eyebrow in question.

"I just came back from using the Visioning Sphere. If I can get the Anunnaki to accept Nita and Satu as my representatives, my voice of authority when I'm away, I wouldn't have to live on Ki," he explained. "I'd just have to make periodic visits. Would you feel better about that?"

Astara grew teary and she nodded.

"We'll still have to figure out what to do while I'm traveling, but you won't have to give up our home here," Enmarsikil asserted. "You can stay here where you're happiest."

Astara lunged forward throwing her arms around his neck. "Thank you," she whispered. "This means so much to me."

He patted her shoulders. "I know, and I want you to be happy."

She pulled back to look at him. "What if I want to visit once just to see what Ki is like?"

"You'd better start Teacher's culture then," he admonished. "I don't want to lose you to your element forever."

Astara nodded. "Have you talked to Satu and Nita yet?"

He shook his head. "But I don't think I'll get any resistance from them."

Enmarsikil rose. "Well, if that's set, I guess it's time to put things in motion. Time to call another gathering."

"Right after a meal," Astara insisted pushing him back down and setting a plate of food before him.

They ate quietly but Enmarsikil couldn't help but notice the shine in her eyes, and the way she smiled from time-to-time. The tightness in his chest eased, and he breathed a sigh of relief.

Once they were done, they headed out for town. Enmarsikil sent out a telepathic message for Nita and Satu to meet them at the Meeting Hall. The brothers were sitting in seats in the top row when the couple arrived. Enmarsikil sat with them quickly explaining his idea. Both men readily accepted his proposal, and Astara went to the tower to ring the assembly bell.

Before long, the siblings were all assembled, and Enmarsikil stood in the well with Nita and Satu. Enmarsikil whistled and the chatter died down.

"It's time to set the next phase of our lives into motion," Enmarsikil announced. "In a cycle, Teacher and I should be leaving for Agade to establish the Pact with Anu."

Astara stood. "It should not be just you and Teacher," she said. "That is their model. Marne should go as well."

He stared at her, a chill running down his spine. "Will you go as well, by my side?" he asked.

Astara smiled. "Absolutely."

Enmarsikil returned her smile then turned his attention back to the gathering. "Because I may not always be on Ki, but Nita and Satu have committed themselves and their team to a long term mission on Ki, I will be taking them to Agade to present them as my formal representatives in my absence."

"What about anyone else who wants to go to Ki?" Marki called out.

"Even to sustain a brief visit requires a full course of Teacher's culture," Enmarsikil replied. "But make this a solemn discussion with your mate first. Not everyone wants to undertake this journey and no one should feel forced into it. And remember, each couple is a unit. You cannot live apart and remain healthy."

344

With that, he dismissed the gathering. Astara, Kienelil, Aiya and Bilnammul approached the men in the well.

"You all need some really authoritative clothes," Kienelil said.

"Yes, I remember how the Anunnaki of different statuses dressed," Astara added.

"All three of you have to appear royal," Aiya concurred.

Enmarsikil nodded. "You ladies did a wonderful job the first time I went to Agade. I'll leave our attire in your capable hands."

The girls followed the men out of the Meeting Hall and across the bridge to Teacher's lab. Once inside, Teacher came out to greet them.

"We're here to start the culture," Astara said. "I think Ki might be worth a visit some time."

Teacher nodded, left briefly and returned with a tray of culture bottles. Astara took one, held it up to her nose, took a whiff and quickly turned her face away.

"That's horrible!" she gagged.

"Are you trying to kill us?" Aiya asked.

"That's what I said," Satu squeaked.

"He said we were tougher than that," Nita added.

"And of course you acted tough and swallowed that stuff," Kienelil ribbed.

"I thought flavoring would help," Enmarsikil offered.

"If you want anyone else to take it, something needs to change," Bilnammul asserted.

"I didn't want to risk destroying the bacteria," Teacher explained.

Astara stared at him. "Oh, please. Conditions in our stomachs are a lot harsher than berries and sweet syrup."

Aiya grabbed the tray from Teacher's hands. "C'mon, ladies. Let's see what we can do with this stuff."

Before Teacher could protest, they spun on their heels and headed for the door.

"Keep it cool!" he called weakly after them.

"And this is what women are for," Nita remarked.

"Yeah, they don't take no for an answer," Satu agreed.

"And they don't feel the need to be tough," Enmarsikil added sheepishly.

"Speaking of 'tough,' are you ready to try out an ecosystem?" Teacher asked.

"Did I need more of that stuff?" Enmarsikil queried.

"Probably not," Teacher replied. "I have yet to figure out an exact

345

dose, and it may be individual."

"I'll give it a try," Enmarsikil replied gamely. "I remember how it felt when I encountered the examples in the labs in Agade. I have a reference point."

Teacher turned and led the way to a series of smaller rooms toward the back.

"Does it matter which one?" Enmarsikil asked looking to the brothers.

Satu shrugged.

"The desert ecosystem was a little more comfortable to me," Nita offered pointing to a nearby door.

Enmarsikil took a deep breath, rubbed his hands together and slowly entered the room. Instantly, he could feel the change in the room though part of that was due to being in a completely unfamiliar environment. He walked about touching rocks, allowing sand to sift between his fingers, touching prickly desert plants. A high pitched buzz rang through his head, which lessened when he stood up. After a while, the heat got to him, and he left the room.

"How do you feel?" Teacher asked quietly.

"My head's ringing, and I'm dying of thirst," Enmarsikil replied.

Teacher proffered the goblet, and Enmarsikil drank greedily.

"Not bad for the first time," Satu commented.

"The ringing goes away," Nita assured him.

"Thanks. Good to know." Enmarsikil paused a moment. "Seems...strange to have had someone try this before me. Good....just strange."

"Another step for facilitatorship," Satu said clapping his elder brother on the shoulder.

"Keep me honest, gents," Enmarsikil admonished. "This is the way we were made to be."

As the men were heading toward the front of the lab, the girls walked in with the four bottles.

"Try these," Aiya suggested. "Each one has different flavoring."

The three men took a sip of each bottle, looked at each other then at Teacher.

"Really, you were trying to kill us," Satu insisted. "This is better."

"Well, you'd better let the ladies have what remains," Teacher admonished.

The men handed the bottles back and the four ladies swigged the culture down. Teacher passed around the goblet and the process began
346

anew. For now, they could only wait, except for those going to Agade. Now it was time to prepare.

CHAPTER 42 - LIVING PACT

Before the cycle was up, the ladies had new outfits ready for those headed for Agade. Enmarsikil and Astara took theirs into their bedchamber to try them on.

"You could always wear the water nymph robe," Astara said pulling it from the wardrobe and holding it up. "Bilnammul fixed it."

Enmarsikil glanced at it and shook his head. "It holds a few too many memories for me in the Agade setting."

Astara pouted and tucked it back into the wardrobe. "But I love the way you look in it."

Enmarsikil hung the shining black coat with gold embroidery the ladies had created for him where he could see it better. "I promise to find an occasion to wear the water nymph coat just for you," he assured her, leaning over to kiss her cheek. "But for this occasion, I want to dress like royalty with an air of authority and just a hint of threat. I think the black will be perfect."

"We could hold a send off dance before you leave for Ki," she proposed. "You could wear it then."

He nodded his agreement. "I'll wear it then. I promise."

Astara beamed happily and held up a new gown. "I'm going to wear black with silver accents," she said holding the column gown up in front of her for his appraisal.

348

"That's new," Enmarsikil remarked appreciatively.

"Mm-hm. I thought it was time for my wardrobe to grow up," she replied. "And I feel the need for protection in Anu's court."

He set his jaw grimly. "After our last meeting with him, this one may be a challenge. At least we aren't going alone."

"Ready to do this?" Astara asked.

Enmarsikil nodded definitively.

"Then let's become royalty," she said.

The couple changed and arranged their clothes and accessories carefully. Satisfied with their appearance, they swept down the hall to the patio before the front door where Teacher, Marne, Nita and Satu waited. Satu was dressed in an elegant, midnight blue robe, and his normally spiky hair was unusually tame. Nita looked handsome as his dark wavy hair spilled over the shoulders of his deep maroon coat. Both outfits had gold trim around the collar.

Enmarsikil eyed them carefully, picked up a box from the nearby table and opened it. He drew round medal seals with his phoenix motif for each, and hung them by broad ribbons about their necks.

"I've seen the Anunnaki do this with those they elevate in status and everyone seems to respect that new status," he explained.

"Here's hoping," Satu said.

Enmarsikil nodded.

Marne set a platform under them and Teacher sifted the dimensions. In no time they appeared just inside the Throne Room doors causing quite a stir. Anu glowered at them from the dais the moment he spotted them.

Without saying a word, the six people approached the throne, courtiers parting for them as they went. At the foot of the dais, they bowed their heads in respect then raised their eyes to meet Anu's.

"To what do I owe this...honor?" Anu asked, his teeth grinding.

"We have a Pact to establish between our people and yours," Teacher said drawing a scroll from a pocket in his cloak.

"Wait!" Astara spoke up. "The queen is not here. Antu was kind to us before. She should be party to this as well."

A red collar began creeping up Anu's neck, but he motioned to a servant who hurried to get the queen. In minutes, Antu entered from a side door, approached the throne and, upon Anu's recognition, took her own seat a little lower than his. She smiled in recognition at seeing the younger couple.

"Once our children were a well-kept secret," Teacher began.

"Your children?" Anu asked. "They are blood of Enki and Ninmah."

"And our blood as well," Marne reminded him.

"After our last visit," Enmarsikil said, "we are certainly secret no more."

"Rather like celebrated," Antu murmured.

"Yes, and you bargained for a large chunk of land, which you got," Anu pointed out. "What more could you want?"

"Sovereignty," Enmarsikil replied.

"You gave back the throne."

"Over ourselves and our lives," Astara stated.

"Yes, and then you'll come after my throne," Anu charged. "You think you're better than me."

Enmarsikil shook his head. "I have no use for your throne, neither do my siblings. No, we agree to leave you alone to rule your people, and you are to agree to leave us in peace. In exchange we would like the authority to partner with your people here and on Ki. Not in a subservient role but as equals."

"And this Pact defines the terms," Teacher added handing Anu the scroll.

Anu opened it and slowly read line-by-line. "And what if I deny the Pact?"

"That Pact is a living entity the likes of which you have never seen. It is designed to ensure that my children are never molested or harmed in any way. Once read, anyone who denies it is automatically sucked into a null universe from which there is no live escape unless they immediately acknowledge the Pact and agree to sign," Teacher explained.

"And what sorts of crafts can you possibly offer to make this exchange worth our while?" Anu wanted to know.

Enmarsikil turned to Astara who held two long, flat boxes. She stepped forward offering one to each ruler.

"Our craftsmen have devised ways to use the purest gold, in the smallest quantities and make the most elegant of items," Astara explained

Antu gasped when she opened her box to discover a gleaming gold filigree necklace. A servant stepped forward and fastened the gleaming gold about her neck. Seeing Antu's gift, Anu was quick to open his box. His eyes bulged in his head as his face was bathed with golden light. Lying in the box was a collar of the purest gold set with bright, clear gems. His servant also lifted the item to his neck and set it in place.

"Your people have considerable talent," Anu remarked

350

appreciatively.

"In this arena and many others," Enmarsikil greed. "We wish a free and equal exchange of talents and ideas."

Anu glanced at Antu who nodded slightly. He took a pen from a servant, affixed his name to the bottom of the scroll and rolled it back up. He held the scroll out to Teacher who took it and tucked it back into his robe.

"You will want to contact Enki, Enlil and anyone else you have placed in charge on Ki," Teacher warned. "We will be presenting the Pact to them as well."

"If you arrive bearing such gifts, I see no one refusing your wishes," Anu told him.

"Just remember," Marne cautioned, "if you ever think to renege on the Pact, it means instant death. We shall energize it and make it so."

"There is one other matter to attend to," Enmarsikil announced. "While I may not always be on Ki with my people who choose to live and work there, my brothers have committed themselves to a full time mission on Ki."

Nita and Satu stepped forward holding themselves at attention.

"On my left is Satuatuini and on my right is Nitadugita. They carry the weight of my authority. Their words are considered to be my words; their voice, my voice. I want this to be clearly understood by you and clearly conveyed to your sons and grandchildren," Enmarsikil said in a tone that would accept no other option.

Anu studied the two other men on either side of Enmarsikil. He noticed the medals with Enmarsikil's seal hanging about their necks and nodded. "I shall make it so," he said at last.

Enmarsikil nodded and with that, the six individuals vanished leaving king and queen to admire their golden gifts.

Once they arrived back at the house and gardens, Teacher and Marne quickly took their leave. Enmarsikil and Astara changed and he immediately sat down with Satu and Nita to begin planning for the trip to Ki. It would require clothes suitable for the climates the lab ecosystems represented. Cloth and clothing makers began working to outfit not only Enmarsikil but the Space Transport and Scout teams as well.

Meanwhile, Astara kept joining the other women in drinking the flavored culture. They watched the men enter the different ecosystem rooms and acclimate easily. However, when the women tried, they had stronger reactions to the Ki elements.

"We will have to study this thoroughly," Teacher told the pioneers.

"It could be that the higher levels of female hormones and their cyclic nature throw off the balance of bacteria."

Astara looked to Enmarsikil with sad eyes. "Doesn't look like I'll be going with you."

Enmarsikil gave her a hug. "I hadn't planned to take you with me this trip," he admitted. "If we didn't need to locate territory for our own settlement, I wouldn't be taking the Scouts, and now I need to be able to introduce Satu and Nita. There's no way to know the reception we'll receive. Father and I alone can handle them, even more so with Satu and Nita. But if you were there, I would worry about your safety."

"You'd be distracted."

He nodded.

"Just come back," Astara begged.

Enmarsikil brushed the hair back from her eyes. "I promise."

Along with preparations for the journey, Enmarsikil couldn't shake the feeling that there had to be a way for he and Astara to maintain contact while he was gone. He tried different things with the memory bubbles, but they all required the use of elements she just didn't possess an attunement to. Satu kept mentioning pocket universes as the end goal of his team's mission, but the idea passed around Enmarsikil until one day, while staring into the water of his fish pond, an image appeared on the pond surface. It was blurry at first but as he stared at it, he found himself looking at himself in another world.

In the vision, he saw himself visit Astara in a village of siblings and Anunnaki. She was miserable, and his heart was sick. He sat outside her house playing with universes until suddenly, he created an opening and entered a perfect bubble. Frowning, he watched himself enlarge it, create portals to it then awaken a sleeping Astara and take her through into it. Without warning, the vision vanished and he snapped back to his reality.

Pocket universe, he thought. *It's as if I did that once before. Perhaps my future self sent me the vision. Perhaps that's how he and his Astara stayed in touch on Ki. Now what would happen if we created one she and I could each equally access, like he did?*

After feeding his fish and working in the garden, he repeatedly tried different applications of the idea. One day, a small universe opened for him. He stepped into it, studied its features and stepped back out. Nodding, he spent some time developing a technique for opening and entering it. Once he had that down, he hurried to find Astara.

"Sweet," he called throughout the house.

Finally, he found her out back returning from the treehouse. She

352

heard him call and broke into a run.

"What's wrong?" she asked worriedly.

"Nothing," he replied, his eyes bright. "I've created something that will help us while I'm gone."

Curious, she looked up at him expectantly.

"I've found a pocket universe we can equally access and make into a space we can enter no matter where we're at," he explained breathlessly.

Astara's eyes widened. "Really?"

Enmarsikil nodded. "Watch."

He made a particular series of motions with his hands and suddenly, a swirl of silvers appeared before them. He took her hand. "C'mon. Step through," he urged.

Together, they pushed into the swirl and came out into a complete little universe of their own. Astara spun around taking it in.

"I'm going to go out this other side," Enmarsikil explained. "That way, it will have two entry portals. You can enter from that side and I can enter from this."

He repeated the hand motions, another swirl of silver appeared and he pushed outside of the little universe. Moments later, he stepped back inside.

"So," he continued. "I'll teach you how to open it from your side. And I can open it from mine."

"And when you're on the ship and on Ki, we can meet here," Astara said catching on.

He nodded.

She threw her arms around him. "Oh, this is so wonderful. I was prepared to miss you terribly."

He held her close rubbing her back. "I know. Me, too. But Satu kept talking about pocket universes till it dawned on me we didn't need to wait to use them."

Enmarsikil took her hand and pulled her back out through her side. He closed the portal then spent time teaching her how to open, enter, exit and close the portal until he was certain she could do it without help.

"We'll have to use telepathy to let each other know when we want to get together," Enmarsikil told her.

"That's ok. Just knowing I'll be able to see you and talk to you while you're gone makes me feel so much better."

"Me, too. Now for the rest of the preparations."

Before they knew it, all was in readiness. The night before they set off, the main gate to the wall around the house was thrown open with tiny, sparkling fairy lights trimming the trees along the path leading to the front door. A steady stream of bobbing lights wove its way across the river bridge from the town to the road along the riverfront. Choruses of song could be heard on the night air wafted by cool breezes.

Inside the house, Didi and other musicians were warming up in the dance hall. Marki, Mirsigmi and Aiya were bustling about the Great Kitchen tasting this, chopping that and checking on the food. In the bed chamber, Enmarsikil put the finishing touches on his blue water-nymph robe. He heard a swish of cloth behind him, turned and let his jaw hang open.

Astara stood before him in a tight, gold-trimmed blue bodice, bare midriff and low slung, filmy blue skirt. Kohl rimmed her eyes dusting her lashes. A subtle red stain just touched her lips and cheeks. She smiled.

"You like?" she asked turning in a slow circle with hip rotations to accent her moves.

"Oh...ahem...I like," Enmarsikil remarked. He held out his arm to her. "Our guests will be arriving shortly. Shall we?"

Astara took his arm and they swept out the door, down the hall and threw open the front door. The air was electric with excitement and the atmosphere was festive. They hugged brothers and sisters in warm greeting, showing them surprise elements of the gardens as they waited for everyone to collect. Suddenly, a bell rang and Marki called them inside.

With a buzz everyone filed into the house and straight into the dance hall to sit at the long tables that had been set up for the meal. Marki and his crew had laid out a long buffet, the aroma from which was mouth watering. The Multi-Dims popped in and Enmarsikil waved them over.

Teacher held up his hand for silence and it worked like magic as it always had. He nodded to Enmarsikil.

"This is a celebration," Enmarsikil announced. "Mudizinizi and Kisikilturkasu are now paired."

The happy couple waved.

"Our home is complete and open to you. Marki, Mirsigmi and Aiya have prepared an absolute feast," Enmarsikil added.

Marki beamed from where he stood at the carving station.

"We have the best musicians," Enmarsikil added saluting Didi and his players. "Tonight let's eat, let's dance and let's sing."

His siblings applauded and immediately filed up to the banquet table. Marki and his crew were kept busy running to and from the kitchen. At one point, Astara snuck away. She poked her nose around the corner glancing about the kitchen, opened her mouth to speak then stopped.

Marki sat on a bench in the kitchen stripping a lobster clean.

"I was going to tell you guys to help yourself," she said.

Marki glanced up. "Someone didn't like lobster. Can't let good food go to waste."

Astara laughed. "Just make sure Mirsigmi and Aiya get to eat."

"We've been taking breaks in turn," he assured her.

"Well, thanks to all three of you for such hard work. The food is to die for," Astara remarked before heading back to the dance hall.

An hour or so into the banquet the musicians stood to play. Enmarsikil and the others raised their hands and the long tables pushed back against the walls.

"Let the dancing commence," Enmarsikil called and Didi struck a lively tune.

Several songs in, Enmarsikil spotted Astara, cut in and whirled her about the floor in a sweeping waltz. The dancing seemed to go on forever and when anyone got too hot, Astara led them out the back and to the treehouse that also sparkled with fairy lights.

In the end, she never knew when people left. She fell asleep in a corner and Enmarsikil scooped her up carrying her to bed. Not too much longer thereafter, the party wound down. After closing the gate on the very last person, Enmarsikil finally joined her. Tomorrow would be a momentous day.

Enmarsikil remained awake lying on his side watching Astara sleep. He reached out, picked up one lock of her long hair and twirled it about his fingers. When that wasn't enough, he edged closer and kissed her neck and shoulders. She murmured and rolled onto her back. He gently smoothed the hair back from her face and spread tiny kisses over her cheek and jaw. Astara blinked, opened her eyes and stared up at him. He picked up her closest hand and kissed her fingertips.

"Trouble sleeping?" she asked reaching up and caressing his face.

"I wanted to remember you," he whispered. "I don't know how long I'll be gone. At first, I thought I'd watch you sleep. Then I thought there was no harm in playing with a lock of your hair. But I couldn't stop. I had to touch you, kiss you."

Astara smiled. "I'm glad you did. I'm going to miss you so much."

Enmarsikil pressed his lips to hers and lay his body directly alongside hers. Before too long their legs were entwined, her bodice was off, their caresses grew more fervent, and their moans mingled. They didn't stop until a bell in the hall warned them that someone was at the gate.

Enmarsikil wrapped her in his arms. "Time for me to go, Sweet."

"I know, but I don't want you to."

He kissed her one last time and went to roll over only her arms encircled his waist.

"You're not making this easy," he protested lightly.

"I never promised to make it easy. I only promised to give you good reasons to come back," Astara said playfully.

"You do, Sweet," Enmarsikil said disengaging her hands and sliding out of bed.

Astara got up, threw on a tunic, leggings and boots and headed for the kitchen. By the time Enmarsikil was showered and dressed, she had a quick meal ready. Afterwards she walked with him to the gate. Outside, a note was posted near the bell pull. Enmarsikil took and read it.

"Looks like everything is in order," he said leading the way past Teacher's lab.

They turned away from the river passing by one of the crop fields. Beyond the fields was a low plain right on the border of their territory. The Space Transport team had already been hard at work with the vehicle nearly complete and all their provisions already stored on board. There was also an entire deck for plants, most of which were food bearing. All of them would act as air scrubbers turning over stale air for fresh.

While the Space Transport team lined up in mated pairs, since they would not physically leave the vehicle, only Ki from the Scout team had sufficiently acclimated to the new bacteria to accompany Kumzubar to the surface. There were hugs all around and, by the time they were finished, Teacher and Marne appeared.

"Are you going, too?" Astara asked her.

"Oh no. They are well suited to manage this on their own," Marne replied.

At last the pairs entered the ship, and Teacher stood in the doorway. Enmarsikil wrapped his arms tightly about Astara.

"Remember to feed the fish and skim the leaves," he reminded her. "And don't hole up alone. Go into town."

Tears trickled down her cheeks and she nodded. She smiled up at him through her tears. "You make them accept that Pact and take care of yourself."

He nodded. "What one thing must a settlement have?" he asked.

"Fresh, clear, running water," Astara replied, "and a waterfall nearby."

356

"You got it."

"Son, it's time to leave," Teacher called from near the vehicle entry.

Reluctantly, the couple parted. Enmarsikil walked up the entry plank, turned at the top to blow Astara one last kiss, then ducked inside the door that closed behind him.

The onlookers instinctively moved back as the engines roared to life. Slowly, the great vehicle rose from the ground, rotated toward the far horizon then took off with a deafening rumble. In moments, it was nothing more than a bright star in the sky.

As the craft broke free of the pull of Nibiru's gravity, they reached orbital height and velocity, circled the planet once and, like being shot from a sling, zipped off into space.

Enmarsikil had made his way to the control deck and watched their progress on the monitors. "We have the most data about the outer planets," he said.

"Should we sift?" Zupatu asked.

"Yes, right up to the Hammered Bracelet," Enmarsikil replied. "At that point we have much less detail."

"And our strategy for getting through that asteroid field?" Gugbubulu asked.

"Bring Erumgal and Ushumgal up here to clear a path through for us. Izishub and I can back up for them if they tire," Enmarsikil outlined.

"Sounds like a plan," Guranmulla said enthusiastically.

"Get ready to leave the star field," Zupatu announced. "Radarkumita, get ready with coordinates."

In moments the entire ship was pulled into the void with Muduabzu and Radarkumita searching for the right coordinates to bring them out this side of the Hammered Bracelet. They entered the coordinates, which lit up on a grid projected at the front of the ship.

"Prepare to fire," Zupatu warned.

"Fire," Gugbubulu commanded.

The ship instantly leapt forward flying through the Field that underlies all. What would have been a journey consisting of many light years turned into a trip of mere cycles. Before long, the ship came out into the overlying reality right on the edge of the asteroid belt.

Erumgal and Ushumgal were called on deck where they strapped into suits that would translate their powers and actions from inside to outside the vehicle. Just in case, the backup suits were brought up, and Enmarsikil and Izishub remained near on standby.

"Going in," Nindulur announced. "Protective shield up."

Namtare stood next to her capturing images of incoming asteroids and feeding them back to the pan elementals. Erumgal and Ushumgal began swinging, their powers firing outside the ship hitting asteroids before they came too close. Suddenly, Izishub jumped into his suit and fired overhead. As each opening appeared, Gugbubulu squeezed the ship through.

Mid-way through the field, Enmarsikil entered his suit and started taking care of straggling asteroids. At one point, he pulled out Astara's Wind Blade and sent it slicing through many ice rocks. They exploded around them leaving the ship unscathed. Finally out of the Hammered Bracelet, the ship moved forward slowly.

"How long will mapping take?" Enmarsikil asked Mudu.

"Not long. I'm tapping into the Anunnaki mapping and navigation system," Mudu replied.

"Plot a course for Ki when you have an entire set of coordinates," Enmarsikil instructed. "Then sift to within orbital distance and make a few passes around Ki to take imaging studies. When that's done, alert me."

Mudu nodded and Enmarsikil headed back to his quarters.

As soon as he entered his cabin, he secured the door with an energetic lock. Immediately, he went through the process of opening the portal to the world he'd designed for he and Astara. Stepping through, Enmarsikil was surprised to find new elements such as a garden, a fountain, a fish pond and a lush bed.

She's been here, he thought. *Why didn't I know it?*

Concerned, he sent out a telepathic call to her. It took several attempts before he saw her portal open and she stepped through. With a squeal of delight, Astara ran to him and wrapped her arms around him. He hugged her to himself, so happy to have her in his arms again. They kissed like air was no necessity finally relinquishing their connection with a soft gasp.

"You've already been here," Enmarsikil stated.

Astara nodded against his chest. "I couldn't connect with you, but when I asked Marne, she tracked you in the Hammered Bracelet," she explained.

"Ah."

"So, I decided to see if I couldn't make our space a little more cozy until you could respond. What do you think?" she asked.

"I love it," Enmarsikil replied.

"How are you doing? Where are you in space?" she gushed leading him over to the fish pond.

He took a moment to add his own creation of a padded bench, and they sat down curled up in each other's arms.

"We just got through the Hammered Bracelet and Mudu is accessing the Anunnaki galaxy maps for coordinates to Ki. They'll sift into orbital range and make a few passes around the planet doing some scans. Then we'll find Enlil's city of Nippur, land, and present the Pact."

"Are you nervous?" Astara asked.

Enmarsikil thought for a moment. "Yes and no. Since mother taught me to read the spaces around the Anunnaki, I can tell their thoughts and ambitions. They can't hide anything."

"That's definitely a skill in your favor," she replied.

"Yes, and one I need to teach to Nita and Satu. But enough about me. I haven't much time. How are you doing?" he asked giving her his full attention.

Astara dropped her eyes. "It's been hard. The house is so big and empty without you. The bed is so cold."

"Have you gone into town?" he queried.

She nodded. "I've stayed with Aiya and Bilnammul some and just gone home to tend the fish. Peenzermi asked me to stay later. I just don't want to be a morose pest."

"I doubt they think you are," Enmarsikil said giving her a reassuring hug.

"Maybe not. I just know I'm really lonely without you."

"Which is why we created this little space for ourselves," Enmarsikil reminded her.

Astara wrapped her arms around him and held him tight.

As if from a long distance, they both heard Nindulur calling his name. Enmarsikil perked his head up.

"That's my cue," he said rising. "We've been in orbit and they've finished the scans."

"You have to go so soon?" Astara asked, her eyes brimming.

Enmarsikil kissed her and rubbed her shoulders. "Now, Sweet. I told you I didn't have much time. I'll contact you again when the Pact has been signed and energized. I promise."

Astara sighed heavily. "All right. I'm just so happy to see you again."

He gave her one last kiss. "Me, too. Now go take Peenzermi up on her offer. I'll be in touch later.

"Ok," she said reluctantly letting him go and watching him retreat through his portal.

Enmarsikil stepped back into his room, headed out into the corridor and was soon back in the control room.

The ship was just moving into an orbit near the planet's equator.

"Anu says Enlil maintains the bond heaven-earth, the Duranki. He is aware of our coming. Find the frequency, make our intentions known and prepare to land nearby," Enmarsikil detailed. "The only landing party will be Teacher and myself for now. I'll come back for Nita and Satu. Everyone else remain with the ship."

Enmarsikil left the control room directly thereafter for his cabin. Once inside, he dressed carefully. Having sifted the timelines and having had Muduabzu and Namtare vision into the future, he knew to carry a large trunk filled with treasure first to be distributed to Enlil, Enki and Ninmah. After that, lesser gifts would be given to their ruling children and grandchildren. The main thing was the workmanship in the gold. That, Anu had assured him, would turn heads and hearts.

Before long, he felt the vehicle set down. Levitating the trunk before him, Enmarsikil left the cabin, threaded his way through the ship and stood waiting as the door opened on a whole new world. Teacher joined him and, together, they left the ship and approached Nippur, Enlil's city on Ki.

The time of reckoning was at hand. If all went well, they would secure the Pact and freedom for their people. And perhaps a whole new species of being would know freedom as well.

CHAPTER 43 - OFF WORLD

Teacher and Enmarsikil approached the gates of Nippur. A quick mention of Anu and a few gold coins and the wards waved them through. Enmarsikil couldn't help but look about them in wonder. Where Agade was obviously a city with history and antiquity, this city was new, colorful and vibrant. He shaded his eyes looking upwards at the bright yellow sun set against a brilliant blue sky.

"The atmosphere is so thin on Ki," he remarked.

Teacher nodded. "It doesn't need to protect this planet from extremes," he remarked. "This planet exists in a sweet spot that supports life year round."

Enmarsikil glanced at the Anunnaki who walked about them. "On Nibiru their hair had a multi-colored sheen. Here it's blond or at least lighter."

"Their hair reflects the environment around them. On Nibiru the thick atmosphere was reflected in the depth of color in their hair. Here, they reflect the bright sun," Teacher explained.

Enmarsikil continued to glance about them in appreciation of the newly discovered changes. Soon they entered an impressive step-sided pyramid in the heart of the city. Armed guards ushered them into Enlil's presence after Teacher produced a seal given to him by Anu.

Enmarsikil studied the man before them. His face possessed hard, angular lines about the jaw and chin. His shoulder length hair reflected the colors in the environment around him. He wore the full beard of a mature Anunnaki. But it was his eyes that drew Enmarsikil's attention the most. Where Enki's eyes flashed with the curiosity of someone possessed of a keen intellect, this man's eyes held others in their gaze as they judged whether or not the other was a threat to be dealt with or could be of benefit and was worth their owner's time.

Right now, those eyes were taking in the black-robed, black-eyed Teacher whose own gaze never wavered, and the intellect behind them was informing their possessor that here was a truly dangerous individual, a clear threat who should be neutralized as soon as possible. When the eyes glanced at Enmarsikil, they narrowed because there was a threat to their rulership, another of King Anu's whelps through Enki.

"You come from my father, Anu," Enlil stated at last. "State your business."

"Where are Enki and Ninmah?" Teacher asked.

"When I have determined the necessity of this business, I will call them," Enlil replied tersely.

"There are matters we must address before we can do business," Teacher replied in a low bass voice.

"I do not have time for long conversation," Enlil replied curtly.

"You will need to take time for this," Teacher said holding out a me-disc Anu had given him. "It comes straight from your father's hand."

Enlil slowly raised an eyebrow, reached out and made to pick up the disc from Teacher's hand. A spark leapt between their fingertips, and he shuddered unwillingly at the power he sensed from that small contact. Quickly withdrawing his hand, Enlil cradled the disc.

"I will review this tonight and speak with you in the morning," he announced casually.

"Now," Teacher demanded.

About them clear hexagonal grids rotated into place locking into an invisible wall of tension that held Enlil firmly in place.

Enlil's face reddened with his futile efforts to rise. At last, he sat back and pulled a me-reader towards him.

"Our mission is classified, of great importance and cannot be delayed," Teacher explained.

Silently, Enlil placed the me-disc into the reader and concentrated on his father's message.

"Enlil, my son, even as my heir and commander of the colony on

Ki, there are things I have had to keep in confidence. This matter is of the most secret nature and to reveal it without authorization brings with it the pain of instant death."

Enlil frowned darkly.

"*Before Alalu announced his discovery of gold on Ki, I was approached by another race of beings from dimensions beyond our own. They came with the offer of advanced technology that they would provide us in order to save Nibiru. They could close the hole in the atmosphere and gave me proofs of their ability. But in order to obtain the technology, I swore to keep it and their existence a strict secret. While our savants and scientists had not been able to heal the hole in Nibiru's atmosphere, these beings have already done so. Their technology is real; their powers great.*"

Enlil scoffed. *This is beginning to sound like a child's fairy tale*, he thought.

"*When I accepted their offer, they hand-picked tow of my savants, two of my counselors, Ninmah and Enki for the project and swore them all to secrecy as well.*"

A jealous glint tinged Enlil's eyes. *My brother and Ninmah knew but I, the heir, was not deemed worthy?* he fumed inwardly.

"*The man in black you see before you we know as Teacher. He is their Seer and leader. It is from him that you will receive the Pact, and to him you must swear the oath of secrecy.*"

Anu's communication continued.

"*The young man with him is the technology we received - he and his siblings. They are hybrids with bodies like the Anunnaki's but with abilities derived from their Multi-Dim parentage.*"

At this, Enlil stopped the me-reader and turned towards the men in his court.

"I am a far more practical man than my father," he began. "This charade of yours has gone on long enough. You will leave my court or I will call my guards."

"Call them," Teacher suggested.

"Guards!" Enlil shouted.

Outside the room, they could hear the sounds of heavy footsteps running towards the doors.

Teacher raised his hands, fingertips pointing towards the ceiling and palms facing the doors. They slammed shut with a loud bang and Enlil jumped.

Enmarsikil stepped out from behind Teacher and focused his concentration on Enlil. With a second sight not primary to his eyes, he saw the Anunnaki's heart field that stretched out about him like an ever expanding donut. With a twist of his hand, Enmarsikil sent this field spinning sunwise. Enlil wobbled and widened his eyes.

Next, Enmarsikil sought a larger field that encompassed the man more in the shape of an egg. With an opposite twist of his hand, he sent that spinning in a motion counter to his heart field. Then, extending his hands towards Enlil, he urged the spinning fields to twirl faster and faster.

Unable to see any of what Enmarsikil was doing other than the motions of his hands, Enlil's jaw dropped and his mouth gaped as he steadily rose off his seat.

"Now," Teacher said in a controlled yet menacing voice. "Hadn't you better see what else Anu had to say?"

The me-reader floated up alongside him, and Enlil pulled it toward him. With one eye on the men before him, he turned it back on.

"These beings are more powerful than anything we know, make up their own technology and have achieved sovereignty of their own estate on Nibiru. They seek the same on Ki and, as the High King over Nibiru and Ki, I have granted sovereignty to them. They will neither seek to rule nor allow themselves to be ruled over. Instead, they seek mutually beneficial partnerships with our people as equal participants."

"Son, having heard this information, you now have no choice but to ratify the Pact with your sign. Present it to your brother and sister. Urge them to sign as well. The Pact concerns the mutually beneficial treaty between our peoples. To refuse to sign means imminent death."

With this the communication ended.

"What could you possibly offer that would be worth my making such a Pact?" Enlil asked disdainfully.

364

Enmarsikil made a motion with one hand and the chest opened. Enlil's eyes flew wide as he saw the gleam of gold from within the chest. One piece in particular rose from the chest and levitated toward him.

"The workmanship," he breathed. "It is without par."

"This...is what we have to offer," Enmarsikil stated. "That and the knowledge of how to create these things."

Enlil reached out, took the majestic piece and turned it over and over in his hands. Finally, he motioned for Enmarsikil to set him down. "For this and the knowledge of its workmanship, I will sign this Pact," he said in awe.

"Call your brother and sister to you," Teacher urged. "They must also sign."

Enlil nodded and Teacher opened the doors to the guards outside. In moments, messengers ran to the quarters where Enki and Ninmah were staying.

"Meanwhile, sign the Pact with your seal," Teacher said handing the commander the scroll.

Enlil took it, went to a desk nearby, melted a thin layer of wax onto the bottom of the scroll and rolled his clay seal over it.

"Read it carefully, Enlil," Teacher admonished. "It restricts you from using these people for your personal gain, from exploiting them in any way, from any form of abuse or restriction of their movements or freedom. In return, they will contract with you and your people as equals during the duration of your sojourn on Ki."

Enlil read through the articles of the Pact line-by-line, carefully rolled it up and handed it back to Teacher.

Footsteps in the hall outside signaled the arrival of Enki and Ninmah. They entered, spotted Enmarsikil and hurried over the embrace him.

"Father said you were coming," Enki remarked. "I couldn't imagine how you would arrive."

"We've developed our own space transports, ones that can be modified and reconfigured at our will," Enmarsikil told him.

"And the others, " Ninmah said. "They are all right? I heard the King took back the Academy."

The corners of Enmarsikil's mouth turned up slightly. "Oh, it was interesting. But we have built our own town and have created our own state where we are sovereign now."

"And yet you seek to come here?" Enki queried.

Enmarsikil nodded. "We have...business to attend to here."

"And right now, that includes having you sign this Pact," Teacher announced handing the scroll to Enki.

Enki read it nodding in places, went to Enlil's desk and set his seal upon the scroll. Minutes later, Ninmah followed suit. As they finished, Enmarsikil handed each a beautiful gold piece in exchange. Enki studied his carefully.

"I cannot believe the quality of this piece," he breathed. "Exquisite is hardly the right word."

Enmarsikil nodded. "Those of us who work in metals have developed their craftsmanship to very high levels. We propose to teach your artisans what we have learned. Some aspects can't be taught because they don't have all the same capacities our people have."

Enki nodded his understanding.

"The gold is beautiful," Ninmah remarked diplomatically, "but what about cloth and healing knowledge?"

Enmarsikil tipped his head to one side. "I had not considered the need for these capacities, but I can certainly discuss this with my siblings upon my return."

"So, you are returning to Nibiru?" Enlil asked.

"After we've scouted out a location for our people while they reside on Ki, I will return to assemble the next teams to arrive on Ki," Enmarsikil told him.

Enlil's face fell. "So, this is a long term plan."

"It is for however long we will it to be," Enmarsikil replied cryptically.

"Well, at least stay and eat a meal with us," Enki encouraged. "It has been too long since I've seen you."

"Yes, please do," Ninmah encouraged.

Enlil sighed heavily and turned to his messenger. "Have the royal cooks prepare a feast. We certainly cannot let them go hungry."

"Please," Enmarsikil replied. "A simple meal. I have siblings awaiting my return and some work still to do before I leave for Nibiru."

Enlil and his siblings nodded and the preparations for the meal began.

Teacher insisted that Enlil's and Enki's grown children be present at the meal as well. The meal was postponed for a couple of days to give the others time to gather. Enki took Enmarsikil on a personal tour of the Edin, land of the pure ones, and his own home away from home, Eridu. Enmarsikil quietly took in all the planning, canal works, bitumen production and mining operations. Every bit of knowledge his Anunnaki

366

father imparted would serve he and his siblings well. They stepped onto one of Enki's boats and began floating down the Euphrates River.

"Anu said you caused quite a stir in the palace," Enki remarked.

Enmarsikil blushed. "Which time?"

"Both, apparently," Enki chuckled. "The people claim you're a hero for fixing the hole in the atmosphere."

Enmarsikil scanned the banks of the river looking for signs of beings like Ginny and Ted. "I and my siblings were created in a lab for the purpose of healing that hole," he said at length. "When everyone else seemed to have forgotten, we did not. We completed our purpose."

"So, that's what it's like to know of your creation," Enki remarked quietly.

Enmarsikil nodded.

"And now?"

"We have our own projects and determine our own destiny now," Enmarsikil replied cryptically.

They returned to Enlil's city, Nippur, and his temple home.

After the tour of the canals, Enmarsikil contacted the ship and met it where it landed. He boarded after stopping in the sterilization room and called Nita and Satu to his cabin.

"This is it," he announced. "We've presented the Pact to Enlil, Enki and Ninmah. Tonight there is a banquet where we will present the Pact to the Anunnaki in our generation. I mean to also present yourselves as my representatives."

Satu rubbed his hands together. "So, this is it?"

Enmarsikil nodded. "I know I have mentioned shifting your vision to ascertain their true intentions before, but it's imperative that you practice tonight. You need to learn what drives them and what their true intentions are."

Nita nodded his understanding.

"Ok, brothers. Go get ready and join me outside. Wear my seal prominently displayed," Enmarsikil instructed.

The men left his cabin for their own. Within fifteen minutes, they came down the landing ramp and stood by Enmarsikil as the ramp retracted.

"Ok, let's go."

They hurried to the city center and the temple. In the banquet hall, several men had joined the others. Enki introduced Enmarsikil to Marduk, his son by his wife, Damkina, as well as Nergal. Ninmah introduced him to Ninurta, the son she bore to Enlil while still on Nibiru. And Enlil introduced him to his own son, Nannar, born to his wife, Ninlil. Yet, a younger man still in his late teens hung in the background watching everything. Enmarsikil couldn't help but notice the boy's keen, observant eyes so like Enki's, though other features reminded him of Enlil. He wandered over to meet him before servants led them to dine.

"I'm Enmarsikil," he said by way of introduction. "I couldn't help but notice you weren't with the others."

The young man blushed. "They are the elder princes in leadership positions," he explained.

"But you will be as well some day," Enmarsikil assumed.

"Perhaps. We'll see. I think I'd rather study science," the young man said candidly.

"You must be a son of Enki, like me," Enmarsikil remarked.

The young man's eyes widened. "Yes. Ningishzidda. I hadn't known I had another brother."

"Half brother at best, and I share your love of science," Enmarsikil replied.

Soon they were called to table, and food and wine flowed freely. After a while Teacher rose, Pact in hand.

"We need the signatures of these young men around the table," he announced.

"On what?" Marduk demanded.

"On the Pact I told you about," Enlil stated.

"Let's see this Pact," Marduk requested.

Teacher handed him the scroll, which he read.

"And you're saying that one of these...beings is here," Marduk sneered.

All eyes fell on Enmarsikil. He studied Enki's eldest son with his second sight. There were layers upon layers of walls about him. It was obvious this man never felt safe.

"I and my brothers are some of these beings, yes," Enmarsikil responded quietly, nodding to Nita and Satu on either side of him.

"And what can you possibly do for us?" Marduk wanted to know.

Teacher reached for the chest but Enmarsikil waved him away.

"For you and your generals, we can create armor that nothing can penetrate," Enmarsikil proposed.

"Show me," Marduk challenged, though Ninurta also leaned forward with interest.

Enmarsikil stood, stepped away from the table and removed his outer cloak revealing a shining mail suit underneath.

368

"Pretty armor proves nothing," Marduk retorted.

"Strike me," Enmarsikil urged. "Prove the armor."

Teacher's eyes narrowed. This was a dangerous game. But Enmarsikil had programmed the armor to be like their space craft, capable of changing its tempering depending upon the weapon used against it.

Marduk stood and in two strides sought to sink his knife into the armor. The knife bent. Ninurta swept up with his sword and charged hacking at the armor; the sword spun away notched. The guards were invited to use spears then arrows. Even Enlil's special energy weapon bounced off harmlessly. Finally, Marduk and Ninurta stood sweating and breathing hard having admitted defeat.

"All right. For armor like that, I'll sign this Pact," Marduk agreed hurrying to affix his seal.

Ninurta looked at Enmarsikil. "I could use that armor."

"And we shall teach your smithies the art as well," Enmarsikil promised.

Ninurta signed with Nergal and Nannar behind him.

"You have one more prince here," Enmarsikil said. "He should also sign."

"He is not of age," Enlil said dismissively.

Teacher frowned. "No, I agree. He has heard the conversation about the terms of the Pact. He has seen these demonstrations. He must sign as well."

Ningishzidda looked about him uncertainly. Enki nodded his encouragement. Ningishzidda reached for the Pact.

"Do I also receive a treasure for placing my mark?" he asked.

Enmarsikil held his gaze. "You will get what your heart desires most."

Ningishzidda mouthed, "Science."

Enmarsikil nodded slightly.

Ningishzidda affixed his mark and handed it back to Teacher.

"Now that the Pact is signed, I would like to introduce my two representatives to you," Enmarsikil announced.

Nita and Satu rose and flanked him on either side. "This is Nitadugita and Satuatuini," Enmarsikil said. "They bear my seal and are my equals. When I am not on Ki or readily available, their words are my words; their voice, my voice. It is covered in the Pact."

The Anunnaki around the table duly took note.

"Come, this is what wasn't done on the parallel timeline," Teacher said quietly.

He and Enmarsikil held the scroll between them. As they did, they built energy between them until they were nothing but a ball of brilliant light. Suddenly, there was a roar and light exploded all around the room. When it finally dimmed, Teacher, Enmarsikil, Nita and Satu were gone leaving the other dinner guests in a state of shock and confusion. Enmarsikil's armor stood beside Marduk's chair.

CHAPTER 44 - NEW LAND

Teacher, Enmarsikil, Nita and Satu found themselves in the void coalescing out of photons. As their bodies came together, two universes that had once overlapped like an enormous Venn diagram slowly moved apart until one jettisoned into oblivion. Teacher placed an energy band around the three brothers and pulled them toward the remaining universe. Images and scenes flew past them in fast forward until they all heard a loud snap. Suddenly, they stood beside the Space Transport in the bright mid-day sun. The brothers blinked and looked about in confusion.

"We need to enter the air lock and decontaminate so we don't sicken anyone inside," Teacher said.

Enmarsikil remained standing in one place.

Teacher stopped and turned. "Son, did you hear me?"

Enmarsikil slowly turned toward him, a shiver running down his spine. "That produced a huge shift. I'm still processing it."

"We energized the Pact sufficiently to completely move the original parallel out of alignment," Teacher explained.

"Do you think they felt it?" Satu asked nodding toward the ship.

"Probably. To the air lock," Teacher urged.

The brothers finally convinced their feet to move and shuffled after Teacher. They levitated up to a portal in the side of the ship, activated the air lock and floated through when it opened. Once inside, they hit a button for an irradiating light to pass over them killing off foreign microbes. When the sensors detected no more, they left the air lock and entered the ship proper. Enmarsikil headed straight for the control room.

"Hey, they're back!" Zupatu called.

The others hurried to the control room to greet him.

"How did it go?" Marki asked.

"We did it," Enmarsikil confirmed. "And this time we energized the Pact."

"We felt a huge ripple in Space Time," Nindulur told him.

"Good. This was the big missing piece," Enmarsikil said. "Any luck with settlement sites?"

"We did an aerial scan," Nindulur related. "We have found several possible areas."

"We may need more than one," Enmarsikil said. "Enlil's people are mostly up in this area including Ninmah. But Enki's people are on a different land mass all together."

"How about we explore the most likely?" Kumzubar suggested.

"Let's see the aerial scans," Enmarsikil requested.

Zupatu brought them up on a transparent screen.

"This location is near here but closer to the mountains to the east," Marki said placing a marker at a location nearby. "There is another mountain range to the west that Enlil favors for space transport."

"Where does he house his artisans?" Enmarsikil wondered.

"Near the mines and where they get bitumens," Ki replied.

"So mostly in the Edin and broader Sumer," Enmarsikil clarified. "That suggests those eastern mountains would be a good choice."

Zupatu marked them.

"Enki's land is far south of here," Enmarsikil said shifting the map to show them. "He's way down on the southern tip of this land and up towards the middle. He has given his sons lands in Khemet along the Nile River all the way to the delta in the north."

"We detected gold mines down in the southern area," Kumzubar told him.

"So gold workers to the south and metal smiths to the north," Enmarsikil surmised.

"Ninmah wanted cloth and healing knowledge," Teacher reminded him from a corner where he stood observing.

"And Ningishzidda is hungry for science," Enmarsikil added. "How shall we do this?"

"Three settlements," Marki said lighting up three areas. "Gold workers to the south, set up a school and let them come to us."

"Metal workers and a school here in the north," Kumzubar said.

"Some of our people can stay near Ninmah working with cloth and healing plants," Ki suggested.

"I can mentor Ningishzidda in Science once Enki teaches him all he knows," Enmarsikil said. "And we can have one site to gather quarterly...here," he said pointing to a large island off the east coast of Enki's lands.

"That could work," Ki agreed.

"How about Kaharsag and Birshutab check the mountains to the east," Enmarsikil said.

The pair nodded.

"Kumzubar and Ki can check in the south in Enki's lands," Enmarsikil continued. "And Marki and I will look into that island. Enki said the planet rotates rapidly; he counts a complete rotation as 24 equal hours. Be back here in seven full rotations."

Satu spoke up. "If it's ok with you, Nita, Barlumgeme, Mamud and I would like to look for our own base."

"We want to try to locate the area where Ginny and Ted will be in the future," Nita explained.

Enmarsikil nodded. "Ok, but rendezvous back here with the others in seven rotations."

Satu nodded.

The groups saluted and headed out while Nindulur took the craft up into low orbit to avoid detection. At the appointed time, she returned, collected the teams and shot back into space.

"It will take a little time to process the data, and the other teams on Nibiru will want to give input. Let's head home," Enmarsikil said wearily.

Nindulur took them out into space and Zupatu sifted them through the solar system. Enmarsikil found his cabin and lay staring at the ceiling as multitudinous questions rolled through his mind. For one, Ki was made up of vast territories. When he had heard it was a smaller planet than Nibiru, he had thought in compact terms. But when the scouts had topped mountain ranges to view the wide-open vistas beyond or had stood on pristine beaches watching the sun set beyond the expanse of waves, his perception of Ki had entirely changed. How in the world could 502 beings cover, support and nurture a planet of that size?

I have more questions than answers," Enmarsikil thought. He knew from speaking with the future Enmarsikil that the Anunnaki hybridized the human species using Ki hominid stock and Anunnaki DNA.

The process forever changed the track those hominids had been on.

On the original timeline, I followed Teacher's advice and further hybridized humans by incorporating our DNA into their species. But was that wise? Did that further alter the course of human life? Is there a way to have that close and interactive a relationship with humans yet maintain the integrity of our DNA and theirs? he wondered.

Restless, Enmarsikil opened the portal to the universe he shared with Astara. He raised his eyebrows as he gazed at her latest additions. A copy of her rosebush stood next to an archway. A canopy stretched over the bed. The walkways were now paved with flat marble stones and birds flitted about.

He dropped down into himself and called to her. It seemed to take more effort, and he almost gave up hope of a reply. While he waited, Enmarsikil created a few trees for the birds to rest in. He also built a wood pavilion to shelter the canopied bed. Just when he turned to go back through his own portal, Astara's opened and she stepped through.

"There you are!" he exclaimed spinning around. He hurried forward and caught her up in his arms.

She wrapped her arms about his neck pressing herself against him. "Sorry. A couple of us got bored and decided to go on an expedition."

Enmarsikil frowned and pulled back to look at her. "Where have you gone?"

"All over," she said. "You secured this huge chunk of territory for us and all we've ever seen is one small corner. We thought we'd find out what else there was to it."

Enmarsikil nodded. "I sent out scouting parties to see how things are on Ki. I took some time to go with one group. It will take a while to process the data so I thought I'd come here. I was missing you."

He sampled her lips in case she doubted him.

"Did you seal the Pact?" Astara asked a moment later.

"And energized it," he confirmed. "We won't be messed with this time."

Astara hugged him. "Oh good!"

He led her over to the pavilion and drew her down onto the bed with him. "Want to see if we can power up here?" he asked, his eyes shining.

Astara opened his tunic and ran her hand over his chest. "Try and stop me."

They had soon shed their clothes and were entwined about one another. Though pleasant, the effect was not quite the same. Finally, they
374

admitted it was time to part. Enmarsikil stood watching her retreat back through the portal. Placing his hands on his hips, he gazed about their little universe.

What makes this place so different? he wondered. *It almost feels sterile compared to Ki and Nibiru.*

Shaking his head, he returned to his cabin and closed the portal.

With his mental gears whirling, Enmarsikil wandered the ship finally entering the herbarium of Nibiruan plants that were the air scrubbers and oxygenators for the ship. He touched the bark of a tree, smelling it and putting the soil from around its roots on his tongue. He frowned pensively before leaving the herbarium and going down into the hold where samples of Ki plants were stored. He repeated his actions with them that he had performed in the herbarium. A nascent thought sprung up but was without sufficient form in his mind.

Crossing his legs and allowing himself to levitate, Enmarsikil went deep within himself wondering at the new possibilities that were opening before him. He let images and words bubble up in his mind observing them and letting them go. Finally, he shook his head, stretched out his legs and settled back to the floor. *I can't quite grasp a pattern,* he fretted.

For a change of view, Enmarsikil went up to the observation deck. He stood staring out at the swirling expanse around them. After a while, he heard footsteps, turned and saw Teacher approaching.

"Your mind is unsettled," Teacher observed.

Enmarsikil nodded turning back to the viewing port. "I do not understand how we can achieve what my future self has requested."

Teacher joined him in observing the vastness that was the vacuum of space only viewed through the layers of dimensional sifting.

"I thought Ki would be this tiny place," Enmarsikil admitted. "Instead, it's vast both on land and at sea. There are too few of us to cover that much territory with the impact required. And we do not reproduce."

"No, and I would suggest not seeking to modify anything so you can," Teacher remarked quietly, sensing his son's train of thought."

"Why not?"

"Because you and your siblings are created from the purest genetics possible," Teacher explained. "All harmful mutations were guarded against. The elements you are attuned to were worked out in intricate, delicately balanced ratios. Were you to develop the capacity to reproduce, there would be no way to monitor and remove harmful mutations, no way to assure the balance of elements. Not only would children be born in a couple of generations that were out of balance themselves, given your impact on the environment around you, great imbalances in nature would occur as well."

Enmarsikil stiffened then sighed, his shoulders sagging. "I had not considered that. I have a silly memory of Astara once seeing the fetus in my old oddities collection. The look on her face when I explained we were all sterile was heart breaking. I thought...it would be nice to give her a child to nurture and help increase our population."

"If you weren't so very technically developed...." Teacher said letting his voice trail off.

Enmarsikil nodded.

"What commonalities have you noticed?" Teacher probed.

"The elements and their representations, the microbes in the soil, water, air and food," Enmarsikil replied.

"Just remember, those microbes already exist inside of you. Your multi-dimensionality you inherit from us," Teacher reminded him. "Is there a reason why you always have to maintain your present form?"

Enmarsikil whipped his head around. "What are you aiming at?"

"Well, many of your siblings can dissolve into their attuned element at will while maintaining the integrity of their identity, thoughts, intentions and will."

Enmarsikil nodded thoughtfully. "Yes, Astara is remarkably adept with water."

"Well, if it's not onerous to dissolve into an element, why not into a microbe?" Teacher suggested. "It is but another form and, unlike other forms, you would then be able to reproduce and spread your awareness across the globe. You would be intimately connected to all life on Ki and still be able to communicate with and awaken humans."

Enmarsikil was a little taken aback but the thought intrigued him. "But how would we communicate with humans and where would we initially colonize?" he wanted to know.

"Step one would be to create a couple of large, technicologically advanced settlements. They would seem magical and otherworldly, even to the Anunnaki, and would attract rulers, artisans and traders from miles around. There will always be catastrophes on Ki when Nibiru's return is closer to the sun. When a sufficiently destructive event is on the horizon, let go of your country and your form. Slip into the form of the microbes and allow yourselves to be deposited in the elements. There will not be a place on the planet where you do not exist."

"I assume you also mean life as a human commensal," Enmarsikil said stiffly, "though how interactions would occur there eludes me."

376

"There is a nerve that runs from gut to brain. The humans will have it, too, because it is common to hominid species. Commensals use it for gut to brain communication, and those humans who learn to quiet their mind's chatter will hear you."

"But what of the Facility my future self talked of...we talked of...in which me and my siblings would need to rest and re-energize some day?" Enmarsikil asked.

"In your present form, it will be a necessity," Teacher affirmed. "In a different form, whether elemental or microbial, the environment itself would re-energize you. No Facility would be necessary, and that could be more to your advantage."

Enmarsikil was still not totally convinced. "I will have to vision around this," he told Teacher.

"Do that," Teacher encouraged. "See where my idea leads."

Teacher turned and left Enmarsikil staring at the nothingness, his mind working through these new ideas.

Enmarsikil remained restless for the remainder of the journey. When the ship finally slowed as it neared Nibiru, he went up to the Command Center watching as the globe before them turned ever so slowly. Mentally, he compared the dusty red, thickly atmosphered orb of Nibiru to the bright blue, thinly atmosphered Ki. He had to admit that the freshness, brightness and aliveness of Ki were very attractive to him.

Gugbubulu found their lands and set a marker on their holographic map. Radarkumita plotted the course and, before long, they were sailing over Agade headed for the plain on the boarder of their territory.

With the landing approaching, Enmarsikil left the Command Center and hurried through the passageways to the exit. He felt the ship rock slightly, heard the whir of hydraulics as the legs extended to the ground and the bump as it landed. The engines slowly died, and he waited impatiently for the door to open. Even before it had completely scrolled up, Enmarsikil ducked under and stood on the ledge at the top of the ramp. Instinctively, he raised his hand to shield his eyes, only to stop with the realization there was no more harsh glare. Nibiru looked almost gloomy.

Scanning the crowd of gathering siblings, Enmarsikil frowned. The face he sought did not seem to be among them. He ran down the ramp and pushed past siblings searching, ever searching for that familiar smile. He got to the back of the crowd and still had not found it. Suddenly, he felt a hand on his arm.

"She's not here," Peenzermi said.

Enmarsikil glanced at her. "She hasn't returned?"

"They have been gone a while," Hashurur said from his place beside Peenzermi's.   Enmarsikil's frowned worriedly.

"They're due back any time now," Peenzermi assured him.

He nodded but looked less than consoled. Wearily, he headed for their home, went straight to the treehouse out back and collapsed into one of the basket chairs. He fell asleep to the sound of water rushing below and breezes fluttering the leaves overhead.

As he slept, Enmarsikil dreamed. In his dream bright sunshine flooded past the waving leaves dappling the light and dancing off the ripples of water. Only he wasn't looking down at the water; he was the water and the mud along the banks. He was the leaves and the cells inside soaking up the sunshine and converting it to energy. Everywhere he turned, he was that which he saw. When an herbivore ate his leaf, suddenly, he was the blood, he was vibrant with life. And when the animal was killed and eaten, he was its consumer as well. At every turn Enmarsikil found himself part of his surroundings vibrating with life yet still fully aware, fully himself.

A voice reached him on the breeze. Was it the predator he had become? He listened harder. No, some other being called to him, and the voice was warm, sweet and welcomed. Enmarsikil sought its owner rising up through the stages of sleep as he slowly released the dream. A moment or two later, he blinked his eyes open squinting till Astara's smiling face came into view.

She all but leapt into the hanging basket beside him, wrapped her arms around him and smothered him in a passionate kiss. Before long, something other than the wind sent the chair swaying.

CHAPTER 45 - EMBRACING CHANGE

After a while Enmarsikil and Astara wandered through their home and into the gardens out front. He stooped down and pulled a particularly thick set of weeds from a bed.

"Sorry," Astara apologized. "Guess I should have had Kisikilturkusa do that, too, while I was gone."

He stood back up. "What did you have her do?"

"Skim the ponds and feed the fish," she replied.

Enmarsikil picked up the pace till they reached the bridge. He leaned on the rail and looked over the edge. A flurry of gaping mouths appeared at the surface.

"Wow, are they big!" he exclaimed running back to the shed for the feed bag.

"You've been gone for almost half a shar," Astara told him watching him scatter pellets to the fish.

He whistled in amazement. "Sorry. I don't know how to count time on Ki, yet. It is such a different place."

"Tell me," she urged.

He shook his head. "For a small planet, it is still vast. We climbed to the tops of mountain ranges to see vast valleys and prairies stretching out before us. On the beach we stood watching the sun set over never-ending waves."

"Wow!" Astara murmured, her eyes bright.

"The atmosphere is thinner, the air crisp and clean, the sun so bright it hurts your eyes. And the colors, Astara!" Enmarsikil exclaimed. "They're so vivid, almost more real than anything here on Nibiru. I confess, I returned home and was disappointed by all the dullness."

Astara curled up on a bench.

"Peenzermi said you led a team surveying our territory here," he prompted.

She nodded. "It was what we could have hoped for."

He frowned noting a less than content tone in her voice. "That doesn't make you happy?"

Astara looked down then off across the gardens. "It's been very strange. Once those of us who had taken the culture acclimated to the Ki ecosystems, Nibiru began to feel less comfortable, less like home. The others found we were dissonant in frequency to them so Marne started having all of us take the culture. This strange listlessness overcame us. I organized the expedition thinking it would make us feel energized."

"It didn't?"

She shook her head. "We came back even more dissatisfied than when we left. I don't think we can stay here," Astara said, a worried frown creasing her brow, "any of us. It's like...we no longer belong here."

Enmarsikil's eyebrows shot up in surprise. "Really?"

Astara nodded.

Enmarsikil pondered this latest news. "I'm not sure I want a mass migration just yet. But if more are uncomfortable here than not, at least it will make the move less painful."

"So, when will we move?" Astara asked.

He glanced at her with his eyebrows raised in surprise. "You want to move?"

She slipped her arms around his waist. "I want something," she replied, "and it's not here. In all my travels around our territory, whatever it is that I'm craving is not to be found."

He held her and gently rubbed her back. "Is that why you went?"

"Partly. And I just had to have something to do with myself. When you're here, I focus on you. With you gone...." she said.

"You needed something else to focus on," he surmised.

"Mm-hm."

"Well, it looks like a meeting is in order," Enmarsikil said leading her off the bridge toward the gate. "We have a lot to present, and I want to hear from the others."

380

They left through the main gate at which point Enmarsikil called up his air skid, and they sailed off across the river landing beside the Meeting House in the center of town. He hurried to the roof to ring the bell and in a matter of minutes siblings began filing in and taking seats. He stood down in the well waiting until the last person was inside.

"Astara has told me you all have taken the culture but in the process you now feel less at home on Nibiru," Enmarsikil opened.

Affirmations came from every side.

"Perhaps sharing my memories of Ki with you will help you understand why," he said drawing out several bubbles from his chest and tossing them into the air.

One-by-one, he touched them letting the scenes play out of seeing Ki from space, landing on the lush planet, walking through Nippur, and roaming over vast stretches of territory. By the time he had shown the last bubble, murmurings could be heard from the ranks of the congregants. Some openly wept.

"I don't understand it," Bilnammul said dabbing her eyes. "I've never seen this place, but viewing your memories makes me feel homesick. I know I have to go there."

Others seconded her perspective.

"What made us feel this way?" Hashurur wanted to know.

"Teacher's culture," Enmarsikil replied simply. "I suspect the microbes from Ki exert a stronger internal force than do those from Nibiru. Given how alive and energetic everything felt to me on Ki, I'd say those microbes within us are homesick and are pulling us toward home."

"But, can we all go?" Aiya called out. "Is there enough room?"

"There is more than enough room," Enmarsikil replied. "The planet is young and not yet heavily populated."

"But what about the Space Transports?" Nadu, a stone man, asked.

Enmarsikil nodded. "Nindulur can teach other foundational elementals to create the bodies of ships. We already know that mated pairs can produce the energy to power the ships. The rest of the navigation team can share the star maps and techniques for piloting the ships and sifting through the multi-dimensional field. I can train strong visioners to use the Visioning Crystal, and we can create several more. It is more than doable to transport all of us to Ki."

"But where will we live?" Zidgu, Didi's spouse, asked.

"Wherever we choose," Marki called out.

"Then when do we leave?" Bilsag, an impetuous fire woman, asked.

A loud clamor arose as others, eager to see a world they mysteriously hungered for, added their own voices.

Enmarsikil held up his hand for silence. When that didn't produce results, a sudden ear-piercing whistle did. While the others ducked and covered their ears, Satu stood behind Enmarsikil wearing an ear-to-ear grin.

Enmarsikil shook his head to clear it. "Thanks...I think."

He created a tall stool, set it in the middle of the platform of the well and sat down. For a moment, he steepled his fingers in front of him resting his chin on his fingertips.

"Ok," he said at last. "There are a couple of ways we could do this. We could all leave at once."

A few people began to shout but stopped abruptly when Satu stood and put his fingers to his lips.

"However, I had always thought of leaving in stages," Enmarsikil continued.

A groan of disappointment went around the room.

"Hear me out," Enmarsikil requested, and the gathering quieted.

"Ki is different than Nibiru," he began. "We already know its microbial composition is different, and the elemental frequencies are offset. The atmosphere is much thinner, and its axial spin is way faster. While we have had great success here setting up our own settlement, I'm sure we'll encounter things on Ki we couldn't foresee."

A few heads nodded in acknowledgement.

"If we start a settlement with a portion of our members," Enmarsikil continued, "we may find there are things the rest of you can develop here on Nibiru and bring with you that will ease life in the Ki settlements. Would any of you be willing to remain here and help with that?" he asked.

Almost the entire Second Generation and part of the Third raised their hands.

"Thank you," Enmarsikil said. "I promise, given the fact the culture has made you feel less comfortable on Nibiru, the goal will be to transfer everyone to Ki."

"Why don't you put it to a vote?" Astara suggested.

Enmarsikil nodded. "Ok. By show of hands, how many want to leave all at once?"

An entire section mostly comprised of First Gens raised their hands.

"How many are willing to make a staged exodus?" Enmarsikil

asked.

Two-thirds of the gathering raised their hands.

"Does anyone have no strong feeling either way?" Enmarsikil queried.

A few hands from the Fourth Gens were extended upwards.

"Thank you," he said. "We will accept the majority decision of a staged exodus. We'll try to keep it to only two or three stages and do this as quickly as is feasible."

With that, the meeting adjourned and the Hall emptied. Nita, Satu, Marki, Enmarsikil and Astara remained behind.

"So where would we start?" Nita asked.

Enmarsikil drew up a holographic globe and rotated it to an area far west of The Edin. "Father Enki spent some time showing me his canal works and land reclamation near his home, Eridu. There is a marshy plain here," he said pointing. "The Anunnaki are less likely to want to use this territory. If we use the techniques Father Enki employed, we could make a settlement there."

Marki frowned. "Sounds like we're using cast off land."

Nita and Satu studied the map in silence.

"I don't think so," Astara said. She waved her hand so fresh, underground water became visible. "There are clearly two underground springs in the center of the marsh. Both are artesian and one seems to be heated by deep underground lava. Plus, there's an avenue between the marshy plain and the sea."

"A canal from the sea to the center of that marsh would provide good access to the sea," Marki mused.

"If we built a series of dikes and water in concentric circles, with the outermost being large and deep enough for a harbor, the others would protect the main portion of the land in the center from high tides and flooding," Enmarsikil pointed out.

"And all the land we dredge out for the canal and those concentric waterways we can pile in the center making a low mountain to build on," Marki added.

"What do you boys think?" Enmarsikil asked looking to Nita and Satu.

"It's a good starting point," Nita said diplomatically.

With those plans laid down, Marki and his team began creating a model of the settlement while Enmarsikil got other teams together preparing what they would need to take with them. Nindulur took three foundational elementals from the Third Gens and began teaching them how to build up and modify Space Transports at will. New navigational teams were trained as well.

Enmarsikil visited Teacher at his labs where he was busy studying vegetation and grain samples he had gathered on Ki.

"So, will we be able to use those for food?" Enmarsikil queried.

Teacher sighed as he looked through his microscope. "They are like everything else on Ki, similar yet just enough dissimilar," he replied.

"The Anunnaki have been eating them," Enmarsikil pointed out.

"And you did ingest them at the banquet," Teacher conceded. "I'm more concerned with long-term effects."

"Like what?" Enmarsikil pressed.

"Come see for yourself," Teacher said straightening up. "The first slide looks at the impact of Ki grain on Nibiruan microbes. The second is Ki grain and Ki microbes."

Enmarsikil put his eye to the microscope and flipped back and forth between the two slides. At last he straightened up.

"The Nibiruan microbes look sluggish...almost ill," he noted.

Teacher nodded.

"What about a hybrid?" Enmarsikil wondered.

"I have one in the works," Teacher responded. "I'm just waiting for the grain to ripen enough to be harvested. I'll let you know the outcome."

Enmarsikil nodded and left the labs for his home just down the road. He entered the gardens and found Astara standing on the bridge surveying their little slice of the world. She turned when she heard the gate open, smiled and held out her hand to him.

He kissed her then slipped his arms around her waist, his front to her back. "Don't worry, Sweet," Enmarsikil murmured. "We can recreate a lot of this. You are coming with me this time, aren't you?"

Astara nodded. "This is the last of Nibiru I'll see."

"You're sure?" he pressed.

"Mm-hm. But I think I'm done with the Academy and reminders of it," she announced.

Enmarsikil straightened up suddenly. "You sure?"

"I am. I'm just trying to figure out what elements to keep," she said.

"I'd still like a garden," Enmarsikil said.

"And my flowering bush," Astara agreed.

"Still want a big room?"

"Definitely. I will never want confined quarters again," Astara asserted. "But I feel more like towers and basements, multiple levels, multiple uses."

"I need a lab," Enmarsikil stated.

She chuckled. "I can't imagine you without a lab or fish."

With their musings at an end, Enmarsikil and Astara began packing and preparing for the long trip across the galaxy. When they were finished with their own preparations, they busily helped others. Before long, the Transports were being created, and their things were being loaded on board.

Enmarsikil made one last stop at Teacher's labs.

"Well, did the hybridization work?" he asked.

Teacher nodded. "It did and I'm sending you back with plants and seeds. These should provide you with food that will keep you healthy."

"Will you be coming?" Enmarsikil asked.

Teacher shook his head. "Not this time. We'll stay behind to shepherd those who remain. When the last of your siblings leave Nibiru, we shall leave as well."

Enmarsikil frowned. "The way you said that makes it seem as if you won't be on Ki, either."

Teacher shook his head again. "We will visit and we will help you whenever you need or want it, but our time of physicality is coming to a close. We created a grand experiment, and it has been a tremendous success thanks to you and your siblings. But, it's time to let it go."

A chill trickled down Enmarsikil's spine. "But where will you be?"

"We'll be in the multi-dimensions," Teacher replied. "It is where we truly belong now."

Within a cycle, it was time for the settlement teams to leave. Space Transport teams for two ships were on board. Builders, gardeners, healers and Satu's entire team went as well. In all, the equivalent of one generation cohort boarded the ships and settled in. To cheers from their siblings left behind, the ramps pulled up, the doors sealed and the transports lifted off the ground. In moments, they shot toward the far horizon like disappearing stars. The first stage had begun.

CHAPTER 46 - BUILDING ANEW

The journey to Ki went a little faster than before now that they were no longer charting the vacuum of space as they went. With two ships, it was easier to blast a large path through the Hammered Bracelet. It wasn't long before they entered Ki's orbit and synched up with the territory they had identified.

"We should find high ground," Nindulur recommended. "The plain is simply too wet to land transports on."

Enmarsikil and Marki studied the surrounding terrain.

"We could blast this hill flat and use it for a landing pad," Marki said pointing a little to the north.

"Looks good. Call Ushumgal and Erumgal," Enmarsikil instructed.

"We have some smaller transport modules they can pilot to the surface," Nindulur said.

Marki nodded and left to get his siblings. Before long three bright, circular pods left the ship and zipped along in a line down to the surface. Marki laid out the dimensions for a flat top and the two pan-elementals immediately got busy. They vaporized the top of the mountain to a level surface then melted the rock together into a solid base.

When Marki was satisfied with their job, they hopped back in the landing pods and raced back to the main transport. Marki jogged back to the Command Center.

"That what you're looking for?" he asked puffing.

"Exactly," Nindulur replied.

She switched the comm to alert their sister ship then had Gugbubulu begin landing preparations. No sooner had their transport landed then the other transport set down beside it. Before long the ramps were down, the doors were open and they eagerly descended to take in their new lands.

"Let's set up camp for now," Enmarsikil instructed. "I had a talk with Father Enki about time on Ki. He has broken Ki's spin into years, months, days, hours, minutes and seconds. Not to get too technical, but the sun crosses the sky in increments of single hours. Father Enki has determined that 24 of these hours make up a day, and seven days comprise a week. He suggests a full day rest on every seventh day to accommodate the hyperspeed rotations of the planet."

"That means we only have a couple of hours till the sun goes down today," Nita remarked.

"Lots to do before it gets dark and we will want campfires," Enmarsikil added.

With all hands unloading tents and provisions, they had a small tent city set up by the time the stars came out.

"If for whatever reason you aren't comfortable out here, we will leave the cabin decks intact," Nindulur announced. "You're welcome to rest inside."

A few couples opted for the comfort of their cabins. Astara stood outside marveling at the array of sparkling dots stretched across the dark night sky.

"We could never see anything like this from Nibiru," she remarked in awe. "They're like millions of diamonds all twinkling."

"They come out every clear night, I promise," Enmarsikil said holding out his hand to lead her inside. "There will be other celestial nights as well," he added. "Father Enki has given me some of his me discs that have the sky data on them. It will be fascinating to watch the moon wax and wane or view comets flying by Ki."

Astara yawned. "I guess a nap wouldn't hurt."

They crawled inside their tent, got comfortable under covers and were soon fast asleep. Even the wolves that howled in the night bothered them little. And before they knew it, the sun rose over the eastern horizon. Others were up watching and Astara and Enmarsikil crawled out to see, too.

She gazed up at him. "This world is so much more alive than

Nibiru. I almost feel reborn."

"Well, reborn or not, it's time to survey the area and get to work on the canals," Enmarsikil told her.

He called the teams together. "Marki, you have the plans and the model. Let's get busy taking a survey. Father Enki gave me a communications device. He said if we needed help with the canals and harbor, he'd send some of his best men."

Marki and his crew headed into the valley on skids while Enmarsikil climbed to a high spot to contact Enki. Within two weeks the Anunnaki workers, barges and dredgers arrived. While Marki's men had begun the canal from both ends, Enki's men set to work and the progress picked up.

By the end of what Enmarsikil now knew was summer, a broad canal led in from the sea. It ended with the harbor, which comprised the first large, outer ring. This was wide and dredged deep to accommodate all manner of ships. A small cut led from the harbor to the next, narrower ring of water. One more set of alternating land and water surrounded the large central island with its ever growing hill.

Marki led forays into nearby caves, discovered white, black and red rock and soon had buildings and bridges created with all different colors of rocks. Bronze, tin and orichalcum were also found nearby. At Enki's advice, they built three concentric walls encircling the main island. The outer one they clad in bronze, the middle one they covered in tin and the inner one they covered in red orichalcum.

Hovering above the growing town on his air skid, Enmarsikil and Astara observed the work.

"We have hot and cold running fountains all over the city," Astara reported. "Your gardens are laid out and the fish look like they're doing well in the inner lake."

"They do," Enmarsikil agreed. "I took a chance bringing live specimens but they seem to have adapted."

"We're getting to the point where more people would be useful," Astara pointed out. "I'd like the full plant and healing team down here."

"We need the full complement of our people," Enmarsikil admitted. "And we need to expand our territory into areas more suitable for different elementals."

"And closer to the Anunnaki," Astara added. "It would seem you made a lot of promises to ensure that Pact."

Enmarsikil sighed heavily. "That I did and if we don't begin to fulfill them soon, the Anunnaki might feel less vested in following it."

388

Back in the Main Hall on the center island of Tukur, those on Ki gathered to wrestle with the decisions to be made.

"So, we agree it is time to accommodate the remainder of our siblings here on Ki," Enmarsikil opened.

The response was unanimous.

"And don't forget the northern territory," Satu spoke up.

"No, I haven't forgotten. In fact many of those from the Third Gens will need the cooler climates while there are many in the Second Gens who will languish without the hot equatorial sun and volcanoes."

"What's the timeframe we're looking at?" Nita asked.

"Nibiru orbits this sun once every 3,600 Ki years," Enmarsikil reminded them.

"So, we're looking at maybe five years out and five years return," Nindulur surmised.

"I'll contact Teacher," Enmarsikil replied. "We need to do better than that."

Within two months, Enmarsikil implemented some structural changes that Teacher proposed, and Nindulur added them to the Space Transports. Plus, he had Marki back-engineer Enki's comms and now they had a more immediate method of communicating with the transports while in flight and with each other around the globe.

When all was ready, Enmarsikil and Astara saw the group that included Nita and Barlumgeme to the ships.

"This will be the last convoy to and from Nibiru," Astara announced.

"Teacher is already working with our siblings and provisions are being made. Ki will be our final home," Enmarsikil added. "Speed safely to and from. We await your return."

Nindulur and company saluted then entered the ships and soon took off.

Satu watched the ships leave.

"They'll be back soon enough," Enmarsikil assured him. "Zupatu, Gugbubulu and I worked on cutting down the transit time between planes in the multi-dimensions."

Satu nodded. "Good. I already feel restless."

Astara chuckled. "You're always restless."

Satu smiled grimly. "This is a different restless."

"I'm afraid I ignite it with my visions," Mamud confessed.

"Well, check out what you're visioning. See what you find," Enmarsikil encouraged. "Just be back here when our siblings arrive."

The couple agreed and left the next day with a handful of equally intrepid souls.

Time flew by, the new transport arrived and Tukur stretched beyond the main city as housing was built to accommodate the influx. A wild celebration broke out at the reunion with their siblings. And when it died down, Enmarsikil addressed the group as one.

"So good to see all my brothers and sisters again. We have territories located and prepared for you where you will hopefully be happiest. Lands in the north even beyond the furthest north where those with frost and ice in their bones will find comfort.

"The real business is the understanding of Ki's cycles I have learned from my half-brother, Ningishzidda. Anunnaki astronomers have timed Nibiru's orbit to 3,600 years, our old shar. But the next three times Nibiru passes close to the sun and our area of the galaxy will bring it increasingly closer to Ki. So, top side cities should be built for the good times, but dig underground as well for when Nibiru's nearness causes upheaval on Ki," he told them.

"And since humans have now been created and are being used by the Anunnaki as slaves, now is the time to observe them, choose those best suited to living free of their overlords and guide them to territory close to our own where we can live amongst them and teach them," Nita insisted.

"My biggest concern of all is how to manage ourselves," Enmarsikil said. "Teacher keeps talking about the need for a Facility, but something about that makes me uneasy. My future self warned there will come a time when the humans will have spread to every corner of the planet and will be technologically advanced enough to breach even our best defenses."

"Some of us may wish to enter our elements and shepherd those aspects of Ki that are similar from within those elements," a newcomer mentioned.

"We have thought long and hard and have several groups prepared to enter pocket universes to be triggered for release later," Mamud added.

"And the other option is to let go of our land, dwellings and even our bodies," Astara remarked.

"Yes, Teacher has frequently mentioned becoming the very microbes that inhabit us so we can multiply and spread around the globe inhabiting everything and, thereby, influencing everything," Enmarsikil added.

Satu stood in their midst. "Let's split how we approach this end game just like we split how we approached our initial projects while training on Nibiru."

"I agree," Barlumgeme seconded.

"Let's work to our strengths," Aiya added.

"If some want to rest and recharge, build a Facility for them," Marki suggested.

"A larger number of us would prefer to enter pocket universes ready to help Ginny and Ted and other humans when they awaken," Nita said.

"Some have grown comfortable living in the form of Ki's plants and elements and desire to live amongst them," Ki proposed.

"And Astara and I have committed to dissolving into a reproducible, multi-dimensional form," Enmarsikil affirmed.

"Then let all paths be prepared with equal intent," Kienelil stated.

At Marne's home of light, Ginny's focus grew more diffuse. It was harder for her to grasp what was being said. Tired from the length of the journey, she began returning to her own consciousness.

"There is still more to see," Marne said, her voice echoing in Ginny's head.

Marne waved her hand showering Ginny with a sparkling cascade of water. Momentarily refreshed, Ginny slipped deeper into the journey. Now she visioned as if from a vantage point in space. She saw the exodus of siblings to an island beyond the farthest north. A second exodus took to a land mass in a southern sea.

Still from a vantage point from space, the view of a complex settlement developing on the island could be seen. After many years, a group of individuals carrying their own Visioning Sphere moved away from the island to another far to the frozen north. A second group with another Visioning Sphere ventured forth to a land mass that connected Enki's lands with those of Inanna's, Enlil's granddaughter, in the east.

As the images continued in fast forward, Anunnaki air ships could be seen approaching and landing in these places. Humans arrived on the scene and were brought to the centers for training.

Gradually, Ginny regained some awareness of herself while observing the scenes Marne was allowing to play out for her and Astara. She could both view them as if from space and see individual events rapidly transpiring in the different settlements simultaneously. One event seemed more important than the others, and Marne slowed time down for the women to observe it more closely as if they were flies on the wall.

In the first settlement Enmarsikil stood on the observation deck of a gleaming white tower in the center circle of land they had called Tukur, the Land Bearer. A now fully grown Ningishzidda approached him bowing respectfully when he reached Enmarsikil's side.

"You called for me," Ningishzidda said straightening up.

"I did," Enmarsikil replied turning and smiling. "You have completed all the training I could possibly offer. What I withheld is that which our multi-dimensional nature affords us and which I cannot confer on you."

Ningishzidda squared his shoulders. "It has been a great honor to learn from you."

"And it has been a privilege to mentor such an apt student," Enmarsikil responded.

"So...what now?"

Enmarsikil's eyebrow raised in question.

"Where do I go with this? What do I do with this knowledge?" Ningishzidda pressed.

"You are the neutral party who mediates between Enlil and Enki, being direct kin to both," Enmarsikil reminded him.

"But since learning from you and seeing the purpose that drives your people, I feel called to join your efforts," Ningishzidda replied.

"Hm," Enmarsikil said thoughtfully. "Let's vision together and see how that might be possible."

The two men went inside descending the tower stairs to the main floor. They walked a short corridor to a round, domed room, sealed off all light and sat cross-legged before the Visioning Sphere."

"I see a path," Enmarsikil remarked at last. "If you are willing, you can mentor humans taking them to higher levels of reasoning, intelligence and spiritual mastery."

"How?" Ningishzidda wondered watching the flickering scenes in the sphere.

"You will be known by different names in different ages. Thoth to the people of Khemet, Quetzalcoatl and Kulkulcan to others just to the west of this island. Each era you will appear to die only to come back elsewhere with a new name in order to carry on your work with a new people."

"How will I keep in contact with you?" Ningishzidda asked.

"There will come a time when I and my people will release these forms and exist everywhere at once," Enmarsikil explained.

"Make it possible for me to remain connected to you,"

392

Ningishzidda pleaded.

"I will give this some thought," Enmarsikil assured him as they concluded their visioning session.

Over the next few weeks, he spent time in meditation considering Ningishzidda's request. After a while, he turned to his lab and finally created a culture for ingestion by his prize student. Ningishzidda swiftly downed the culture then Enmarsikil sent him away to be one of those to help lead humans to settlements in the north where siblings living in Iginimmatumer, beyond the farthest north, could educate them. The process was going on all throughout the world.

One pass of Nibiru was close and drove many into underground settlements. Still Enmarsikil held their settlements together having visioned an even greater worldwide disruption. With the next pass of Nibiru 3,600 years later, he sensed the catastrophe was upon them that they had been waiting for. He called all of the siblings together to Tukur. There they said their good-byes in their physical form. In a few months, Nibiru's giant orb took up the entire sky as it neared the Sun and Ki inordinately close. The ground rocked, storms swept the planet and this time even the Anunnaki were preparing ships to leave Ki.

Some of the siblings decided to remain in form longer in order to save groups of humans in their care. They headed out, took small bands and placed them into submersible vehicles or deep inside mountain tunnels. Other siblings created parallel pocket universes in which to hide and wait in a timeless environment. But the majority embraced Enmarsikil's plan.

On the day that the skies opened and torrential downpours let loose, the day the aquifers of the deep sent up sky-high geysers of water, the day the tectonic plates groaned and shifted, Nita and Satu brought their groups to Tukur for a last good-bye. Siblings hugged all around, then Enmarsikil and Astara stood back. Bubbles of time-out-of-time opened up and the dedicated groups of siblings entered the ones they had helped to design. Nita and Satu were the last to go.

"Hold to your purpose to disperse," Nita admonished.

"We have made your personal frequency our homing beacon," Satu added.

"When there is a sufficient accumulation of your essence in humans for them to awaken, it will trigger the portal and we'll step through. Then we can guide and support them and others we may find."

"We will not fail," Enmarsikil assured them.

Nita and Satu stepped into their bubbles, turned, waved and slowly disappeared.

Enmarsikil and Astara joined their siblings in a line on the coast. As the waves of a giant tsunami crashed over the cliffs, they let go of their homes, their buildings, and even their physical forms. When the waves receded, they, their cities and their islands were gone.

Ginny and Astara felt cool air rush past them as they were sucked out of the timeline and back into Marne's house. They stood in her journeying room with tens of thousands of years' worth of experiences spinning through their brains.

"How all of that plays out to your time period," Marne said from the platform above, "is determined by how well we empower and seal the changes we saw outpicture."

She held out her hands levitating the women up to the platform beside her. Giramusen, Emissary, Zalkur and Teacher joined them. The Multi-Dims placed the two women in the center and surrounded them.

"Once we energize this change, the old timeline will depart and the new timeline will be your only experience," Teacher warned them. "Are you ready?"

Ginny and Astara nodded.

The Multi-Dims held hands and began to glow, first in the color of the elements they were attuned to but gradually growing whiter and brighter. With a deafening roar, the light exploded and Ginny felt nothing more.

After a while, she became aware of the darkness of her room. She moved her hands feeling the covers of her bed where she lay. She ran her fingers over them allowing her awareness to return in its own time. Finally, she removed her eye mask and turned off her drumming music. She sat up slowly feeling disoriented and dizzy. It took several deep breaths for the spinning sensation to stop. At last, she swung her legs over the edge of the bed, planted her feet on the floor and stood up.

Wondering at the long journey and what changes she might notice now, she headed straight outdoors. Ginny shaded her eyes with her hands as the afternoon sun shone bright about her. The red buds on the rosebushes climbing the arbor caught her eye. Bright Blue Jays and Cardinals zipped back-and-forth overhead as they took turns at the bird feeder on the deck. As she turned about drinking in the deep green of the grass and leaves, the world suddenly felt more alive than it ever had before.

Ted came outside and joined her. When they looked into their main garden, they saw a shimmer in the middle that grew larger and larger until suddenly a swirling doorway opened and familiar faces appeared. Satu, Nita, Barlumgeme and Mamud stepped through, their smiles as bright as the sun.

"Welcome and well done," they chorused. "We knew we'd see you again."

Inside both Ginny and Ted, Astara and Enmarsikil surfaced but as part of them, not as separate entities. They walked under the arbor and into the garden sitting on their cast iron bench in deep conversation with those who had waited so long. A new era had begun; a new mission had been engendered. And the promised help and support was all in place. That night as the moon grew full, other portals opened, others siblings approached. A new age for humans had begun.

APPENDIX

In the following appendix, I've included the names of the Guardians and Masters I've learned. While the names are all of Sumerian origin, I don't promise any are grammatically correct. If anything, they are the best translation into Sumerian and then English I could devise. When you see them broken by syllables with dots in between, that is a common method of showing the individual words making up the names. And from what I've learned through research, it would seem that Sumerians liked long names that were very descriptive of the individual and often full sentences. I'm sure they didn't use the full name every single time they talked to each other, so a few of the siblings are introduced first by their full names and then by shortened versions later.

Pronunciation:

"The vowels may be pronounced as follows: 'a' as in *father*, 'u' as in *pull*, 'e' as in *peg*, and 'i' as in *hip*...."

"Of the special consonants, 'g' [with a diacritical mark[is pronounced like ng in *rang*, 'h' is pronounced like the ch in...German [*Bach*] or Scottish *loch*, and 's' [with a diacritical mark[is pronounced like sh in *dash*." *Sumerian Lexicon, Version 3.0 by John A Halloran (http://sumerian.org/ sumerlex.htm)*

Example: Enmarsikil = En (short e like in hen). mar (as in Mars). si (like the i in hip). kil (like in skill)

Along with the amazing Sumerian Lexicon that John Halloran has produced, which I also have in paperback, I was super fortunate in college to have a Latin professor who was also one of the very few people worldwide who knew extant Sumerian. After Latin class, I would frequently ask questions about Sumerian and he was always so gracious to answer my questions.

APPENDIX A

MEMBERS OF MISSION TEAMS

Mission #1 Seal the Pact with Anu
>En.mar.sikil - (M) Lord of the Pure Sons
>Teacher

Mission #2 Pact with Leaders on Ki
>Enmarsikil
>Teacher
>Sat.atu.ini - (M) Flowing Mountain Water and Wind
>Nita.du.gita - (M) Reedlike Loving Male Friend

Scout Future Settlement Sites
Space Transport Team (by partnered pairs)
>a. Gu.anmul.la - (M) Starry Sky Space Man
>   Radar.ku.mita - (F) She Who Determines the
Enduring Darkness

>b. Mudu.abzu - (M) One Who Knows
Limitlessness
>   Nam.tare.gibba.rabu - (F) Future Seer

>c. Gug.bubu.lu - (M) Direction Finder
>   Tumer.merm.shun.ni - (F) North Star Woman

>d. Zu.patu.rabu - (M) He Who Knows How to
Substitute Dimensions
>   Tumer.ad.hal - (F) North Diviner

>e. Izishub - (M) Flame Thrower
>   Nin.dul.lur - (F) Lady of the Protective
Foundation

>f. Imgiri - (M) Lightning Storm
>   Mu.uru - (F) Thunder Storm

>g. Erumgal - (M) Pan elemental man
>   Ushumgal - (M) Pan elemental woman

Settlement Scouts
  a. Mar.ki.mudim - (M) Pure Earth Builder
     Mir.sig.mi - (F) She Who Flattens out Anger

  b. Kum.zubar - (M) Hot/Liquid Metal
     Ki - (F) Attuned to Earth

  c. Ka.har.sag - (M) Keeper of the Mountains
     Bir.shu.tab.lalhar - (F) Light of the Magical
Lakes

Mission #3 Establishing Tukur [Atlantis]
     Enmarsikil (Facilitator)
     As.ta.ra - (F) Beloved Water Woman

Space Transport #1
  a. Gur.anmul.la - (M)
     Radar.ku.mita - (F)
  b. Mudu.abzu - (M)
     Nam.tare.gibba.rabu - (F)
  c. Gug.bubu.lu - (M)
     Tumer.merm.shun.ni - (F)
  d. Zu.patu.rabu - (M)
     Tumer.ad.hal - (F)
  e. Izishub - (M)
     Nin.dul.lur - (F)
  f. Imgiri - (M)
     Mu.uru - (F)

  g. Erumgal - (M)
     Ushumgal - (F)

Set up Dwelling Team
  a. Shi.dim.gal - (M) Architect
     Ga.dug.dug - (F) Very Happy House

  b. Ki.derin - (M) Builder in Cedar
     La.tesh - (F) Luxury in Harmony

c. Kab.sar - (M) Stone Carver
Zalag.du.mu.dim - (F) Luminous Quartz

d. Markimudim
Mirsigmi

Mission #4 Expanding Tukur; Establishing Iginimmatumer [Thule]

Space Transport #1
a. Gur.anmul.la - (M)
Radar.ku.mita - (F)
b. Mudu.abzu - (M)
Nam.tare.gibba.rabu - (F)
c. Gug.bubu.lu - (M)
Tumer.merm.shun.ni - (F)
d. Zu.patu.rabu - (M)
Tumer.ad.hal - (F)
e. Izishub - (M)
Nin.dul.lur - (F)
f. Imgiri - (M)
Mu.uru - (F)
g. Erumgal - (M)

Plant Growth Team
a. Astara (F)
b. Ush.an.i.a.bu.gabtil - (M) Bird Who Opens His
Wings to Catch the Wind
Aiya - (F) Commands Water to Rise [Creates
Steam]

c. Gir.a.lil.er - (M) Fiery Air Man
Bil.nammul - (F) Bright Spark

d. Kumzubar
Ki

e. Kid.ag.da.a.gar - (M) His Arms Embrace with

Love
　　　　Ki.ene.lil - (F) Woman of Earth and Sky

Cloth and Clothing Team
　　　　a. Hashuru.ur - (M) Cypress Tree
　　　　　　Peenzer.mi - (F) Hearth Tending Woman

　　　　b. Kid.erin - (M) Builder in Cedar
　　　　　　La.tesh - (F) Luxury in Harmony

　　　　c. Hu.mudi - (M) Water Bird
　　　　　　Kia.tug - (F) Beach Cloth

　　　　d. Giraliler
　　　　　　Bilnammul

　　　　e. Diri.ges - (M) Excellent Tree
　　　　　　Tir.kiri - (F) Country Garden

Settlement Scouts
　　　　a. Mar.ki.mudim - (M)
　　　　　　Mir.sig.mi - (F)
　　　　b. Kum.zubar - (M)
　　　　　　Ki - (F)
　　　　c. Ka.har.sag - (M
　　　　　　Bir.shu.tab.lalhar - (F)

Ice and Cold Climate Peoples (Partial List)
　　　　a. Ul.kur - (M) Mountain High
　　　　　　Muru.amagi - (F) Mist of Ice

　　　　b. Sed.maagatu.kur - (M) Cold Falling Mountain
Water
　　　　　　Anedin.sadu - (F) High Mountain Water

　　　　c. Gissu.gillim - (M) Shadow Dancer
　　　　　　Se.sudin.en - (F) Yellow Butterfly of Change

　　　　d. Ra.men.ishku - (M) Ruler of the Far Mountain

400

Lands
        Pa.teema.ta.lukal - (F) Cleanser of the Blessed
Summits

   e. Ten.she.ur - (M) Cold Glimmer
        Gissulal - (F) Cover with Dark Shadow (Make
Invisible)

   f. Anshem - (M) Cool Water
        Zi.kur - (F) Soul Shelter

   g. Ten.adug.senga - (M) Cold Fresh Water Rain
        Igi.igi.bar.an - (F) Face Looks to the Sky

   h. Na.pal.kar.gissu.pa - (M) Broad Shadow Wing
        Il.la.harsag.ga - (F) High Mountain House

Mission #5 Free Humans from Anunnaki Slavery

<u>Free Humans</u>
   a. Nitadugita (M)
        Bar.lum.geme - (F) White Cloud Woman

   b. Satuatuini (M)
        Mamu.sag - (F) Dream Healer

   c. Didi.lu.gigida.da - (M) Man Who Plays a Reed
Flute
        Zidgu.babar - (F) Fine White Flower

   d. Pa.ki.shude.harsag - (M) Apex of Earth's Oath
        Mash.tulki.da - (F) Spring of the Promise of
Earth's Vision

   e. E.hala.bur - (M) Grantor of Future Generations
        Dur.e.ten - (F) Keeper of Past and Future
Generations

   f. Nam.tar.mas.su - (M) Destiny Advisor

Mu.inzu.gur - (F) Woman Who Teaches the Wisdom of the Circle

g. Anesh.zi - (M) Anointed Heavenly Soul
An.ta.mush - (F) Close Companion of Discernment

h. Tum.ta.sinnu.elenu - (M) Messenger of the Sky
Sida - (F) Bestower of Defenses

i. Nir.un.ta.du - (M) Prince of Purity in People and Nature
Deb.ik.tu.ma.ran - (F) Exalted Leader of Spiritual Cleansing
j. Shim.ur - (M) Aromatic Tree
Nin.abnu - (F) Lady Stone

Mission #6 Final Mission Held in Pocket Universes

Primary Scouts
Ba.bu.lu - (M) Searcher; Who Searches

Awakeners
a. Ti.da - (M) Promise of Life
Suh.ka.tu.lama - (F) Woman of the Fortress of Cleansing

b. Mana.tam.se.ka - (M) Gate Keeper
Si.tum.ta - (F) Giver of the Truth of Nature

c. A.zu.ad.hal - (M) Diviner of Healing
Sar.gilim - (F) Herb/Plant Dancer

d. Keshda.ki.essutu.ki - (M) Man Who Mends the Knots of Life
Girpodna.sag.ki - (F) Bone Knitter

e. Kim.sa.la - (M) Call to Abundance
Tur.ne.dara - (F) Invigorating Power of Eternal

Youth

      f. Sag.sha.har.man.tila - (M) Call to Beginning
Life

         Ku.u - (F) Throw off a Load

      g. Bar.tah.u.di - (M) Inflame the Spirit from Sleep
         Gish.tuku - (F) Hear a New Voice

      h. Ash.gid - (M) Curse Remover
         A.de.lil - (F) Fresh Wind

Grounders

      a. Shim.ur - (M) Aromatic Tree Trunk
         Nin.abnu - (F) Lady Stone

      b. Na.du - (M) Stone that Was Raised UP
         Ul.gu.a - (F) Sound of Joyful Water

      c. Lu.gul.lam - (M) Crooked Tree
         Ir.gid.zu - (F) Sweet Smelling Fine Flower

      d. Ka.har.sag - (M) Keeper of the Mountains
         Bir.shu.tab.lalhar - (F) Light of the Magical Lake

Portal Openers

      a. Zil.imi.er - (M) Gentle Wind Man
         Ir.lil.mi - (F) Fragrant Wind Woman

      b. Imgiri - (M) Lightning Storm
         Mu.uru - (F) Thunderstorm

      c. La.ta.ku.ses - (M) Brother Who Determines
Abundance in Nature
         Nin.esh.buru - (F) Woman of the Bountiful
Harvest

      d. Zal.nanna - (M) Bright Full Moon

Dara.suena - (F) Dark Moon

e. Annisig.sa.ki - (M) Blue Sky, Red Earth
Zi.ersetu - (F) Breath of Air

f. Anshem - (M) Cool Water
Zi.kur - (F) Soul Shelter

g. Anni.siga - (M) Beautiful Blue Sky
An.dur.ab.ba - (F) Evening Sea

Protectors

a. Mana.tam.se.ka - (M) Gate Keeper
Si.tum.ta - (F) Giver of the Truth of Nature

b. Tum.ta.sinnu.elenu - (M) Messenger of the Sky
Sida - (F) Bestower of Defenses

c. Allan.agal.abadgal - (M) Mighty Protective Oak
Adug.senga - (F) Fresh Water Rain

d. Lil.nasaru - (M) Air Guard
Nu.nasaru - (F) Fire Guard

e. Saha.nasaru - (M) Silt Guard
Mudi.nasaru - (F) Water Guard

Communicators

a. Didilugigidda - (M)
Zidgubabar - (F)

b. Kin.sal.la - (M) Call to Abundance
Tur.ne.dara - (F) Invigorating Powers of Eternal   Youth

c. Pu.imi.ndu.dugnamtar - (M) Whistle
Communicator
Geshtug.galga - (F) Listens to Counsel

d. Sig.ili.mi - (M) Quiet Cuddly Breath
     Ban.sed.ad.sha - (F) Spirit that Soothes by
Singing

Earth Bound

a. Satuatuini - (M)
     Mamudsag - (F)

b. Nitadugita - (M)
     Barlumgeme - (F)

d. Mud.izi.nizi - (M)   Blue Water Waves
     Ki.sikil.tur.ku.sa - (F) Girl of Gold and
Sweetness

Space Bound

a. Guranmulla - (M)
     Radarkumita - (F)

b. Muduabzu - (M)
     Namtaregirrarabu - (F)

c. Gugbubulu - (M)
     Tumumermshunnu - (F)

d. Zupaturabu - (M
     Tumeradhal - (F)

Healers in Himalayan Facility

a. Ti.da - (M) Promise of Life
     Suh.ka.tu.lama - (F) Woman of the Fortress of
Cleansing

b. Gal.a.ti.mummu - (M) Eldest Born son of Life
Giving Water
     Da.van.mu.i.ra - (F) Source of the Perfume of
Vitality

c. A.zu.ad.hal - (M) Diviner of Healing
     Sar.gilim - (F) Herb/Plant Dancer

d. Izi.ri.ri.shag - (M) Kindle Fire in the Heart
     Zi.sag.ki - (F) Breath of Life Restorer

e. Keshda.ki.essutu.ki - (M) Man Who Mends the
Knots of Life
     Girpodna.sag.ki - (F) Bone Knitter

Bringers of Magic/Science

Gur.kala.gis - (M) Tall Strong Tree
U.zal.ushum - (F) Dawn Dragon